ONTARIO LACUS

A Novel by

J. Matthew Neal

Cover photos from Cassini Orbiter courtesy NASA/Jet Propulsion Laboratory/Space Science Institute.

Printed in the United States of America
Dunn Avenue Press
Muncie, Indiana 47304
ISBN 978-0-6152-1127-5

"When you marry a man, you also marry his family and friends . . ."

Bonnie Mendoza remembered that old saying before she married Alexander Dirk Darkkin, and she happily accepted his clan's little idiosyncrasies. But, in "Ontario Lacus," she quickly finds that the melding of the two families may be more than the world can take.

In this sequel to "Specific Gravity," Bonnie and Alex go on the adventure of a lifetime to stop a sports steroid scandal, which is soon revealed to be something far more ominous—a master plan for genetic annihilation and the creation of a legion of super-soldiers. But what role have Bonnie's colorful new relatives unwittingly played in the genesis of these horrific plans? And does one of hers have skeletons in his closet as well?

Journey with them from the days of the dinosaurs, to the lavish casinos of Las Vegas, to the White House, to the hallowed stadiums of professional football, and to the surface of an alien world with wonders beyond imagination. Don't miss this eclectic crew's amazing mission to make everything right again, before it's too late for mankind. But who among them will pay the ultimate price?

"J. Matthew Neal does it again with his second book . . . even though this book is full of technical information, it is written in a reader-friendly format. I always enjoy reading this author's works, because I learn so much while reading a great story. His real life experience as a physician gives him an insight that most authors do not have. This story plot includes murder, romance and very high technology. . . I am so glad that the author continued on with these characters. This page turner kept me up reading through most of the night, because I could not put it down before I found out how it turned out! 'Ontario Lacus' is definitely one that thriller fans will not want to miss reading."

—*Cherie Fisher, Reader Views*

"One day at a time—this is enough. Do not look back and grieve over the past, for it is gone; and do not be troubled about the future, for it has not yet come. Live in the present, and make it so beautiful that it will be worth remembering."

—Ida Scott Taylor

"It is not the strongest of the species that survives, nor the most intelligent that survives. It is the one that is most adaptable to change."

—Charles Darwin

Prologue

Sixty–five million years ago
Ontario Lacus
Southern hemisphere of Titan

Eight hundred and eighty–four million miles away, the 870,000-mile-diameter spectral class G2 main sequence star fused the hydrogen isotopes deuterium and tritium to helium fiercely; of light's visible spectrum, however, only the bizarre, orange-red rays filtered through the dense nitrogen and hydrocarbon atmosphere, which was at a pressure of 1,460 millibars—nearly one and a half times that of Earth's. The yellow star was dwarfed by the beige oblate spheroid which glowed in the foreground, whose most famous feature—its fabulous rings—were barely visible, as its huge moon was in the same plane. Indeed, the beautiful rings were less than 100 feet in thickness, man would discover in the late 20th century.

The ominous orange shadows of the sky and plains that contrasted with the black liquid methane and ethane which constituted dark, tar-like Ontario Lacus would be seen—if any human had existed at that time. The swirling winds produced by the moon's seasons would also be terrifying to those who could hear the eerie howls.

However, as striking as the landscape was, no living being could conceivably survive on the surface of the giant Saturnian moon—the only body in the Solar System besides Earth to have a nitrogenous atmosphere and well-defined bodies of surface liquid. *Homo sapiens* would, sixty–five million years later, name the giant hydrocarbon lake after Lake Ontario, whose size and shape it roughly resembled. The Cassini orbiter flyby in July 2008 confirmed that it contained large amounts of methane and ethane.

Titan, or Saturn VI, was perhaps the greatest discovery of Dutch astronomer Christiaan Huygens, and was by far the largest satellite of the 5.68 x 10^{26}–kilogram ringed planet; Spanish astronomer Jose Comas Solá first raised the possibility of the moon having an atmosphere in 1903, when he observed that Titan appeared brighter at its center than at its poles. His explanation was that light reflected toward Earth from the poles must have traversed more of the giant moon's atmosphere than that reflected by its center.

The existence of an atmosphere was confirmed in 1944 by Gerard Kuiper at the University of Chicago, who identified methane in its spectrum. But the composition of the odd, orange body's atmosphere and surface evaded detailed description because of its thick haze; it would not be until the early 21st century that the man-made Huygens probe would land on its surface, in an attempt to unlock its centuries-old mysteries.

A bolide over twenty kilometers in diameter had struck the third planet from the sun sixty–five million years ago, in an area that would later be part of the Yucatán Peninsula in Mexico in the town of Chicxulub, creating an impact crater over 180 kilometers in diameter. This created an extinction-level event for most life-forms there, spewing a hundred billion tons of debris into the atmosphere.

The debris cut off all sunlight for over two years, thus destroying the plant vegetation on which the giant herbivore dinosaurs subsisted. And, after the herbivores perished, the carnivorous dinosaurs died, since they required the flesh of the herbivores for sustenance. Only insects, microorganisms, and small mammals would survive, signaling the end of the Cretaceous Period and heralding the Age of Mammals.

Scientists would eventually ponder whether or not that event alone had destroyed the giant lizards; certainly, the eruption of multiple volcanoes in India and severe climate changes had contributed—but the meteor had certainly played a major role. Tyrannosaurs and velociraptors would soon be no more,

The meteor's impact had sent millions of large chunks of Earth into the atmosphere, about two hundred thousand of which were propelled with enough force to reach escape velocity—the speed where the kinetic energy of an object equaled the magnitude of its potential energy in a gravitational field. Such a velocity would allow escape from Earth's atmosphere, at 11.2 kilometers per second.

Over thousands of years, these fragments eventually made their way towards our neighbors in the Solar System, many to the gas giants Jupiter and Saturn; most in that vicinity had been sucked into their large gravitational pulls. Sixty–seven pieces, however, had escaped the giant ringed planet's gravitational pull and had descended into Titan's atmosphere—a primordial smog of nitrogen and methane.

The large meteors floated through the thick haze into the lakes, illuminated by the eerie, glimmering orange of Titanian dawn. The lakes weren't water, but liquefied hydrocarbons, at minus 289 degrees Fahrenheit—a very cold place to be, indeed. By the time the Terran fragments reached Titan, the dinosaurs had long since perished. The heat generated by the meteors on reentry into the thick atmosphere had produced enough heat to melt some of the ice, however; survival of any known life form was impossible without water.

If man were witnessing this event, he surely would reason that any prehistoric life forms present on the meteor would have quickly died on this exotic yet environmentally hostile world. The similar fragments sucked into Saturn, Jupiter, and the Jovian moon Europa certainly suffered that fate. They were only primitive unicellular organisms, after all—in the vastness of the universe, the significance of this singular incident seemed less than apocalyptic.

But a lot could happen in sixty–five million years. And, life was always unpredictable, scientists in the 21st century would learn. Could the occurrence that led to the greatest mass extinction on Earth somehow be linked to a similar event in the future?

Chapter One

Thirty–nine years ago
Belle Epoqué Casino
Monte Carlo, Monaco

The incandescent lights of the mammoth, ornate building reflected from the Mediterranean Sea like dancing, shimmering orbs as the large man entered the fabulous building—a privilege reserved only for the upper crust of society.

The glimmer from the six–five, dark-haired, bearded man's $2,000 tuxedo caught several pairs of heavily made-up female eyes as he entered the establishment, and he brushed away the many attendants who flocked around him like flies. He gave them little notice, as he didn't have time for riff-raff wanting a gratuity; he was a man on a mission for one thing—and it sure as hell wasn't gambling. A more elemental urge was calling his name.

Despite his relative youth, the thirty–year-old American with the codename Röntgen was already a man of immense importance—and, more importantly, money. The big southpaw had just come in from outside, after a particularly close call—some thug had been following him, he knew from a tip-off by headquarters. Bad luck for that guy, he thought as he wiped the crusted blood from his left, rock-hard fist that had just a few minutes earlier smashed the burly Italian man's face into pulp.

But the lackey they sent was fortunate to have only lost a few teeth, and not his life. That latter fate was reserved only for higher-ups—this was the message the large man gave to the minion, to give to his bosses. Don't mess with him ever again, he said—or the consequences would be lethal. His favorite Montblanc Meisterstück 149 fountain pen was also damaged in the scuffle—now *that* pissed him off more than anything. The elegant, piston-filled West German device was a "special issue" that could shoot highly corrosive acid and poison gas, the lab guy had said; but he simply liked to write with the huge, cigar-sized stylus (made of a lustrous "precious resin"), the secret composition of which was known to only a select few.

The hard-drinking, fast-living man peered down at the large, diamond-encrusted gold Rolex President Day-Date watch on his meaty right wrist, one of many such fine Swiss timepieces in his impressive collection. Nine o'clock—the night was just getting under way, and he had to make up for lost time.

He was considered handsome in a rugged sort of way—the beard hid several scars he had received during his many scuffles, souvenirs of a hardscrabble existence. Women knew instantly by his appearance that he was a real man, not some poor imitation.

The man hadn't been in the small country since the Monaco Grand Prix the previous year—how he remembered the fine ladies from that weekend. The finest scientists in the world were gathered for a prestigious conference, and he'd had a long day of his favorite activities—discussing nuclear equations, eating filet mignon and lobster, and fighting. It was time for rest and relaxation in the best way he knew possible. And he had primal needs his fellow atomic scientists couldn't meet.

He winked at the many beautiful females who caught his eye; he knew that he certainly caught theirs, as he was quite the charmer. He knew a lot of things, but most of all, how to please the ladies. Years of experience had honed those skills. But he wanted something a little different tonight, and smiled as he spied the voluptuous red-haired woman seated at the roulette table, nursing a drink. And roulette was his game, as were women. He was an expert at both.

"*Здравствуйте.*" The bulky muscular man said hello in Russian, in a Southern drawl distinctly peculiar to the small European monarchy. "Is this seat occupied, beautiful lady?"

She looked at him and sighed. "No, it is a free country. You may sit where you wish, sir."

"I wish to sit right here, next to your loveliness."

She stared at him intently. "You are American? Your accent is different . . . from the gentlemen I have known from New York and Chicago. And how did you know I am Russian?"

"I am very perceptive, and quite different from anyone you've ever met. It's my job to pick up on small clues." The big, callused left hand, capable of smashing flesh into pulp, fondled her necklace delicately, as if holding a fragile porcelain doll. "The jewelry, for example, which you bought at a small shop in St. Petersburg, near Nevsky Prospekt. I recognize the unique design."

She opened her mouth wide. "Hmm, I may have underestimated you. Do you know more Russian than 'hello,' or are you just trying to impress me?"

"I don't have to *try* anything, lady—I'm the real deal. I'm fluent in Russian, as well as German, Portuguese, Italian, Spanish, and Mandarin Chinese." He then rattled off several passages in Russian, which sounded odd due to his accent. "And if you're not impressed, it's your loss, in more ways than meet the eye."

She nodded her head. "How fabulous. My husband is American as well. I don't trust him."

"My wife's British—so what? They aren't here. We are."

He sat down as she pulled a long cigarette from the gold case in her purse and put it between her red lips. He pulled a gold lighter from his pocket and lit it for her as he stared at the dancing flame.

She blew a cloud of gray smoke into the air, and the aromatic smell of the burning tobacco was enticing as his eyes opened wildly. But he was ready to start another kind of fire.

She looked at the blood on his left hand. "What has happened to your hand? An accident?"

"Heh, yeah, a little 'accident,' that's it. Nothing of any concern to you."

"Oh, no—was anyone hurt?"

He laughed as he took a swig of his amber blended whiskey, served neat in a glass. "Yeah, somebody out there needs a dentist, doll. He's lucky to be alive, and next time, he won't be. No one screws with me twice—no, heh, guy, that is, if you get my drift."

She frowned. "I see—a ruffian, are you? How crass."

"Just defending what I represent—America the beautiful. Sorry, no offense." He shook his head. "I save the world, so you don't have to. You really don't want to know about it."

She paused and took another drag from her cigarette. "What's your name, my rugged-looking American friend, who saves the world?" she said as she exhaled.

"W. Conrad Darkkin—Rad for short. My parents chose to name me after Nobel physics laureate Wilhelm Conrad Röntgen, who discovered the X-ray."

"*Rad*? That's a very peculiar name. A 'rad' is a unit of radiation exposure, yes, in English? We generally use the 'gray' unit here in Europe."

"You catch on fast. Like gamma rays, I'm powerful as well as deadly, in ways you can't see until it's too late. The name matches the job, baby—I'm a nuclear physicist. And what you see is what you get—pure atomic excitement."

"My." She exhaled several smoke rings. "How fascinating you seem. My husband is a scientist, like you."

"I bet he's, heh, *nothing* like me. What's your name, anyway?"

"Katrina. Katrina Argon." She flicked an ash into the expensive marble ashtray.

He took another swig of his bourbon. "Argon—sure. You must be Malachi Argon's wife. The bio-geneticist. We were at Princeton together."

"Yes. He is quite brilliant."

He let out a hearty laugh. "Compared to what? Not to me, he isn't. Nobody can measure up to Rad Röntgen, baby."

"Perhaps. We all have our faults. One of yours seems to be a lack of humility. You think you are more talented than he?"

He laughed. "You have no idea." He took her left hand and kissed it. "So, why isn't old uni-dimensional Chi here with you? Got some experiment to do? You look like any guy's cup of tea."

"Cup of tea? I don't follow you."

"You're beautiful and sexy." He pulled a Dunhill from the gold cigarette case in his pocket and lit it with his matching twenty–four karat, gold-plated lighter.

"Well," she shrugged, taking a sip of her drink. "Malachi is very involved with his work. A lot of classified things, and I do not know much about it. He does not have time to attend to my needs. Currently he is attending some conference with the world's greatest minds."

Rad stared at her generous breasts. "Hell, that can't be, since I'm pretty much the smartest guy around. What's ol' Square Chi studying? Heh, Square Chi, Chi-Square, get it?" He laughed.

"Yes, how funny. He is interested in fossilized life on other planets, specifically, moon rocks that might have contained life at one point."

"Studying moon rocks, what a loser. I'm a man of the future, as I study the atom, not some damn fossils. But I can help meet any needs you want, lady."

"You can? What needs do you believe I have, Rad?"

"Needs only my equipment can provide. I do classified work too, babe. Work on weapons."

"Weapons? How terrible. What kind?"

"Stuff a lot of people would kill to know, but I'll start off by showing you the one in my pants. Shit, it's so top secret, it's probably treason to show it to a Russian. I'll have to kill you afterwards. But I guarantee you'll enjoy it."

She frowned as her finely manicured right hand crushed out the cigarette in the expensive ashtray. "How crude. You are inferring that I would enjoy seeing your . . . gun, is it?"

He laughed. "I know so, and it's a pretty damn dangerous one. Don't know if you can handle it after being used to Chi's sorry junk. For a big guy, he's pretty sad with the ladies, I heard."

"Is that correct? How fortunate for me. As I have told you, though, I am married to him."

"So what? I'll show you something you'll never forget."

"You would cheat on your wife?"

He threw his hands down. "Damn, it sure ain't the first time. Looks like you ain't here for the gambling, either. Too bad—we could've made a bundle." He stubbed out his cigarette and walked with her from the casino to the elegant hotel lobby.

Dr. W. Conrad Darkkin and Katrina Argon took the elevator to the penthouse, where he planned to show her some of his classified items.

• • •

A few minutes later, they walked off the gold-plated elevator and went to the door of his lavish accommodations.

"A very nice suite, Dr. Darkkin," she said. "You must be a man of significant means."

"Money ain't no good unless you can spend it, lady."

They went inside the opulent four-room suite, with full bar, den, hot tub, and, of course, a fabulous bedroom—the focal point of any Rad Darkkin-endorsed dwelling.

"You live very elegantly, Rad. Our suite is much less opulent. Of course, Malachi is not there much, so it matters little."

"Aww, what a pity. Always live life to the fullest, that's my credo. Tomorrow, I'll probably be dead, so what the hell?"

"An interesting philosophy. Shall we have a drink first?"

"Hell, we can drink later. Let's have a little fun. I can't wait."

She peeled off her outer clothes as he gaped in anticipation. God, she was filled out, he thought. His wife Marianne was okay looking, but kind of plain. And the proper British woman didn't like wild stuff. The kid at home kind of cramped his style, too, and the wife said she wanted another one.

They always said guys like him shouldn't take a wife—the best and most loyal companions were probably a bottle of booze and a carton of smokes, with some ladies on the side for those inevitable testosterone surges. Yes, this was where he was in his element—an exotic location in the Mediterranean, plenty of gambling, the best of food and drink, and a stacked Russian gal. Things couldn't get any better.

He'd show science geek Malachi Argon's neglected wife a time she'd *never* forget. Passionate lovemaking was one thing the well-endowed man was the best in the world at. And he was talented at a lot of things.

Chapter Two

Twenty-six years ago
Mendoza Flores Residence
3217 San Ysidro Blvd.
San Diego, CA

The unmistakable smell of the newly sharpened yellow No. 2 Ticonderoga pencils produced a pleasant melody as the small eight–year-old girl sat down to help her brother and his girlfriend study for their advanced algebra midterm on Sunday afternoon. She knew she was more tolerable to him than their mother, who would be most unhappy he had left his studying to the last minute.

The aroma of freshly cut cedar and graphite evoked vivid sounds and colors as she lined them up like soldiers in her pencil box—everything had to be just right for the Herculean task at hand, one for which there seemed little chance of success.

She grew increasingly impatient as the teenagers continued to waste valuable study time, loitering in the living room. There was *nothing* more important than homework, she thought as she yelled at him, as he and his girlfriend sat on the sofa of their family's modest suburban ranch home. The clock in the kitchen, which featured, ironically, a drawing of the famous mathematician Euclid (one of her favorite heroes), showed valuable time ticking away, like precious temporal sands disappearing through an hourglass.

She was shocked to discover, as she peeped through a crack in the door, that they most definitely were *not* solving linear equations. How terrible—and with an examination tomorrow, even.

"I am waiting, and my time is valuable," the diminutive female said in her shrill, piercing voice. "In case you are not aware, I am charging you by the minute."

"Aww, shaddup, dork," her oldest brother yelled, rudely interrupted from the activity he was pursuing with his friend Penny while they were listening to the top hits of 1984 on the stereo. "Hold your horses. We'll be there in a minute."

"You should not have procrastinated on your algebra portfolio, Jaime. You will *never* be prepared for your calculus at this rate," the wiry dark-haired girl exclaimed as she shook her head and cackled hysterically at the pitiful, soda-stained scribblings he had made on the sheet of graph paper. "How comical! You cannot even graph these simple cubic equations properly. I did better at age two."

"Who the heck cares? I've got more important things on my mind," the six–one, handsome sixteen-year-old said to the busty female to his left as they walked into the kitchen. "Much more important, get my drift?"

She ignored him. "First, we shall work on solving simultaneous and quadratic equations. I have created an outline with several examples that will be challenging. Then we will discuss their relevance to differential and integral calculus."

"No time for all that. Just show me how to do one and that'll be it." He yawned as he took a gulp of orange soda.

"No time?" She stood and stared up at him. "Duh! You cannot just memorize it, you must understand the principles behind it!" she said vehemently. "Maxima and minima problems will be more important to you than this other activity. Just you wait and see how useful they will be—there are many applications in football."

"I want to get the 'maxima' results with the 'minima' effort," he laughed as he smooched with the attractive girl. "And I doubt they'll be more important. Some day you'll understand, I hope."

"Humph, how juvenile," the little girl exclaimed, hands on hips. *"Qui non est hodie cras minus aptus erit!"* she then admonished, pointing her pencil at them like a miniature sorceress casting a diabolical spell with a hexagonal, yellow, pointed wooden wand.

"What'd she say, Jay?" the grinning girl on his arm whispered. "Your sister's a weirdo. You sure she's not an alien?"

"Ha, you've got that right. Some Latin stuff, I think. She's pretty geeky," he whispered back. "She's got some serious issues."

"I heard that!" the pint-sized tutor exclaimed. "I have very good hearing." She crossed her arms in a futile attempt to appear imposing. "The quotation means, 'he who is not prepared today shall be less prepared tomorrow.' Appropriate, is it not?"

"Yeah, like, whatever," the older girl said, giggling.

"Tomorrow, it will not be so humorous to you, Penelope. The darkness of mathematical failure will descend like a grim cloak of death upon you both. How sad."

"Shaddup. Hey, Penny, come look at dweeb-face's stupid Einstein clock. You ever seen something so dumb?" They both laughed hysterically as Jay pointed to the unusual timepiece hanging above the kitchen table.

She gasped in horror. "He is the great Euclid of Alexandria, not Einstein, you idiot—how dare you talk about him that way?"

"Haw. He looks like some old homeless wizard dude to me."

"Shut up. I will tell Mother about how you insulted him."

"Whatever. And no more smart remarks out of you, peewee. I'm paying you ten bucks to do this."

"If Mother finds out, she will be very angry at you for failing *again* to meet your potential."

"Mom's clueless about it, and I just care about right now, Boney Bonnie," Jay said as he kissed the girl again. "You're skinnier than that pencil."

"I am not! You take that back."

"Get to work. I'm not paying you to lecture me."

"I doing your work will not earn you the top marks on your exam you require to get your new car. Father said that only a B+ or greater will qualify." She snickered. "There seems to be little hope."

"As long as I pass, that's all right with me. You don't help, you don't ride in it, remember."

"Mother says 'B' is for 'bad,' and 'A' is 'acceptable.' 'C' means 'crappy,' you know. 'D' is 'disgusting,' and 'F' means, well—I cannot speak it!" She put her hand over her mouth, feigning fear.

He pointed his finger at her. "Hey, you may think I'm scared of Mom, but I'm not, so shut up. I'm not afraid of anybody."

"Well, you should be terrified. Of Dad, too."

He chuckled. "Sure, right. I'll just turn on the old Jay charm, like

I usually do."

The abrasive, dark-haired, precocious pre-teen shook her head in disgust, because she knew he was right.

"So, Jay, what was it you had to do last night?" the brunette girl asked. "I really wanted you to come over."

"Had a special football practice, hon."

"On Saturday night? I thought there was some rule you weren't allowed to practice then."

"Yeah, sorry, wish we could've gone to that thing with your folks. I was really looking forward to it, too. But Coach wanted us to go over the new plays for the Eagles game next Friday."

The short girl shook her head as she detected the subtle odors and colors of his speech. At that time she noticed, as she had many times before, the sunlight from the window split into the seven Newtonian, or named, colors—red, orange, yellow, green, blue, indigo, and, finally, violet.

The violet rays began swirling and formed her friend Oogly-Googly, the helpful ectoplasmic purple blob, as he appeared on her right forearm. No one else could ever see him, but he was always there when someone was lying.

"You should not fib, *hermano*. You were at no such thing!"

"What? I was, too. And how do you know, dummy? Mom took you to the movie last night," he said nervously. "You were in bed when I got home. I didn't even see you."

"I have no firsthand knowledge of your whereabouts, but I just know when you are lying," she said confidently, looking down at her right arm. "Oogly-Googly always knows."

The teenage boy got up and shoved her in the back. "Shut up, you little creep, before I put some tape over your mouth. You and your dumb imaginary friend. What a retard."

She stuck her tongue out at Jaime and made a face. "Oogly-Googly is not dumb, he is smarter than you!"

"Is that true, Jay? Were you really at that football practice? You weren't out with Christy Jenkins, were you?" Penny asked angrily.

He put his hand over his chest. "Of course not. I wouldn't do that. How could you think that of me?"

The smooth, shiny purple blob jumped up and down, as he often did, casting a shadow from the sunlight on her arm. "Yes, he was!"

she said as she pointed her finger at him. "Such a faithful boyfriend you are to her. For shame."

"Thanks a lot, idiot. You need to keep your mouth shut."

"Sorry, but you know I cannot allow lying to occur."

"I'll remember this next time you need something," he said as he pointed to his sister angrily.

Penny gathered her books, jacket, and purse. "Jay, we'll talk about this later. Right now I need to leave before I get really mad."

"Penny, wait. I can explain."

"Yeah, right. Bye, Mr. two-timing football captain. I guess what I heard about you from the other girls was true."

Bonnie chuckled heartily as the angry girl stormed off.

"What're you laughing at? If you weren't so little, I'd pound you into the ground, you little rat!"

She stuck out her tongue at him again. "I will tell Mother about this. You know I am her favorite. You will be in *sooo* much trouble."

"Why did you do that, anyway? You wouldn't have done that to Mike."

"Miguel takes pride in his homework, unlike you, and is respectful to his girlfriends. Had you shown more initiative, this particular event might have turned out differently."

"Yeah, right. Mike's thirteen, what does he know about girls? Someday, I'll be a millionaire, and I won't give you any of it."

"Yes, dream on, Jaime. And someday I will be a superhero, and I will not save you when you are in trouble. What do you think of *that*?" She heard the front door open and grinned. "Oh, oh, Mother is here. Too bad for you. Wait until I tell her what happened, and the bad things you said about Euclid."

"Euclid's a dork, just like you."

Chapter Three

Present Day
San Diego Children's Hospital
Mendoza Flores Rehabilitation Center
San Diego, CA

The six–year-old boy with leg braces smiled as he slowly moved towards the physical therapist at the children's rehabilitation center, one of the best in the country. He was short and stocky, his red cheeks puffing out as he smiled and laughed. Tommy Wilkinson was the third child of his family, a bit different from his brother and sister, but unique in his own way, his parents had learned.

Tommy had Down syndrome, his parents learned shortly after he was born, and had more than his share of problems—he had trouble walking, and was more developmentally delayed than the typical Down child; he also had a profound hearing deficit, and had a heart defect which had to be surgically repaired at age three. But you wouldn't know to look at him that he had suffered such hardships; he was just one of the gang at home, playing with his older siblings. Each small step forward was a giant triumph.

The three late-twentyish pediatric residents were rounding with their program director, Dr. Brenda Mortland; all were attempting to dodge the workers and construction cones on their way to rounds on the crisp April morning. The new wing would be wonderful, they all said—when it was finally done.

Dr. Mortland asked the senior resident some questions as she spied, out of the corner of her eye, the large white-coated blonde coming briskly down the hall. She always enjoyed Chief's Rounds, although the residents were usually scared out of their gourd by the friendly, boisterous, and physically imposing Chief of Staff.

"Wake up, guys," Brenda told the two female and one male resident sharply. "Admiral on the bridge."

"Oh, crap," the female senior resident said. "I didn't read my journal club assignment."

"Then you better be good at bluffing," Brenda said. "Or you could just plead insanity."

The entourage of medical personnel attending to Tommy Wilkinson parted like a scattered flock of sheep before a lion, as Dr. Mary Gwendolyn Williams came up to the small boy and picked him up in her arms. The boy smiled as he recognized the familiar, friendly, freckled face.

"How's my big boy today?" she said in her deep voice. "Looks like you're going to be running the 100-meter dash soon."

"He's doing well," the male physical therapist said. "He should be walking independently, we hope, within a year."

"I know he will," she said as she turned to the senior resident. "Dr. Huang, who described Down syndrome, and in what year?"

If Dr. Lisa Huang could have shrunk and disappeared, she would have done so, it seemed—but that was beyond her capabilities. "Uh, Dr. Down?" she uttered in a barely audible tone.

Dr. Wendy Williams, standing over a foot taller than the five-one resident, frowned at the sheepishly grinning woman.

"*Down*? What an astute answer." She put the child down and turned to the tall male resident with immaculately pressed slacks, Armani shoes, and starched white coat. "Dr. Esterbrook, do you have a more detailed answer to my query?" she asked sweetly in her deep Southern voice.

The tall male intern held up his Clystarr pharmaceutical pen. "Naturally. Down syndrome was described by British physician John Langdon Down in 1866, and was recognized as the trisomy 21 chromosomal abnormality in 1959 by Lejeune."

"I see. What is the gene regulator of interest, and what two controller proteins are elevated, Doctor?"

"You would be referring to NFATc, and the proteins are DSCR1 and DYRKIA, of course. The latter two are elevated by fifty percent in Down syndrome."

"Somebody's read their article for today. Good job, Dr. Esterbrook. I am confident that any further probing of your knowledge would serve no purpose, correct?"

"I hate to presume anything, Dr. Williams, but that is very likely to be the case."

She nodded. "Confidence is a good thing to have. Just make sure you don't let it turn into arrogance. Humility is one of the best virtues to have." She gestured to the patients in the rehab facility. "If you can't learn that here, then you might pick another specialty."

"Yes, Ma'am," Esterbrook said. "Humility it is."

Wendy bent down and whispered in Dr. Huang's ear. "And, Dr. Huang, this is my clinic day. Good probability that I might show up. Better be prepared next time."

"Yes, I will, Dr. Williams. Thanks."

"And give your gunner intern there some nice scut work to do. He needs to be cut down to size a bit."

"My pleasure."

Wendy left the group to talk to Tommy's mother, who was standing at the side of the large room.

"Thank you, Dr. Williams, for all you've done with Tommy the last two years. I'm so glad Bruce got relocated here so that we could get the care you've given," Christina Wilkinson said to Wendy as she shook her large hand.

She beamed. "I appreciate that, but this is a team effort, and I'm only a small part of it. You and Bruce are the real heroes." She watched the laughing Tommy as he rambled down the carpet towards the therapist. "And Tommy, of course."

"So many people told us how sorry they were. How they wished Tommy could have been 'normal.' I didn't know what to think at first. It kind of shocked me."

"A lot of people don't understand—most of them don't mean to be unkind, they're just saying what they think is right."

"I know," Tommy's mother said as she watched him play with a red toy truck. "They said Tommy would never make it, that he wouldn't reach his third birthday, with the heart defect and all."

"They were wrong. Not the first time."

"But he was a gift, so special, so many things he can do now.

They may not seem like much to most people, but his milestones are as important to us as anything."

"Of course they are. The things he's done are amazing. That's why I love this job."

"People ask me, if I could take him back, have a 'regular' boy, would I do it? Would I have had him at all? Why not just have an abortion, they said, since we knew about it?"

Wendy laughed. "Since we can't alter history, it's kind of a moot point. But I know what your answer would be, Chris."

"I know you do. It would be to have him as he is. He's made such a difference in our lives, to appreciate the little things . . . I wouldn't trade it for anything. I know his life will be different than Ben and Audrey's."

"Different doesn't mean better or worse. There are lots of differently-abled people who contribute much to society. God has given you a gift—he wouldn't have given Tommy to just anyone. His life will make yours more fulfilling."

Chris Wilkinson hugged the larger woman as she brushed away tears. "I know he will. Thanks for being not just a doctor, but a friend to us and Tommy."

"I wouldn't want it any other way," she said as she walked away. "Carry on, troops," she said to the group as she departed through the construction tunnel to the main wing of the hospital.

• • •

Wendy exited the rehab unit and walked back to her office in long strides. She ran into the director of nursing, Dana Emmerson, on the way.

"Hi, Dr. Williams," the fortyish woman said, tightly grasping the morning newspaper.

"Dana, how's it going?" she asked cheerfully. "My, you sure look excited about something this morning."

"I am." Dana held out the April morning edition of the San Diego Union-Tribune. "Look, *he's* on the front page!" The shorter woman swooned as she pointed to the photo of the handsome Hispanic man shaking the hand of the pro football commissioner. "Isn't he marvelous? So nice-looking, with that sexy mustache."

"Gee," she said in an underwhelmed tone. "*He* certainly is. In the paper again, I see, as usual. What's up this time? Did he break up with Fabiane Carrera again?"

"He was just named head coach of the new Las Vegas pro football expansion franchise." Dana punched her in the shoulder. "I still have his swimsuit poster. I hear he's still single, too."

"Yep, sure is." She nodded. "Like the number π, the speed of light, and Planck's constant, you can always count on certain things in life to always stay the same. Glad I don't have to worry about stuff like that."

"I'd give *anything* to have a date with him."

Wendy patted her on the shoulder. "Some things aren't as great in real life as they are in your imagination. Just speaking hypothetically, of course."

"Wow, maybe you could get me tickets to a game, an autograph, and an introduction? That's a lot to ask, I know, but you do know him, I heard."

"How true." She stared at the grinning man's photo—one that she'd like to place on a dartboard and launch pointy projectiles at. A good-time Joe if there ever was one—a guy who certainly liked to spread the "good times" around. Her own brother was somewhat dysfunctional and arrogant, and she'd come to terms with that—but Alex's sense of self-importance didn't hold a candle to that possessed by the egotistical sibling of her best friend. But she was, admittedly, a bit biased.

However, the new coach had given millions of dollars to the hospital, and she had to put her petty personal grievances to the side. And *she's* the one who chose to be Chief of Staff here, at the place that would soon have his picture plastered all over.

"Hey, Dr. Williams? Isn't it great?" Dana nudged her on the arm, shaking with excitement. "You don't seem too enthused about it."

Wendy looked up from her daydreaming and smiled sardonically. "Oh, trust me, it is simply *fantastic,* I just don't want to fully demonstrate my exuberance in a public place. I can't wait to go, too, and I'll see what I can do."

"That sounds really keen. Well, gotta go. See you."

"Sure." She looked out the window on the way, over the debris and chaos around the construction of the new, $20 million rehab center. So many more children could be helped now, she thought, with the new facilities. It was twenty years ago, at age eighteen, that she had decided on a career in medicine; of course, the facility was much smaller then, when she began volunteering as an activities coordinator for deaf children.

It was there that she met the wiry thirteen-year-old patient who helped her with math homework and swindled her at card games, the little cheater. Bonnie almost died when she was eleven, and had to learn everything all over again; she had, in the following two years, become a skilled runner and recovered most of her uncanny intellectual abilities. The profoundly deaf girl's speech would, however, never again be normal, although, paradoxically, she sure liked to talk a lot—slowly, of course.

Where was her best friend and sister-in-law right this moment? Knowing her, she was probably in some kind of unusual predicament somewhere, as she sure had a knack for that.

But she turned her thoughts to her upcoming trip to Washington with Senator Jill Quigley—something she had been looking forward to for a long time. She strolled in long strides down the corridor on the way to her office, to take care of whatever "crises of the day" might arise.

Chapter Four

Palomar Observatory
Palomar Mountain
San Diego County, CA

The reedy distinguished professor mumbled angrily to himself as he impatiently waited for his turn to speak on the outdoor amphitheater of Palomar Observatory, as he looked at the birch and California black oak trees illuminated by the sunset. The weather was always a little cool at the observatory's 5,618-foot altitude this time of year. Bah—he couldn't wait until this debacle was over.

Palomar was arguably the most famous, if not the largest observatory in the United States, located in northern San Diego County, about two hours' drive north of the city. Palomar was owned and operated by the one of the world's preeminent scientific universities—the California Institute of Technology (Caltech). Palomar was a world-class center of astronomical research, home to five telescopes (the largest being the 200-inch Hale Telescope) that were used nightly for a wide variety of scientific purposes.

Recently, a public relations program had been created to increase public interest in astronomy, much to the professor's chagrin. Dr. Jasper Bennett didn't care much about the ignorant masses cheering for his canvas-bound colleague dangling over a smoking vat labeled "SULFURIC ACID"—a stunt straight from the tacky movie serials of his youth.

But his boss, the Dean, *did* care about such things—the main reason he was here tonight. Everybody had a boss, even him, it seemed.

Having tenure only meant they couldn't fire him, he discovered; they could still tell him to do crappy events like this, if he wanted to keep his private secretary and nice corner office in Robinson Hall.

Dr. Bennett, distinguished astrobiologist, was to speak to the Friends of Palomar Observatory this crisp April evening, at a special, $35-per-ticket lecture. But he was a famous scientist who was certainly not accustomed to following someone else's presentation. He grumbled at Dr. Annette Carson, director of the observatory, about the unorthodox prelude to his presentation.

"Things certainly weren't like this thirty years ago," Bennett said harshly. "When I was young, professors had respect for each other. Distinguished faculty didn't have to take a back seat to a greenhorn assistant professor . . . who's doing magic tricks on the grounds of this hallowed place of science, for God's sake. What's this world coming to, Annette?"

The heavy-set, fifty–one-year-old brunette smiled. "I'm sure she has respect for you, Dr. Bennett. You just don't give her any credit, do you?"

"Well . . . we never had female faculty, either, not in *this* department. Not focused enough on their work."

"What's that? 'Not focused on their work?' That's a pretty good one to tell at an observatory." She laughed.

"Yes, yes, quite funny." He peeked out the tent. "Look at that cartoonish outfit. Padded and everything."

"You may not like the outfit, but I assure you there's *no* padding. She's really built like that," she said as they waited in the tent area. "And I'll trade my body with hers any day."

He shook his head and laughed dryly. "Whatever."

"We all have to pay the bills. You might not have to worry about that, but I do."

"That is inconsequential administrative drivel."

"You're *so* special, Professor. But she can draw far bigger crowds here than any faculty member ever did before. The melding of pure science and media—they're curious and want to see something they perceive as dangerous. Aren't you impressed?"

"Not particularly. Straitjacket escapes over a tank of acid, how campy. The crowd is mostly young males wearing rock T-shirts. We would've worn suits and ties in my time."

"It's not real acid, merely some water with dry ice in it. It's just entertainment. Don't you like fun?"

He grunted. "Palomar is no amusement park for 'fun' with the kiddies! She's incredibly bright, I'll give you that. But a scientist has to be completely dedicated to his or her profession, and she just has too many 'hobbies.' How do we know Caltech's not just another passing fancy? I gave up everything, lived in a tiny apartment while I went to graduate school, ate stale bread and beans out of a can—"

"And walked ten miles to classes in the snow, I know. You also worked three jobs to support your widowed old mother, who raised you in a one-room shack with your fifteen siblings."

He scowled. "Yes, make jokes. I didn't have time to be on television—hawking vitamins and kids' cereal, doing celebrity races and boxing, being on Super Gladiators, and guest-starring on the Forensic Files. I was doing real work. Plus, she's not even in the astronomy department. Disgraceful, I say."

"I didn't think television existed when you were her age."

Bennett looked at her angrily. "I won't tolerate such insubordination. Whom do you think you are addressing?"

"A blowhard. And those *summa cum laude* physics faculty are pretty worthless. Did you know every penny of her media earnings went to charity? Get your facts straight before you start criticizing."

He grumbled. "No, I guess not, but still—"

"That was also several years ago, you know, and I asked her to do these quarterly shows—she didn't want to do it. But I see you're driving a new BMW, Professor. Nice ride for a monk-like academic who gave up everything."

Bennett pointed at her angrily. "That's *way* out of line, Annette. Nothing wrong with me doing a little private consulting, it's all in the best interest of science, not some outlandish . . . circus show. And I've earned it." He gestured with his hand.

"No offense, Jasper, but when's the last time there was standing room only to watch you do an experiment? The Friends of Palomar program's enrollment has tripled since I got Bonnie to do PR shows. And if you want to know about giving up things, maybe you should get to know her. She's overcome obstacles you couldn't possibly fathom."

He grunted. "Sad, when science becomes second fiddle to this kind of theatrics. How unladylike."

"Get ready. You're about to go on."

"It's damn well about time."

The five–nine, muscular, blue spandex-clad, black-haired female with the stylized "M^2" on her chest moved away from the large "acid" tank she had just been dangling over as she took the microphone. Bennett stared at the shiny bodysuit, which it appeared a liquefied Dr. Bonita Mendoza had been poured into. No professor in his day would ever be seen in public like *that*. For someone who claimed such disdain for her attire, he certainly seemed to have an intense interest in staring at it, though.

"I am pleased that you have enjoyed my little show," the deaf woman said in her typical slow, high-pitched, lispy voice, which required some effort to understand. "Before I go, I must tell you of my last visit to my physician. She placed the stethoscope on my chest and said, 'big breaths!' To which I looked down sadly and said, "Thank you for trying to make me feel better, but they are the same tiny size as always."

The members of the audience, as usual, groaned at her signature, self-deprecating "deaf joke," as several workers removed her paraphernalia from the stage.

"But that is not the reason you are here, to see me doing tricks. We have before us today one of the greatest minds in the world of astrobiology, one who has authored over one hundred peer-reviewed publications as well as four textbooks.

"He is Distinguished Professor of Astronomy at Caltech, and a man who needs no introduction in the celestial world. I am honored to occupy the same stage as him. Let me introduce . . . Dr. Jasper Bennett." The crowd applauded with one-tenth the amplitude that existed when she had completed her death-defying "escape" ten minutes earlier.

Bennett took the podium, apparently humbled by the marvelous introduction, yet dismayed he didn't receive more applause.

"Thank you, Dr. Mendoza. It is my pleasure to be here today." He pressed the remote, beginning his PowerPoint presentation as the previous performer exited the stage. "As you know, we humans have always fondly fantasized about life on other worlds. Traditional life is carbon-based, made of left-handed, or L-amino acids. But the concept of other types of life also exists."

He brought up several diagrams of various molecule types. "Ammono, or NH_3 life, would be an unusual possibility. Arsenious life would be another peculiar consideration. Arsenic mimics phosphorus, a necessary component of life, and is therefore poisonous; but scientists are interested in the possibility of arsenic-based life, to which phosphorus, ironically, would be toxic."

He showed several additional animated slides of atoms and molecules. "The most exotic of potential life forms would be with another atom that could form four bonds, like carbon—its closest four-valence neighbor, silicon. Although alien to us, silicon-based life could possibly exist on other planets.

"But where would it be found? Fiction writers such as Edgar Rice Burroughs had once felt Venus, our 'sister' planet, to be a place where life, even intelligent civilizations, might be found. After all, it was closer to the Sun, and temperatures there were probably a bit warmer, but capable of sustaining life, they thought. The gravity is 0.9 that of Earth's as well, another ideal quality."

The audience watched the only photos of Venus' surface available—a set of grainy Soviet Venera probe images. "How wrong they were. The second planet from the sun, named after the Greek goddess of love, was literally the closest thing to hell one could imagine. Venus' surface features are obscured by its crushing atmosphere, with ninety-three times the mass of Earth's. And Venus lacks a natural satellite to stabilize its wobble. The atmosphere is hardly supportive of life-forms; it's mostly carbon dioxide, with no biomass on the surface to create a carbon cycle.

"And, the unusual highlights in the atmosphere were found to be something different than the beautiful place early writers had envisioned; they were large clouds of toxic sulfuric acid. Scientists always thought Mercury to be the hottest, most desolate place in our Solar System, but the thick, carbon dioxide-heavy Venusian atmosphere created a massive 'greenhouse effect,' resulting in surface temperatures exceeding 900° F—hot enough to melt lead.

"Efforts at exploring Venus proved horrifically difficult due to the harsh environment. The Soviet Union had sent its Venera probes there in the sixties, most of which did not survive descent onto the surface. Finally, Venera 7 landed in 1970, and lasted only twenty-three minutes before being crushed by the atmosphere—but not before transmitting several photos of what was the first successful landing of a spacecraft on another planet."

Photos of our smaller red neighbor filled the screen. "Mankind then looked to Mars as the most likely place to support habitable life—the temperatures could get as high as 90 degrees Fahrenheit, but as low as minus 190 degrees; nevertheless, certain life-forms *might* exist there.

"But Mars suffered a different fate than Venus; again, it lacked substantial satellites, and its lack of a significant magnetosphere failed to protect it from the streaming, deadly ionized particles known as the 'solar wind,' resulting in most of its atmosphere being stripped away." He pointed to the next slide excitedly. "But, on Mars, there *did* seem to be one thing necessary for life—water, contained mostly in ice at the polar caps.

"The Viking and Pathfinder missions failed, however, to find any evidence of life, although their instrumentation was relatively crude. The lifeless Martian surface did seem to lack a vital component for supporting life—organic molecules. A Martian meteorite named ALH 84001, discovered in Antarctica in 1996, was found to possibly contain evidence of life; this was later disproven, however." He showed several slides of the various meteorites.

"We have always thought life had to exist in climates similar to Earth, but, in fact, the most Earthlike place in the Solar System, chemically and geologically speaking, is not a planet at all, but a moon of our second-largest planet."

He advanced to the next slide, which showed the hazy orange sphere. "Indeed, many scientists were excited in October 1997, when the Cassini orbiter was launched from Earth, for eventual rendezvous with Saturn in 2004; attached to it was the Huygens probe, which was launched towards the giant Titan, whose composition had baffled astronomers for centuries. What would it discover? Would it be a place that would unlock the secrets of a primordial Earth? Or a colossal disappointment—a barren place similar to Venus or Mars? The encounter of Huygens with Titan in 2005 was one of the most eagerly-anticipated events in astronomical history."

Bennett showed additional photographs of the Mars missions as well as those from the Cassini orbiter and Huygens probe; these included maps of Titan plus the few surface photographs available.

He continued to discuss the various possibilities for life on other worlds—all of which were simply theories at this point. He finally concluded his presentation and took questions from the audience, most of whom were somewhat bored by this time, as the most entertaining performer had already stepped down.

A young, sweatshirt-wearing man waved his hand. "Dr. Bennett, thank you for the talk. I'm *so* interested in the Huygens mission. But you left several questions unanswered in my mind. Was there any real evidence of life on Titan or not?"

"That's a good question. We did find evidence of organic molecules such as methane and ethane lakes, and there are a variety of hydrocarbons in the outer atmosphere, but we can't confirm the presence or absence of more complex compounds. The Huygens probe wasn't sophisticated enough for that, but we certainly learned a lot about the surface composition."

"Will there be subsequent missions to Titan?"

"Well, if my colleague here can raise enough money, perhaps," he said condescendingly. "It would have been nice to discover definite signs of life there, but for now, we'll just have to be content with the wonderful things we did discover."

Another young man, obviously science-oriented, raised his hand. "What about the Pluto Express? I was, like, so looking forward to that."

"Pluto? I don't think there's life there, but the Pluto Kuiper Express was cancelled due to budgetary reasons. The New Horizons spacecraft was launched in 2006 and is scheduled to reach Pluto in 2015. We hope to find out fascinating information about the dwarf planet."

"Cool, dude," the young man said, smiling. "But it's just wrong that it's not a planet any more. It just doesn't feel right."

"Ah, yes, well . . . any more questions? I have many copies of my book, 'Titanic Titan,' here for purchase, if anyone wants a signed copy. Are there any more comments or questions?"

A third young man, wearing a rock band T-shirt, held up his hand. "Yeah. M-Square rocks, professor dude! I wanta see another cool show!"

Afterwards, Bennett watched as the group of geeky, testosterone-saturated young men flocked around the slick-suited Bonnie Mendoza, apparently seeing a kindred nerdy spirit at heart, albeit a muscular one who looked like she stepped right out of a comic book (except that most comic book heroines were a tad more busty than the flat-chested magician). They wanted to see the limber physicist do more escape tricks, some acrobatics, and sign autographs. One even asked her out on a date.

In contrast, only two people wanted Jasper Bennett's autograph and a signed copy of his book, he noticed as he grumbled and stepped off the dais. No, sir—things weren't like this in his heyday.

He was simply glad he was now working with some people on the side who could appreciate his real talent. And they paid pretty well, too. Even a distinguished professor's salary only went so far in Southern California.

Chapter Five

Atlas Warehouse
3410 Rampart Street
Washington, D.C.

The April rain poured down incessantly on the rainy, cold evening on the seedy street of the nation's capitol on Friday, as the man and woman converged under the awning of the dilapidated old warehouse. Each was carrying a small parcel, each apparently a bit apprehensive about spying the other, both looking around suspiciously as they met at the clandestine location.

"You got the stuff?" the thirtyish, tall, blonde woman, wearing a trench coat, asked. "I don't have a lot of time, Bobby Joe."

"I got it, Connie." He held up the plastic bag. "You don't know how dangerous this shit was to get. I'm taking a big risk here. I've had this job for a long time."

"Hell, for fifty grand, you deserve to take some risk." The overweight man handed her the small plastic bag, as the tall woman handed him a leather satchel. "Just like you wanted—non-sequential bills, mixed denominations, everything."

His hands shook as he looked at the bag. "Well, the Secret Service will shoot my ass if they find out, and I'll go to federal prison."

"But you need the money, right? That's always more important. They'll never know, and it won't hurt anybody. It's just some hair."

Bobby Joe nodded his head. "I guess so."

"Looks like you just gave yourself a raise. But trust me—you won't be needing much," Connie Dawson said smartly.

"What the hell's that supposed to mean?" the portly man asked in a perplexed tone as he eagerly counted his cash. "How do you know how much money I need?"

"Aw, never mind." Connie shook the man's hand. "All there, good buddy?"

The heavy-set man hesitated and wiped the rain from his face. "Yeah—looks like we've got a deal. I got no goddamn idea what you want with the President's hair, though. Gonna sell it on E-Auction?"

The attractive blonde woman laughed and pointed her finger at Bobby. "You've figured it all out, Bobby Joe. Thanks. Now get the hell out of here."

"Yeah. I hope I never see your sorry face again, you asshole."

"Hah. Don't worry, you won't." She walked back down the street and got into her black Cadillac sedan, while Bobby Joe went back to his old Ford pickup truck, badly in need of new tires and a fresh coat of paint. Hopefully that would change now, with his new windfall.

Bobby Joe Thompson was the White House barber, whose small salon was located right underneath the Oval Office. He was proud to have cut the hair of many Presidents—Johnson, Nixon, and Ford; during the Carter administration, he was moved briefly to another building, as that President wanted to bring in "real" hair stylists; in 1980, however, he returned to the White House, as Ronald Reagan wanted a true barber to cut his hair, not some "sissy stylist."

He and the missus would have a great time with that fifty grand, he thought. Europe would be great next summer, and he could finally buy that classic 1966 Dodge Charger he always wanted. Yessir, things were looking good, he thought as he drove back to his old house. He'd tell Sally he won the lottery—she'd believe *anything*.

• • •

Bobby Joe Thompson's House
4702 Quincy Drive
Washington, D.C.

At home, two days later, the overweight White House barber was breathing heavily while doing a spring clean-up of the yard of his small home. Those damn oak leaves never disintegrated, he muttered to himself as he raked them. He hoped his vegetables would come in better this year. But he sure was out of shape, he thought, as he started wheezing.

"What's wrong, Bobby Joe?" his wife asked him. "You been smokin' again? Doc told you to quit those damn cancer sticks."

"No, having chest pain," he said in a gravelly voice. "I can't breathe."

"Doc Walker said you were fine two weeks ago. Probably your acid reflux again. You can pay the neighbor boy to clean that yard, too, and plant your seeds. No sense in doin' it yourself, at your age, and it's still too cold."

"Goddamn it, Sally, call an ambulance or something. It feels like a weight sitting on my chest."

"Come on, you just had too much to eat. Two pieces of cherry pie for lunch."

"It's not . . . the pie, dammit. Call the hospital now!"

Bobby Joe turned blue as his wife finally grabbed the portable phone out of her pocket and dialed 911.

"911 dispatcher. Can I help you?"

"Please help me—my husband . . . he's having a heart attack."

"Is he breathing, Ma'am?"

"Barely. He's turning blue."

"What's your address?"

"4702 Quincy."

"Do you know CPR?"

"I don't know. I'll try."

Sally Thompson remembered the many medical TV episodes she had watched and began chest compressions and mouth-to-mouth resuscitation. It didn't seem to be doing much good, as he was now unresponsive.

Five minutes later, the paramedics arrived and took over resuscitation. The heart monitor showed asystole—a flat line.

"I'm sorry, Ma'am. It looks like he's had a heart attack. Your husband's dead."

"I know," she sobbed. "How could that happen? He didn't have no heart problem."

"He's what, seventy? He must've had an undiagnosed heart condition. It's not your fault—he probably didn't know," the paramedic said as she gave the grieving widow a hug. "I'm so sorry."

"His doctor just did that fancy treadmill test. He was the White House barber, you know. Everything was great. Got the report right here."

The paramedic perused the report. "I'm sorry, lady, sometimes tests can be wrong. I hate to ask, but I need it for my report, but . . . was he on any, well, performance-enhancing drugs?"

"Bobby didn't take no drugs. He smoked and drank a little, but not that."

The paramedic paused. "No, I mean . . . medications to help him have sex. Some of them can be dangerous if you have a heart condition."

"*Sex*? Heck, no. We haven't done that in years, and he didn't have no heart condition, I already said that."

"I'm sorry, but I had to ask."

"I can't believe it. He was so happy, doing so well . . . and now he's gone."

She put her arm around her. "If it's any consolation, it looks like it happened pretty quickly. I don't think he suffered."

"What happens now? I'm really confused."

"Do you know which funeral home you want?"

"I don't know . . . Gibson's, I guess."

"Okay. We'll go there, I assume you'll make the arrangements."

Sally went back inside while her neighbor consoled her, and prepared to call their daughter and her family. It was then that she noticed the leather satchel partially under the bed. She pulled it out and opened it.

"Betty, come here," Sally Thompson screamed.

The thin, fiftyish neighbor rushed into the small, cluttered bedroom. "What, Sally?"

"This," Sally pointed to the contents of the satchel. "I haven't seen this before."

"Money," Betty said. "How—how much is it?"

Sally Thompson went through the crisp green bills. "Tens, twenties, there's gotta be forty, fifty thousand in here, at least."

"My Lord—where do you think he got it?"

Sally wept and sat on the bed. "I don't know. He was always as straight as an arrow. We've had some money problems, but I can't believe he would steal or anything."

"What are you gonna do with it?"

She closed the satchel and sat it on the bed. "Only one thing I can do, Betty. No one knows about it, and Bobby Joe didn't have much life insurance. I'll give you half if you keep it quiet."

"I . . . don't know."

"What will it hurt? He's dead now."

"But, Sally, whoever gave him that money might come looking for it now. You can't just spend it."

"Not right away. We'll hold onto it for a few months, then spend it. No one will ever know."

Chapter Six

National Cherry Blossom Festival
Presidential Reception
National Gallery of Art
Washington, D.C.

The pink cherry blossoms were in full bloom in mid-April at the nation's capitol as a large VIP crowd gathered for a special reception during the two weeks in spring that comprised National Cherry Blossom Festival. The statuesque blonde woman strode into the main atrium of the grand museum, after presenting her identification to a guard and passing through a metal detector.

Wearing three-inch, size thirteen pumps, she stood slightly over a stately six–four. Although her conventionally-measured body mass index of twenty–nine bordered on "obese," her body-fat measurement (measured by dual-energy X-ray absorptiometry) was only twenty–three percent, well within normal female limits—which meant there was a lot of lean muscle mass in there.

But she certainly wasn't *underweight*—she did, after all, like to eat, she thought as she spied the numerous delicious comestibles on the ornate tables, ready for her consumption. The stunning Cerulean blue gown was a designer original and, of course, was custom-made. Dr. Mary Gwendolyn Williams couldn't buy any decent clothes "off the rack." Most women that tall were thin—not 223 pounds, with a fifty–inch DD bust.

California Senator Jill Quigley met the blonde woman and patted her on the arm as she walked into the room.

"Wendy, it's great you could come. I know it's tough with your job and your son."

She shook the shorter Senator's hand. "No problem, my husband is pretty helpful, most of the time."

"You're lucky. My ex was a real jerk."

"And I really appreciate your inviting me to this fund-raiser. I guess I need to circulate more. And I haven't been here for Cherry Blossom Festival since high school. I forgot how pretty it was."

"That's right. I know how you like to meet people."

"Is the President here yet?" Wendy whispered.

"Yes, he's over there, next to Speaker Watson."

"Ohmigod, I can't believe it. I actually *know* some of these people. Isn't that the Vice Chairman of the Joint Chiefs over there?" Wendy asked, pointing to the six–foot, gray-haired man in dress Army uniform.

Jill nodded. "Yes, that's General Gallagher. Would you like to meet him?"

She scowled. "Not particularly. He has some, well . . . different thoughts on things than I do. Know thine enemy, I always say."

"Oh, nonsense. If you want to play this game, you need to deal with people from all walks of life. No better time than the present. The military types are just like us."

Wendy laughed. "Not hardly."

"Let's go."

"Uh, I don't think . . ." It was too late, as Jill took her by the hand and walked over and found Gen. Gallagher at the seafood table.

"Hello, General Gallagher," Quigley said to the six–foot man wearing three stars on his dress uniform.

"Senator Quigley. It's so nice to see you." The two shook hands.

"General, I have someone I would like you to meet. Wendy, this is Lt. Gen. Brant Gallagher. General, Dr. Wendy Williams of California."

He looked up at the blonde with the shoulder-length hair. "Yes, I believe I have seen you on television, Dr. Williams."

Wendy laughed. "Not singing on my old kids' TV show, I hope," she drawled. Her superb rehabilitation team employed dozens of speech therapists who could work wonders with speech-impaired children, yet they couldn't help her get rid of that damn Tennessee accent. She wasn't particularly proud of that heritage.

"Hmm, I don't believe I'm familiar with that, as I don't have children. But I've seen you on some commercials, I believe, and at some fund-raisers."

"Probably so."

"How do you know Senator Quigley, Doctor?"

"I'm president-elect of the California Medical Association. I'm a pediatric rehabilitation specialist, and will be moving to Sacramento next year."

"Politically active, I see." Gallagher took a sip of his champagne. "Good for you. Most professionals aren't."

"Certainly. If you don't want someone else to drive your car, you'd better drive it yourself, General, or the world will pass you by, right?"

Gallagher paused and took a bite of his shrimp cocktail. "Interesting paraphrase—a woman of great perception, I see. You also know Senator Orson, I understand?"

"Yes. I have a special interest in his genetics bill, to protect against unsafe experimentation and use of genetic information. Someone has to regulate the exponentially growing technology we have available today."

"A conservative. So, who is watching the watchmen, right? To make sure we aren't creating Frankenstein's monster?"

"Something like that." She laughed and winked at him. "Let's keep Pandora's box closed, shall we?"

"You therefore believe we shouldn't be doing things to make the world better? This isn't about making super-soldiers, contrary to what image I might portray in my military capacity. We want to identify those with disabilities or genetic defects, and spare them the agony of going through life like that. Correct the problems at an early stage."

"Interesting point you have, General," Jill said.

Wendy stared down at the trim, six–foot general, as her mouth opened wide. "So, who decides what constitutes a defect—*you?* 'Sparing them the agony?' What the hell's that supposed to mean? And why do you care?"

Gallagher took a step backwards in amazement. "What do you mean, 'why do I care?' I care about human beings, just like you.

Don't stereotype me because of my uniform."

"I'm sure he didn't mean anything, Wendy," Jill said.

The general crossed his arms and paused. "No, it's okay, Jill. You sure speak your mind, don't you, Dr. Williams?"

"I meant no disrespect, General. However, I am passionate about my work, as I'm certain you are about yours."

"Yes, I most certainly am. But let me, for one moment, play the devil's advocate."

"Shoot. I'm all ears."

"What if a great scientific development, in genetics, for example, was quashed by bureaucratic red tape? Wouldn't that be just as sinister as what you're suggesting?"

"Sir, if your 'great development' includes 'eliminating' defective people, then, hell no."

"Wendy . . ." Jill said nervously.

She ignored the senator, as the line in the sand had been drawn. "Have you ever met one of those 'defective' children? Looked into their eyes, held their hands?"

He laughed. "Personally, I have not, but what does it matter? I welcome the opportunity to debate my case. Dr. Williams, you take care of children with, for example, Down syndrome, born with cystic fibrosis, inborn errors of metabolism, cerebral palsy, right?"

"Of course. Most of the children I see have special needs. Many are accident, illness, or burn victims, though, and don't have genetic problems. I had a TV show which featured several characters of different ethnic backgrounds with disabilities who taught the wonders of science to children. Everyone is unique and has value. Maybe not to the military, though."

"And you try to make them better, right? Walk, talk better? Live independently?"

"I suppose so, but don't try and twist what you're proposing to be the same as my rehab team helping disabled kids. You have no idea what they want, what their joys and sorrows are, or the wonders they bring to their families." She scowled at him.

"Those seem pretty obvious. Mentally retarded, those who can't walk? Come now—what kind of life is that to have in the 21st century? Blood tests combined with ultrasound can identify Down syndrome with ninety percent accuracy by twelve weeks. The aberrant pregnancy can therefore be terminated in time."

"*Aberrant? Terminated*?" she yelled, looking at him angrily. "I see—you have made yourself God, who has the right to determine life. And where do we stop, General Gallagher? Ethnicity? Skin color? The concept of liberal eugenics to enhance human beings is repugnant, and selective termination of fetuses with chromosomal abnormalities is disgusting . . . beyond my comprehension as a human being."

"I don't follow you, Doctor," the gray-haired general said dryly. "I am appreciative of people of all origins. And two white people talking about racism seems to be a ludicrous discussion."

"Yeah, I guess a blonde Aryan like me fits into your concept of what's 'right.' Just like Adolf Hitler and his perfect regime."

"*Excuse me*?" Gallagher said as he stepped back. "I don't think I heard that. Did you just call me—"

"I believe you heard me, General. My voice carries pretty well." The aquamarine eyes were piercing as they stared down at him, as he stood there, speechless.

"Well," Jill interjected. "This has been an interesting discussion. I need to take the general to meet Rep. Zachary over there. He's been dying to meet him."

"So nice to meet you, Dr. Williams," Gallagher said coldly as he shook her large hand limply.

"Yes, likewise," Wendy replied back.

Jill Quigley took Gallagher to meet Rep. Zachary in the corner, then came back, and went with Wendy to the appetizer table.

"Wendy, those were *not* the most appropriate things to say. Gallagher's the Vice Chairman of the Joint Chiefs of Staff, and some feel he'll make a run for the Democratic presidential nomination in 2012. Don't embarrass me—this *isn't* how it works."

"So? We're Republican, in case you didn't know."

"It doesn't matter. You or I might need his influence at some point. What if you need a favor from him someday?"

She blushed. "I'm sorry, I don't know what got into me, but I just can't take that eugenics crap. That's the wrong button to push with me. And I'll ask someone else for favors."

Jill patted her on the arm. "I know, but, if you want to be a politician, you need to make nice. He disgusts me too, but that's

Washington. It's not like San Diego or Sacramento, where it's sunny all the time. Get with it."

"I don't have to do anything for anybody. And why'd you take me over there, anyway? This was some kind of test, wasn't it? To see how I'd react?"

"No, it wasn't—are you kidding?" Quigley looked up at her massive protégé. "I've known you for almost ten years, and you used to be able to suck up like the best of us. But you may want to reconsider—is this really what you want?"

Wendy looked away and smiled. "I really don't know. Maybe this isn't it, after all, if I have to swallow my principles."

"It isn't about that. We all have principles, but you can't use social opportunities to prove your point. I loathe Gallagher and half of the other people here, but you have to see the big picture. Can you do that?"

She looked away for a few seconds, then snapped back. "Yeah, I hear what you're saying, Jill. I'll be a better team player next time."

"Good. Now let's go meet some other people."

"Can I meet President Graham?"

"Well . . . I'll ask his aide what his agenda is. Why don't you get a drink?"

• • •

Wendy walked back to the refreshments table, obtained a virgin Piña Colada, and looked at the people she knew, and the fascinating world she wanted to be a part of. She was immersed in thought when she felt Jill tap on her shoulder.

"Mr. President . . . Dr. Gwendolyn Williams."

Wendy gasped in shock. "It's nice to meet you, sir," she said softly in the highest voice she could muster.

"It's nice to meet you as well. I've heard a lot of good things about you, such as your charity work with disabled children. I know the Governor thinks highly of you."

She almost fell backwards, not used to being on high heels. "You've heard of *me?* I can't believe that."

"Don't underestimate yourself, Doctor. It's my business to know people."

"I know you meet a lot of people. You met the Super Bowl champions a few days ago, I heard."

"You seem to really know what's going on, Doctor. We might need a new Surgeon General one of these days."

"Oh, sure." She laughed. "I know, for example, that you like football—you were a pretty good player at Ohio State."

"That's right. It's one of my greatest pleasures, meeting those fellows. Football's a fantastic game."

"It is. I watch it all the time."

The tall African-American president tapped his finger on his chin. "I just remembered . . . you're related to the new Conquerors head coach, aren't you? The Hall of Fame wide receiver."

She hesitated. "Uh, sort of. Nice fellow."

"Yes, he was a great player. I heard you were a pretty good athlete yourself."

"Past tense, sir. My days of powerlifting and flinging heavy steel spheres are over. I like to spend my time helping the less fortunate achieve their goals. *Without* genetic experimentation."

"Yes, about that . . . I heard you had a somewhat loud discussion with my best friend General Gallagher."

"Oh, your friend . . ." She thought of some way she could shrink or disappear like her magician pal Bonnie. "Mr. President, I had no idea, and am very sorry if I offended you. However, I stand by my comments on his views."

Graham laughed. "Relax, that jerk would be the last person in the world I'd want for a friend. I admire your brass, standing up to him like that."

"Thank you. I feel strongly about those things, sir."

"Yes, I . . . agree." Graham became diaphoretic and mopped his brow. "It's . . . hot in here, don't you think? I—"

"Mr. President? Are you okay?"

Suddenly the patrons in the room started gasping, as a large number of Secret Service agents began clearing out the area.

"What's going on?" one of the agents asked.

"The President—it looks like he's having a heart attack!" she exclaimed.

"Get him out now!" the senior agent yelled, pushing her away.

"I'm a doctor. I can help," she said as the men in black quickly ushered her and the other guests out of the museum. She watched in horror as the team of well-trained agents attempted resuscitation on President Graham, to no avail, as she began crying. She had difficulty seeing through the crowd as she was whisked outside with the other patrons, but the tearful physician knew one thing for certain.

Andrew W. Graham, the forty–fourth President of the United States, was dead.

Chapter Seven

Four months later
Las Vegas Conquerors Training Complex
Las Vegas, NV

"Come on, do it better this time!" the perturbed head coach bellowed at his kickoff return unit. "That last series was a piece of crap. I've half a mind to get out there myself and show you how it should be done."

The six–one, dark-haired, forty–one-year-old man watched as Number 9's size thirteen right foot applied a peak of 10,500 Newtons of force to the 0.41-kilogram leather prolate spheroid, launching it at a velocity of 121 miles per hour in a parabolic trajectory down the grassy field. At least that's what the irritating, blue spandex-clad placekicker on the "Football Fizzics" episode of the kids' science show *Dr. Wendy's Science Squad* said about the average kickoff, he remembered from his boxed DVD set.

The subtleties of drag coefficients and angular momentum were hopelessly lost on him, the nerdy girl maintained sternly when he was a teenager. But he really didn't care about a Wilson F1010 football's mass, elastic modulus, or moment of inertia—he had too many other problems to worry about right now, such as how much harder this new job was than he thought. What kind of mess had he gotten himself into?

The kick was fielded at the five-yard line by the returner, who promptly fumbled the ball into the end zone, while a member of the kickoff team recovered it for a touchdown. The special teams coach had to keep the normally poised head coach from rushing onto the field and killing his players.

"That was disgraceful," he screamed as he kicked a pile of dirt and threw his cap onto the field. "Do it again and get it right, or we'll be here forever."

"It's been a long day, Jay," the special teams coach pleaded. "Let's start up again tomorrow. Don't you have a date?"

"Yeah, but that can wait. Get them back out there for another series, Dave." The special teams coach grumbled and motioned for the teams to assemble again. And his gorgeous girlfriend Danielle would have to take a back seat to his first love: football.

The infrared radiation emanating from the setting sun was stifling to the massive men rambling down the practice field in early August. Training camp for the new expansion Las Vegas Conquerors football team was in mid-cycle, and the team was preparing for their first preseason game next week. The desert was always hot this time of year, and today was no exception. But the coach would work the special teams unit until they got it right.

Rookie head coach Jaime Mendoza Flores wasn't terribly pleased with his players this scorching day. Expansion teams by definition weren't very blessed in the star department, and were often a bunch of rookies and second-string players scrounged from other teams. But his expectations had always been high, and a heavy weight had been placed upon him for his first year in pro football.

The fact that he went to the Pro Bowl for several years, was Most Valuable Player of Super Bowl XXXI, and was just inducted into the Pro Football Hall of Fame didn't mean squat any more. Like all coaches, he would be judged by his team's performance, not by the glories of years past. In this day of the fickle sports fan, no one much cared about "Jettin' Jay" any longer.

He kept asking himself why he'd given up a comfortable life to coach a bunch of expansion team losers. He was handsome, articulate, and intelligent, and had been a senior analyst for ESPN. This gig was actually a cut in pay, and a huge jump in time commitment and responsibility.

He coached Division I college football for several years, and led the University of Missouri to the Fiesta Bowl in 2006, where they lost to Oregon on a last-second field goal. His friends thought he was crazy. But not his family, who knew that the competitive drive would never go away. And pursuing the unusual seemed to be a trait for members of the affluent, athletic, academic Mendoza Flores family.

He looked up as the punt return team prepared to field a kick. A pretty good punt, about sixty yards, he thought, was fielded at the five-yard line by Rodd Edmondson, a second-string utility back he got from San Francisco. He took off down the field and was promptly knocked flat by one of the defensive players. Edmondson got up and started shoving the tackler.

"Hey, break it up out there," Jay said loudly. He always told people to call him "Jay," because the proper Spanish pronunciation of his first name, "Himey," never seemed very glamorous. "This is just practice, Rodd. You deserved that hit, the crappy way you were running." Edmondson looked at the coach angrily and took his place on the field again.

Jay looked out at the sky again, and noticed that the odd bluish haze was there—easily separated from objects in his vision, but nonetheless present. It was another blue Monday; Mondays were always that color, everything glowing with the pale hue. Tuesdays were orange, Wednesdays green. Sundays were bright magenta—his favorite. The colored days were a secret between he and his little sister, who understood about the colored days, although hers were different; all synesthetes—those rare persons who had unusual "blended" sensory experiences—had differences in perception.

His mom was a synesthete, too, although she didn't see the colors as vividly as he and Bonnie. He remembered how his *Lita* (Grandma) Flores told him about the smell, taste, and colors of musical notes. Bonnie and his mom were both quite adept at mathematics, the former being a genius in that regard—while he had the mathematical acumen of a brain-damaged chimp.

Some people even thought a few synesthetes were clairvoyant, with the ability to sense the future, although research had never been able to confirm that. Certainly, he had been a great receiver and kick returner mostly because of his God-given speed. But he also had the uncanny ability to sense what was going to happen next with the defense. And he knew it wasn't his innate ability to read defenses—he was terrible at memorizing his playbook.

Somehow, he always had a sense as to what might happen next—on or off the field, and became a top-notch Division I college coach and premier pro sportscaster because of that. His sister could always pick the game winners by using her colossal mathematical abilities—committing to memory all sports statistics known to man, and analyzing them in every way possible. A "brute force" solution. But the more artistic sibling did almost as well by simply guessing—a fact which made him one of the most popular sportscasters around. And gambling was a no-no in his family, even before he got the coaching job.

He was the consummate playboy, never in a serious relationship. Sure, he had lots of opportunities, but they were all superficial. He came close to marriage once, but that blew up in his face when he couldn't stop playing the field. He wasn't complaining, though—he decided to live his life that way, and had no regrets.

But he always thought about the one that he might have let get away. Looks fade with time, after all—true beauty lies underneath, he thought as he looked dreamily into the pastel desert sky. Maybe it was time to grow up and settle down with someone like that. But *she* was off the market now.

The six–one former wide receiver still walked with a slight limp, a consequence of the injury that had shredded his knee twelve years ago. He attempted a comeback after multiple surgeries and saw limited action on special teams, but never recovered the blazing speed that set him apart from the other players. But he learned to be grateful for what he had, which was more than most; a special person showed him that you could always have less than that.

He jumped back to reality, as he realized that what he had *now* was a team who was likely to get their butts kicked in their preseason opener if they didn't get in gear. And he didn't want to be the laughing stock of the coaching world. Some things needed to be left in the past, because you couldn't go back.

• • •

Jay went out to the practice field early the next morning to work with the receivers. He had especially high expectations for one of his wideouts, Jason Lee Torpin. Torpin, a somewhat troubled player prone to behavior problems and substance abuse, was felt by management to be a worthy "reclamation project." He had once been suspended from the league for one year, and his old team, Indianapolis, was fed up with both his on- and off-field antics, and released him on waivers.

Another of Torpin's problems was that he had torn his left anterior cruciate ligament three months ago, and probably would need to sit out a year. Miraculously, however, he made an astounding recovery after reconstructive surgery, and team physicians declared his knee as good as, if not better than, before.

During training camp, Torpin had again showed flashes of the brilliance that had earned him the Heisman Trophy seven years ago, but also demonstrated much of the inconsistency that plagued him through his seven-year career. And the new head coach's patience was wearing thin this morning.

"Hey, Torpin," the fiery coach demanded, "get your fricking lazy ass in gear. I'm not paying you for that kind of crap. Even my little sister could kick your tail."

The six–two African-American receiver ran up to the coach and stuck his finger in his chest. "What'd you say to me, Mendoza? Go to hell, you has-been. How you got this job, I'll never know."

The assistant coaches gasped in horror as Jay stepped back in disbelief. "What the hell did you say to me?" Jay shoved the slightly larger man back. "Get off the field before I really do kick your ass. $10,000 fine, and if you *ever* touch me again, I'll fire your sorry butt."

"You gonna make me, loser? Just 'cause you got into Canton, don't mean shit to me. You didn't deserve it."

Jay pointed his finger in Torpin's face. "Get out and cool down, now. I've been through wars out there too, punk. Bad knee, doesn't mean I can't take you on." He was still in pretty good shape, and had sparred enough with his two pugilistic siblings to take care of himself.

"Bring it." Torpin came at him swinging and knocked him against the wall, as Jay tried to throw a right cross. A group of other players and coaches stopped the melee.

"Goddamn it, Torpin, what's wrong with you?" receivers coach Buck Stellwag yelled. "You know what happened last year!"

"Yeah, right, that's how I ended up on this loser team. I don't like smart pretty boy here, that's all. I grew up in the ghetto, not with a silver spoon in my mouth."

"Get used to it. You don't like me, then go." Jay pointed to the gate. "Don't let the door hit you on the way out."

"Move it out of here, you sorry sack of shit," Stellwag yelled. "You're gone."

"Fine with me, asshole." The assistant coaches escorted the infuriated Jason Lee Torpin back to the locker room, while Stellwag remained to talk to Jay and walk back to his office.

• • •

"Don't know what the hell's gotten into him," the early-fortyish Stellwag said as he took a seat in Jay's office. "You gave him a shot to start again, clean slate, and now this. Brags about his championship ring from last year, but he ended up a scrub, 'cause he couldn't keep his big mouth shut. So they traded his ass."

"Yeah, lucky us." The tall former wide receiver walked around and thought pensively. "No question, though—it looks like 'roid rage' to me. Seen it before, back in the day when lots of guys were users. You remember how it was." He picked up the thirteen-inch, dark-haired, blue-clad female action figure from the display on his cluttered credenza and began playing with it. "A bunch of the fellas were on the juice."

His old college and pro teammate laughed. "Yeah, right, Jay. How's he gonna do that? League's testing processes are tight as a drum. He's just an arrogant asshole, and you don't need steroids for that. And he's not the sharpest in the brain department, in case you didn't notice."

"I mean it, Buck. I can smell it, and I saw it in his eyes. I'm going to find out what's going on."

"You and your damn intuition's gonna be the end of you. You got a team to run, so let the management deal with Torpin. I've known you a long time, now."

"Damn straight, and that boy isn't right. He's on something."

Stellwag took a sip of the coffee he poured from the pot in the corner. "So what you gonna do?"

"Don't know. But I'm going to find out why he's so buzzed up. And I know just the person to help me."

"Uh, who's that? Hope it's not your little heroine friend there."

He shook his head as his eyes opened wildly. "Nobody. Just don't tell anyone else. I don't want to start a ruckus."

"You need to call the commissioner's office if you have a concern. Don't do it, man, you'll get in all sorts of trouble."

"Not yet. Just roll with me on this one, Buck. I need your support." He put the darker-skinned doll back on its stand and turned his interest to the taller, heavier-set blonde female doll standing next to it on the display.

"Okay, you're the coach, but just don't get my ass fired along with yours. Just remember, though—those superheroes are for kids. They aren't real. Life is." He watched Jay pick up the blonde action figure, part of a limited edition collectors' set. "Now get your head out of the clouds and put *that* one down, buddy. The past is gone—you can't get it back by wishing."

"Huh?" He threw his pen down angrily. "What the hell is *that* supposed to mean?"

Stellwag grinned. "*You* know what. We go way back, remember? You broke a lot of hearts, pal. That one, you crushed."

Jay sighed as he put the full-figured, round-faced blonde doll back on its stand next to sappy TV show companions *Mendoza Milagroso, Admiral Ampere, Gravi-Golfer,* and *Chemical Cowboy*. "Yeah, I wish it had never happened, especially now. Women never forget, and it's awkward."

Stellwag laughed. "I'll bet, especially after she found you in bed with her roommate that afternoon. You're lucky she didn't break you in half, JJ. She's pretty frickin' strong."

"She didn't get the chance. I could run the 40 in 4.1 back then, and speed isn't one of her attributes."

"Hell, I wish I'd had those kinds of problems, with women falling all over me. I should be so lucky."

The glamorous Mexican-American man looked out his east bay window towards the rising sun. He had dated exotic supermodels, actresses, even a European princess at one point—but he couldn't forget *her*—the girl he dated while he was a senior at USC and pursuing the Heisman Trophy. And she didn't, as Stellwag had suggested, "fall all over him;" she was one sassy gal he had to put on his "A" game for, as she wasn't easily impressed.

She was as tall as him, although a couple of his supermodel girlfriends were, too; but they weren't heavier and stronger. She certainly wasn't beautiful in the traditional sense, but the freckle-faced, countrified blonde was pretty darn bright—and his family was no slouch in that department.

The down-to-earth Southern gal was like one of the guys in a lot of aspects, and certainly enjoyed sports, both as a spectator and participant (football and wrestling in particular); but she could, he was delighted to discover, meet those "special" needs his teammates couldn't. She worked and played hard, a driven yet curiously self-indulgent young woman who enjoyed all of life's pleasures to the fullest—particularly rich food, loud music, and, best of all, a good roll in the hay.

The fun-loving, Falstaffian female named Mary Gwendolyn Gallinsworth was a strength athlete on a partial scholarship to San Diego State—a place far away from home, which was fine with her. The eighteen-year old new friend of his sister helped him gain twenty pounds in his senior year, making him a first-round draft pick in 1990 and runner-up in the Heisman Trophy voting.

They dated for a year, and it was her first serious relationship. Pro football beckoned after that, and he tried to forget about her, but it was hard. In a bizarre twist of fate that no one would have possibly predicted, she was, ironically, now part of his family—but she had moved on, and now had her own husband and child.

And now it was time for him to move on. He had his current smoking-hot girlfriend, Dani, to think about. There was a heck of a lot of fantasizing he could do about *that* succulent body, if practice would ever end. It was going to be a long day, and it had just started.

Chapter Eight

Two days later
Geneseo Casino
Las Vegas, NV

The five–nine, cinnamon-colored woman strode into the lavish casino at eight PM on the hot Saturday evening. The woman wearing the red dress hadn't been there in, what—seven years? It had been *too* long. She cut a striking figure, the red pumps adding about three inches to her height; a horde of men craned their necks as the muscular, obsidian-haired woman passed.

Most of the sounds of the bustling establishment escaped her, but the two cochlear implant receivers affixed to her large ears allowed the deaf woman to perceive some speech. The irony made her laugh—big ears which couldn't hear. But the assistive devices worked best in quiet environments. It was much different in a noisy casino—one reason she didn't like going there any more. But certainly not the main reason, she thought as she fixed her gaze on the hundreds of patrons playing roulette, craps, and blackjack, and thought about the life that was once hers.

The taste and smell of the casino were especially enticing this evening as she strolled inside and looked around. The large security man in the main lobby received a call on his earpiece as she walked briskly past him in the corridor.

"Yeah, boss?" he asked.

"I don't believe it. Bogey on the main floor. Please intercept."

"Who is it? Some wiseguy trying to con us?"

"Not exactly, but it's someone we really don't want here. We'll get cleaned out, and there's nothing we'll be able to do about it."

He sighed. "I need a description, Boyce. There are thousands of people in the casino this time of night."

"No, you don't. She just walked right past you. Pay attention."

The man thought for a few minutes, then slapped his hand on his forehead. "Oh, man, you've gotta be kidding. Not *her*, after all these years."

"You got an image in your head? Then get going so we don't get fired," the loud voice on the transceiver said.

The security man's partner looked at him curiously. "What is it, Big Mo?"

"Lady we really don't want in here. A legend."

"A chick? A nice piece of ass?"

Morgan laughed. "Yeah, if you want to end up on the ground in pieces. Trust me, you stay *away* from this piece of booty—it's tough and grisly. Look, but never touch."

"Huh. This, I gotta see."

The portly Morgan and his partner walked down the main hallway into the atrium where they interrupted the fast-moving woman's locomotion.

"May I help you gentlemen?" she said in a slow, high-pitched voice.

"Ah, Ms. Mendoza. It has been a while. I did not really expect to meet *you* again. Not here, anyway."

The deaf woman watched his lips carefully, stared at him, and noticed a garlic smell. "It has been many years since I visited this fine gaming establishment—Morgan, isn't it?"

"Very good with names, as always." He stared at her dress. "You seem to have a little better taste in clothes these days, as well."

"Yes, my exclusive tailor makes appropriate selections for me. But it's *Dr.* Mendoza now."

He put his hand over his chest. "Oh, my apologies. A healer of the sick. Congratulations."

She laughed. "Not that kind of doctor, but the research kind. A physicist, to be exact. I completed my thesis and other requirements one month ago."

"Of course. May I inquire, however, as to the nature of your business here, Doctor? I do not believe we have any magic acts booked tonight."

She laughed. "No, I am *Mendoza Milagroso* no more, except for special performances. I am only interested in finding a suitable companion for the evening and consuming intoxicating beverages. Is there a problem with my consumption of ethanol? I am over twenty–one." She had actually just turned thirty–four less than a week ago, although she looked younger than that.

"Not at all. You are always welcome to imbibe in our refreshments and to search for companionship. Perhaps I can help you find that special someone—do you prefer male or female?"

"Huh?" She thought for a moment. "Well, I believe I will try a virile, handsome man tonight."

"These days, you have to ask."

"Maybe I will try the other kind tomorrow. And I will find my own, thank you."

"Didn't I hear that you were out of circulation, though?"

She looked at him for a minute in puzzlement. "My circulation is fine. I watch my cholesterol, take my chewable vitamins, and exercise every day."

He smiled. "No. I meant that I heard you were married now. Lucky man."

"I suppose he is. But tonight, I seek something adventurous and different. You certainly can understand that, no? This is 'Sin City,' is it not?"

"Certainly. But you must understand that we will not be allowed to sell you chips."

"What? How rude—I will eat all the chips I want if I so choose. It is none of your business what I consume."

"Uh, no, the other kind of 'chips' we sell here. Certain activities are, eh . . . off limits to you, shall we say?"

"Oh." She laughed. "Of course. To suggest otherwise would be unsportsmanlike, and certainly unprofitable for you. And not in my best interest either. Fox in the henhouse, so to speak."

"Understood. Very well, then. Enjoy yourself." The slow-spoken, strangely verbose woman left the large man and walked off towards the bar, and looked in awe at her former avocation, the one she now was glad she had left behind.

She was a compulsive gambler—but not the kind who lost everything and became penniless. She realized in college that she could use her rare mathematical abilities to make a lot of money. Money she didn't need, because her family was well-off financially. But the addiction had enticing allure.

Despite her amazing number abilities, Bonita Mendoza wasn't the best at monitoring her money, however; she had a vague idea how much she had, and allowed her brother-in-law, a finance professor, to invest it and set up automated bill payments.

Her husband, for example, in their first year of marriage, noticed that she had earned $440,000 one year; he told her he thought perhaps she had been gambling again; but he learned from the bank that, no, that was just interest on one of her several certificates of deposit—at six percent, almost eight million dollars in principal. And there were other investments and royalties from her security patents she had sold to several companies.

At the insistence of her best friend Wendy, she entered a rehab program eleven years ago and had stayed clean for years. She was just here for a little fun and a rendezvous with a handsome man. She was certain that one would be along any minute.

• • •

The glimmer from the six–two, sandy-haired, forty–year-old man's $2,500 tuxedo caught several pairs of heavily made-up female eyes as he approached the opulent lounge area of the lavish Geneseo Casino—a place reserved for only the upper crust of society.

He had just come in from outside, after a particularly close call—someone had been following him, he knew from a tip-off. Bad luck for that guy, he thought as he wiped the coffee from his right hand. He had accidentally spilled some on the unfortunate gentleman just a few minutes earlier; he was a headhunter who had been harassing him for weeks.

The tall man had told him he wasn't interested, and the recruiter they sent was fortunate to have only suffered a ruined shirt, courtesy of a double latte. The good doctor had earned some rest and relaxation, he thought as he brushed away the attendants who flocked around him like flies.

He looked at the stainless steel Omega Seamaster on his left wrist, one of many fine Swiss timepieces in his collection. Eight–thirty—the night was just getting under way. He winked at the many beautiful women that caught his eye; he knew that he certainly caught theirs. He knew a lot of things, but most of all, how to please the ladies. He had tried to leave his hard-drinking, fast-living life behind, and had achieved some success in that regard over the last few years. He sometimes missed those days.

He had a beard at one time, but his wife made him shave it off. Dang, she was bossy, he thought. But he wanted something a little different tonight, and smiled as he spied the athletic, dark-haired woman at the bar, nursing a margarita. He was an expert at women. Gambling, he knew very little about. Maybe the *Latina* who appealed to his dangerous side knew about games of chance. He savored the opportunity to impress her with his multilingual repertoire.

"*Hola,*" the well-dressed man said in a Southern drawl to the interesting-looking woman. "*¿Qué pasa, Senõrita?*"

She turned around, apparently annoyed. "Beg pardon? Are you addressing me?" she said as she put her right hand on her hip. "And it is *Senõra*. Leave me alone, quaint yokel," she said as she looked away, indifferently.

"Look sharp. I'm talking to you, *chica*."

"Is that all you can say in Spanish?" The deaf woman spoke slowly in her the high-pitched, lispy voice. "How pathetic you must be, like a lowly *hormiga*."

"Hey, I'm not one of those, but I thought you might be—"

"A *hormiga* is an insect of the family *Formicidae*—an ant, moron. I will stomp on you."

He looked at her red stilettos. "Hey, I might like that."

She looked away and took another sip of her drink. "I am certain you would. What has happened to your shirt, lummox?"

"You don't want to know about it. It's pretty dangerous."

"I bet. It looks like you spilled coffee on yourself."

"More than that. But I know a few more phrases, if you'll just let me get a word in. For a deaf person, you sure talk a lot."

She laughed in a shrill tone. "Please. I am fluent in Spanish, French, Italian, Latin, Portuguese, German, Greek, Russian, and Romanian. How could you possibly impress me?"

"I'm sure a dead language like Latin is really useful."

"All knowledge is useful, but I can see that you would not know about that, one of limited intellect." She took a sip of her drink. "You are from the South, correct?"

"That's right. Born and bred in the great state of Tennessee."

She sneered. "I see—a hillbilly. My husband is one of those. I don't trust him, as he is quite perverted. All he thinks of is sex. I hope you have more intellectual interests."

"What a coincidence. My wife's *Latina,* like you. Unlike you, she's straight as an arrow, which drives me nuts, and I like some action."

"A 'man of action,' eh?" She said, looking bored. "So, what is it you require, dolt? You are bothering me." She removed a long stick of red licorice from her metallic Zero Halliburton purse and put it into her mouth, sucking on it. "I am easily irritated by intellectual simpletons."

"That's a pretty mean-looking metal purse, lady. You got secret spy stuff in there?"

"I have many items in my aluminum alloy purse, whose shell can withstand a gunshot and a drop from 50,000 feet. More than meets the eye."

"You look pretty hot. You want some action, lady? I'm the guy to give you some."

"Are you propositioning me?" She took another sip of her cocktail. "What is your name, ignoramus?"

"Dirk."

"Huh? Dork? It suits you."

He wrote it out on a piece of paper. "D-I-R-K."

She laughed as she took a sip of her drink. "Dirk? What a pitiful moniker, derived from the Scottish term for a small dagger. It undoubtedly refers to the stature of the tiny appendage inside your trousers."

"Hey, lady, that's insulting. I'll show you what's in my pants." The bartender raised his eyebrows.

"Right here? How indiscreet. I am far too cultured for such debased crudity. You must be of the species *Homo erectus.*"

"Well, I thought we could just go to my hotel room."

"Ha. I do not hardly think so. Your room is probably the janitor's closet with a cot inside. Not very comfortable for my delicate skin."

He put his hand over his chest. "What've you got against me? I'm here because the concierge told me your services are available, for a premium rate."

She watched intently as she read his lips. "Am I understanding you correctly, that you wish to play with me for remuneration? How dare you insinuate that?"

"That's the general idea." He reached for his wallet, but couldn't find it in any of his pockets. "What the heck?"

She laughed again. "Do not tell me that you have no money. I have heard that one before. No pay, no play."

"Uh, I can't seem to find it. Will you take an I.O.U.?"

The amateur magician pulled a black leather wallet from her unimpressive cleavage. "You should not leave your things within my undergarments. How it got in here, I don't know." She removed five hundred dollar bills and stuffed them down her bra, which was an easy feat, as the small-breasted woman had plenty of spare room.

"I will keep this for my aggravation. Perhaps save for a desperately needed mammary augmentation."

"Hey, you stole my wallet. I should have you arrested."

"I merely have recovered what you have carelessly lost. And you had better not be threatening arrest again, cretin." She pulled a set of gleaming gold Smith & Wesson Model 100 handcuffs from the metallic purse. "Keep it up, and you will be wearing these tonight." The bartender opened his eyes wide and finished drying his glasses.

"Well! What'd you have in mind—I assume you're not a cop or something, because those don't look like standard issue. And I thought this kind of stuff was legal here in Nevada."

"A common misconception. Such promiscuous activities are legally permitted only in the brothels, in cities with populations less than 400,000. But, for many years, I was with the police . . ." she said with a dreamy look in her eyes. "All those years of excitement."

"So, what happened, lady? Get fired for being stuck-up?"

"I thought it would be more challenging to become a theoretical physicist. I study the topological movements of subatomic particles at Caltech."

"Really? I'd like to exchange a few particles with you."

"You are bothering me. I should slap you for that crude comment."

"What's your name, anyway? I've seen you before—you've been on television."

She laughed. "Yes, I am famous, of course."

"I think it was on the local children's access channel. Anyway, I hear you're pretty dangerous stuff. My wife is pretty dangerous too, if she ever caught me having an affair."

She rolled her eyes and ignored him. "Whatever."

"I do classified work too, babe. Work on combating medical errors. Top secret."

"Is that correct? It sounds so exciting—is one of those 'medical errors' inside your pants? A mistake of nature?"

"Hey, that's insulting."

"As I have told you, though, I am married."

"So am I. What's the big deal? I'll show you something you'll never forget."

"I probably will want to forget it, sadly." She threw the bartender fifty dollars in exchange for a bottle of tequila. "This will help numb the pain." She put the 750 mL bottle to her lips and drained the entire contents in less than five seconds, as onlookers gasped. The bartender's eyebrows rose again as Dr. Alexander Dirk Darkkin and Dr. Bonnie Mendoza walked off towards the hotel lobby, as the tawny magician tossed him the empty bottle.

When he agreed to get married, he promised he would never cheat on his wife. Before today, he had never broken that promise.

And, after today, he still hadn't.

• • •

They went up to his hotel room and slammed the door, as he wrestled her to the bed and quickly unfastened her dress straps, eager to see what was underneath.

"A very nice suite, Dr. Darkkin," she said. "Perhaps I have underestimated you. You must be a man of significant means."

"Money ain't no good unless you can spend it, lady."

"But should we be doing this, amorous Dirk Darkkin? I have a husband, whom I promised to cherish. Sometimes it is difficult."

"You didn't promise to obey?"

"I changed the wedding vows."

"That was pretty sneaky."

"I suppose you have a point."

"How can you still be conscious after drinking that whole bottle of booze? Even I can't do that."

She snapped her fingers. "It has disappeared, due to my magical powers." She flipped him over and threw him onto the bed. "Now I have you where I want you."

"Rough, huh? I like rough. You look like you work out."

"You really do not wish to see." She ripped his shirt open. "You look like you work out a little bit too. I emphasize the 'little' part."

"Wait till you see what's down below."

"I tremble with the anticipation." She unzipped her dress and slipped it off as well as her bra. Perfectly formed, yet tiny breasts. The almost flawless cinnamon-colored skin. Deltoids that looked like small melons. This was not your average scientist, he thought to himself as she held him down. But he knew that quite well.

"Your set of gold hardware—I assume they are working models?"

"Of course. I have a collection of several hundreds. Old, new, large, small, pink, gold, green, ruthenium-plated—"

"Cool. What else do you like to collect?

"I have a collection of elements, if you would like to see those. Also stuffed animals and scientific calculators."

"Can we play with them and see if they work?"

"I did not bring any exotic elements, yet I always travel with an RPN calculator." She pulled out the green calculator from her purse and turned it on. "Reverse Polish Notation is a method of symbolic logic developed by Polish mathematician Jan Lukasiewicz, and is used as an operating system in advanced calculators."

He rolled his eyes. "No, lady, the first item."

"Oh." She grinned at him sheepishly. "I did not know you liked to play cops and robbers. How juvenile."

"Sure is. But I want to be the cop this time."

She frowned. "That's not fair. You always do."

"That's because you look like a pretty dangerous, desperate criminal."

"How true. I am like the moonshine your family fancies—toxic and illegal, yet simultaneously invigorating."

Alexander Dirk Darkkin's wife, despite her uptight demeanor, could actually be quite fun and theatrical, and he knew that she enjoyed their fun little games. The trip to Las Vegas was planned on short notice—and he knew it might not be the best place for either of them. Sex was probably the safest activity for either of them in this town.

He stared longingly at her mesomorphic physique. Long, athletic, muscular limbs. A lot more than meets the eye, as she had said. Tiny, yet perfectly formed dewdrop-shaped breasts. He knew that quality, not quantity, was the most important attribute of any asset.

Alex Darkkin had been with a lot of women in his life, but none as intriguing as his wife. Mild-mannered scientist to the world, with a passionate side no one knew. The deaf woman constantly sputtered verbose, terminology-laden sentences in her slow, high-pitched speech, but it was what was *not* said that was important. She was, in one way, like a powerful tigress. But, in another way, she was of almost childlike simplicity.

He knew that she liked to wrestle. Even in a closed room, where his larger size theoretically gave him an advantage, her speed and knowledge of martial arts made her a formidable bedroom companion. He knew she used to fool around with her police officer brother Mike and his "little" sister Wendy (who could still knock him around pretty well). The woman who collected stuffed animals, elements, calculators, and manacles also had a quirky, bizarre side to her—and *that* really turned him on.

There was something about her, he knew, that wanted to be conquered, to be overpowered. She rarely performed as her campy "alter ego," amateur magician *Mendoza Milagroso* ("*Mendoza the Miraculous*" in English), any longer; the Caltech doctoral program in physics had proven to be too challenging for that. He always thought she did that for fun, and to help his politically motivated sister raise money for sick and disabled children; after all, she had been one herself. But she always had a sense for the dramatic—if not on stage any longer, in the bedroom, at least.

Chapter Nine

Las Vegas Conquerors
Team Offices
Las Vegas, NV

Alex and Bonnie drove their rented Lexus sedan to the main gate of the Las Vegas Conquerors team offices on Sunday morning. The rest of the team was at training camp, but Jay asked them to come up to the main offices on Sunday for a private meeting.

They drove up as Jay waited for them outside. Alex parked the car, and they exited and walked up to the entrance. Jay shook hands with Alex as Bonnie kissed him on the cheek.

"Nice digs," Alex said as they walked into the sprawling new complex. "Never been in a pro football office before."

"Yeah, it's pretty cool. New stadium will be ready to go by next summer." Jay pointed to the west, where construction was under way. "State of the art, with the best turf, luxury boxes, and everything."

They went inside the mammoth building, the only pro football team's headquarters decorated in a Southwestern motif.

"The architecture is fabulous," Bonnie said. "It needs more color, however."

"Subdued, yet strong. That's my mantra."

"*Subdued? Mantra?*" She laughed. "You are about as subdued as a strand of flaming magnesium. And 'subdued' and 'mantra' are pretty big words for you."

"Well, that's what management wanted, anyway." Jay showed

them around the meeting area, training area, and conference area, and then took them to his plush office.

"Some bright reds and blues would be nice, though," Jay said. "You guys want some coffee or something?"

"Sure," Alex said. "I would never turn down caffeine."

"Only if it is of sufficient quality," she said.

He quickly made a pot of Indonesian coffee and poured it for them as they went into his 400-square-foot office.

"Nice office," Alex said. "Sure beats the heck out of mine at Lutheran Hospital."

Bonnie stared at the plush leather sofa, overstuffed chairs, and huge mahogany desk. "Very modest, as I would have expected." She took a seat in a large leather chair and put her head back. "So, what is it we can do for you? Surely you do not want my advice on football. You never did take any of it."

"No, I don't want that, I know plenty about football, thanks." Jay pulled out a photo of his talented yet mercurial wide receiver and handed it to Alex. "I need something else from you."

Alex studied the picture. "Jason Lee Torpin. I heard you got him on your roster. All I can say is . . . I'm sorry, bro-in-law. You want us to kill him for you, is that it?"

"Ha—the other day I would've taken you up on that. A great talent, with speed like you wouldn't believe. Our guys really thought they could make him a sort of 'reclamation project,' but he's been exhibiting even more erratic behavior than usual."

"How can he even be in training camp? I thought he needed surgery on his ACL," Alex said.

"We thought that too, but he made some incredible recovery. Sprints and weight room workouts are fantastic."

Alex stared at the photo. "No offense, Jay, but what did you think? He's always been a hothead and a distraction. What else is new?"

"Like Bonnie, I always believe the best in people. And, yeah, he's always been a bit temperamental, and shot his mouth off a lot during TV interviews and stuff. But he's a rare talent."

"So what is different now?" Bonnie asked. "Am I now a psychologist capable of altering fundamental dysfunctional behavior?"

"You aren't getting it." Jay shook his head. "I don't want you to fix him, I want you to get dirt on him. I think he's on drugs or something."

Her eyes brightened with energy, like a child spying a bowl of candy. "What kind of substances? Cocaine? Marijuana?" she asked as she dangled the size nine Liz Claiborne shoe from her foot. "And when did I become your private detective?"

"Performance-enhancing drugs, like steroids. And I happen to know you don't start teaching until winter semester."

Alex laughed. "Surely he's been tested, Jay. And why would he risk it, anyway?"

Jay walked across the room. "Yes, it's a broken record—the league office says he's clean as a whistle, and they say I'm overreacting, even paranoid. But people risk a lot of things when their career's on the line. He tore up his knee pretty badly, not as bad as I did, but some experts didn't think he was going to make it back. But here he is, better than in his prime. It simply isn't physically possible."

"Remarkable recoveries have happened." She pointed to herself proudly. "Look at yours truly."

Jay snickered. "There's no freaking way he could come back from ACL surgery in three months. Alex?"

"That sounds about right."

Bonnie pointed her finger towards the ceiling. "Perhaps he is simply motivated by his new chance, and he is trying harder than before to maximize what may be his final opportunity."

"I could maybe buy that, but I've seen the 'roid rage' in him. Damn near attacked me in practice last Monday, just because I told him to put it in gear. Took three guys to get him off me."

"And you're certainly not the kind of guy to start a fight," Alex said. "You're a pretty mellow guy."

"Quite correct," Bonnie said dryly. "Jaime is known far and wide as a lover, not a fighter."

"Stop it," Jay said as he stared at her, then turned back to Alex. "No, I'm not, but I expect respect from my players."

Bonnie crossed her arms. "I assume, then, that you want me, a new doctoral graduate without teaching assignments until winter semester, to scour the training complex looking for incriminating evidence of steroids and similar drugs."

"That's pretty much it. I guess I need to know if that's even possible," Jay said.

She thought for a minute. "The best thing would be to obtain access to his blood and urine. Blood, we cannot obtain discreetly. I can hook up a radio-controlled trap on a urinal or toilet for use when he urinates."

"Are you serious? You're kidding," Alex said.

"No, I am not. There are many ways of obtaining evidence, and I know more about secret passages and hiding things than anyone. I can do metabolomic studies of things he touches—his helmet, footballs, water bottles—in this heat there will be much perspiration."

"Metabolomics?" Jay asked. "What the heck is that?"

"It is the science of detailed examination of body fluids, using various spectroscopic methods. If Jason Lee Torpin is on steroids, I will soon know it."

Alex shook his head. "How are you going to do it, hanging around here? It's not like you won't draw attention—you stick out like a sore thumb."

"We do have an opening for another maintenance worker. You'll blend right in," Jay said. "You better do a good job."

"Wonderful. Looks like I need to obtain a haircut. I have wanted to try it short for some time."

• • •

Jose Hernandez, the new Mexican maintenance worker for the Conquerors, started his new job two days later. Smartly dressed in his blue pants and teal shirt, he made his rounds, cleaning the bathrooms, washing equipment and uniforms, gathering small fragments of hairs and siphoning perspiration from various sites. He mixed in pretty well with the other workers, and played card games with them during lunch breaks—which he lost on purpose, to please his new friends.

Bonnie learned much about the art of disguise during her years as an expert stage magician, much of it from her former assistant Wendy, a theater enthusiast who took pride in her ability to disguise herself as various interesting personalities.

No one seemed to notice her, now with shortly cropped hair. She had a fairly tomboyish figure anyway, and was not particularly well endowed in the mammary department. She was able to hide the cochlear implant processors under her Conquerors cap, so no one would notice.

"Jose" would blend in seamlessly with the other Hispanic workers; the synthetic voice processor she and Wendy previously used for magic shows would deepen her voice by two octaves, and she would pretend to only know Spanish when spoken to. Wendy had an amazing three and a half octave vocal range, but hers was much more limited. Being a talented magician seemed to have its hidden benefits.

After three days, "Jose" took her collection of samples and headed with Dr. Alexander Darkkin 270 miles west to Pasadena, to run some tests at the California Institute of Technology. It was a place the recent doctoral graduate knew well. She could do it anonymously, with the finest equipment available in the world.

The excitement grabbed her like a vise. They were on the trail of a mystery again—although pro sports and steroids didn't seem terribly glamorous, compared to her previous cases as a San Diego forensic scientist.

But you have to make the most out of your opportunities at hand, Bonita Mendoza de Darkkin thought to herself. She rarely used her full name; like most Hispanics, she had two surnames, and used the first (her father's first *appelido,* or surname) after marriage, and had, per tradition, dropped her mother's (Flores).

That concept was almost as confusing as quantum mechanics to some people.

Chapter Ten

Parthenon Condominiums
1222 S. Collier Blvd.
Marco Island, FL

Illinois Senator Theodore Orson looked in awe at the tall woman standing in the bedroom of his penthouse suite at the Parthenon Condominiums on Marco Island. Collier Boulevard was a beautiful place to be this time of night—especially without his nasty, henpecking bitch of a wife, who wasn't due in town for two more days, because of some lousy charity event she was attending.

How he loved the white sand beaches, the lovely smell of the Gulf in mid-August, and watching the sun set. He hated sucking up to all those superficial bastards—the one thing he disliked about being a United States Senator. He needed some rest and relaxation from Washington.

The other perks, though, he enjoyed immensely. Orson watched in anticipation as Tammy Preece took off her clothes in the hotel room. The fourth-term senior Republican senator was a heavy advocate of a bill against human cloning and fetal stem cell genetic research; as a steadfast Christian, he simply didn't believe that some things God made should be tampered with.

And right now he was about to enjoy Nature and all its bounty; he knew that God meant some things to happen naturally, even though he needed a little help from the wonders of modern pharmacology. He also, conveniently, forgot about the Seventh Commandment: *thou shalt not commit adultery*. Hell, he was entitled to an occasional forgetful "senior moment" at his age.

Damn, she was a sight to behold, he thought as he looked at her five–ten willowy body, those long legs that seemed to go on forever. She was maybe thirty–five, but looked younger; the luxurious brown hair, her complexion smooth as a baby's bottom. A tiny amount of peach fuzz was present on her face and body, and not even a shred of pubic or armpit hair. It didn't look like she shaved it, either. Thick hair like he had never seen before.

He knew she had brought the black leather boots and bodice. He liked that. As feminine as Tammy looked, he knew she could wrestle him down like no one he'd ever been with. Unbelievable strength for someone so soft. A lot more enticing than his fat slob of a wife, who never wanted to do anything fun. She was so boring. But his constituents liked boring. He, on the other hand, liked something else during his sunny Florida retreats.

The full, pink breasts became engorged with excitement, and he kissed her as he took his purple Energme tablet. Things didn't work as fast as they used to, he thought, but thank the stars for modern science and Clystarr Pharmaceuticals.

He had reservations about screwing around with gals like this, but what the hell? He had the money and power to do almost anything he wanted, even if she was the pro football commissioner's daughter. Pro sports answered to Congress. Many cities used taxpayers' monies to build their stadiums, and you couldn't have the government involved on one hand, and ignore it on another.

God, this was wonderful, he thought as they rolled around in the lightly scented king-sized bed. That new Clystarr pill was good stuff, even if it did cost five bucks a pop; his friend the Clystarr lobbyist gave him plenty of samples, however, which he would make optimal use of before his wife returned in a couple of days. She was about the most inept person in the world, he thought. How he dreaded her arrival. But now he could forget about it, as his balding head disappeared between the gorgeous brunette's breasts.

• • •

Three days later, Orson was at the condo with his wife, who had just arrived. If that wasn't bad enough, he wasn't feeling very well.

Weak and run-down; even his morning shower had exhausted him terribly. Probably some virus or something, he thought. Great—what a fine time to have to deal with *her*. At least he hadn't been sick when Tammy was around; what a waste that would've been.

"What's wrong, Ted?" The five–four, 190-pound Stella Orson asked sarcastically as she began to unpack his things. "Must be tired again. Too much drinking, not enough rest."

"I . . . don't know," the sixty–year-old replied in a shaky tone. "I was just feeling woozy, but now I'm having chest pain . . . going down my left shoulder."

"I told you to stop taking that Energme, you asshole."

"You just got here. Why would I be taking that?"

She threw her purse down and threw a glass at him. "You damn cheating son of a bitch, I'm not stupid. I've tolerated it all these years for your career, but now—"

"It isn't funny, Stel. I'm in real pain." He lay back on the bed and became diaphoretic.

"You faker, trying to get sympathy from me again. Well, it won't work. I've had it. I'm calling my lawyer tomorrow."

He was sweating profusely. "I'm not kidding this time, call an ambulance."

"Sure." She smiled, then turned and looked at him in horror. "Oh, my God, you *are* having a heart attack."

"That's what I . . . said, you dumb bitch."

She panicked, dialed 911 and waited for the dispatcher, and knew the odds weren't good—the nearest hospital was over fifteen miles away, in nearby Naples. Marco Island, despite it being a playground for the wealthy, wasn't the best place to have a sudden coronary. Senator Orson writhed on the bed as his skin became blue, as he finally lost consciousness. The Collier County, Florida dispatcher answered a few seconds later.

"Yes, I'm at the Parthenon on South Collier. Penthouse. My husband just had a heart attack—I think he's dead. He turned blue and isn't breathing." She hung up the phone and sobbed for a moment, then began smiling.

Chapter Eleven

Dr. Wendy Williams' Office
San Diego Children's Hospital
San Diego, CA

Wendy sat down in her modest office at Children's Hospital at eight AM and read her morning e-mails. She still was shaken up about the sudden death of Senator Orson, whom she had met once and even served with on a genetics ethics panel at a Congressional hearing.

She looked up all the information she find online regarding his death, which wasn't much; she had never been to Collier County, Florida, but saw the profile of the sheriff, Sandra Rodriguez, a name that was vaguely familiar—although pretty common. She then decided to call the private cell phone of a person she knew well, high up in the chain of the San Diego Police Department.

The person on the other line answered after four rings. "Lt. Mendoza."

"Hey, Mike, it's Wendy. You have a minute?"

"I'm in a meeting."

"It'll just take a minute."

He sighed. "All right, just give me a second." He paused for a few seconds, and she heard a door slam. "Thanks for getting me out of the boring administrative meeting with the captain. What's up?"

"I was curious about this Senator who died in Florida, and saw the county sheriff was Sandy Rodriguez. Is that the same Sandy you worked with?"

Mike laughed. "Yeah, the lucky dog, she got elected on the first try, can you believe it? That's a pretty sweet gig down there, not a lot of crime, mostly helping out all the senior citizens with various things. She's got lots of other family down there."

"Well, this one strikes my curiosity."

"Aww, I'm really busy, Wendy, and I haven't spoken to Sandy in over two years. What is it you want me to do about it?"

"Can you call her to get some information?"

He sighed. "I suppose so . . . it is about a Senator, so it's probably pretty confidential."

She sighed. "I know that, or I wouldn't be calling."

"Naples, Marco Island, dang, I wish I could be there now. This job isn't always as exciting as I would like it to be."

"Why don't you take a few days off and go down there, then?"

He laughed. "Are you kidding me? I don't have time to do that kind of stuff. Why don't you get my super crime-solving sister to do it? She knows Sandy, and probably has time on her hands—isn't she taking some time off after graduation before she starts full time?"

"That's a good idea. Thanks, Mike. I'll see you at the dedication next week."

"Okay. Gotta go, hope it works out. Bye."

Wendy pulled out her headset microphone and dialed Bonnie's home number through the Internet. Her deaf sister-in-law with bilateral cochlear implants used to do reasonably well with telephones, but recently had stopped using them for the most part.

Alex and his friend Jim Krakowski were excellent software engineers, and had adapted speech-recognition software for use with the deaf; she could simply speak into the computer, and her speech would be translated into text on Bonnie's end. Bonnie would then type her reply into the special keyboard connected via a wireless link to her land or cell phone, allowing her to immediately answer. There was some delay, of course, but it was certainly better than the TTY devices of yesteryear. And it was another DarTech software patent which was quite profitable. You could never have enough money, she thought. Unfortunately, most of *her* business ventures had not been very successful, her husband was quick to point out.

• • •

Darkkin Mendoza Residence
4552 Eagle Point Blvd.
Pasadena, CA

Bonnie gathered her things for her and Alex's trip to Southwest Florida to speak to an old friend about Senator Orson's death, after which they would go back to Las Vegas. She had completed her Conquerors studies, which revealed interesting findings; she couldn't wait to share them with her brother. She went into Alex's den to look for a pen; she always liked to borrow his expensive ones, as they seemed to work better than the cheap ones she used.

She and her husband shared most everything—she was fortunate to have found her soul-mate, a person who enjoyed many of the same interests. But sometimes her curiosity got the better of her. She always had the irresistible urge to open locked doors and drawers, and thought about Alex's desk. He was at the hospital, taking care of some business, and wouldn't be home for a couple of hours.

She looked around the den in their spacious three-bedroom condominium and went over to the mahogany credenza. The top drawer was always locked. What did he keep in there? He kept all the important papers—insurance policies, birth certificates, etc., at the bank safety deposit box, so the drawer's contents seemed tantalizing to the curious physicist.

Did it contain a secret stash of alcohol? He had been, amazingly, "on the wagon" for several years, but she knew that the odds of alcoholics relapsing were high. She didn't think he was smoking again, either—she had one of the best senses of smell in the world, as measured with an olfactometer (a device for quantitatively measuring the ability to smell).

He'd never told her *not* to look in there, and the drawer was secured with a simple pin-tumbler lock—she was picking those open when she was seven. So, in her estimation, it was fair game.

She opened a paper clip, the only tool she would need to get it open—wearing latex gloves, of course. After a couple of minutes it was unlocked, and she pulled it open. It was empty except for a large manila envelope with the word "DARKKIN" written on the outside.

She gulped as she thought about whether or not to look inside.

What would it contain? Pornography? Something worse, such as photos of a secret girlfriend? She knew he had no criminal record (she had checked while at SDPD, of course), although he had a much richer past social history than she did; he, like her own brother, also had a reputation as a ladies' man. She didn't begrudge him the occasional men's magazine or X-rated video, as she knew virile men like him often fancied such things; but this might be different, even illegal. But she wondered why his surname, an uncommon one of English origin, was printed on the back.

She took a deep breath as she slowly opened it. It was a CIA file—the former deputy director of forensics for the San Diego Police Department had seen many of those before, and it appeared genuine. Although Alex liked excitement, being involved with the CIA seemed a bit too much to swallow. But he wasn't the only person with the Darkkin name, she remembered.

She perused the file. Secret documents. Surveillance. And many photos of the bizarre man named W. Conrad Darkkin. Why was *he* connected with the CIA, more specifically, its techno-weaponry branch, the Directorate of Science and Technology (DS&T)? For all she knew, Alex's father was just an alcoholic retired physics professor from the University of Tennessee who later worked at Oak Ridge National Laboratory in the cyclotron lab. He'd made a good living, Alex said, but much of their money was from stock in the Darkkin whiskey distillery Rad's father started.

She had, actually, only met him once—at Wendy's wedding fourteen years ago, since Alex and Wendy had become alienated from him because of his outrageous behavior and treatment of their mother. She often thought there was something terribly dangerous about him—she somehow knew that about people. She had dismissed it because of his intimidating size and demeanor—but, somehow, she wasn't surprised at what she found.

She examined the documents, and, instead of being shocked, smiled and reclined in the leather chair. She understood now why Alex had kept it secret, but, in a way, she was paradoxically pleased that her father-in-law hadn't been the loser she thought he was.

At least he was the best at his chosen vocation, even though Alex apparently felt too ashamed to share that information with her. She smiled as an odd sense of pride overcame her. Rad Darkkin had an interesting past, one that wasn't just about women, alcohol, or drugs.

She didn't really care, as it wasn't like she was ever going to deal with him again; but, on the other hand, one could always use an interesting father-in-law like that in a pinch. It was a sigh of relief, actually, to know that it wasn't something else.

She closed the drawer and re-locked it, being careful not to leave any traces she was there. Alex would not approve, she knew.

But he didn't have to know about it. It would be her secret. Everyone had them, she knew.

Chapter Twelve

Collier County Sheriff's Office
3301 Tamiami Trail East
Naples, Florida

The Lincoln taxi drove Bonnie Mendoza down Tamiami Trail in Naples, a beautiful gulf community which, along with Marco Island and the Everglades, comprised the Paradise Coast. Alex had decided to play a round of golf at one of the country clubs, while she went to visit an old friend, at the request of another. The driver pulled up to the city government complex, and she got out and went into the sheriff's office.

Collier County Sheriff Sandy Rodriguez welcomed Bonnie Mendoza to her office a few minutes later. Sandy, a compact five–three woman in her early forties, extended her small hand to her larger friend, who was wearing a lime-green suit and matching hat.

"Bonnie, it's nice to see you again. I miss the old San Diego haunts. You look great. Still fond of bright colors, I see."

"Thank you. I am sure that life here is quite hard and laborious. Congratulations on getting elected to this fabulous position." Sandy had worked for several years with her brother Mike at the San Diego Police Department. "You deserve it."

"Oh, I'm surviving. Not a lot going on—the usual emergencies, minor accidents, people losing keys, you know. Not much crime. Pretty weird, what happened to Senator Orson, though."

"Yes, I am investigating my brother's own problem, as an independent expert. He again requires my assistance, just like when we were children."

"Mike? I figure he could solve his own case."

She laughed. "No, my *bon vivant* football brother. He has some goings-on with his new team which are puzzling. The league office and local law enforcement personnel have not been very helpful."

"That's right—I heard Jay was head coach of the Las Vegas expansion team now." Sandy looked at the large ring on Bonnie's left hand. "I also heard you're married now. I never met your husband. Can I see a picture?" Bonnie showed her a photo of the handsome, sandy-haired man. "Hey, he's pretty good-looking."

"Yes, he has his positive attributes. I am quite fortunate."

"How's Wendy doing? After, you know . . ."

"It's been hard for her. Can you imagine watching the President perish right before your eyes?

"It was all over the news. She was right there, I understand."

She took a sip of her coffee. "Yes, the event troubles her to this day. But she stays busy, always involved in a thousand different things, you know. Her son's at the 99th percentile for size, of course."

"It must be pretty neat having them around."

"It is. Pasadena is less than two hours away." She sipped her coffee. "What can you tell me about the Orson case, though? Wendy knew him, as he was active in the California Medical Association. She is part of the reason for my cross-continental trek to Naples, because of her concern she is a jinx or something."

Sandy leaned back in her chair. "Not a whole lot to tell. Orson was up in his penthouse at the condo with his wife, getting ready to do it, she said, when he apparently got sick and had a heart attack. I certainly don't think Wendy's acquaintance with him is anything more than a coincidence."

"Any history of heart disease?"

"No, pretty healthy guy, only sixty. But you know, anything can happen. Wife said he started grasping his chest."

"Anything found on his autopsy?"

"It looks like he had pretty bad undiagnosed heart disease. Big thrombus in the left main artery."

"How can this be possible? Did he not he see his personal physician regularly?"

"Yeah, he did, had regular physicals at Walter Reed. But it looks like they missed it, screwed up big time. I guess there's going to be a big investigation."

"Were poisons or drugs detected?"

"A little alcohol, only 0.02 percent. Small amounts of caffeine. No other drugs or toxins, except for that new ED drug, Energme."

She leaned over and stared into the sheriff's eyes intensely. "There are organic poisons which leave little trace."

Sandy smiled. "He's a fricking senator, Bonnie, and the FBI was all over it. Trust me, there's nothing there. The dude had a bad ticker which went south when he got a boner. Not the first time you've seen that, I'm sure."

"No, of course not. But it seems to be a recurring theme, with both he and President Graham. There may be things we don't know about. Anything in the room suspicious?"

"No, nothing. He was just dead when we got there. Looks like a pretty clear-cut case. Wouldn't lose any sleep over it."

"Was there any DNA found?"

"Now *that's* interesting," Sandy said, leaning back in her chair. "Word is that they found a few long brown hairs with a male genotype. And Orson sure didn't have hair that long. Looks like he had a very special guest there that night, if you get my meaning."

She raised her eyebrows. "I suppose the secrets of Orson's private life died with him. I'm sure that this rumor will be kept quiet."

"Oh, yeah. But, hey, enough shop talk. Let me take you to lunch. There's a great Mexican place down the road that people line up down the street for. You'll love it."

"Uh, well . . ." She gulped in horror. Growing up on her culinary-impaired mother's inedible Mexican cuisine was not something she fondly remembered, and she continued to have an aversion to the foods of her ancestors.

She became nauseated as she reminisced about the acrid smells of tacos and burritos, burned beyond any sign of recognition. Even her desperate attempts to get Pythagoras (the family dog) to eat them had been futile. Luckily, she had an understanding father who secretly snuck in hamburgers and pizzas later; otherwise, the family might have starved.

But she would be a good sport and try to eat it, nevertheless. She was taught *never* to be rude to a host.

Chapter Thirteen

Argotech Industries
U.S. Bio-Genetic Research Facility
Cairo, West Virginia

The sun began to set over the horizon, disappearing quickly behind the misty Appalachian Mountains in early September. Dr. Malachi Argon had picked up Army Lt. Gen. Brant Gallagher at the nearby airport, and they talked as they rode in Argon's yellow Hummer H3 to his North American research complex.

"Nice wheels, Chi," Gallagher said snidely. "I guess we're paying you too much."

"You don't pay me enough for the risk I'm taking."

Gallagher took a sip of brandy from his flask. "Aww, you act like we made you do this. As I recall, you're the one who sought out funding for your secret project."

"We have a symbiotic relationship, how about we leave it at that? We both benefit."

"That's how it is, huh?" Gallagher replied. "Back to specifics—I need to know the progress on Project Ortho-Man. I've thrown a lot of cash your way, Chi. I have to give the higher-ups some info, because their patience has its limits."

"Higher-ups, right," he said as he choked on his coffee. "Real patriotic types, I'm sure."

"Of course they are. Like you, they want what's best for America. This country's become soft, led by a bunch of bleeding hearts who don't have the fucking balls to do what's necessary."

"And you do, eh, Brant?" he said as he took a sip of coffee. "Rebuild our greatness? Almost sounds like something a Republican would say."

Gallagher laughed. "We're going to make history, Chi. The USA's been pushed around too damn long, the Middle East and Chinese flaunting their money. Time to get back on top."

"Good. I want you to see how Travis is progressing."

The general took a swig of his coffee. "Yeah, but he's just a prototype. We can't use him, he's not going to make it, right? Gonna croak, I heard." Gallagher laughed.

"He won't die. I'm working on options now."

"Yeah, you care so much about your son, I know. Just need him around so you can experiment on him some more, right?"

He looked at Gallagher angrily. "That's a low blow, you SOB."

"Haw. Sure." Gallagher chuckled. "About the others—the testosterone levels needed are too high, you said yourself, unless they have that one gene. We don't need a bunch of roided-out super-soldiers out there. No more football players—you proved your point with that stuff."

"The player analyses were mostly for your mission, but they may serve another purpose, Brant. After it's done, I'm finished with football. Once I've found what I need."

Gallagher laughed. "If you say so, but I still say it's crazy. You're looking for the proverbial needle in a haystack, and won't find a match for him there."

"You military guys talk a good line, but you have no vision—you forget my prototype women. They're immune to the testosterone effects, and have greatly augmented strength after we give them OT-45. It's not just about Travis."

"Pretty weird. I never quite figured that out, Chi."

"It's a genetic endocrine anomaly. The high levels have no effect on Tammy Preece, Connie Dawson, or the others, because their bodies lack testosterone receptors. They can carry the toxin without detection."

"But their strength, after OT-45 augmentation, doesn't approach Travis', you said. About three times normal, about that of a real strong guy. Not impressed."

"Unlike Travis, though, their appearance is virtually normal.

Tammy's five–ten and looks 150, but weighs almost 225. She could kick your ass, Brant. Connie, too."

Gallagher laughed. "I doubt it."

"Tammy's multiple sclerosis was to the point she couldn't work any longer. *Now* look at her. I'll arrange a demonstration if you like. And Rita, who was paralyzed, in a wheelchair."

"What a great favor you did your buddy the pro football commissioner. But I don't give a shit about your disease research, Rita, or Tammy. I want my army built, goddamn it. We gotta get rid of all the undesirables, to get back in front. The damn Chinese are kicking our butts academically."

They continued driving down the old dirt road, the rural location picked because of its remoteness. "You'll get it. The island facility is working around the clock. Best people available. And pretty soon, we won't have to worry about those Chinese sons of bitches anymore."

"And no one suspects?"

Argon laughed. "No one. As you know, the opposition to our little . . . research has been dealt with. And now Orson's history. That new guy I hired for security is dangerous as hell."

"Yeah. Willie Chalfant was a real good Special Ops guy. A shame to lose him to you."

"He's created nearly impermeable defenses around the island. No one can stop us."

"And . . . I still have trouble thinking about what we did. I was right there," Gallagher gulped. "Right there at the art gallery, three days after . . . you know."

"Patience—like I said, he was dealt with. Get some goddamn balls. It was your idea, for Chrissakes."

"My balls are solid brass. But I just don't like it, Chi. Murdering *him*. I'm a fucking lieutenant general in the U.S. Army. It just feels wrong somehow, even if he was black."

"What do you want to do, Brant? You want to run for President, don't you? Wasn't going to happen with that one, and Reardon's a lame duck who'll never win re-election. Once we create your legion of Ortho-Men, your super-soldiers—the sky's the limit. Once we get rid of the undesirables, that is." He laughed.

"Yeah, we sure as hell don't need their kind." Gallagher patted him on the arm. "I guess I misjudged you, Chi. You could've done a lot of good with this . . . thing you found. Instead, you were a perfect capitalist—used it for your own gain. I love it. It's taken a lot of money to hush it up, though. You'd better come through."

"I've done a lot of good for Travis. And Rita, don't forget her—she was in a wheelchair a year ago."

"And for yourself, for your Parkinson's. You're such a bleeding heart. No, you're a cold-hearted bastard, just like me. That's why I like you so much."

They turned into the entrance of the industrial-looking complex in West Virginia. But the real action wasn't there, but at the secret island complex in the Caribbean. One that cost billions of dollars of laundered government money, as well as funding from his hand-picked "private" investors. Like shareholders, though, they expected a return on their investment, and they had yet to see many results.

Yessir—America was going to soon be a great country again, run by Americans. And Malachi Q.Z. Argon, M.D., Ph.D. would be one of the richest.

• • •

The six–five, 450-pound man turned up large clouds of dust under his feet as he sprinted towards the end of his ten-mile run, which he had completed in just over fifty minutes. He didn't look like he weighed that much, and certainly didn't look like he could run a five-minute mile.

The slightly shorter, graying Dr. Malachi Argon watched out the window as his son Travis worked out on the grounds of his heavily guarded West Virginia laboratory complex. He'd promised his son everything, and tried to give him something to hang onto, but those days might be coming to an end. He took a sip of his coffee as he watched the sun set amidst the grassy mountains.

Travis was his greatest achievement—a man of amazing strength, almost unlimited endurance, and the intellect of a brilliant scientist. He was also, tragically, Argon's greatest failure, in another way, he thought as he reflected on project *Ortho-Man*.

The renowned bio-geneticist, founded the biotechnology firm Argotech Industries in the late 1970s. He had taken on several promising projects in the 70s and 80s, but fell into disfavor with the government after suggesting that bio-engineering experiments be done on humans. In particular, there were several genetic experiment opponents in Congress, the most rabid being Illinois Senator Theodore Orson, who had recently died a mysterious death, fortunately. There had been others as well, including the President—but even Andrew Graham wasn't a problem any longer.

Argon's assistant, Dr. Rita McPherson, came in and handed him a clipboard. Rita had been with him three years, and was one of his most recent, and most successful, "experiments."

"Well?" the graying scientist asked. "Status update."

"Travis looks better today. His strength is up about ten percent, and he pressed 1,900 on the bench press machine. Way more than Tammy or the others. Ran under five minutes per mile for three miles—less than last month, but still pretty good."

"I don't give a damn about that stuff, Rita. What about the cancer cells?"

"The current peripheral cells are not dividing, but past experience has shown us that a relapse is inevitable at some point, Dr. Argon. We've pretty much tried every treatment and genetic manipulation. A bone marrow transplant would be an option, but there are no good matches or new potential donors, as you know."

His team had done extensive gene therapy—the means by which genes were inserted into a person's cells to treat a disease or condition. There were two types: germ line gene therapy, and somatic cell therapy. In germ line therapy, germ cells (sperm or ova) were modified by inserting altered genes; because the changes were in the germ cells, the changes would be passed on to later generations.

He realized when he saw Travis' strength as a young man that he might possess something special, and proposed a protocol for his enhancement, an experiment no "legitimate" center would ever have condoned. Travis was the first full-scale human genetic experiment using retroviruses as a vector, or method of insertions. Retroviruses were RNA, or ribonucleic acid, viruses—which infected host cells by introducing their RNA into the cell. The retroviral enzyme reverse transcriptase produced a deoxyribonucleic acid, or DNA, copy of the virus' RNA, which would be inserted into a host cell by the viral enzyme integrase.

Unfortunately, the technology used by Malachi Argon in the late 1990s to make his genetically correct, perfect, "orthogenetic" man was not without immense risk. A problem with retroviral techniques was that integrase could insert the desired genetic material into the wrong position; if this occurred in even a small number of cells in a part of the genome regulating cell division, rampant division—malignancy—could occur.

Argon knew that something was wrong when his son started having fevers and fatigue for no reason, and his white blood count rose to over 100,000 cells/liter (normal being 5,000-10,000). The terrible diagnosis was ALL (acute lymphoblastic leukemia), which had spread throughout ninety-eight percent of his bone marrow. This type of leukemia was typically seen in children under age fifteen, for whom the prognosis was relatively good—but there were few successful treatments known for adults.

Argon thought about the donor possibility. He was a large man himself, and never had a reason to doubt that he was Travis' biological father; he found out, however, that his paternity was impossible after he and his wife tried to have another child. The irony had been difficult to fathom: the world's most prominent human geneticist was infertile. His beautiful wife had many sexual liaisons during his frequent absences, and he had no idea who the father was.

Travis had responded remarkably well to initial induction and consolidation chemotherapy, but no suitable bone marrow donors could be found; his mother Katrina had since passed away from breast cancer, and there were no known siblings, of course. And Argon was not, he discovered, a suitable genetic match, either.

The next quest was the Holy Grail man had sought for millenia: cell regeneration, or immortality. Was there a way to regenerate Travis' bone marrow, and, more importantly to Malachi, treat his own progressive Parkinson's disease? Lower animals, such as urodele amphibians (salamanders), were well known to have amazing regenerative abilities; the animal could re-grow the limbs and tail after amputation. But humans were far more complex. The only organ known to regenerate itself substantially in adulthood was the liver, which could regenerate from as little as twenty percent remaining functional tissue.

That was, until he uncovered perhaps the greatest scientific discovery of all time—the primitive alien organism with the ability, gained through millions of years of evolution, to regenerate, to survive, in the harshest, most toxic environment imaginable.

He could have shared that discovery with the world, won the Nobel Prize, and would have become famous beyond comprehension—but he saw an opportunity to instead have unmatched power. But even that wasn't enough today, as he looked back up. He had his own mortality, too, to think of, as well as that of his adopted son.

Rita continued. "The true identity of his biological father remains a mystery. We have no idea if he's even still alive, or if there are any half siblings. Even if one were found, we would need fetal material for the creation of stem cells."

"Yeah, with his sleazy mother, who knows." Argon paused and walked around the room. "For that reason alone, I wish that lousy bitch was still alive. What are the options, then?"

"We can continue experiments with the *Orthogeneticus titania* protein, but we need fetal tissue that is undifferentiated, with enough genetic similarity to his family line to incorporate into his DNA."

"Goddamn it, I know that, Rita. I can't just manufacture a fetus from nowhere. We've tried other fetuses with no results." The initial treatments had failed, and he resorted to advanced genetic manipulation two years ago with the help of OT-45—and the money to keep the lid on those experiments was substantial.

He tried to save Travis' life, but now he was going to die. He had invested his life's savings and enormous time in Project Ortho-Man. The experiments had extended Travis' life, but it was all going to end. Despite the hatred of his deceased wife, he did care for his only son. He knew Rita thought he was self-serving, but it wasn't entirely true. And he didn't care what others thought.

The oily, liquid methane and ethane sludge of Titan's Ontario Lacus would make him one of the richest and most powerful men in the world, after his pal Brant Gallagher got his new job.

And it wasn't because the lake was a nearly inexhaustible supply of hydrocarbon fuel. No, the remarkable tar pit contained something more fantastic than he had ever dreamed possible. It would be good to have a best friend who lived at 1600 Pennsylvania Avenue. One who would always be in his pocket.

Chapter Fourteen

Williams Residence
5547 Davidson Blvd.
San Diego, CA

The slim, five–seven, sixty-two-year-old woman patted her platinum hair in the mirror as she strolled into the living room of her daughter's Colonial-style home, sat down next to her, and perused the morning paper after donning her reading glasses. There wasn't much of a physical resemblance between the woman and her towering daughter, who took after her lumbering father in physical characteristics. They did share the same fair complexion and blue eyes, although both her children had her light hair. In most ways, though, most people thought they were quite different.

"Interesting headline about that White House barber who they found dead at home of a heart attack in April. Why is that worthy of press now?" Marianne Gallinsworth said in a crisp British accent. "Oh, I see, they found out he stashed $50,000 of counterfeit money at his house. His widow was spending it on a holiday and new cars, it seems. Perhaps someone did him in?"

"Gee, Mom, what a fantastic sleuth you are. Don't know and don't care. Lots of worthless stuff in the news these days," Wendy drawled as she went through the day's mail. "The White House really isn't my favorite topic, okay?"

"They did an autopsy, I remember hearing that—his heart was all lousy. That's what smoking and high cholesterol do to you, you know."

"All broken up about it. People die of MIs every day. Jeez," she said, breaking apart one of her blueberry muffins at the coffee table. "He probably was selling drugs or something, and got some funny money."

The older woman continued flipping through the paper. "My, this Senator Orson chap's dead, too. What do you think of that? Didn't you know him?"

Wendy slurped down her heavily sugared coffee and scowled at her mother condescendingly. "What the heck do you think I think of it—that it's good? Of course it's horrible. I was on that genetics discussion panel with him. Ironically, the sheriff down there at Marco used to work with Mike and Bonnie at SDPD . . . she went down there for a couple days to talk to her, as a favor to me."

"Weren't you on C-Span with this Orson once?"

"Yeah. We were both advocates of President Graham's genetics bill, designed to improve the safeguards of genetic research in children, and the knowledge that is disseminated." She dropped her head in sadness.

"It's too bad, what happened." Marianne put her arm around her daughter. "You don't talk much about it. Do you still have the nightmares, the thoughts, about . . . you know . . ."

"Sometimes it's bad. I'm trying to forget, but know I can't completely."

"How do you feel now?"

"I was the last person to see the President alive. How the hell would you feel? Going through the investigation, being questioned by the Secret Service . . . let's talk about something else. Your degree is in English literature, not psychology."

"Speaking of Bonnie . . . how's Alex like his new job?" the older woman asked her plus-sized daughter as she took a sip of Earl Grey. "Haven't talked to him in a spell."

"Oh, it's okay. Not as exciting as he would like. Director of Medical Affairs at Lutheran Hospital in Pasadena . . . gets to do a lot of credentialing stuff and stomp out disruptive physicians."

"Disruptive? I suppose he would have a lot of insight into that," Marianne said snidely. "A world expert."

"Give him a break. He's trying, but it's not the jet-setting, crime-solving job he thought it might be."

"Wow. Does he really have the finesse to pull something like that off? He isn't the most tactful of individuals. Rather matter-of-fact and to the point, he is."

"You haven't been around him much lately. He's really polished and has sort of mellowed out, you know. Spends a fortune on clothes, like his wife. At least he can pick out his own outfits and doesn't have to dress by number like she does."

"He always was the dapper one. But he's stayed on the wagon this time, I assume?"

"I believe so. I think the penalties for non-compliance with that would be too severe to comprehend."

"Censure by the medical board?"

She chortled as she put her right fist into her left palm. "Worse. Censure by a 170-pound enraged physicist who could beat the stuffing out of him. Oww."

"Oh, yes, I forget that sometimes. She always seems so demure and sweet."

"One of many illusions created by *Mendoza Milagroso*. Like a glimmering coil of titanium wire—exotic and pretty to look at, yet wiry, dense, and tough."

Marianne paused for a few seconds. "You say they're gone for a few days? I wanted to stop by."

"They went up to Vegas for a few days, to see a couple of shows. They'll be by after that."

Marianne paused as she drank her tea and opened her eyes wide. "Las Vegas . . . is that really the best place for them to go? Either of them, with their history? Good Lord."

"Alex is on the wagon, like I said. Bonnie hasn't been to a casino in years. That's not why they're going, anyway."

"To see shows, you said. Neither of them has ever been much into that, Bonnie especially."

"Mainly to see Jaime. He wanted Bonnie's opinion on something to do with science. That's not his strong suit."

"Jay? That's right, I remember about him being the coach of the new team up there. Never had much interest in this football. Is he doing okay? He had such a good job on the telly."

"Same Jettin' Jay as always, I guess. I really have no idea, Mom. Why would I be talking to *him?*"

"You seen him since the wedding?" Marianne asked sweetly.

She stood up and stared down at her passive-aggressive mother as her voice deepened. "No. Why do you think I'd want to see *him*, of all people?"

"Don't bite my head off, I'm just curious. He is still Bonnie's brother."

"Well, I don't have a clue. He's probably dating the latest Brazilian supermodel or Vegas showgirl. He's going to be on 'Superstar Dancing' on TV this year, I hear tell."

"You know, I *am* your mum. I care about you. You were both just college kids, and it was a long time ago."

"And I'm a doctor, and know about re-opening old wounds. I'm also a big girl now. I've got a husband and a five–year-old child. What's the big playboy got?" The speech became faster and faster as her voice decreased another octave in pitch.

"Whoa, keep your wig on. I'm not trying to start—"

"Yes, you are. Bonnie and Alex may need their high-priced shrinks, but I don't. I'm wonderful. You can be pretty irritating, do you know that?"

Marianne stood up and stared into her daughter's liquid blue eyes. "You listen here. I used to tell your irresponsible brother this, but just now, I've never seen *anyone* look more like your father than you at this moment. Just remember who your dad is, Wendy. You can't ever change that."

"I try to forget, every day. Got rid of that name. Even tried to get rid of this damn accent."

"I've come to terms with it, and have forgiven him. It's the Christian thing to do. You haven't seen him for what, five years?"

Wendy threw down her hands. "Six. How can you forgive him for what he did to you? The lying, the cheating, the affairs—what he did for a living? I still don't know if I believe it all."

"Anger doesn't solve anything. In many ways, he was a bastard. But I know he had some things that were . . . beyond his control. And he thought he was doing the right thing for America. Someone had to do it."

She snickered and shook her head. "Yeah, right, his terrible inner 'demons.' What a great way to excuse everything. Should've went to get help, then, Mom, don't you think? Alex has his bad problems, too, but he cleaned up his life, didn't he? Bonnie too. Good ol' God solves everything, doesn't he?"

"Don't you dare make fun of the Lord that way. Do we all get help for our problems? Think about the people you're close to."

"He could've. Well, I tell you what—I'll forgive him too, in about thirty years. Long after he's dead."

"Whatever he did to me, with all the lying, know that he always loved you both. If you needed something and had no one else to turn to, he would be there for you."

"Yeah, right. Excuse me if I don't share your optimism of how he felt about me. Please change the subject, Mom. I don't want to talk about him any more."

Wendy stormed off to take a shower as she thought angrily about the philandering man who was her biological father. She couldn't change that. But she didn't have to see him any more, and further contemplation of Dr. W. Conrad Darkkin's colorful life would occupy no more of her valuable time. She had too many other important things to do, she thought, as she kicked the bathroom door open so that she could take a shower.

• • •

Stan Williams came into the den an hour later. The rangy six-footer was wearing blue jeans and T-shirt on the warm Saturday afternoon in August. Their son Jake was at a friend's for a play date, and Wendy and Marianne were watching television.

"Marianne, would you excuse us, please?"

"What?"

"I need to talk to Wendy alone, if you don't mind."

Marianne shrugged. "Uh, of course, Stan. Everything okay between you two?"

"Just fine."

"Off you go, then," the slender, platinum-haired woman said as she went into the kitchen.

Wendy stood up and stared down at him. "So, what's your problem today? And why'd you ask Mom to leave?"

He sat down and slapped his hand on the coffee table. "I get tired of all this, Wendy. Everything has to be about you and what you want."

She rolled her eyes. "What do you mean?"

"All your activities, your fund-raising. When is there going to be time for me?"

"Well, you're a big boy. Go finish your finance doctorate, if that's what you want." She gobbled down a chocolate chip cookie. "I'm sure not stopping you."

"Yeah, you do—every day. All your activities going on, almost every night. I get to baby-sit."

She broke apart another cookie and munched on it. "Jake's your son, too—in case you didn't know, that's being a dad, not baby-sitting. I'm sorry you dislike spending time with him."

He looked up at her. "Do you have to eat while I'm talking? Quit stuffing your face."

"I don't have to take orders from some liberal Democrat," she garbled as she chewed her high-calorie snack. "I guess what they say is true—these mixed marriages really don't work."

"And that's not what I mean, about Jake. You think everything's about you. Even after Bonnie moved to Pasadena and the TV show and magic fundraisers went away, you found other things to do. The stupid *Squad* merchandise—the action figures, the vitamins, cereal, lunch boxes—all that crap cost us a fortune, while you lied and told Bonnie how successful it all was. What a waste."

"So, I'm supposed to change everything because you feel left out, poor guy. You knew about that stuff when you married me. You don't like it, go marry someone else," she said as she popped several cheese puffs into her mouth.

His mouth opened wide. "You surely don't mean that."

She laughed. "I don't, but . . . if you don't like it, go find yourself another meal ticket, Stan the Man. Take your twenty–five percent interest in Milagroso Security and buy yourself a new house."

"At least that investment makes money." He stared at her in disbelief. "The good times seem so long ago, Wendy. Now you're talking about running for United States Representative."

"Well. How'd you hear about that?"

"Oh, come on, I hear things, you know. That's a decision both of us need to make."

"Got a darn good chance at winning, too, so you'll be married to a Congresswoman! That'll help your low ego. Oops, it'll be a Republican one. The shame may be too much for you."

He shook his head. "You really think you can win, don't you? Besides, I don't need that kind of ego fulfillment. I made some calls, and I want you to go to counseling with me. My friend Paul, he suggested a really good—"

"*Counseling*? God, you sound like my nagging mom. The rest of my family may need some stinking therapist, but I sure don't."

"Maybe she's got something there. There's no shame in it."

She choked on her glass of milk. "Yeah, she's done a great job herself, hasn't she? Good at solving everyone's problems except her own with the old-time religion."

"She left him and made a better life for herself, just like you did. Stood up to Rad's garbage for all those years."

"Yes, just like you're doing now—isn't that what you're implying? The apple doesn't fall far from the tree? Don't you *ever* give me an ultimatum."

"And don't put words in my mouth. I don't think you're like Rad at all. I'm just tired of being second fiddle."

She gestured, as if strumming an imaginary violin. "Aww, sometimes you're just so needy. I can't help it if you feel inferior to me. But, it's not your fault—most people would. It takes a special person to appreciate someone like me."

"You know, you sound more like your brother used to every day. I don't feel inferior, and don't have low self-esteem. I simply have a realistic view of who I am."

"Yeah, you got that right—someone who's boring." she said as she yawned and turned on the TV to a home shopping channel. "My mind is at a higher cerebral level, obviously."

"I'm going fishing for a few days with the guys before classes start. Your mom wants to play with Jake anyway while you're up in Vegas hobnobbing with the rich and famous."

"Jay's family now, and I haven't seen him for years. Bonnie was always my family. You're the one who doesn't want to come."

He put his finger in her face. "You think I'd just get in the way."

"That's probably true, come to think of it." She looked up and rolled her eyes. "Maybe I'll be on 'Superstar Dancing' too, as fit and athletic as I am."

He paused for about thirty seconds. "You know, I used to really dislike Alex. But, I'll at least say this for him—he never pretended to be anything other than who he was—a self-absorbed jerk. What you saw was what you got. But he's tried like hell to change himself. You, though, are full of bullshit."

"I was under the impression that you didn't think very highly of my obnoxious sibling."

"That's just it—he's evolved into something better, while you keep pretending to be something you're not. Someday, you're going to wake up from this ego high and find out things have changed."

"I'm not waking up from anything. I'm the best there is." Stan watched intently as his wife began dancing around the room. "I hope you come along for the ride, because it's gonna be fabulous. If not, that's your choice."

"I'm going to a movie. I hope you're in a different mood when I return."

"There's nothing wrong with my mood," she said in a melodious voice. "Don't hurry back."

"I won't, trust me." Stan picked up his wallet and keys, walked out the side door, which he slammed behind him.

Marianne returned to the room. "Are things okay?"

"Never better," she said softly. "Why?"

"I had a marriage fail, and I can't bear to see my daughter's going all pear-shaped. I overheard what he said about counseling. You should go."

She laughed and made a throwing motion with her hand. "Oh, he's just having a fit. He feels inferior to me, most people do. And why would I want to change what I am, Mom? Why would you want to mess with perfection?"

"I don't think most people feel that way. No one's that great, Wendy. Not you, not Conrad, not Alex, nobody."

"Well, they would be, if they had some self-confidence. And I *am* that great."

"Don't take things for granted. Stan's a good man and father, I know—I had a husband who wasn't."

"You've sure got that right. Maybe I just want something more, and don't want to wait until I'm old to have it, like you."

Marianne opened her mouth wide in amazement and looked at

her daughter. "I'm glad you think so highly of me, all the things I gave up for you and Alex."

"Save the whining, Mom. I don't need it right now. You made your choices, and don't blame them on me, because you never asked what I wanted. You stayed with him because you're weak and couldn't make it on your own."

"Wendy, I—"

She walked into the kitchen to find something else to eat and slammed the door, leaving her perplexed mother behind. She didn't need to be lectured by anyone.

Chapter Fifteen

San Diego Children's Hospital
Administrative Board Room
San Diego, CA

The group of six sat during an informal meeting in the hospital's board room, debating the expansion of the pediatric residency program. The five–four, thin woman in the blue-skirted suit finished giving the PowerPoint presentation from her seat in the front.

"Thanks for the presentation, Dr. Mortland," Roger Corben, the hospital CEO, said curtly. "We thank you for your time."

"Thank you," the mid-thirtyish Dr. Brenda Mortland, program director of the pediatric residency, said as she sat down.

The portly, balding man in the wrinkled gray suit spoke up. "I know we agreed to meet with you about this," Tom Quincy, the chief financial officer of the largest children's hospital in San Diego, said. "I'm sorry, but, at this time, we will not be able to fund—"

"We need the extra positions for the pediatric residency program, Tom. You know that," Wendy Williams, wearing a well-tailored tan suit, said loudly. "You and Roger committed to that, remember?"

"Well, difficult decisions have to be made, Wendy," Corben said. "The bottom line is always the most important."

She pointed her finger at him. "I don't think you're sorry at all, and you lied to me, you SOB. I'll remember this."

"*What* did you just call me?"

"It's an acronym, of which you probably know the meaning."

The other men in the room looked at each other as Corben continued. "Insults aside, the big financial picture, which you don't understand, is—"

"I don't give a crap." The four men in the room were taken aback as the powerfully-built woman rose up to her full height. The voice had deepened from its usual mezzo-soprano to contralto and had become much louder. "You don't lie to me or this medical staff. *Ever.* Got that?"

Corben started shaking his hand nervously. "Wendy, you're way out of line, and I suggest you change your tone."

"*Change my tone?* You wouldn't have told the previous medical staff president what to do, but you'd tell a girl. Try to bully me, and, mark my words, you'll be sorry."

"Backing it up with muscle, huh?" Corben said as the other men in the room snickered hesitantly.

She laughed. "No, sir—backing it up with the California Medical Association—which I am president-elect of—and the Governor, the editor of the Union-Tribune, Mayor Anderson, Senator Quigley, and dozens of others. Try taking that on, and you'll have a fight you really don't want." The room quieted. "Not so funny now, is it?"

"I guess your buddy the President isn't on that list any more. And you're only the Chief of Staff because your old boyfriend gave all that money to the Foundation. Must be nice."

The spindly hospital vice president spoke up softly. "Roger, maybe we should just talk about—"

It was far too late for talk, as the gauntlet had been thrown down, and she stuck a large finger in his face. "You piss-ant misanthrope, that's pretty low, even for you. And leave Jay out of it—they elected me because I'm the best. You want to take it to that level, you got it, mister. Bring it on, it'll be a pleasure." She clenched her fists.

Corben looked at her blankly and remained silent.

"Well, what'll it be, Corben? Put up or shut up. The back alley awaits. I've taken your shit for the last time, you asshole."

Roger Corben paused for another half minute. "I . . . didn't mean to insult you. But the program director here understands what we're proposing. Everybody else is on board."

"What choice did Brenda have? She works for you." She got in Corben's face and peered down angrily. "You listen here. I represent this medical staff, and I'm not one of your suck-up yes men, Roger.

Tom here made a promise to fund the five additional positions, and I'm going to hold you to that. If you don't like my 'tone,' then you'll have to do something about it. You gonna do it? Huh?"

The four men stared and looked at each other. "I guess I, well, misjudged you. That's what we're doing, then," Corben said sheepishly as his hands shook.

"Damn right that's what you're doing."

The men cleared the conference room quickly as Wendy and Brenda sat back down.

"Wendy, thanks. They tried to bully me before this meeting. I don't know if I could've stood up to them by myself."

The tall blonde put her hand on the shorter brunette's shoulder. "Don't worry, they're just bluffing. You can see how they backed down. Nobody pushes *me* around."

"Yeah, I'm pretty impressed. I've never known you to be so, well, forceful. I was almost a little bit . . . scared."

"Haw. Scared? Of those wimpy jerks?"

Brenda paused for a moment, her hands trembling slightly. "No, Wendy . . . of you. That was a little, well—over the top for me. For a minute I thought you were really going to pound Corben into the ground."

She looked at Brenda wildly for a few seconds, then smiled. "Oh, come on, are you kidding?"

"Honest?"

"Of course."

"It was pretty weird, if you want my truthful opinion. You never use that kind of language, at least from what I know."

"You just don't understand about management yet. Men understand talk like that, and you have to stand your ground. I wouldn't *really* do that."

"I suppose not. That wouldn't be . . . very professional."

"Just remember you don't know what you can do until the situation arises." She rose from her chair. "Anything is within your reach if you try."

Brenda changed the subject. "I can't wait for the dedication ceremony tomorrow. I'm glad this is all finished."

"It'll be a great time," she said in an uncharacteristic quiet tone. "Let's go get some decent coffee. I'm buying."

Chapter Sixteen

San Diego Children's Hospital
Mendoza Flores Rehabilitation Center
San Diego, CA

Jay Mendoza adjusted his $300 blue tie in the mirror of the men's room of the center's conference room, about fifteen minutes before the ceremony was to begin on the sunny Saturday morning. Satisfied with his appearance, he exited, and collided with the blonde woman of equal height but greater mass. She stared at him for a few seconds and moved back.

"Hey, Wen," Jay said. "It's been a while."

"Yeah . . . a while. Alex and Bonnie's wedding. You're on the go so much, it's hard to keep track of you." She gave him a sisterly hug, which he returned a bit hesitantly.

"You're lookin' good."

"Ha. Diet's a killer. Lost about fifteen pounds, starving myself to death."

"Be careful. Don't want to get anorexia."

"I'll keep that in mind. No Darkkin's ever died of that, to my knowledge, as alcohol has too many calories. Not that I would know, of course, being one who abstains from spirits."

He looked away towards the window. "I'm kind of embarrassed by all this pomp and circumstance. I didn't want something big like this."

She turned around, surprised. "You, not wanting a big to-do? Don't kid me. The new addition will be fabulous."

"It's not television, it's a kids' hospital, for the little Bonnies of the world. I'm a humble guy, deep down."

She chortled. "Yeah, right. Hey, congrats on the new job, by the way. I haven't had a chance to tell you in person."

"Thanks. It's a challenge, but a lot of fun. *And* a hell of a lot of work."

"I know you can do it."

"How's Stan? How come he didn't come?"

"He wanted to go fishing with his buddies. Sometimes he just feels a little out of place."

"Why would he feel that way? Everything all right with you two?"

She looked down at her blue pumps. "I don't really want to talk about it, Jay, okay?"

He looked up at her slightly. "Yeah, sorry. Anyway, thanks for your support. It means a lot to us. You're like family."

"And it means a lot to me that you helped with this. It'll help a lot of people. You always gave a lot."

"Me? Hah. I spent and wasted a lot, too. It's you and Bonnie who gave a lot to this hospital, all the charity fund-raisers, all the crazy stunts."

"The good old days. She's moved on to grown-up stuff, at least most of the time." She stared at him. "We've all moved on, it seems."

"I guess so."

"By the way, I hear our super sibling spouses are helping you on your little problem with the team."

"Trying to. Not much to go on so far, but we'll see. Crime-solving's a lot harder than I thought."

"You've got that right. I promise I'll come up and help next week, too. It sounds interesting."

"Come on. You don't have to do that."

"You proceed from a false assumption. It's not awkward for me, you know. It was a long time ago."

"Maybe it's awkward for me, Wen. You ever think of that?"

She took him by the arm. "Come on. Let's go outside."

• • •

The Mendoza Flores Rehabilitation Center was a newly renovated, state-of-the-art children's rehabilitation complex, the largest such facility on the West Coast. Jay and Bonnie had donated undisclosed sums for its construction. Mayor Sharon Anderson was there, as well as Pro Football Commissioner Gerard Preece. The family members were gathered on the outdoor stage as the mayor took the podium.

"It's my pleasure to announce the dedication of the new Mendoza Flores Rehabilitation Center, a rehabilitation complex that will greatly aid the health and welfare of children in the Southwest. This family has given so much to the city of San Diego. I would not do them justice, so I will turn over the microphone to someone who knows them better than anyone—the current Chief of Staff at San Diego Children's Hospital, Dr. Gwendolyn Williams." The crowd let out a cheer for the instantly recognizable popular physician, science TV show host, and enthusiastic fund-raiser.

"Thank you, Mayor Anderson," Wendy said as she took the podium, adjusting the microphone for her height. "You don't know how honored I am to be here today. As you may or may not know, I first started working here as a volunteer when I was eighteen years old, and had the pleasure of working with a very special patient here. It was then that I decided to go into pediatric rehabilitation, and it has been a great career. But, enough about me—let me introduce these wonderful people to you.

"First, Dr. Carlos Mendoza, who was a lieutenant with the San Diego Police Department for years, before he became a professor of criminology at San Diego State. Dr. Mendoza has been extremely active in educating children about crime and drugs in our community, and has worked tirelessly to improve physical fitness by promoting various events." The six–foot Carlos stood up and waved at the crowd, and was greeted by hearty applause.

"Next, a person who has given a lot through education and volunteerism, Elisabeth Flores, daughter of the late musician and composer Gabriela Flores. Elisa has been the director of the Mathletes mathematics championship program for many years, and has been the head judge for the city science fair the last ten years. An excellent golfer, she has also organized many charity golf tournaments." Elisa stood up to another round of applause.

"Up next is Lieutenant Mike Mendoza of SDPD. Lt. Mendoza was a champion sprinter at San Diego State University and joined the SDPD force after graduation. Like his father, he has been extremely active in anti-drug education and charity fund-raising for the community." Mike stood up and received a hearty round of applause and waved to the cheering crowd.

"The next person is most special to me. I first met her when she was a patient, recovering from a near-fatal illness, felt to have little hope of recovery. But she overcame those obstacles to become valedictorian of her high school class at St. Martin's Academy. She was an NCAA champion in the hundred meters at San Diego State, and is the current women's heptathlon world record holder for the deaf. She was deputy director of forensics at SDPD for several years, and currently is assistant professor of mathematics and physics at the California Institute of Technology.

"You may, of course, also know her as the mentalist, magician, and TV personality '*Mendoza the Miraculous*,' who has raised many a dollar for the underprivileged in the community, who has donated all her winnings to charity. Presenting my intrepid sister-in-law, the amazing Dr. Bonnie Mendoza."

The crowd let out a cheer for the geeky, socially inept scientist, who Wendy and others had made into an unlikely media sensation with a sort of local cult following.

"Finally, this man is known the world over. He was runner-up for the Heisman Trophy, NFC Offensive Player of the Year in 1997, MVP of Super Bowl XXXI, multiple Pro Bowl selection, and Pro Football Hall of Fame member—former TV sportscaster and the new coach of the Las Vegas Conquerors, Jay Mendoza."

The crowd cheered the most for the handsome coach, one of the most eligible bachelors in the Southwest. He stood up and waved to the crowd, as he took the podium on behalf of the family.

"Thank you, Dr. Williams. It is indeed a great honor to be here and is humbling to have this named after our family. But the true heroes are not us, but the patients and their families whom we serve, who work tirelessly towards their goal. I have learned through people like my sister that the greatest gift you can receive is good health, and we should never lose sight of that. If what we've done here today can help even one child improve the quality of his or her life, it's all been worth it."

The crowd cheered again as the family stood up, with Wendy standing next to them. Yeah, he sure was nice looking, she thought. Everybody cheering for him, while her own husband was off fishing somewhere, just another mediocre guy. She did promise to go up to Vegas for a few days, to hobnob with her flashy relatives. Stan and her mom could stay home and take care of the mundane things.

• • •

"Hey, Wendy," Mike Mendoza said as he saw the tall woman in the hallway after the event..

"Looking good, Lt. Mendoza, sir." She saluted the slightly shorter man. "Haven't seen you for a few months, bud. Thanks again for the tip on Sandy down at Marco. She was very helpful to little sis."

"Sure, hope it worked out. By the way, you look great, too."

"I feel great, too. I've got more energy than I've had in years."

"Wish I could say the same."

She punched him in the arm. "What's wrong with you? You made lieutenant. Youngest in history, I bet. Beat your dad by five years, I heard. And he was a legend."

"I guess so. Hard to meet expectations in *this* family."

"Chief of police someday, or FBI if you want it. Why so down? We're almost exactly the same age. Whole life to look forward to."

Mike looked around. "What the heck do you think, Wendy? Look at this. Mendoza Flores Rehab Center. Three of us, and I'm the odd man out."

"It represents all of you. What do you mean by that?"

"Jay's a fricking superstar, on TV, head football coach, donating millions. Bonnie's a genius, super athlete . . . heck, they've both met the President, and—" he said, stopping in mid-sentence. "Oh, God, I'm so sorry. I didn't mean to bring that up."

She smiled and put her hand on his shoulder. "It's okay, Mike, I'm dealing with it. But Jay made his money catching a football and returning kicks for touchdowns. Nice job, but hardly the ultimate benefactor of humanity."

"They're both great heroes to lots of kids. Bonnie did all the charity stuff and everything."

"And made a fortune winning world poker championships on television, and patenting lock designs for security companies. Plus, you and I have helped out on quite a few of the escape tricks. Every bit as important as the performer."

"Those two are vastly different people, yet theatrical and flamboyant in their own ways. I'm the calm, composed one who had to keep them on Earth. Me and Dad and you, while Mom and the two of them were in their fantastic Technicolor world, thinking their big thoughts we mere mortals can't comprehend."

She laughed. "And if those two were in trouble, they'd call you so fast you couldn't believe it. They wouldn't be anywhere without your stability."

"Yeah, right. Look at Bonnie and Jay up there on that podium, signing autographs. The people love them. I'm happiest for her, though. All those years, she felt so down, couldn't really talk again until she was fifteen or sixteen."

"I remember. Now you can't shut her up."

"Just how she was before she got sick, only talks a lot slower. I can't imagine what it was like—she never fit in, was like the biggest geek in school."

She laughed. "She may appear different, Mike, but she still doesn't fit in, and still is *el geeko supremo*. An illusion. Alex tries to do a good job picking out her clothes and things."

"I know you're right. I'm glad she's happy with Alex now. She deserves that, after all she's been through."

"On the other hand, my family has *so* much to be proud of. D.T. Darkkin & Sons Distillery—what a fine legacy. That really scored lots of points with the guys growing up."

"Could have been worse."

"Oh, but it was. At least my grandfather just made whiskey. My dad had the distinction of having built thousands of nuclear weapons, made nerve gas, lots of other fine humanitarian stuff, in between all the drunken, drug-laden affairs—how can you top that?"

"About Rad . . . does Bonnie know about that stuff?"

"No. Alex said she had enough problems to be burdened with that, after she almost died, *again*, a few years ago after trying to catch the guy who hacked into all those medical records. Even my mom doesn't know it all. It's not like we can change any of it."

"Maybe that's just as well."

"Yep, what fine memories. Hey, it's 'Bring Dad to School Day.' Johnny's dad's a fireman, Tommy's is a banker, Anna's sells insurance. Finally, let's meet Wendy's pop, who blows people up, when he isn't cheating on her mom, taking LSD, and swilling the famous family fermentation. What a fella." She clapped in mock applause.

"At least he was good at it, you have to admit." Mike laughed. "A legend. Somebody had to build weapons of mass destruction. Might as well be somebody you know."

"I agree—he was truly the best piece of crap dad a girl could have. But you have a fabulous wife, Bella and Jose are wonderful, beautiful kids . . . can Jay say the same? You think he's happy?"

"He's happy. Not everyone wants what you and I do. You should know that better than anyone."

"Yeah." She looked down sadly at her shoes again. "He made his choices."

"We all do. Life's a compromise. You can't have everything."

"But, hey, Mike, you don't need anyone's approval." She pointed to her chest with her right thumb as her demeanor switched from glum to exuberant in a flash. "I sure don't. I'm going to start doing things that I want, because I can. And I *can* have everything." She beamed with the glow that she suddenly felt, knowing that she could illuminate a dark room with her brilliance.

He stared at her in interest. "You seem so full of confidence these days. Not that you didn't have any before, you just seem so . . . sure of yourself."

"Some of my brother rubbing off on me. Always thought he could do anything. The future is pretty rosy these days."

"You always said Alex was the black sheep. That the apple didn't fall far from the Darkkin family tree."

"Maybe I was wrong about him, and he was right about some things. Wendy Williams is going places, you can be sure of that."

Mike hesitated for a moment. "Just be careful, Wen. Don't make the ride a bumpy one."

"I will miss the warm weather when I move to D.C., though."

"Yeah. Where you going now?"

"Mama Ciccini's with the super-sleuths for lunch. Got a lot of catching up to do."

Chapter Seventeen

Mama Ciccini's Restaurant
San Diego, CA

"You seem to be having some trouble with processing speech," Alex asked his wife as she looked at her breadstick in the posh Italian restaurant, where they were having lunch with Wendy. "Batteries low or something? I've got your spares."

"So, how are things here at home? Have you picked out a Halloween costume yet?" she asked Wendy in between bites of her Caesar salad.

"It's only mid-August, and your handsome hubby is talking to you, M-Square." Wendy pointed at her brother.

"What?" she turned to him, irritated. "Have you something truly important to say?"

"I just noticed that sometimes you seem tuned out lately."

"Perhaps it is because you bore me incessantly with irrelevant droll, which desensitizes me." She turned back to Wendy. "Well, what about Halloween? It is your favorite holiday, since you like to disguise yourself."

"I don't know, haven't thought about it. Too much on my mind," Wendy said as she ate a pepperoncini. "Gotta think about my big political future. Don't be so childish."

She pointed at her friend sternly. "Only a little over two months to go. Here is an idea—Stan could go as a syringe, and you could go as a medication bottle. It would be cute."

Alex choked on his coffee. "Say what?"

"Thanks a lot, pal," Wendy said. "You think I'm shaped like a medication vial? Geez, I've tried to lose weight, too."

Bonnie pursed her lips. "No, that's not why, and you look quite good. It would be entertaining because—"

"I think we all understand the basic concept," he said, laughing. "At least I do."

"Duh, it is funny because Wendy is a doctor, correct? And ectomorphic Stan is rather thin," she said as she looked around sheepishly. The blank stares from the other two were piercing. "What? I don't get it."

"Oh, come on," Wendy said. "How dense."

She bit her lip and looked at Alex and Wendy almost rolling on the floor in laughter. "I just don't get why you are laughing. Tell me—sometimes humor escapes me."

"Okay," he said. "It's an advanced scientific concept, but you may have heard of it. When a boy and girl get to a certain age, they become attracted to one another and start kissing, and eventually that leads to something else."

"Hickeys?" Bonnie rolled her eyes.

"After those. I can draw a picture if you want."

She thought deeply for several minutes as they curiously watched her think. "Yes, the 'birds and bees,' I am aware of this principle. Yet, I still cannot see the obviously mirthful connection with that and Wendy's theoretical costume."

Alex gestured with his hands. "So, what does the syringe do to the bottle, and how can we relate that event to this Halloween costume?"

She crossed her arms. "The syringe removes its protective cover and pierces the bottle with its needle, of course."

"Right! You're really bright."

She looked around, puzzled, for a minute or two, and finally her mouth opened wide, then held her index finger up. "How crude. I did not understand immediately, because I think on a much more sophisticated level than you bucolic bumpkins."

"It was your joke," Alex said.

"Humph. For your information, it is *hardly* the same at all. The syringe draws liquid from the vial after removing its cover. However, in the hypothetical activity between the boy and girl, a liquid is injected *into* the receptacle, not withdrawn; and sometimes a insulating cover is worn, rather than being taken off. So, as you can see, they are fundamentally distinct concepts, leading to my confusion. Get it right."

"Gee, I hope you never become a stand-up comic," Wendy said. "Only you would think what you said wasn't hilarious."

"I agree. I am afraid I would starve if I had to make a living that way. Sometimes I am funny by accident, luckily."

"That's for sure, and I'm glad that's settled. How about some dessert? I'm still starved," Wendy said.

"Yes. A large slice of chocolate cake with ice cream would be optimal right now."

"So, what happens now with the Conquerors?" he asked. "I can take a few more days off, but then I've gotta get back to work at Lutheran. Their patience has its limits."

"We must still determine the mechanism by which Torpin and friends are being given anabolic steroids. I must return to the team office with my new information."

"I can help," Wendy said. "I'm due to take some time off, too, and can come up in a few days."

"Yes, that would be of immense aid to us. Three heads are better than two, I think. I have interesting information to discuss in my detailed report to the Conquerors staff."

Chapter Eighteen

Las Vegas Conquerors
Team Offices
Las Vegas, NV

"Look, Coach, there's no way Torpin is on steroids or anything else," pro football Assistant Commissioner Tamara Preece said to the Conquerors coach in his plush office the day after he returned from the rehab center dedication ceremony. "We've been through this over a dozen times." The five–ten, attractive brunette, daughter of Commissioner Gerard Preece, was second-in-command of the administration of pro football. A formidable woman, indeed, most thought.

But Jaime Mendoza, a man used to making his living outrunning 275-pound linebackers, wasn't easily intimidated by anyone. He knew that was one of the reasons they hired him—coaching an expansion team was certainly no picnic.

"I tend to agree with Tammy, Jay," Conquerors general manager Patrick Dunlap said. "We're wasting a bunch of time here. They tested Torpin again, and the results are conclusive. Drop it. This is becoming a distraction, and there's a lot of higher priorities."

"Higher priorities than our players on drugs? You've gotta be kidding," Jay said.

"I really don't want the media getting hold of this," Dunlap replied. "Could really hurt us in our first season."

Jay laughed. "I see, the truth comes to light. This is all about the publicity and your image, isn't it?"

"Coach Mendoza, I concur," the five–seven, wiry African-American woman standing next to Tammy said. "Ms. Preece is correct. I don't see any evidence of tampering," DEA Special Agent Jacqueline Levickis said politely. "We've been over the testing procedure and results."

Jay crossed his arms. "Despite you all ganging up on me, I know you're wrong, and my expert's going to prove it. Some people are smarter than you, believe it or not."

"Coach Mendoza," Tammy Preece said authoritatively as she stood and looked up at him. "You are *not* authorized to conduct any type of investigation into this matter. I have looked at the information, and conclude that there has been no drug doping. DEA has even loaned Agent Levickis, an illicit drug expert from the Los Angeles division, to corroborate my findings. Her reputation, as well as mine, is impeccable. She has extensive experience in drug abuse in sports."

"What's going on, Jay? I didn't know about this," Dunlap said. "What 'expert'? These people are the best in the business."

"You'll see in a minute." He looked at his sports chronograph, hoping his "expert" wasn't lost on the other side of the city—or worse, playing poker in one of the casinos.

Dunlap paused for a second, then opened his mouth and pointed his finger at the coach. "It had better not be what I'm thinking, or you're in big trouble."

"Relax. Everything I've done is legitimate science, done by the best in the business."

"I can fine you if you keep this up, Coach. I don't want to, with your sterling reputation and popularity, but don't push me," Tammy said angrily.

"Do, it, then. I don't like threats. Look, with all due respect, ladies—I don't care what you think. My intuition tells me otherwise. And it's almost always right."

"Your intuition didn't help you avoid that knee injury, Jay," the shorter, overweight Dunlap said snidely.

Jay pointed at the general manager. "That's a low blow and you know it, Patrick."

Dunlap stepped back. "Didn't mean you to take it that way, just indicating that you're not always right. Don't be so arrogant."

"I'll show you arrogant in a few minutes."

The doors suddenly parted as the sunglass-wearing, five–nine woman in the thousand-dollar red skirted suit came into the Conquerors' coach's office, as heads turned. Behind her was her sandy-haired, six–two, forty–year-old husband, dressed in a blue pinstripe suit.

She was a master of illusion, and one of her best was manipulating the appearance of her size, to the point of almost appearing to shrink and grow at will. At sixty-nine and one-quarter inches, the *Latina* with the twenty–six-inch waist could look downright thin—most people would guess her at no more than 135 pounds.

But the woman with thirteen percent body fat and forty–two-inch chest weighed in at a rock-solid 170. Some days she appeared small and thin. Today, she wanted to be big, boisterous, and threatening, which might not have been the best choice with the DEA and pro football administration in the room.

"Hey, what's going on? We were just talking about you," Jay said. "Thought you might've gotten lost in the casinos or something."

"Jesus, all we need," Dunlap yelled, stomping his foot as he pointed at the dark-haired guest. "The circus is now officially in town. All we need now is a TV crew."

"Uh, actually, there are some Channel 7 reporters at the front gate," Alex Darkkin said as he shrugged. "Trying to get an interview with Torpin, go figure."

"Dammit!" Dunlap yelled, pointing at Jay. "Look at all the trouble you've caused already."

"I believe this is a private meeting," Tammy Preece snidely insisted. "Not a family reunion with the life-size version of Coach's little dolly over there."

"I am here by invitation and have come at my celebrated sibling's insistence," Bonnie declared dramatically, like a slow-spoken stage actress making a grand entrance. "I have a complete report of Torpin's body spectroscopy and metabolomic analysis of hairs for everyone's perusal." She passed out several detailed, full-color reports to the group, each member reluctantly taking one.

"What the hell is *this?*" Jackie asked as she looked through the report. "Who ordered it?"

Tammy Preece's eyes lit up. "Torpin's *what*? I didn't understand you."

"Raman spectroscopy from hairs on his body, as well as other measurements. His skin density, muscle fiber thickness, and so on, and analysis of perspiration and urine, are consistent with an athlete abusing anabolic steroids and possibly human somatotropin, and furthermore—"

"Rom-what?" Dunlap asked. "I didn't understand a single word you said."

Bonnie put her hand on her hip and looked at Dunlap condescendingly. "Raman spectroscopy, duh! I would not expect *you* to understand my perspicacious methods."

"Hey, I don't need this crap from you in my own building," Dunlap said. "Be quiet or I'll ask you to leave."

"This is not *your* office, Mr. Dunlap, so I will do what I wish. And RS is a technique used in condensed matter physics and chemistry to study vibrational, rotational, and other low-frequency modes—"

"I'm sorry, Coach Mendoza," Tammy interrupted, angrily throwing her hands down. "Agent Levickis and I have already conducted an investigation, and your procurement of this conveniently available 'independent expert' is outrageous and totally inappropriate."

"But not illegal," Bonnie said officiously. "I merely studied sweat and urine samples and examined his spectroscopic images. Well within the law as applied to private detectives."

Jackie laughed. "Except you aren't any private detective. I should give you a citation for doing those things without a PI license."

Bonnie put one hand on her hip, lifted her sunglasses with the other, and peered down at the five–seven Special Agent. "*That* is impossible. Your police powers extend only to federal drug-related offenses and other felonies; you cannot even issue a traffic ticket here."

Jackie pointed angrily. "Hey, you'll see what I can issue, girl."

"Nevertheless, you think me to be unprepared, eh?" She fumbled through her small cluttered purse for a couple of minutes, dumping out items that seemingly would have occupied a purse five times as large. "I will procure my credentials momentarily. Sorry, it is amazing how much paraphernalia is in here."

"You going to pull a rabbit out of there next? Look, the show's fun, but we're really busy, Mendoza," Jackie said.

"*¿Conejo?* A lagomorph?" She walked around Jackie several times. "You should know that the name of the country *Hispania,* or Spain, is derived from the Punic word *Span,* which means rabbit."

"Why would anyone care about that?" Jackie said, turning to Tammy. "The geek squad's here."

"*Greek*? I am of Mexican origin, although fluent in Greek."

"*Geek,*" Alex signed to her.

"Hah. All knowledge has potential value." She finally pulled out a photo ID card. "Here. My California private investigator's license."

"Let me see that. Did this come in your cereal box?" Jackie said as she plucked it from Bonnie's hand and snickered. "Well, that's nice, Mendoza, but we aren't in California, are we? This is Nevada—your geography lesson for today."

"I am certain the great state of Nevada will grant me reciprocity." She yawned. "It is no concern of yours, anyway."

"Got a little toy badge, gun, and handcuffs to play with in there too, I bet."

She threw down her hands. "Of course I have no badge or gun, are you loco? Guns are dangerous." She pulled a pair of glimmering red anodized bracelets from her small handbag and handed them to Jackie. "Please accept them as a gift, with my compliments."

Jackie took the expensive manacles amusingly, then broke out in laughter. "Oh, my. They match your outfit—what a laugh."

"Of course. They are the 'Debutante Detective' model, for dress occasions. A good choice for your annual holiday ball."

"Uh, thanks . . . I guess. Never had red ones before."

"You are welcome. Did you know that the Spanish word *esposas* means both 'handcuffs' and 'wives'? There must be a connection."

"Who gives a crap, Mendoza?" Jackie said, staring at her.

"And these are *not* toys. Toy ones will break and you have to file or drill them off when they malfunction." She moved towards Jackie and whispered in her ear. "I only carry nickel-free models, as my husband is extremely allergic to that metal. He gets terrible welts."

Jay started laughing. "I would give up if I were you."

"I've had it. Comedy club's over, Coach. You're real close to a fine," Tammy yelled, grimacing.

Bonnie sneered and pointed her finger at the two women. "I will have you know that Torpin's plasma testosterone is estimated at over 2,400 ng/mL—staggeringly high. What say you to this finding, Special Agent and Assistant Commissioner?"

The agent turned to Bonnie and pointed back. "No offense, but I don't need Nancy Drew and Hardy Boy over here to tell me my business." Jackie then looked at Alex. "Hey, you mute over there? What you got to say for yourself, Jethro?"

"I'm just watching and enjoying the show."

Bonnie frowned and looked at her husband. "What did she say to me?"

"*She says you are Nancy Drew,*" he signed in ASL, as it often took her a while to comprehend the speech of a new acquaintance.

Bonnie puffed out her chest and pointed her finger again. "The fictional children's sleuth? How insulting. Beg pardon, but I am no teenager on an amateurish quest. I will have you know that I have a vast amount of experience in forensic scientific analysis."

"That may be. As I understand it, though, you no longer work for the police, which was in San Diego, by the way. You have no authority here, despite your pretty little license." Jackie laughed.

"Nevertheless, I must maintain that the chemical residuals are quite incriminating. I challenge you to prove me otherwise."

"I don't have to take orders from you. As entertaining as your little theatrics are, your findings have no significance here."

She looked down at Jackie intensely and put her hand over her chest. "Do not allow your pride to obstruct the true findings here. There is no shame in being wrong, you know. Believe it or not, I have made a mistake once or twice in my life."

"Hey, who do you think you are? Some of us have to do real work, and don't have the time or money to dabble in playing cop."

"Uh, can I talk to you for a minute, Jay?" Dunlap put his arm around the taller coach and guided him across the room. "Need a meeting of the minds here, pal."

• • •

Jay and general manager Patrick Dunlap went into the conference room and slammed the door, with the former still laughing.

"Look, Jay, it isn't funny. Agent Levickis and Tammy are right.

I don't need this soap opera shit around my team in its first season, and don't want to mess with the commissioner's daughter. Tammy has a lot of influence. Torpin's already talking to the TV crew."

"*Your* team? You own it? It's my team too, and what does that mean, Patrick? You want our guys juiced up on drugs? Remember the women's Olympic track steroid scandal of 2000, the dog-fighting crap, and baseball and the Mitchell report, for God's sake. We all just want the truth here."

"You know what I mean. A lot of people didn't want you for this job, because they felt you were too, well . . . unseasoned."

"*Unseasoned*?"

"Immature is the word they used, actually. But I went to bat for you, because I believe in you. Their first choice was to bring Bryce Pickering out of retirement, but I talked them out of it. Don't let me down."

Jay threw down his pen. "*Pickering*? That frickin' zombie's so catatonic he's almost in a coma. No personality. His clothes look like they come from the Salvation Army store."

"But he's a coaching genius with two championship rings."

Jay showed Dunlap his own ring. "What the hell do you call this?"

"It wasn't for coaching. Your playing days are over, buddy. Win one for coaching, then you can put Pickering down."

"What the hell's wrong with me? I'm a legend. I've been in big action movies."

Dunlap laughed. "You were in *one* movie. *Death Match* sucked, and you *were* a legend. You're a head coach now, so act like one—an adult, that is. Your family seems to thrive on theatrics."

"I'm damn good, and put a face on this sorry bunch of guys."

"Don't you understand? We're in Las Vegas, and we don't need Bonnie, of all people, and her meddling husband in here causing trouble. They both have a reputation for that, and seem to thrive in the limelight. The papers get a hold of this, we're toast."

"She has nothing to do with this, and Alex isn't meddling. They're vertebrates, unlike your species," he said, pointing his finger at Dunlap. "You should try getting a backbone sometime, you spineless suck-up."

"Shut up, Jay, I'm still your boss."

"Wish the hell I was back in Titletown. At least there the town owns the team, and didn't have to kiss the owner's ass, like you."

"Settle down. The league is strongly anti-gambling, and plucky little sis, darling as she is, isn't exactly the poster child for that. I realize that she's a celebrity, and I'm willing to extend a great deal of courtesy, but you must understand I can't allow some crazy, unauthorized investigation to go on."

"But wasn't the original name of this team supposed to be the Las Vegas Gamblers?"

Dunlap paused and frowned. "Not funny, Jay."

"So she was a big poker and pool champion. She did it legally, and it had nothing to do with me, and she gave it up long ago. We've all made mistakes, and she got help and cleaned up her image."

"I know, but . . . the guys upstairs had their concerns. The media always did love you, so just keep everything level."

"Don't worry, I can handle her. Always could. She's brilliant, but horribly naïve, and will believe anything I tell her. Just gotta know which buttons to press."

Dunlap twiddled his thumbs. "That's fine, but what about Darkkin? The guy looks like he could be a real pain in the butt. Unpredictable."

"That may be more of a challenge, but I'll take care of it."

"You'd better. Don't need the DEA and FBI on our case."

They left the conference room, went back into his office, and turned on the old charm.

"I think we all need a break from the heat out here," Jay said. "Lunch at Fensterman's for me, my sister, and fine brother-in-law in a half hour. Dunlap here's buying with his expense account."

"Thanks, Jay. I'll get you for this."

"Relax. You're getting off cheap."

Bonnie put her finger into the air. "As long as it is not Mexican food. It is horrific. Jaime remembers how bad it was."

"Great. Got a few things to take care of, we'll go in a half hour or so. I want to talk to Tammy and Agent Levickis for a moment."

• • •

Jackie Levickis met Bonnie outside the Conquerors conference room ten minutes later, before they left for lunch. Jackie displayed a significantly different demeanor after speaking to Jay.

"Dr. Mendoza, I'm sorry, I didn't mean any disrespect. I guess I only knew about you from the popular media, and wasn't fully aware of your qualifications. But I have a job to do here, and have to do it the best way I know how. I don't . . . like to be second-guessed."

"I also did not mean to blow a fuse. I know you are just doing your job, and understand about having pride in your work. I am also prone to grandstanding and obnoxiousness at times."

Jackie grinned. "It's okay. You're actually pretty entertaining."

"Thank you. I am not easily offended, as I have been attacked by the most vicious people in the universe—inhumans who show no mercy to their victims."

"Yeah, I've dealt with some really bad criminals, too."

She shook her head randomly like a bobblehead doll. "No, no—I am referring to the lowly life-forms called attorneys. I have been to court numerous times to take their abuse during my forensic director days, Special Agent."

Jackie laughed. "You're a hoot. And call me Jackie. Answer me this, though—why does a Caltech physicist have a PI's license?"

"A what?"

"Private investigator license."

Bonnie shrugged. "Oh, I do not know. I was qualified, of course, with my forensics background. I guess I thought it was a way to sort of keep a portion of my past life. They do not let deaf be regular officers or federal agents, you know, which is what I wanted."

"Sorry about that. Anyway, I know a lot about you. Pretty talented—not just in science, but in sports, too. You can do everything, it seems." Jackie sat down and sipped her coffee.

She shrugged again. "An illusion—I have numerous flaws which I hide well. Anyway, my world heptathlon record in the Deaflympics doesn't get a whole lot of press. 'The world's greatest deaf athlete'—hah."

"I'm curious about that. Why the heptathlon, anyway? You were an All-American sprinter in college with world-class speed, and might have made the Olympics in the hundred meters. Why do the deaf heptathlon?"

She laughed. "You are not deaf, so you cannot possibly understand. I did not do that for me, but for the deaf community, who are my true brothers and sisters. I had my own significant . . . personal problems to deal with at that time."

"I guess I can understand that."

"Short sprints and hurdles, I'm pretty good. Longer races, I cannot 'hear' runners behind me to make lane changes. But I gained almost thirty pounds of muscle in college—I am probably faster now than then. And much stronger."

They sat down in the lounge and poured more coffee. "I'm impressed by your forensic science background. The techniques you describe are cutting edge."

"I have been out for a few years, but keep in touch with colleagues back home."

"Why'd you leave that?"

"Maybe I was doing it for others, and not for me. Saving the world is not my thing. I can accomplish much greater good in the worlds of mathematics and theoretical physics."

"So, how did you come to get involved in this?"

"Habit, I suppose. And my nosy husband, who fancies himself an Appalachian version of James Bond. And Jaime, who was always there for me. When he summoned me, I felt the urge to respond."

"Yeah. You seem to hear pretty well, I noticed."

"It is not 'hearing' as you define it. I can only manage so much information at once. I cannot perceive music, for example. It's not just that the processors can't handle it well, but also because my own brain doesn't understand it. I was in high school before I could speak intelligibly at all."

"If you don't mind my asking—were you born deaf?"

"No. I almost died after contracting meningitis at age eleven, and lost my hearing after that, as well as most of my memory. I could not walk or talk, and had to learn to speak all over again. The slow speech you currently hear is the result of over twenty years' and hundreds of thousands of dollars' worth of speech therapy. I could not have done it without Jaime or my best friend Wendy."

Jackie stood up. "So, what's next, Mendoza? What kind of tricks have you got up your sleeve?"

She took out her pen and started taking notes. "First, I desire to tour the drug testing complex. If there is a way to defeat it, my husband and I will find out. The next order of business is to determine why certain players are taking drugs, and to network and find out similar information about other teams."

The agent scratched her head. "How the heck are you going to do that?"

She made several notes on a legal pad. "I will simply use a CCD-based dispersive Raman spectrometer, using 785-nm diode laser excitation, to analyze sweat from the players."

Jackie nodded. "Got it. Just what I was going to suggest."

"Really?" she said in a surprised tone.

"Oh, sure. I do that Raman diode stuff all the time, as a hobby, when I'm not doing calculus."

She smiled and opened her mouth wide, displaying a toothy grin. "Me, too. We seem to have much in common."

"Yeah, sister," Jackie laughed. "If you say so."

"And the heat will aid my investigation. Not as good as directly analyzing urine, but it may give us some direction."

Jackie extended her hand. "This is gonna be fun as well as educational for me, I'll tell you that."

She looked up proudly. "Of course. One must learn something new every day."

Chapter Nineteen

Champions Testing Center
Las Vegas, NV

Bonnie, Jackie Levickis, and Tammy Preece went down the corridor of the league's Las Vegas testing center, as Tammy gave them a detailed tour of the complex.

"Dr. Mendoza, let me show our procedures to you," Tammy said. "The athlete to be tested strips down to his shorts. They then go into this special room, and the tester's clothing is actually searched by a security officer before going in. I'm sure you're familiar with the procedure."

"Yes, but what about the testing room itself?" Bonnie asked the slightly taller but slimmer woman.

"I'll take you to a representative room." They walked down the corridor and into a testing unit. "I understand from your FBI file that you are a very good magician and escape artist, and therefore very adept at hiding things, so, in a way, no one could be more credible than you. I want you to see if you can figure out a way to hide something in here. In other words, I am actually asking your help."

"That is one thing I can do well." She carefully went over every inch of the room for over an hour, meticulously examining every nook and cranny. Everything in the room was designed like a well-furnished jail cell—there was nothing that was removable or that could be taken apart without specialized tools. That was one reason she always enjoyed escaping from old jail and prison cells—apart from the nostalgic appeal, they simply had a lot of defects which could be exploited. This room's design, on the other hand, was a masterpiece—like a modern-day prison cell.

"Are you satisfied?" Tammy asked cheerfully.

She nodded reluctantly. "For now, perhaps, but there is always a way, if you want to do it badly enough. But I cannot detect a method to bring contraband body fluids in here easily. But I will."

"Exactly what I thought you'd find—nothing. You are welcome to try and find another way."

"This is an absurd query, but why couldn't the tester simply give his or her own body fluids in place of the athlete's? That is one method of circumventing the process. Assuming the tester was an accomplice, of course."

Tammy smiled. "That's a good question, and the reason why the tester is always female—for male athletes, of course."

"Huh? Come again?"

"Female. We test the samples for the presence of a Y chromosome. If the sample was switched and came from the female technician, that obviously wouldn't be the case."

"I see, because they would be XX. Why not perform a complete DNA test, then? Verify that against the athlete's true profile?"

Tammy laughed. "You ran a forensics lab, and should know how expensive that would be—testing a thousand athletes a year. And confidentiality prohibits us from collecting their DNA profiles. The players' union would go crazy. The chromosomal analysis suffices, don't you think?"

She thought for a minute or so. "I suppose. That's actually quite brilliant, though. Whoever thought that up should be commended for ingenuity."

Tammy took a bow. "It's my system. I thought it up. We can't be too careful, what with the Olympic sprinter scandal of 2000, baseball steroids, and such."

"How many such testing centers are there like this?"

"Nine. Vegas, San Diego, Cincinnati, Philadelphia, New York, Atlanta, Seattle, Tampa, and Dallas. They all go to one of those centers. You are welcome to go to one of those if you want. You'll find just what you found here."

"It looks like you have put a lot of effort into the procedures. Are you *that* worried about steroid and other drug abuse?"

"Pro football has to be beyond reproach. You can't trust anyone these days."

"Perhaps other sports should look into a similar system. And the legal and penal system as well."

"We are looking into marketing it to them, rest assured."

She certainly knew that steroid abuse still existed, and her brother's intuition was seldom wrong; the metabolomic analyses of Torpin did suggest steroid abuse. There had to be a way. She and her creative husband just had to figure out how.

• • •

Excelsior Hotel
Las Vegas, NV

Alex and Bonnie were sitting in the living room of their hotel suite a half-mile from the team complex.

"So, who else on the fantastic, championship-contending Conquerors squad is on steroids besides Torpin?" he asked as he sat the two large coffee cups down on the table.

She didn't answer, and finally looked at him.

"Where is the coffee? You said you would procure some, as I am severely xanthine-deprived."

"Coffee?" He pointed to the cups on the table. "It's over there, and I just asked you a question." He signed the previous sentence to her.

"I cannot test the injured players, but my crude metabolomic analysis from the field reveals two others. Non-crucial players."

"Who?"

She showed him the team roster. "Rodd Edmondson and Quell Yarling. Steroids, but no evidence of growth hormone or other drugs. Jay did say that Edmondson blew up in a practice at training camp."

He looked at the list of Conquerors players. "Both are late-career guys who played for Indy last year, like Torpin, but they were subs. Edmondson's a second-string punt returner, Yarling a long snapper. Mediocre players at best, and the team let them go to relieve salary cap room. Torpin's the only star."

"Why Torpin, though?"

"Makes no sense. Jay says his rehab has been phenomenal. He should've needed six more months to get in this kind of shape, and he's faster than he's ever been. He benches over 400, the trainers said."

"Why did Indy let him go, then?"

"The injury, of course, and his salary's sky-high. And the fact that he's an overpaid asshole adds bonus points. You've seen him."

"Many people are passionate. Such emotion does not diminish one's worth as long as one produces."

"He can't produce if he's getting into fights with the coaches all the time, can he?"

"In any case, what is the connection among those three? That they both played for Indianapolis? What is the significance of that?"

"Three players from the Super Bowl champs. A volatile star with an injury, almost magically reborn. The other two, fringe players, second-stringers with a limited future. It doesn't add up."

"Perhaps there are others whom we have not yet identified."

He took a swig of his coffee. "Why the Conquerors, anyway? Other than Torpin, who no one wanted, they've got no stars. Hardly contenders for the division."

"Gambling takes many angles, Alex. The point spread, for example. Anabolic enhancement of key players could alter that enough for someone to profit. Unlikely, but still possible. A small advantage is often all that is necessary to achieve a profit."

"Come on—game an expansion team, in Vegas, of all places? No one would buy that, it's too risky. And improbable."

"*Adversus solem ne loquitor*. Do not waste your time arguing the obvious."

"What, that someone would juice up a bunch of losers to gain a few points on the spread? I don't buy it."

"The benefit, admittedly, seems unworthy of the potential legal and health risks. Perhaps they are simply random players, intent on illicitly enhancing their careers during their twilight years."

"We're assuming they're doing it intentionally. But what if they don't know they're taking a risk?"

She laughed. "Duh! For a doctor, you are so stupid. Anyone with half a brain knows the health risks of taking steroids."

"No, I mean, what if someone's giving it to them without their knowledge?"

"Testosterone may only be given by injection. Why would they not know they are getting that? They think they are getting vitamins instead, like the players in the baseball scandal? Hello!"

"Untrue. It is absorbed well orally but is degraded rapidly by the liver. There are some preparations, namely testosterone undecanoate, which can be taken orally. There are transdermal preparations, too. Maybe they're being told they're something else."

"To what end? They surely must be noticing some adverse side effects of it."

She didn't know the answer, but there had to be some reason why they were taking anabolic steroids. As fantastic as it seemed, it had to be some reason besides the athletic enhancement. But what?

Chapter Twenty

Las Vegas Conquerors
Team Offices
Las Vegas, NV

Bonnie and Jackie were sitting in the conference room the next morning, going over some files on current pro football players.

"I appreciate your support, Jackie. I am working on some interesting findings which may assist our investigation."

"That's okay, I want to give you a fair shake. I don't trust Preece either, but she wanted me to stick around. I got no problem with that. Or with you."

"That's fine. I have nothing to hide."

"But I don't get it," Jackie said. "What is the gambling thing with you all about?"

"My past has not been always . . . shall we say, constructive. I am an addict, a compulsive gambler. Card games such as poker, mostly. I played on television. I am also a very good pool player."

"Pool? *You* were a pool shark? Don't take this the wrong way, but you don't seem the type."

She smiled. "Just what 'type' of person do you expect a gambling addict to be?"

"Usually a down-and-out middle-aged guy who loses everything. You seem, well, a little too educated and high-class for that sort of stuff."

"Gamblers, like alcoholics, come in all shapes and sizes. But, about pool, it merely involves coordination and knowledge of physics. Simplest thing in the world."

"To you, maybe. So, you came to Vegas to gamble often?"

"Yes. It became an obsession in my early twenties. An illness, and a gross misuse of my gifts."

"Gifts?"

"I can beat the house at almost any game that involves mathematical probabilities, such as blackjack or poker, by using my native cipher powers."

"Huh. If you're so good, why is it a problem, if you don't lose?"

"People always ask that, and wish they were me. You don't want it, trust me."

"I sure wish I could do that."

"Be careful what you wish for—you may just get it. I amassed a small fortune—I don't know how much, as my husband manages my money—but it was a waste of time. What possible good would I be doing for society that way? A shallow waste of my second chance at life."

"Second chance at life?"

"I almost died when I was eleven. Resulted in this." She pointed to the aural processors. "I almost died, again, three years ago, after taking down a desperate criminal. A decision of extremely poor judgment on my part."

"Huh—I guess I can see your point. Can you show me how you do it, though?"

"Why?"

"Just curious. If we're going to work together, I'd like to know who I'm working with."

She scowled. "What do you want me to do? I'm not fond of demonstrating it—I want to leave it behind. You would not ask a drug addict to smoke crack."

"It's not quite the same. Can you do sport outcomes?"

"Yes. I am not going to do it, though, for you to gamble. I hope that's not what you are suggesting."

"Of course not. As a federal agent, I certainly don't gamble. I just want to see it. You're the one suggesting a sports scandal. I want to know the real odds."

Bonnie reluctantly took out a legal pad. "Okay. You can reduce every known parameter of an athlete to a statistic. I studied the various stadiums, the noise levels, etc. You cannot plan on injury, but I am the best in the world."

Bonnie took about fifteen minutes and perused several sports almanacs and schedules, and hurriedly made a list for Jackie.

"I made a list of my picks for tomorrow. Give me your word you will not use them for your own gain."

"I told you, I can't gamble." Levickis looked at the list. "You *really* think the Conquerors will only lose their first preseason game against Arizona by a field goal? Line is two touchdowns."

"The enhancement of Torpin and the others gives them the advantage. My prediction is not perfect—it is the probability of an infinite number of games played between the two teams. Since the outcomes of football games are normally distributed, the mean of all games should be by that margin."

Levickis shook her head. "You kind of lost me. And you're still on Torpin, aren't you? Can't you just accept that he's made a phenomenal comeback, and leave it at that?"

"I hope you are not in the commissioner's pocket. That would disappoint me greatly. And I do not trust this arrogant Tamara Preece woman. She seems evil, somehow."

"Hey—Jackie Levickis is no one's patsy, I assure you, and I don't like that chick, like I said before. But I have to get more proof than your . . . metabolomics, is that how you say it?"

"Yes—an evolving technology. The DEA should be aware."

"But it's surely not admissible in court."

"Not yet, anyway, but just wait. You should read some of my monographs on that topic."

"Wow. I can't wait to see those," Jackie said in a caustic tone.

• • •

Jaime Mendoza's Home
7732 Cactus Way
Las Vegas, NV

Alex and Bonnie watched some video clips on Jay's widescreen TV at his expansive Las Vegas home, while their host pulled a VHS cassette from the entertainment center cabinet.

"Please do not show it," Bonnie pleaded, recognizing the tape. "We were not a good team. Alex does not know of it."

"Yeah, but he's gotta see this," Jay said. "They even showed the clip on ESPN before one of my games."

"What is it?" Alex asked.

"Bonnie played football in high school, you know."

"I didn't know that. Why didn't you tell me?"

"We were last in the conference. Hardly stellar moments in sports history."

"Ah, yes, but her last game was great. She played football at St. Martin's Academy her senior year—it's a private prep school."

"No way. You had to wear a school uniform?"

She shrugged. "It simplified my clothing choices."

"Anyway, they needed a kicker, and I suggested Bonnie to the coach. Her senior year, they were playing this much bigger school, Rutledge, who was on its way to a perfect season. But St. Martin had scored a touchdown with thirty seconds left to trail by only six points."

"She really was their placekicker?"

"You bet. She could have played as a wide receiver or defensive back, but coach wouldn't let her because, well, she was deaf. He did let her kick, with the understanding that she not tackle anyone."

"What happened?"

"Bonnie kicked off, their returner fielded it at about the seven. He got some good blocks, and took off down the sideline, and had beaten ten guys, and was at the St. Martin thirty. Beat everyone except the kicker."

"The kicker, huh?"

"She took off after the guy and ran him down, coach screaming at her . . . of course she couldn't hear him. She hit that 200-lb dude at full tilt, lifted him off the ground, knocked his frickin' helmet off. As nasty a hit as I've ever seen, and I've seen a lot. Ball popped loose, backwards, into the hands of a St. Martin defender, who ran it back for a touchdown. They lost, and Bonnie ruined their 'perfect season,' even though it was only the second game they won all year."

"Coach upset she tackled that guy?"

"Actually, no—he said that a football player *should* play like that. My folks were furious with her, although she just got the wind knocked out of her. With that speed, she can generate an amazing amount of momentum."

She smiled. "He was right. A football player is to play, no? A kicker should not be given special consideration. If only I had been allowed to smash more."

"But that showed me something I always knew was true," Jay said.

"What?" Alex asked.

"She's the meanest competitor I've ever seen. Absolutely no fear, and will beat you to death at anything. I've faced a lot of stiff opposition, but she's the one that always scared the heck out of me, even when she was a little girl. That look in her eyes."

"Come on," he replied. "You were eight years older than her. I don't think she would have been too threatening."

"Didn't matter. She could be sweet as honey to Mom and Dad, then nastier than a snake to me, always plotting something. It's amazing I'm nice to her at all."

"I can't wait to hear all those stories."

"I will have some to share about Jaime, as well."

Jay turned on the video player as the three of them watched the final game in the brief, illustrious football career of Bonita Mendoza.

Chapter Twenty–one

Sam Boyd Stadium
Las Vegas, NV

The next day, coach Jay Mendoza watched as 11,211 fans filled the 36,900 available seats of Sam Boyd Stadium in Las Vegas for the team's first preseason game. Construction was almost complete for the new Conquerors Stadium, but they had to play their games there until the final touches were completed for next season. Jay was worried that the capacity would be too small. But he frowned as he realized he'd played to bigger crowds in high school.

Jason Lee Torpin, despite Jay's concerns, was having a great game. He had returned a punt for a touchdown and caught a sixty–five-yard touchdown pass from quarterback Grant Sawyer, a third-string castoff from Tampa Bay last year. And Sawyer wasn't that great, he knew.

Alex, Bonnie, and Jackie watched eagerly from the Conquerors' sideline with low expectations for an exciting game.

"First time I've been on a pro football sideline," Alex said. "Kind of cool."

"I agree," Jackie said. "Not much of a crowd, though."

She yawned. "How droll. I have been on one many times."

"Yeah, freezing your tail off in Green Bay," he said.

"I wished I could play. I always dreamed of it. I kicked a forty–two-yard field goal, once."

"Those old clips were impressive. Ever think of trying out for the pros?"

"What?"

He signed it in ASL. *"Pro football. You could play. And you don't seem to be hearing as well. I've told you that several times."*

"You jibber-jabber so much, it is hard to pay attention. No, I have no desire to play pro football. And women are not allowed to play in the pro leagues. A few have played in college."

"Really?"

"Yes, really. It is no place for a female."

"Darn. I wanted to see you in full gear."

"Huh? King Lear? I do not like Shakespearean tragedies. I prefer the comedies, such as—"

"You need to go see Dr. Traylor and get your processors checked," he signed in ASL.

"It is probably a minor malfunction. Sometimes maintenance and software upgrades must be done."

They watched the agonizingly unexciting game, as both teams traded a pair of touchdowns over the first three quarters, Eventually, fifty–eight minutes had passed on the clock, and they were down to the two-minute warning of the fourth quarter. The Conquerors were down to their new division rivals, Arizona, by only three points.

"I told you, Jackie. Three points."

"I don't believe it. It has to be partly luck. On the other hand, you also correctly picked the winners of the other nine games which have been played so far. Damn."

"There is always some element of random chance, to be sure, but I win more times than I lose. I would normally be within the point spread, however."

The clock finally ticked down to zero. Final score: Arizona 17, Las Vegas 14.

"If you had gambled on your prediction, how much money would you have made?" Jackie asked.

She frowned. "A lot. I don't want to think about it. But there probably was not a lot of action on this game."

• • •

Excelsior Hotel
Las Vegas, NV

"So, what did you find out from the Arizona game?" Alex asked his wife as they met in their hotel room two days later, as she had just returned with new laboratory findings.

"The results are very crude," she said. "Normally, we would do high-performance liquid chromatography on body fluids. But we have discovered that hair tends to accumulate steroids, and your brashness seems to have paid off. I cannot believe you paid off their trainer to look inside the players' helmets."

"Yeah—about half had some hair which could be extracted, which I placed in bags for you."

"None of it is legally admissible, of course."

"What does it show?"

"The testosterone/epitestosterone levels range anywhere from 2.3 to 5.7—within normal limits established by testing authorities. All except for Rayden Mang, a starting left guard. His ratio is 12.2 to 1, highly suggestive of anabolic steroid use."

Alex looked up the player roster. "Mang . . . 6-3, 322, pretty big fella, even for an offensive lineman. First-year player for Arizona, his fifth year in the league. First round draft pick out of Alabama. But guess what?"

"He played for Indianapolis last year."

"You are getting more perceptive."

"But why? Random players here and there, none of whom are stars, save for Torpin, who's a liability."

"I don't know. Wendy's going to come up for a few days, and we'll see if she has any ideas."

She pondered the findings and considered the possibilities—none existed that made any sense. But she knew that sometimes events had a way of unfolding on their own.

Chapter Twenty–two

Argotech Industries
U.S. Bio-Genetic Research Facility
Cairo, WV

Dr. Rita McPherson walked up to her desk, sat down, and retrieved several reports on her computer terminal at the Argotech West Virginia complex. There was a lot of work to be done in her fifteen-hour work days, but it was a job she relished every moment, the chance of a lifetime. A biochemistry scholar who had graduated with honors from Harvard, she was heavily recruited by Dr. Malachi Argon to join his "team." But the stellar geneticist wasn't recruited just because of her intellect and education, but because of another reason.

The thoughts of a life that could have been passed through her mind. Talented, pretty Rita was a junior in high school when the habitual drunk driver (driving without a license) ran the stop sign and smashed into her boyfriend's car while they were on their way home from the prom.

Her escort was killed instantly; the intoxicated driver, ironically, suffered only minor injuries. She was rushed to the emergency room, with a broken leg and badly lacerated foot. But she couldn't feel those injuries, which paled to what she would learn about later.

The neurosurgeon at the trauma center gave her and her parents the horrible news: she had suffered a T5 vertebral crush fracture, which resulted in paralysis from the waist down. She was on the high school volleyball team, but that all came to an end that night.

Family and classmates flocked around her, but Rita McPherson wouldn't be pitied by anyone. She threw herself into her studies, graduated from high school on time, and earned her undergraduate and doctoral degrees in biochemistry at Harvard University on a full scholarship.

She was pursuing her post-doctoral fellowship at Harvard when she was approached one day by the tall, distinguished geneticist she had read about in prestigious scientific journals: Malachi Quincy Zachariah Argon. She had numerous job offers from pharmaceutical companies as well as universities, but Argon claimed to have something to offer that others didn't. Something that only he, equipped with one of the greatest scientific discoveries of all time, could accomplish.

Argon—the famous professor whose textbooks most students of the biological sciences had used at one time—inspired great awe. Yet he was here, wanting to work with her. And what he offered her was priceless. But she wasn't stupid, and thought what he suggested was ridiculous. Until he showed her irrefutable proof, that is.

He could make her walk again, he claimed. It sounded ludicrous, as she had heard the claims of quackery before. But he had his own medical problem, he had confessed; the disabling Parkinson's disease had been getting worse by the week, and had begun doing genetic experiments on himself to alleviate the symptoms. And, it had *worked*—he was now nearly back to normal.

He had another reason that few people knew about. His son Travis, a standout college athlete, had been diagnosed with leukemia a number of years earlier; he had tried various experimental therapies without success. But the genetic experimentation on Travis had reached a peak, and Argon needed some new ideas.

Travis Argon was, she learned, his greatest experiment in human genetics. Argon had long hypothesized about replacing certain amino acids in the body, improving upon what humans had been given. The massive computer servers at his disposal continuously performed manipulations of the human genome, predicting what certain mutations would do. And Travis, he said, would be saved from death to become that man—an "orthogenetic" man, one whose genes were "perfectly aligned" for maximum strength and efficiency. He was a physical marvel, but the treatment was not without flaws, and his malignancy was back.

The therapy Argon recommended for her was based on a protein from a unique microorganism. But not one she had ever encountered; the DNA of this novel organism, related to the denitrifying archaebacteria, had been discovered in possibly the most hostile environment ever discovered by mankind. *Alien* was, rather, a more appropriate adjective. The remarkable growth factor produced from *Orthogeneticus titania* (at a cost of many billions of dollars) seemed to possess the ability to restore damaged nervous system cells to an extent never thought possible before. The animal models he used showed startling recovery; the chimps who underwent spinal cord transection recovered seventy percent of their function within six months of treatment.

She was the fifth spinal cord victim to be treated with OT-45, as Argon called it. Some of the others experienced the return of varying degrees of function; the first died, she second didn't improve at all, and the others improved moderately. After three weeks, she began experiencing motor function and sensory return in her legs, and was able to walk again, slowly, after six weeks. Argon had come through on his amazing promise.

But what was she asked to do in return? Argon had always treated her well and paid her a handsome salary, but the project called *Ortho-Man* was far more secretive than anything she had ever imagined. Argotech was a military contractor, and she didn't want to know what Travis and any like him would be used for, if he even survived.

She eventually, by accident, learned that Travis' disease was actually caused by Argon's own genetic experimentation, prior to the discovery of *O. titania;* the *O. titainia* protein was his salvation, his redemption. But she also wondered if Argon cared less about her and Travis than himself and his own disease. Why had he experimented on his son in the first place? Surely he wouldn't have agreed to that willingly.

She was in far too deeply to go back now, she knew. Walking again was her greatest dream, and she had achieved that remarkable feat. But at what price? And what was Argon's mysterious "silent partner"—Lt. Gen. Brant Gallagher—going to do with the classified information?

She was a trusting sort, and put her skeptical thoughts aside, because she just *knew* that the brilliant Dr. Argon was doing what was best for mankind. Her parents said that she had made a deal with the devil, that nothing came that easily—and that somewhere, sometime, payment would be required. It was hard for them to understand how charitable such a brilliant man could be. After all, their daughter, a brilliant and successful scientist, was walking again.

Chapter Twenty–three

Benny's Coffee Bean
Las Vegas, NV

"Okay," Alex said to his sister as they sipped coffee at the Las Vegas coffee shop. She had flown in the previous evening, and was staying at a nearby hotel. "I know they're feeding Torpin and those two other guys 'roids, and maybe Ray Mang from Arizona, but can't figure out how. Preece and Levickis even took Bonnie to the testing lab, and she couldn't figure out any way to do it.

"That doesn't mean it's impossible."

"I know, and she's the first to admit that there's always a way."

"So, the tester's always female, right?" Wendy asked after pausing for half a minute. "That's how they verify the sample came from the player, then."

"Right. If a male were the tester, he could switch the samples with the athlete. Guys dressed up as girls, maybe?"

"Alex, that's really dumb. The testers undergo a complete physical, Bonnie said. She also said they were pretty attractive women."

"What does she know? For a former forensic scientist, she can be pretty gullible." He took a swig of his twenty–ounce caffeinated beverage. "But I guess that wouldn't work."

"You think?" Wendy laughed. "One way around it, though—they could have a bunch of ladies with testicular feminization syndrome collecting the pee and blood. They would have a Y chromosome for sure."

Alex turned his head up. "Huh? Testicular what?"

"Male pseudohermaphrodism, which refers to a female with a male genetic structure. It's one way you could defeat it—complete androgen resistance syndrome, or testicular feminization."

"No way. That sounds pretty bizarre."

"Right up your alley. But it's actually pretty common, about 1 in 50,000, and even some celebrities have it. Girls grow up perfectly normal, except they have no hair on their bodies."

"Why don't they have hair? I forget."

"Because all body hair, except on the scalp and eyebrows, is testosterone-dependent, dummy. They have plenty of testosterone, because they have testes, but the body can't use it, so just a little peach fuzz on the face and body. Generally not picked up until 15 or 16, when they're brought to the doctor for never having had a period."

"I . . . guess I remember hearing about that in endocrine lecture hall. Some of them are pretty hot. I guess that sounds pretty weird, since they're really guys, aren't they?"

"God, you think anything with a female form is hot. And they're not guys, simply females with a Y chromosome, and the testes are removed at an early age. And they look perfectly normal, except they can't have children, of course, because they have no uterus."

"Interesting, but that's an absurd theory."

"*You* saying something is absurd? But it's one way of getting a Y chromosome in there," she chortled. "I don't see you or M-Square coming up with something better."

He got up and walked around the room for a minute or two. "Do you really think it's possible? I think you've got something there."

"What? Alex, I'm kidding. Jeez."

"You said it was pretty common, so why couldn't you do it? Get some gals with T-fem in there to collect the stuff, then they substitute their own."

"Gotta be more sophisticated ways to do it."

"That sounds pretty high-tech to me. I didn't think of it, and I'm pretty smart."

"But why? To win some ball games?"

"Winning games can make you a heap of money. Ask my well-heeled wife."

Her eyes opened wide. "Yeah, maybe you're right, they could've done it that way. I can see it."

He was taken aback by his sister's change in attitude, but he knew she was often like that. "Really? You think so now?"

"I guess so. You're gonna have to get that sinister Darkkin mind going to think of how to prove it, though."

"I'm working on it, but I think I'll need Crazy Jim to help me."

"Ah, I was wondering when you were going to call him in on consultation. We need some more weirdness."

"You still good with the magic stuff? Just between us."

"I guess so. I just thought about something special, something the amazing M-Square wouldn't approve of, I'm sure." She took a sip of her coffee.

"I can't wait to hear about this. And did I hear you right when you ordered? When did you start drinking decaf? That's heresy."

"Caffeine's not good for you, Doctor. It causes all kinds of ailments. I'm on a health kick now. Look at all the energy I have."

"Yeah, I can see, but I can't believe you're saying that. Bonnie once tried to get your name legally changed to Juanita Valdez."

She stood up and raised her hands into the air. "I gotta find my old buddy in the prosthetics lab, who likes challenging projects. This one's gonna cost a bunch, but he owes me a favor. And it'll involve some hacking, just so you know."

"Great. Haven't done any good computer espionage in some time. Crazy Jim will have to be on high alert."

• • •

Jim Krakowski's Residence
Poway, CA

Jim Krakowski's phone rang at one AM at his cluttered apartment in suburban San Diego. He spied the caller ID on the phone and immediately started cursing.

"Darkkin, what the hell do you want? It's one AM, you moron!"

"Hey, I really need your help, or I wouldn't be calling this late."

"Am I an emergency service? You're the big doctor. Oh, I forgot, you don't actually see patients anymore, just push pencils around."

"That's not a very nice thing to say to your best buddy."

"Don't you think it could have waited till morning?"

"No. And I am technically your boss, in case you didn't know."

"And you're a dumb ass. I'm a private consultant for DarTech. It doesn't include calls in the middle of the night."

"I guess maybe you're right. Maybe I just wanted to hear your pretty voice."

Jim laughed. "So, whaddaya want, anyway, weirdo?"

"We need to make a road trip. I'm paying."

"Oh, man, not to Iowa City again, I can't take that place. Nothing but cornfields."

"The world's largest truck stop wasn't fun? No, a slightly finer establishment. The Plaza."

"Plaza? What the hell's that? Some sleazoid strip joint?"

"No, *The* Plaza, in Manhattan."

"You kiddin' me?"

"Nope. I'll fly into SD and meet you in the morning."

"I hate to ask, but what is it we're going to be doing?"

"You don't want to know. It's pretty dirty, and involves the assistant commissioner of pro football."

"Football? Sounds cool."

"I'll fly by and meet you at the airport in the morning. I've already booked the flights."

"They sure better be first class." Jim hung up the phone and thought about his old friend, with whom he had shared more than a few adventures. He hoped this one would be enlightening. Any trip with Alexander Dirk Darkkin had to be more exciting than watching old reruns on TV, he thought as he went to look for some clean clothes, a seemingly impossible task for the disorganized bachelor.

• • •

James Allen Krakowski was Alexander Darkkin's best friend. Born in New Castle, Indiana, the bright young man had earned an academic scholarship to Vanderbilt University. Always prone to mischief, he did things that almost got him expelled from school on several occasions, including running a non-FCC licensed "Radio Free Test Answers" radio station from the trunk of an old sedan than he kept hidden in an old storage shed.

A democratic sort, he felt that all test answers should be in the "public domain," and hacked into professors' files to obtain the answers, which he broadcast on AM and FM radio bands, so that anyone with a simple radio could listen to the answers. He was smart enough to build several repeaters around Nashville, so that the exact point of transmission couldn't be found; they might find the repeater, but never the true source.

He was a genius at thinking up devious things to do, without getting into trouble. At Vanderbilt, he knew that certain advanced scientific calculators were not allowed on examinations because they were too powerful; many high-end models could be programmed and could deal with complex mathematical functions (differential and integral calculus, complex numbers, advanced polynomial factoring, etc.). He found that some of the 'low-end' calculators of the same manufacturer had a similar faceplate bezel, and created a micro-industry of "hacked calculators," with the innards of the advanced models swapped with the cases of the "allowed" models.

The modified calculators were so good (and pricey) that only detailed inspection could determine the difference. A paranoid sort, he only dealt with money orders and P.O. boxes, and had complete deniability in case the deal went sour.

Jim graduated with a degree in computer science, and later earned his masters' in computer engineering. He worked as a consultant for many years until he worked with Alex on a bizarre investigation three years ago, regarding the poisoning of a pharmaceutical executive with heavy water. It was then that he realized that his old friend worked with some pretty cool stuff, and he and his strange better half sure had a wild sense of adventure.

After that caper, he decided to stay in San Diego and manage Alex's radiology imaging software company, DarTech, and became a regional expert in medical informatics. And, of course, he was best man at Alex and Bonnie's wedding over two years ago. Alex had little time to run the company, as he was busy trying to solve the ills of medical administration at Pasadena's Lutheran Hospital.

He had always liked pro sports, and Las Vegas was a fun place all year. He was never a very good gambler, though, but he hoped his luck might change. He was also looking forward to whatever illicit hacking might be involved in uncovering this new information.

Chapter Twenty–four

Tamara Precce's Residence
320 Park Avenue
New York, NY

Alex Darkkin always liked New York City, although this was a quick trip—something he had to do without his wife. Bonnie had other business to take care of, and Wendy had other plans, so he was on his own with his best friend Jim Krakowski. And this was a caper right up their alley. It demanded some forethought, to determine what day trash was picked up, so they didn't have to wait several days. But the two of them were good at spying and gathering information; they spent a lot of time doing those things in college.

Alex wore the crisp uniform of a New York Sanitation Department worker on the fine September day, as his best friend reluctantly drove the large truck. They had "borrowed" the truck for thirty minutes from the two workers, who were more than willing to loan their equipment after Alex flashed five hundred bucks.

They came to the residence they were looking for: the posh brownstone on Park Avenue, located up the street from pro football headquarters. Alex found the green trash can and pretended to empty it into the truck, but instead held onto it as he got back into the cab with Jim.

"When you said 'dirty,' I thought you had something else in mind," Jim said. "Perhaps involving strippers and dollar bills. Marriage has altered your basic cognitive functions, my friend."

"It does change your perspective, that's true. Trust me, you don't get away with much with a snoopy wife who used to run a big forensics lab. It's like living with a policewoman."

"Uh, I hate to ask, but what's so special about that bag of trash that we had to fly all the way here for and masquerade as sanitary engineers to collect?"

"It's special trash, trust me. It's the assistant commissioner's trash, which contains astounding information."

Jim twirled his hand in a circle. "O-kay . . . whatever floats your boat, my man. Your private fetishes are your own business, I guess. At least I got a nice room and a couple of meals out of it."

They drove the truck back to the trash collectors, removed the overalls, and took their bounty down the street where they went into a corner coffee shop and sat down, everyone staring at them, a few laughing and pointing.

Jim tried desperately to hide his face. "You look like an imbecile, Darkkin. Jeez, everybody's staring at you."

"I don't care." He ignored Jim as he looked through the trash eagerly. "None of their business."

"What are you looking for in there? Credit card receipts? I'm done with computer crime, you know. Got a thing for the assistant commish's panties?"

"Razors and tampons, or the lack thereof, hopefully."

Jim shook his head. "God, you're really a sicko. You need help bad. I heard of a doctor somewhere in Amsterdam that can do wonders with guys like you, but she's expensive."

"No," he laughed. "It's to confirm a medical condition. It's the easiest way to do it, trust me, as outlandish as it sounds."

"Huh. If you say so."

Alex finally found what he was looking for—a week's worth of trash with no razors or tampons. He knew from cleaning up his own garbage how unusual that was.

"This confirms it," he said proudly, holding his bag of trash high. "No question, that's how they're getting the steroids in there."

Jim picked up Alex's coffee and smelled it. "You putting a little joy juice in there? Steroids and Tammy Preece? You lost me."

"I'll tell you on the way home."

• • •

Excelsior Hotel
Las Vegas, NV

"Tammy Preece has some interesting garbage," Alex said to Bonnie and Wendy at the hotel in Las Vegas he had rented by the week. Jim was off at one of the casinos, probably losing money, he had told them.

"My brother, the garbage man. Always did have a mind in the sewer," Wendy said.

"It was a lot of fun, wearing the uniform and all. The guy let me have the trash truck for only five hundred bucks."

"That is so repugnant. What of interest did you discover, anyway?" Bonnie asked, sticking out her tongue. "What a waste of my good money."

"Hey, it's not all yours, and don't boss me around. But it's what I *didn't* discover that's significant. A whole week's worth of trash, and not one razor or tampon."

"It wouldn't be unusual for the latter, if she wasn't on her period, stupid," Wendy said.

"But no razors? Come on, you've seen her. Arms and legs smooth as silk. In contrast, Bonnie waxes and uses several razors per—"

"Shut up right now," Bonnie said as she kicked him in the shin. "And there could be another explanation. A chemical depilatory, for example. Or perhaps she utilizes waxing."

"No, I don't believe that. I think Tammy Preece has complete androgen resistance, or testicular feminization. Consistent with the hypothesis Wendy developed, I must add."

"At least your're giving me some credit," Wendy said.

"Tammy has a daughter, duh! Doesn't one require a uterus for that?"

"About that . . . I can't prove it exactly, but there's no medical records anywhere around the time of the daughter's birth," he said.

"Her father is the pro football commissioner. That information surely remains confidential," she said.

"It also means the daughter could be adopted."

"Yeah, so what?" Wendy asked. "I heard Tammy had multiple sclerosis, but appears to be in remission, so maybe she couldn't have any, and she's divorced now. Lots of people adopt kids, and Tammy doesn't even do the testing."

"You believe that multiple women with T-fem are doing the testing? How ludicrous."

"That's exactly what I think," he said. "It's a perfect setup, don't you see? With the assistant commissioner in on the whole thing. After all, she's the one who developed the whole process, while she had a way to conveniently circumvent it all along."

"I suppose . . . it's possible," Wendy said. "T-fem is pretty common. She could conceivably round up enough 'testers' to supply the whole league."

"But why?" Bonnie asked. "I have analyzed the players we detected, and they confer no logical advantage to the team. Why do this for random players of mediocre skill levels?"

He pointed his finger at her. "That's too narrow-minded. Don't assume the reason has to lie with gambling or money, despite us being in Vegas. No, the secret has to lie somewhere else. There are other legitimate uses for testosterone and its derivatives. Certain types of anemia and other things, like hereditary angioedema."

"Oh, yes, the elusive hidden secret," Bonnie said sarcastically. "I am certain that vast knowledge or treasure awaits the one who deciphers the clues."

"You're the one who found the testosterone," he replied.

"You are correct, so *I* should be leading this investigation. But I am seeking sports enhancement, not some endocrine anomaly."

"I doubt those guys have health problems, Alex," Wendy said.

"Then there's another reason. A protein or something else that requires high amounts of testosterone to function. But what is the hidden link? Testosterone is anabolic. Some growth factor, perhaps unrelated to the other metabolic functions. The Indy Super Bowl team is the only common denominator."

Bonnie saw that her husband had that look in his eye again, while his sister beamed enthusiastically, and knew that it could mean trouble from both. But right now she had to focus her attention on herself.

She had a check-up coming up tomorrow, and hoped that her otoneurologist could repair her aural processors; she kept denying it, but she wasn't processing as well. She knew that electronic devices sometimes needed maintenance and upgrading.

Chapter Twenty-five

Dr. Raymond Traylor's Office
1050 B Avenue, Suite 300
Coronado, CA

Alex and Bonnie took an early flight from Las Vegas to San Diego, rented a sedan, and traveled across San Diego Bay on the Coronado Bridge to visit the office of prominent otoneurologist Dr. Raymond Traylor. There weren't many otoneurologists around—such a specialist was one who dealt with the profoundly hearing-impaired and those with other inner ear disorders. Bonnie, as well as most in the deaf community, considered the adjective "hearing-impaired" to be pejorative, as if being deaf meant impairment of some sort. Suggesting that Bonnie Mendoza was "impaired" in any way would surely elicit a painful, one-way journey to Black Eye City.

Bonnie had seen Traylor for over twenty years, ever since she was first implanted in 1989, when the technology began coming of age. She did extremely well, and gradually learned speech again with the aid of extensive therapy over many years. She finally received a procedure reserved for only a small number of people with cochlear implants: a second device. The thought was that it would allow her to discern direction and process sounds better than the single implant.

They arrived at his office and took a seat in the well-appointed waiting room. She sat and read a fashion magazine in the exam room, confident that a microprocessor or some other electronic device was malfunctioning, although it seemed unlikely that both processors would be failing at the same time.

After a few more minutes, she looked up as the late-fiftyish Traylor came into the room to review the audiogram findings and results of other tests.

"Hi, Bonnie," Traylor said. "Alex, how are you doing?"

"Good, thanks." Alex shook the otoneurologist's hand.

"What is the verdict, Doctor? I assume I have a device failure of some type. It is probably time to upgrade, anyway. Another seventy–five thousand dollars for you."

The graying, heavyset man put his hand on her shoulder. "I want . . . to send you to Chicago for some more tests."

"Chicago? What do you think's going on?" Alex asked. "Tell us."

"I can speculate, but we need to be sure, Alex. Walt Zellner at Rush is the world's expert."

"What?"

The white-coated doctor paused for a few seconds, sighed, and looked into her dark brown eyes. "You've always wanted it straight, haven't you?"

"Of course. Do not mince words."

Traylor put his hand on her shoulder. "Okay, I know for sure what's going on, but just want a second opinion, for what's at stake."

"What do you mean, 'what is at stake'?" she asked.

Traylor looked at the pen in his right hand, then up at her. "It's not a device failure at all, Bonnie. They're functioning fine, and your CT and other neuro tests look normal."

She was perplexed. "If not that, then what could it be?"

Traylor pulled out an anatomical diagram of the brain. "As you know, cochlear implants require functioning auditory nerve fibers to work. When you had your first implants, they were fine. You've done better than any patient I've ever had, with the coma and all. You were, in essence, a prelingual person—due to your brain injury you had no knowledge of speech or hearing as we know it, yet you've regained a phenomenal amount of speech, when most thought you'd either die or be severely brain-damaged. A living miracle."

"*Mendoza Milagroso—Mendoza the Miraculous.* That's how I got that name, not because I am a good magician."

"But you were implanted over twenty years ago, and the nerve fibers appear to be slowly degenerating."

"*Degenerating?* Why?" Alex asked in dismay. "She's only thirty-four."

Traylor shook his head sadly. "I don't know. It could be a delayed response to your original meningitis. The other tests rule out any type of systemic neurological disease like ALS or multiple sclerosis—something I was remotely worried about. You're fit as a fiddle, except for this. I have one theory, though."

"What?" Alex asked.

Traylor hesitated for a few seconds. "Most likely, it's a result of the anoxic brain injury you suffered over three years ago. You were in a coma for over a week, and still have some amnesia."

Alex remembered what happened—she had run down, against advice, a criminal at the hospital Charity Ball, and was stabbed. Only her superb physical conditioning and he and Wendy's makeshift surgery saved her life. "But why no problems until now?"

"It's probably been occurring slowly, with not enough damage to cause a perceptible problem until now. You probably compensate with lip-reading more than you realize. Remember, you've been out of the forensic science world, where you were constantly interacting with people, going to court—since then you've pretty much been doing physics at Caltech. And you've really done very little stage or television lately, as I understand, save for some performances at Palomar Observatory."

"So, what are we going to do to fix it?" Alex asked. "New implants? Cost is no object."

Traylor shook his head. "We *can't* fix it, Alex. It's a degenerative process. There are many deaf persons who can't be implanted in the first place because of poor quality nerve fibers. Brainstem implants do exist, but they're risky, and provide only one or two channels of sound."

"One or two channels?" she asked. "And putting electrodes in my brainstem? I think not. I enjoy breathing, thank you."

"Your CIs are state of the art—over a hundred thousand dollars each, and provide twenty channels bilaterally. Not in any way approaching normal hearing, but enough to discern most speech, after training. The brainstem implants allow only the discernment of crude sound, and it's a risky procedure. I don't recommend it."

Bonnie got up and walked around, and finally looked back at Traylor. "Is that all it is, Doctor?"

"What do you mean? Did you understand what I said?" Traylor asked. "Bonnie?"

She looked back out the window at the blue sky for a couple of minutes. "Only one more question. Will I die?"

Traylor shook his head in puzzlement. "*Die?* Of course not."

She smiled. "That is all that matters to me, then."

Alex looked at her and grabbed her by the shoulder. "What do you mean, 'is that all?' He just said you'd be totally deaf."

She looked out the window. "Deaf? Do you believe me not to be deaf now, just because I have adaptive technology? For as long as I can remember I have been deaf. The CIs do not change that. Just so you know, I was worried I had a brain tumor or something else that was very bad."

"Don't you understand? This *is* bad."

"Not to me, it's not. Every day of life is a gift to me. Before my illness, I had everything—and afterwards, I had nothing. I was once so weak I had to use a motorized wheelchair until I learned to walk again. You could not possibly understand."

"I'm sorry, Bonnie," Traylor interrupted. "I'll get you an appointment with Dr. Zellner at Rush in Chicago right away. He's an old friend of mine."

She paused for a half minute. "That will not be necessary, Dr. Traylor. I respect your opinion."

"We'll go, Dr. Traylor. Please make the appointment."

"No!" she yelled, pointing at him. "Leave it alone. It is my problem, not yours."

"Okay. Please call me and let me know if that changes. I do want to see you back in a few weeks." Traylor left the room.

"I'm sorry. I had no idea something like this could happen. We'll get another opinion. We'll—"

"I said that will not be necessary. I trust Dr. Traylor."

"I say it is."

She finally broke out crying. "I do not mind losing the implants. I can live a happy life with lip-reading and signing. I do not remember anything else besides being deaf, and don't care. But your reaction makes me know it is something else I will grieve."

"What?"

"That you will not want me any longer, because, to you, I am defective. Your reaction confirms this fact."

"That's insane. I love you more than anything in the world. I just feel badly for you."

"Then answer me this—would you have married me if I didn't resemble you? A hearing person, able to verbalize and discern your speech?"

"Yes, of course."

She shook her head angrily. "No, you would not have—you feel bad for yourself, the prospect of living with me forever."

"Of course I want to live with you forever."

She stared at him. "Nothing is forever."

"You know what I meant."

"Understand this—I never saw deafness as a problem, something that needed to be fixed. My well-meaning parents saw it differently. They wanted more for me. Everyone helps little Bonnie be the intellectual giant, Wendy helps me be the star of stage and crappy TV, be on a cereal box, a stupid action figure, on billboards, and—"

"They were just trying to help you. Without the implants, you might have never regained coherent speech."

"*Speech?* Who the hell cares?" She stared at him, then shoved him away and pointed. "It has already started—you feel there is something wrong with deaf who cannot or choose not to speak. Many deaf communicate only in sign language. I can verbalize much faster in ASL than *your* language."

"I didn't mean it that way."

"Yes, you did. Maybe not intentionally, but you are prejudiced whether you believe it or not. But I am proud to be deaf, and I never viewed it as a disability to be overcome. I felt bad, at times seemingly rejecting deaf culture."

"I wish I could get it back for you."

"In a way, I am happy. I will no longer be the great superhero others wanted me to be. Many in the deaf community have resented me, feeling that I have turned my back on deaf culture, essentially functioning as a hearing person."

"What you do with your life is no one's business. You don't have to do anything for anyone, least of all me."

"I have only wished for one thing for the part of my life I can remember. To remember things from my childhood, as they used to be, if only for a moment. If I can do that, I'll be content the rest of my days."

Alex hugged his wife as they prepared to leave the doctor's office. He knew that their lives were going to change. But he and his quirky wife had been through a lot together in the last four years.

"Just promise me this," she said.

"What?"

"Do not tell anyone yet, not even Wendy. I know it will be devastating to her, but I want to tell her on my own terms. I still have some time left, he said."

Chapter Twenty–six

Champions Testing Center
Las Vegas, NV

The six–one athlete was busily deadlifting a 450-pound Olympic barbell set in the training room at the drug testing center. Not bad, although certainly not the best the power athlete had ever done. It might be time to do some squats, he thought as he looked at the other two men sizing him up. He was sizing them up too, but in a different way, it seemed, as he stared at their groin areas.

"Bryan Lykens," The tall, dark-haired female testing technician wearing a "Linda" name tag said as she looked at her clipboard. "You're next."

"That's me," the blond athlete said in a Southern accent. "Call me Big Bry, sweetie."

"Don't call me that," she said harshly. "You're a walk-on, not a contract player, and I'll kick your butt out of here, pal."

"Yes, Ma'am," he said, making a salute.

The tester looked over his file and laughed. "That's a pretty heavy lift. Where'd you play last year?"

"Arena League. Used to play with Hamburg, but they closed the European league a few years ago. Didn't pay much, anyway, but the beer and girls were sure mighty fine over there."

"What happened to your knee?" She pointed to the scar on his left knee.

"ACL tear. Had to have a complete reconstruction. Thought about playing in Canada for a while, but don't like the cold. Damn field's too long, too, but they do a lot of punting, with only three downs."

"What position are you?"

"Punter, like I said. Was pretty damn good in college. Thought I might walk on with the Conquerors. Always liked this town, you know, the shows, the money, the ladies—" Lykens winked at her. "Yessir, I could sure live in this burg."

"Have you any questions about the drug testing procedure?" the businesslike woman, smartly clad in white blouse, navy skirt, matching pumps, and white lab coat, said.

"Done it before. Give me my cup and let me tinkle in it."

"It's a little different here. Time to take it off, Mr. Lykens."

"*Everything*? Gotta be kidding me—I do it right in front of you?"

"Yeah. No problem with that, I hope."

He laughed in a loud Southern drawl. "Hell, no. I ain't got no problem showin' you my junk, if you got no problem lookin' at it."

Lykens pulled off his shirt, revealing a muscular chest moderately hairy with light brown hairs, and then removed his shorts. The tall female stared at his generous genitalia.

"Like it? More than meets the eye, huh? Most don't expect it from white guys like me, but there ya go. Some got it, and some—well, don't. God's gift to the ladies."

"Oh, sure. Don't get excited, I see these all the time."

"I bet it's a fun job for ya." He urinated in the specimen bottle and allowed her to draw a blood specimen from him. "Here ya go, little lady. If you'd like to experience the Lykens magic in a different way, just let me know."

"I think I'll pass on that for now, Bryan, thanks."

"You're very welcome. How soon can I start?"

"Testing'll be done in a couple of days, then we'll send a report."

"Fantastic. Can I have your phone number?"

"No. Last time I'm warning you before I write you up."

"A guy's gotta try, you know."

Linda the tester shook her head and left the room. "Get dressed, Mr. Lykens. You've had your jollies for the day. You'll have to find another girl."

"Damn. Thought I might get lucky tonight."

"Mr. Lykens, with your equipment, I don't think you'll have a problem with that."

"Hell, you got that right, lady!" Lykens said proudly.

• • •

Coach Mendoza's Office
Las Vegas Conquerors Complex

Alex, Bonnie, Jay, and Wendy were sitting in Jaime's office at the Conquerors training compound the next day. Jay looked at the three of them from across his large mahogany desk while they sipped coffee, and prepared to discuss the latest findings.

"I appreciate your help, but I think we've hit a dead end here, guys. I'm really getting hassled by Preece to stop snooping around and accusing my guys of steroids. It's weird, like she's covering up something."

"That snippy, uppity woman. I do not like her," Bonnie said. "Very irritating."

"She kind of reminds me of you," Alex replied to her.

"What?" she said.

"You and Tammy Preece are a lot alike," he signed. *"That's why you don't like her."*

"Well, she is probably just efficient at her job, as I am at mine."

Jay looked at his sister. "I appreciate your help, but you really haven't been able to come up with anything else."

"Have faith, Jaime. Alex claims to have additional information. I am as anxious as you, and his sleuth-like skills have improved immensely over the last three years. He may actually have something of use to us."

"She's right." Alex opened a large manila folder. "Jim helped me hack into Tammy Preece's server, and I got the report on Bryan Lykens, an 'addendum' to your 'official' one."

"Who's that?" Jay asked, taking the folder and looking at the digital photo. "Six-one, 235, huh? He looks vaguely like somebody I know, but I can't place him."

"This should be interesting," Wendy said. "A first for medical science."

Jay looked at the files, shaking his head. "I never heard of this guy, and didn't ask for a drug test, and certainly did not authorize you and Krakowski to do anything. And I didn't ask for a punter tryout. The one we have is fine."

Bonnie stuck a finger in the coach's face. "Your punter is mediocre, and obviously lacks even the most rudimentary understanding of spheroid physics. I even created a special handheld calculator for you to compute kicking parameters. Special teams are critical, and I have warned you that soon a price must be paid for—"

Jay stuck his right fist out and showed her the gleaming diamond ring. "In case you didn't know, I have a championship ring, while you don't, so don't tell *me* about football, shorty."

She stuck her chest out. "I have a gold medal, and you do not."

"Huh. A Special Olympics gold medal. Big deal."

She stood up, peered at him across the desk, and threw a pen at him. "Deaf Olympics, not Special Olympics, dullard. They are not the same. And do not dare make fun of the Special Olympics. Those participants have more fortitude than you will ever have."

Jay laughed. "Okay, I'm sorry, I just couldn't resist that one."

"And you should receive a medal for retarded brothers whose sisters do their analytic geometry homework because they are too stupid," Bonnie sputtered. "What is your degree—Bachelor of Basket-Weaving? How shameful to our academic family."

"I have a business degree. At least I can drive myself to work."

"Were they always like this?" Alex asked Wendy, whispering.

"Of course. I guess it was really bad when she was little. Look familiar?" she replied, socking him in the arm.

"At least she probably never beat him up like you did your brother."

"He deserved it, especially after setting my dolls on fire."

"Making them 'walk the plank' into molten cerrobend alloy was the best, though. The smell of burning plastic makes me reminisce." Cerrobend was a eutectic fusible alloy of bismuth, lead, tin, and cadmium, known for its low melting point of 70° C, used in radiation experiments. His nuclear dad always had a bunch lying around, conveniently enough—and it was a great way for an adolescent boy to melt his sister's dolls.

Wendy put her arm around Bonnie. "Don't worry, pal. Bryan's not that great, anyway," Wendy said. "And his short career's over. Trust me."

Jay looked at Wendy intensely. "You *know* this guy?"

"Pretty much, yeah. Known him almost forever."

"Bryan has a high-normal testosterone level of 730 ng/mL, and his pituitary hormones are in the normal range, too," Alex said. "He must have a high libido to go with it."

"He does, believe me, I know," Wendy replied. "What about the chromosomes?"

"46, XY." Alex put his hand on his sister's shoulder. "I knew there was something wrong with you. I want to know how the hell you had a kid if you have a Y chromosome. I need to write it up in the New England Journal of Medicine."

"I was meaning to tell all of you," Wendy said. "Don't tell anybody. I'll lose my state shot put record and NCAA medal if they find out I'm really a man. Stan will really be upset."

"You guys are going all scientific on me. I don't get what you're talking about," Jay said as he looked at Bonnie. "Something funny's going on here, I can smell it."

Bonnie put her hand over her chest. "Do not look at me. I am as perplexed as you. Please explain this cryptic statement, siblings."

"Look," Alex said. "It's not rocket science. Here's Wendy's true chemistry panel and chromosomal analysis, which I had run. Her serum testosterone's 32 ng/mL, normal range for a female her age, and karyotype is XX, of course. Someone replaced her urine and blood with a male's in the testing center. It's the only way."

"What do you mean, 'replaced her urine'? Wendy's? Where?" Jay asked.

"The testing room."

Bonnie crossed her eyes, deep in thought. "Was Wendy helping the tester with Bryan Lykens, as a guest doctor? That must have been an interesting experience for you."

"Oh, my God," Alex said as he put his hands over his face. "How dense can you be?"

"Two X chromosomes?" Jay shook his head. "You mean this punter, Bryan Lykens, is really . . ."

Wendy nodded her head. "You Mendozas are a brilliant and deductive bunch. Takes you a while, though."

"I can't believe you guys did this, it's crazy." He threw a clipboard across the room. "You didn't really—"

"You are the one who contacted us, Coach." Alex stood up and pointed at him. "You said you weren't going to ask questions on why or how, as long as we got results."

"I know, but you're all insane."

"Excuse me, *hermano,*" Bonnie said, "I do not claim to know these demented people. Do not group me with them."

Jay began sweating. "You really went in there disguised as a punter? Stripped down and everything? Why and how the *hell* did you do that?" He mopped his damp brow with a towel. "On second thought, I don't want to know."

"Some things are better left to the imagination," Alex said.

"It proves they didn't use my urine and blood in those reports. They replaced them with someone else's, just like we thought they did." Wendy stood up. "The bio-prosthetics are pretty advanced these days. The body and facial hair were, of course, synthetic. The chest harness was a tough one, especially with my, well—generous boobs. The junk downstairs was a challenge."

"You . . . actually peed through some . . . rubber thing?"

"Yeah. Ouchie. But if she and I were the only ones in the room, it means the blood and urine were hers, and she has complete testicular feminization syndrome, like Alex and I thought."

"Say what?" Jay said as he pointed to his sister and stared down at her. "I'm really disappointed in you. I trusted you and asked you up here to help me, not turn this into some circus, like Dunlap said would happen. You'll make me look like a moron."

"Jaime, I plead ignorance to this haphazard caper."

"I'm not surprised by some stupid-ass stunt from these two hillbilly clowns, but you? You know how much trouble I could get in for screwing with the drug testing office? Do you?"

She put her hand over her chest. "What, you think that I, champion of law and order, had anything to do with this?"

"Don't con me. You cheated me too many times at cards for me to believe you."

She opened her mouth wide. "I am offended at your distrust. I assure you, the Tennessee Two here surely thought this grandiose scheme up on their own. Perhaps hospitalization for acute mania is in order. A double room."

Alex got up and stared at Jay. "I know you're upset, Jay, but I knew you'd never agree to this stunt, and we couldn't figure out any other way. But we proved our point, did we not? Their testing setup is a sham. And it wouldn't have proven anything if I did it, since I have a Y chromosome."

Jay stared at his coffee and paused for a few seconds. "I suppose I would agree. But why? And surely they knew it was a joke."

"Not a joke—a scientific experiment," Wendy said.

Bonnie got up and started shaking her head. "I have seen some of your gender-changing disguises, and have been to strange bars with Alex, but this . . . I will need urgent therapy. I must text Dr. Elsevier immediately to arrange an emergency appointment."

Wendy stood up and stared down at her. "You disguised yourself as a maintenance man in this very building, so who's talking?"

"Humph. I happen to be a licensed private investigator."

"And you sure didn't need much of a disguise with *that* figure. Most of those guys probably had bigger tits than you."

She sputtered. "Why, you corpulent—I merely wore a fake mustache and overalls, not artificial genitalia. How perverted!"

"You do what you gotta do," Wendy replied back. "Sometimes you have to think outside the box."

"My frickin' head feels like it's gonna explode," Jay said as he took four ibuprofen tablets from the bottle on his desk. "All of you, out . . . right now. I don't want to see any of you three around here for a long while."

The three stood sheepishly in the doorway.

"I mean it . . . all three of you, out, now, before I have you thrown off the grounds."

The doe-eyed woman looked at him sadly and pouted. "Surely you do not mean me, too, Jaime? Your sweet baby sister?"

"Let's count. One, two, three—that includes you. 'Bryan Lykens' and all his relatives are banned permanently from my office."

"I guess we're not wanted here any more," Wendy said.

"Got that right. Out!"

• • •

The three left the Conquerors complex and went out to their car before the head coach had them thrown out. Bonnie was obviously fuming and was pummeling Wendy repeatedly in the shoulder.

"*¡Cuñada estúpido!* That was the most idiotic thing you have ever done, my moronic sister-in-law."

"Hey, quit punching me. I thought it was one of my better disguises. Cost a bunch, too. Nobody appreciates a true *artiste*."

"And my own husband was in on it—I am ashamed to show my face. My brother welcomes us into his training facility, and you repay his hospitality by conducting this embarrassing spectacle."

"We found out something we couldn't learn any other way," he said. "A bit theatrical—but you, the big-shot magician, had your chance to find out how they got the specimens out, and you came up short. The urine and blood must have belonged to that tester."

"But it makes no sense. Why would they want to do that, Alex?" Bonnie asked.

"I don't know. But I'm going to find out, for damn sure."

"I suppose this means we're not welcome in the VIP boxes for the San Diego game next week," Wendy said.

"I'm sure it would have been a crappy game," he replied.

"How jocular you both are. What are we going to do now? I suppose our investigation is over," Bonnie said sadly. "Meanwhile, everything in my life is going straight to hell."

"Don't count on it. He's just mad and will get over it, then we'll be invited back. I'll let Levickis know about it," he said.

"I do not think so. I thank you both so much for your expert assistance," Bonnie said, her voice now trembling. "Just leave me alone, Darkkin dullards."

Wendy turned to her shorter friend and put her hand on her shoulder. "Look, I didn't mean to cause any problems, I just wanted to help. I still think it's useful information. I'm sorry."

Bonnie started crying. "If *this* is your idea of help . . . I don't need it or you right now, thank you. What you did just makes everything worse."

"I don't understand." Wendy turned to her brother. "I've done dumber things than this, Alex. Something's wrong."

"Yeah, about that . . . I think we need to go have a little talk. There's something you need to know."

Chapter Twenty–seven

Argotech Industries
U.S. Bio-genetic Research Facility
Cairo, WV

"Dr. Argon. I have something you have to see right away," Dr. Rita McPherson said excitedly as she ran into her employer's office.

"What is it, Rita? I'm busy." The gray-haired scientist came over to her, obviously annoyed by the intrusion.

"You told me to look out for something that might help with Travis. Paulsen found something in the football chemistry panels."

He shook his head. "Damn football shit. That was for Gallagher, anyway, to get rid of Graham and Orson . . . I don't care about it, unless we find someone with the gene and enough HLA matches. It's like Gallagher said—finding a needle in a haystack. And, for obvious reasons, men won't really help that much. We need to shut that operation down, too. It accomplished what we wanted."

"Then prepare yourself. The 'needle' has arrived."

"What? There isn't anything that can help him. Even the protein from the Ontario Lacus organism that allowed us to create those DNA-specific poisons can't help any more, despite his strength. If I could locate some fetal tissue . . . with some DNA that is similar enough, that might help me regenerate his bone marrow. But we know that's impossible."

She sighed. "That's what I'm trying to tell you. The ACTN7 gene, which appears to convey the potential for great strength. This individual is homozygous for the gene."

"So are a few of the football players we studied. Doesn't mean anything, Rita. The matches just aren't good enough."

She pointed at the LCD screen. "Don't be so sure. Look at this information. Match is closer in DNA to anyone we've ever seen before, almost uncanny. Six of six HLA haplotypes."

"*Six?* That's impossible. Who is this man?" He looked at the screen for a few seconds. "I've seen that face somewhere before."

"This is the information I have on this 'man.' A surprising amount is available in the public media. Get a load of this."

"Just get on with it, Rita."

She pulled up a clip of C-Span on the monitor at his conference table. "The day of the President's death, she was standing right next to him. And, here, on that Republican genetics panel, sitting right next to Senator Orson. Facial recognition of the photo is a 97.4 percent match, correcting for the makeup."

"A *woman?*" Argon stared at the full, round freckled face of the blonde woman. "I don't believe it. Are you certain? This can't be random. She *must* share first-generation lineage with Travis."

"Absolutely. Former California heavyweight powerlifting champion and NCAA champion shot-putter—deadlift over 550 pounds, squat 500, bench press 375. Blood typing and DNA confirms it. Human chorionic gonadotropin levels are sky-high. It's real."

"My God. The β-hCG is over 200,000 mIU/mL." He looked at the screen. "Williams, maiden name is Gallinsworth. That doesn't make any sense—I don't know anyone by that name. How could she possibly be related to Travis?"

"That *wasn't* her birth name. I did some investigating—she changed it to Gallinsworth when she turned eighteen."

"What's the birth name, then? As if that helps."

"I think it will. I found the original birth certificate, using linguistic technology to narrow her accent's origin to Appalachia—eastern Tennessee, specifically. The birth name is Darkkin."

"*Darkkin?*" He stared at Rita and knocked a set of half-full beakers off the counter. "Is *that* why we didn't know about this? Is he even . . . still alive, after all these years? I heard he was dead."

Rita shook her head. "We can't confirm or deny that. There have been no financial transactions in his name in the last five years, so he may well be dead, or out of the country."

Argon looked at the computer screen. "I didn't know that low-life hillbilly son of a bitch even had a daughter. I never would have thought of that, but it's so logical. It explains everything."

"It's fantastic, but true."

Argon walked around the office, perplexed at this amazing new information. "But what the hell was Darkkin's pregnant daughter doing in the drug testing center posing as a football player?"

"We don't know, but the coach of the Las Vegas team is a relative through marriage. The limited information on her father suggests a history of rather . . . bizarre behavior. Perhaps it is genetic."

"No, not entirely," he yelled. "She's somehow figured it out, at least partly. If she's inherited even a fraction of her father's intellect, that could be big trouble."

"I've heard rumors about him. Was he really that good?"

He frowned. "I was from a long line of professors and doctors, and he was from a family who made whiskey and ran a zinc mine. Yet, he always got the best grades, the best girls . . . everything, while I came in second. That rotten bastard."

"It sounds like you hated him. I didn't know any of that."

Argon looked at her angrily. "Yes, I did—but I think how my dislike of him spurred me on, to be the best in the world. I guess, in a way, I owe Rad Darkkin for who I've become. Well, I'm going to repay him in my own way. He won't laugh at me now."

"What do we do now?"

He held his right fist out and shook it at Rita. "It all fits now. Katrina, that goddamn whore . . . no matter. Providence has brought us the means to our salvation."

"I agree. Should I inform General Gallagher of our discovery?"

He looked down and smiled. "Not just yet, Rita. I'm going to pursue this one on my own. Travis is going to enjoy it, too."

"You're always so sure he'll do what you want, aren't you?"

He leaned back in his seat and smiled. "Of course. He's my son. He knows I just want what's best for him." But only if it was best for Malachi Argon.

He was, as an ancillary benefit, going to have his revenge on the bastard who screwed around with his wife and made fun of him in college—if he was still around, that is. And Travis was going to help him do it. Life was sweet.

Chapter Twenty–eight

Williams Residence
5547 Davidson Blvd.
San Diego, CA

Wendy burst into her home to find Stan sitting at a table with a thirtyish, red-headed woman, and was not very pleased. What was he doing, bringing this attractive woman into their home? She just learned that her best friend would no longer be able to "hear" in a few months, and Stan had a strange woman here; could things possibly suck any more?

"What's going on, Stan?" she demanded. "Who the hell is *this*?"

"You remember Lisa from the faculty-student mixer, hon. She and I are going over the teaching plan. We have 'A-Core' coming up, and need to get the curriculum revised. I told you about it."

She smiled and pointed at him. "You didn't expect me home from Las Vegas so soon, I get it now. Well, I'm sorry I broke up your little rendezvous."

He scowled at her. "Are you nuts? This isn't anything, we're just working on lessons. Jeez."

She started singing. "Oh, I see. Well, whatever. Where's Jake?"

"Uh, your mom took him to the children's museum."

"Great." She started eating a cookie. "Did you get my colored rollerball pen refills like I asked? You better have."

He shook his head. "Sorry, didn't have time. I'll go by Office-Mart tonight. It's no big deal." He ignored her, turning back to the mountain of paperwork spread across the dining room table.

"*No big deal*?" She knocked their papers off the table. "Don't you ever dismiss me. I don't ask for much, but my fricking colored refills would be nice. Is that so difficult?" she yelled.

"Maybe I should just leave, Stan," Lisa said as she rolled her eyes. "This doesn't seem like a good time, you know?"

"No, just hold on." He turned to Wendy and pointed. "What's your problem?"

"Nothing at all. You and pretty friend Lisa go about what you're doing. Don't interrupt on my account." She turned to the smallish woman. "I'm just his horsey wife, and you're nice and svelte. More his type."

Lisa shook her head in puzzlement and got her purse. "I think that . . . we better do this later. Somewhere else." She waved good-bye and left. "Good luck. I'm so outta here."

"Yeah. Looks like I've really got my hands full here."

Wendy went into the other room as Lisa slammed the door.

Stan went after his wife and stared up into her big aquamarine eyes. "What the hell's your deal? The answering service called three times looking for you because you don't answer your pages. The residents had questions about two patients in the emergency room, and they had to call someone else who wasn't even on call."

"Oh, that can wait. I've got better things to do with my time."

"You'd better call the ER back right now."

"I will, after I take a nap. I will have one of the underlings take care of it. I'm the Chief of Staff, so what can they do to me?"

"Not so fast—I need to talk to you about the credit cards. You spent over $2,000 the other day at Horton Plaza, at a dress shop. What's up with that?"

She stared into his eyes and shook her right index finger at him.

"You're spying on me, that's it. How dare you?" she demanded in a deep voice.

He stared back. "I get a notification via cell and e-mail if there's a purchase over $1,000, you know that."

She looked away. "Well . . . it's none of your business. I'll get my own credit card in my name—it's mostly my money, anyway."

"We agreed to discuss large purchases like that."

She threw herself onto the sofa. "If you want to go spend two grand on fishing poles, I really don't care. That's a dumb rule, because I should have whatever I want. I deserve nice things."

"We can't reach our financial goals we want in life if we do that. Come on."

She fluffed a pillow behind her head and stretched her long frame out. "Maybe what I want has changed, did you ever think of that?" she said melodiously.

He looked at her intently. "Yeah, maybe some rest is a good idea. Then we're going to see your doctor. Maybe Patty can find us someone who can straighten you out. You can see Bonnie's doc."

"I don't need any stupid doctor. They're all a bunch of quacks, especially her weirdo hippie shrink." She jumped to her feet with speed that belied her stature. "On second thought, I'm not tired at all. I'm going for a little drive in my beautiful, upscale silver minivan. Perhaps I'll go buy a new Ferrari, too."

"I've had enough of you," Stan said threw down his hands and went to the basement. "Don't go anywhere."

"Don't you tell me what to do," she yelled as she picked up her car keys and went out the door and got into the minivan, the interior of which was strewn with toy cars, crayons, empty juice boxes, and DVD discs. She deserved better, she thought as she pulled out of their addition at seventy miles per hour, leaving her bewildered husband at the front door.

She turned up the 80's music on the oldies station as she soared down the road and noticed how bright and vivid the colors were, how intense the smells of early autumn seemed. Reds so vivid, greens so saturated, blues like her eyes—fabulous.

Her argument with Stan was soon forgotten as she realized she never had so much confidence in her life. She was so happy, flying down the road at eighty mph, on the way to the fashion mall, to that special lingerie shop. No one was going to tell *her* what she could and couldn't buy.

She was Dr. Wendy Williams, Chief of Staff and Congressional hopeful. She could do *anything*. She used to feel down in the dumps a lot, but the samples the new Clystarr Pharmaceuticals representative gave her helped more than she could ever imagine. Could anyone ever feel so good? The sky was the limit. And she was going to go get something she'd wanted for a long time, feelings she had kept suppressed. It would be a big surprise.

• • •

Jaime Mendoza's Home
7732 Cactus Way
Las Vegas, NV

Jay left his sprawling home on Thursday afternoon to travel to the private airport, to take a chartered flight back to San Diego for the evening. He gave the team the day off because of their stellar play in the first preseason game, even though they lost. He rarely bothered with regular flights; he had the money to fly wherever he wanted. Getting there an hour or two early for a first-class flight, the hassles of the airport—heck, he could drive there in four hours. He thought once about buying his own jet, but that was a little extravagant, even for him.

He was still furious about what his outrageous in-laws, the dysfunctional Darkkins, had done the other day, with that fiasco in the testing center. What were they thinking? He fully expected Tammy Preece and her minions to show up, declaring some humongous fine, because he would surely be blamed for it.

Amazingly, he hadn't heard anything yet, so Wendy's disguise must have been pretty good; or maybe heartless Tammy did have a sense of humor, after all. He felt badly about throwing Bonnie out, as she probably was being truthful that she didn't know about their plan. Still, he couldn't condone that kind of shenanigans, and was glad he was getting away, if even for the day.

He boarded the private charter with his luggage and took a seat in the luxurious executive jet. He pulled out the note he had received, along with a box of chocolates, from the gorgeous Danielle Weatherly, anchorwoman for one of San Diego's major TV stations. He leaned back and popped open a beer as he thought about the brunette's svelte, five–eight, lightly perfumed body—she was built like a brick house, that was for sure. Suddenly, the troubles seemed to simply melt away.

But, somehow, he knew there was something waiting which was unexpected. He liked surprises, and couldn't wait for this one. She said in the note that it would be something he would really love.

Chapter Twenty–nine

Dr. Jasper Bennett's Office
California Institute of Technology
Robinson Hall
Pasadena, CA

Dr. Jasper Bennett was stopped in the hallway by the huge, black-clad man at 11:04 PM. There shouldn't be anyone here this time of day, he thought—and he sure didn't look like Carl Benson, the regular night janitor.

"Excuse me, this building's closed," the smallish, gray-haired professor said. "You need to leave, sir, or I'll call security."

"Haw. Not to me, it isn't," Travis Argon said in a deep voice. "You and I have some discussing to do, about keeping your mouth shut, you old fossil."

He stepped back in fear. "Who are you?"

"I believe you may know my dad, who paid for that nice new Beamer out there. I'm sort of like the repo man. The 'Grim Repo'—what a laugh."

"How . . . how did you get in here?" Bennett asked. "This area's locked, and the perimeter patrolled."

Travis picked up a steel chair and bent it into a pretzel. "I pretty much can do anything I want, thanks, in part, to you."

"Oh, my God—please don't hit me with that chair."

Travis laughed. "Are you kidding? I sure as hell don't need any chair to kill you. My bare hands are fine."

"Kill me? Are you crazy?"

"Not at all. I'm perfectly aware of what I'm about to do."

Bennett ran off, with Travis right behind him, and ran into his office and locked the door. He fumbled with his telephone, but couldn't get the campus police to answer. He watched with disbelief as the thick oak door was torn from its hinges.

"You know too much, Bennett," Travis said. "Can't have you around any more."

"I haven't told anyone anything about Titan that isn't in the mainstream. Read my book."

"You're a liar, and I know better. But it doesn't matter—you won't be telling anyone anything ever again." Travis picked him up with one hand, lifting him off the floor.

"That . . . you're . . . not human. No one can do that."

"You're right about that—I'm sure as hell not human." Travis broke his neck and dropped him to the floor. "I'm better than human, you stupid old man. I wanted to say 'thanks' in person."

Travis rummaged through Bennett's files and tore open his safe, and found what he was looking for—anything that looked like it contained information on Titan. They would find him dead the next day, but what was anyone going to do about it?

He was stopped by the two campus police officers who stopped him just outside the building. "Freeze, mister," the female officer said. "Get down on the ground. Hands behind your head."

"Shut the hell up, lady," Travis said, brushing her aside.

The male officer pulled his weapon. "Sergeant Turner gave you an order, punk. Get on the ground!"

Travis covered the five feet between he and the male officer in approximately 0.11 seconds and threw him thirty feet across the parking lot, into a garbage bin.

"Oh, my God," the female sergeant said, drawing her weapon. She fired two shots into Travis' chest, which were absorbed by the lightweight Kevlar.

"I said to shut up," he said as he ran over to her and crushed her right hand into a bloody pulp as she let out a scream. He then smashed her head against the stone wall, as her blood and grey matter stained the colorless walls. "Not so tough now, huh, cop?"

The efficient assassin sped off into the night as quickly as he came. He was damn good at what he was engineered and trained to be—the greatest killing machine man had ever envisioned. There was nothing that could stop him, Malachi Argon and General Gallagher had told him. And now Jasper Bennett could tell no one about the secret Ontario Lacus research, as all that information had been destroyed. Of that, Travis Argon, the Ortho-Man, was certain.

• • •

Alex and Bonnie walked past the police line after she showed her credentials to the uniformed officers outside. She had been called, as a courtesy, by the Pasadena Police after Bennett's body had been discovered.

"Who was this Bennett guy again?" Alex asked.

"Distinguished Professor of astrobiology."

"You know him, I assume?"

"Yes. He did some private consulting work with NASA, on some secret space project. It was pretty classified, as I recall. He wasn't my biggest fan, I can tell you that."

"Say again?" Alex asked.

"He thought the things I do on the side were not befitting a physics professor. A carnival show, he said."

"At least he's observant," he said, drawing an evil look from his wife. "Are you in this building much?"

"Not every day, but often. We were housed in Lauritsen Hall."

Alex and Bonnie approached the detective standing outside Bennett's office.

"What the hell happened?" Alex asked.

"Some people killed him, plus two campus police officers. Murdered them in cold blood, like some animal tore into them," the police lieutenant said. "It was horrible. The cops' bodies were found outside, the female's right arm was crushed, and her skull was smashed to bits." He pointed to the tape outlines where the bodies once lay. "Makes me want to puke."

"You confidently say 'some people,' as if you are certain multiple assailants were involved. It could have been one person," she said. "One man could have gotten in and out easier than many."

"No way, Mendoza," Pasadena Det. Lt. Darian Adams said, shaking his head. "There must've been at least three or four men.

That male cop was thrown across the parking lot."

"Any possibility of us looking through his office, Lieutenant?" Alex asked.

"You guys? You're pulling my leg, aren't you, Darkkin? This isn't a hospital for you to fight crime in. Go fix some of those medical records at Lutheran, where you belong."

"I resent that, as I know proper police procedure," Bonnie admonished. "I am also a licensed private detective."

The lieutenant paused for a moment. "I know you are, but I've got rules. You should know that."

"We're all after the same thing here," Alex said. "You said you didn't find anything. Maybe we can help."

Adams paused for a few moments. "Well, I do know your dad. Went to a seminar of his at the state capitol. I guess it would be okay."

"Thank you," she said abrasively.

Alex and Bonnie looked through Bennett's small office for the next thirty minutes, while Lt. Adams looked on. Most of the office had been ransacked, and the computer destroyed, with the hard drive ripped out.

"No subtleties here," Bonnie said as she examined the door. "The lock is a Brinson, a simple one to pick, yet the perpetrator smashed the door open. Why?"

"Must've been one pretty strong guy, too," Adams said.

"Duh! You think?" She examined the hefty deadbolt lock and oak door of the old office. "It is impossible for a normal human to have knocked this down; this oaken door is nearly two inches thick."

"Are you an expert in that?" Adams said sardonically.

"Actually, she is," Alex replied. "She owns several patents for lock design. Milagroso Security Co."

"Oh," Adams said sheepishly. "I guess didn't know that was your company."

"But if a machine broke it open, there would be marks. The same goes for the outer doors." She pointed to the ceiling authoritatively. "There is only one possibility: one very powerful individual, with the strength of many men, performed this dastardly deed."

"*Dastardly deed?* You sound like some frickin' cartoon." Adams howled with laughter as he clapped his hands. "We have a break-in by an alien being with super-strength, is that it? *That's* your explanation? I would've expected something better from Carlos Mendoza's daughter."

"As ludicrous as it seems, yes," she replied. "Someone with enough power to apply at least 120,000 Newtons of force in a single blow. As Sherlock Holmes once said, 'once you eliminate the impossible, whatever remains, however improbable, must be the truth.' You can provide a superior explanation, Detective?"

"Sherlock Holmes, what a laugh. Martial arts could do it," Adams said. "Pretty strong guys out there."

"Is that so?" She removed a one-inch thick maple plank from Bennett's bookshelf, placed it between two large textbooks, then shattered it into several pieces with her right hand. "Like that?"

"Holy crap," Adams said, backing away from her cautiously. "I'll be damned."

She pointed to the scraps of wood. "My point is that it could not have possibly happened that way. See how a focused blow splinters the wood in a certain pattern? The wood fibers on the door, conversely, were not shattered, but instead *pulled* apart."

She then removed a compact disc from his desktop player and saw that it was labeled "A Magical Horn." She then replaced the CD and pressed the "play" button.

"What is this? French horn classical music?" she said as she turned up the volume to its maximum setting.

Alex covered his ears. "Yeow, it's damaged or something. Just static," he said. "You really can't tell it's not music?"

"I guess not," she said as she put her head down. "Again, it seems I do not meet your expectations."

"I didn't mean anything by it," he said as he patted her on the shoulder.

"Yes, right," she said, pulling away angrily.

He then removed the CD from its tray and handed it to her. "What do you make of this?" he said to her.

She looked at it carefully. "Just a CD. It is bluish on the bottom, meaning that it is recordable, made by laser phase-shifting."

"Correct. So, it didn't come from a commercial distributor."

"But many limited-distribution CDs are burned rather than stamped these days. That does not prove anything."

Alex turned on his laptop and put the disc inside.

"What is on it?" Bonnie asked. "Perhaps it contains data."

He shook his head. "Don't know. Computer says there is no data on this disc."

She scowled. "You meant to say, 'there *are* no data.' Data is a plural noun. Datum is the singular form. How embarrassing."

"Yeah, right, whatever." He removed the disc, which looked pristine. "Not a scratch on it. There are other operating systems than this, you know."

"But why does the title say 'A Magical Horn,' with a photo of a French horn on it?" she demanded.

"Don't know."

"While you two keep working on your little music CD, I've got to find out who murdered these people and why," Adams said sardonically. "Someone's gotta do the dirty work."

"I'll call Jim and maybe you two can work on it at the house. I reason you know more about Bennett and what's on that disc than anyone."

"Ugh. Do I *have* to work with him? He is not my favorite."

"Don't worry, it won't be for long. You'll have it figured out soon, and then you'll be rid of him."

"I sincerely hope so. The less time I have to spend with him, the better."

Chapter Thirty

Renaissance Super Motel
3342 Mesa Blvd.
San Diego, CA

Jay pulled up to the Renaissance Super Motel at nine PM, parked his rental car, and went up the old metal staircase to room 222, for which he had the room key; it had arrived by messenger yesterday, along with the note. The seedy old motel was probably named that because it was built during the Renaissance Period, he thought.

The coach went upstairs in anticipation as he opened the door to the room, expecting to find Dani Weatherly inside. She was a little minx who liked to play cute games, and a secret rendezvous at a neon-signed "No-Tell Motel" was a different, but welcomed, twist; there would certainly be no paparazzi *here*. He especially liked that deep, sultry voice. He was about to get such a voice.

He opened the door with the corroded old key and discovered, however, that the woman inside was someone quite different than he had hoped for. He'd had only one Corona on the plane, after all, and couldn't be drunk enough to be hallucinating *that*. He then wished he'd had nine or ten beers, or, better yet—stayed home.

He gasped as he saw the big six–one woman lounging on the pink vibrating bed, in a red nightgown, getting ready to take even that off. What kind of crazy joke was this? His surprise turned to anger, as he'd had just about enough of *her* crap after that stunt at the football complex.

"I hope you're not disappointed," the busty, scantily-clad blonde said to him. "I wanted it to be a surprise."

"What the *hell* are you doing? Have you lost your mind? Wasn't that stupid stunt you pulled at the training complex enough fun for you? I can't believe you guys did that."

"Like Bonnie said, she had nothing to do with it. Just trying to fix your crappy team, lover. It needs it."

"I think . . . I need to leave. I was supposed to meet Dani here. You've lost it, and this isn't funny any more. You've really pissed me off." He kicked at the vintage 1971 bright green shag carpet with his right foot.

"You don't want Dani, and she's not coming. This was a little surprise for you. I love you, Jay." She pushed herself up to him and threw him down on the bed.

He tried to push away, to get leverage, but there was one small problem—she was *way* stronger than him—he certainly remembered that now. When she was eighteen or nineteen, Wendy was probably one of the five strongest women in the world. He knew—she used to help him weight train, and he likely wouldn't be in the Pro Football Hall of Fame if not for her. What would she be—thirty-eight now? But she seemed in better shape than before. And she had that wild gleam in her eye, which he had seen many years ago, if only momentarily—but this time it wasn't going away. She was obviously possessed by a force beyond her control.

"Get the hell off me. What's wrong with you?" Now he really was stuck and couldn't get her off; he thought about laughing, because Wendy loved to play practical jokes, and, at any other time, this might be funny—but he knew that something was seriously wrong, and he was now getting scared. Unlike Bonnie, one of the more gullible people in the world, he usually knew the score.

But doing something about it was a different story. He was a great athlete, but was, as Bonnie had said, a lover, not a fighter—he didn't have the hand-to-hand combat skills his police-trained, black-belt brother and sister had, and didn't want to hurt her, anyway. Yeah, right, if that was even possible.

He did have the gift of gab, however, and surely could talk her out of this. It certainly didn't seem as if she wanted to hurt him, and there seemed to be only one thing on her mind. It was indeed something he had fantasized about for some time. But not this way, like this. The problems this little scene would create could never be overcome, and no one would believe he wasn't in on it.

He could just see himself lying dismembered, in a pool of blood, in a squalid Las Vegas alley, at the hands of either Rad Darkkin (if he was still alive) or, worse, his sister—whichever colorful figure got to him first. Neither option sounded very appealing. Bonnie wasn't real pleased with him right now, anyway.

"Hold on there, sport. I don't think your husband would approve of this. For that matter, I don't approve of it, either."

"I don't care about him. He's so whiny and needy. I want a *real* man. I remember how good you were."

"Uh, my little sis would probably have a problem with it, too."

"So what? I can whip her. And there's nothing wrong with me. I'm perfect, and we're going to have a perfect night."

"How many drinks have you had? You're pretty messed up." He stared point-blank at the nearly naked endo-mesomorph's powerful physique. "Let me call Mike to send a squad car to take you home, so we don't have to call Stan. He'll get you sobered up. Nobody has to know about this."

She got up, stood in front of him, walked a straight line, and touched her fingers to her nose perfectly, and did a pirouette. She always was pretty coordinated for her size, he remembered, as he realized with dismay that she wasn't intoxicated, and she wasn't the type to do drugs.

"As a shareholder of D.T. Darkkin & Sons, I get freebies, but my illustrious daddy has imparted to me an aversion to drink. Nothing wrong with me. Everything's right."

"Stop it, you idiot. We've got to get out of here. Something bad's going to happen." He felt the compulsion to scribble three words that popped into his mind; he wasn't certain at that time what they meant. They said he couldn't *really* see the future, but he knew he had the ability to sense when something undesirable was about to happen. This was one of those times.

"Oh, very bad, indeed. I'm a bad girl, you just didn't know it. Here, I took these from your sister's magic stuff. She won't miss one pair. Lookit, they're pink, and very expensive." She dangled the gleaming rose-colored metal devices she had "borrowed."

"I mean it, Wen. We've got to go. *Now.*" Yeah, right. She was back on top of him, with that glazed look in her eyes. He wasn't going anywhere.

"I know you fantasize about it. Just give in, Jay, you know it's what we both want."

At that point, the door smashed inwards, off its hinges. The six–five bulk came at them with ferocity, with a five–ten brunette woman by his side.

"What the hell?" Jay said. The large man picked him up with one hand and lifted him into the air. "Oh, my God." The hulk then threw him against the wall.

"Take that, Mendoza, you asshole, for 1995. Payback time."

Wendy was preoccupied with her new-found female adversary. "I'll tear your head off, Preece, you bitch. You picked on the wrong lady. In an enclosed space, I'll break your neck like a twig."

"You sure?" The five–ten woman looked up at Wendy, who threw a punch. The shorter but much thinner woman easily stopped it with her right hand. "Better check that again." The woman flung Wendy into the wall, then took out the tranquilizer dart gun and shot her in the neck. The large blonde woman slumped quickly to the floor. "God, she's a wild one."

"Yeah. That was a blast. I busted Mendoza good."

"Did you have to be so rough, Travis? This isn't about him."

"I don't take orders from you, Tammy. I do things my way. You got a problem with that?"

"A hell of a mess to clean up. But we got what we came for."

Travis looked at the unconscious Wendy on the floor, whom Tammy loaded into a laundry cart. "That's . . . her, huh?"

"Yeah. What'd you expect? Some little pretty girl?"

"It's just weird, meeting someone like this for the first time."

"It's not like you have a choice, Travis. Malachi told you that."

"I know. Sometimes I just don't like what I've become."

"You're alive because of him. And, with her help, you'll continue to be. Your dad really cares about you, you know."

Assistant pro football commissioner Tammy Preece patted Travis Argon on the shoulder as they whisked Wendy to their van, leaving a bloody Jay Mendoza for dead, bleeding on the green shag carpet.

• • •

SDPD Det. Lt. Marcus Owens was on the scene at the Renaissance Motel at eleven PM and watched as Bonnie ran up the decrepit old staircase, in front of Alex by about twenty feet.

"My God, Marc, what has happened here? Where is Jaime? Miguel went to the hospital with him, he told Alex on the phone."

"Mendoza, I'm sorry, but I don't have any further news. Your brother was found beat up and unconscious in the bed here," the fiftyish, six–four African-American man said, peering down at her through his bifocals. "He's still alive, but barely."

"I appreciate your help, Marc. How did you come to be summoned here?"

"Another motel guest saw the door smashed in, and a uniformed patrol car came. The officers found Jay, and as soon as they knew who it was, they called Mike. They let me know because of our friendship. The rental car out there is Jay's."

Alex walked in and stared in disbelief. "Why in the hell would he be staying at a seedy motel in San Diego? Carlos and Elisa live less than fifteen minutes from here."

"Perhaps to be discreet . . . he does have a reputation for liking the ladies, does he not?" Owens replied.

"Sure, but . . . this crappy place? He can afford a lot better," Alex replied, looking around.

"That behavior is unlikely at this time," she said. "Football is his current obsession. Any other information?"

"CSI is gathering some evidence. If his companion had any clothes or anything, they're long gone. Look at this—the damn door looks like it's been ripped right off its hinges. But that's impossible."

She looked at the door. Like many old motels, the construction was heavy-duty. The steel had been sheared, not bent, like it would have been, had a tool been used to force open the door. Just like the one in Jasper Bennett's office.

"The strength needed to open this door is enormous," she said.

"Oh, no, here we go again," Alex replied.

"No one man could've done this, Mendoza," Owens said. "The door must've been defective."

"I will see when I examine the hinges at the lab," she said as she took a screwdriver and removed the bent hinges from the door.

"Hey," a uniformed officer said. "You can't do that."

"Yes, I can. *You* are going to stop me, patrolman?"

Owens laughed. "Let Mendoza be, Walters. She knows what she's doing. We found these, too. Don't see ones like this every day."

He held up the gleaming pink manacles, which weren't cheap toy models painted pink, like those found in "adult" novelty shops; they were, instead, composed of a glimmering, outlandishly expensive lanthanoid (rare-earth metal) alloy.

"Huh? Are you kidding me?" She plucked them from his large hands, searching for the serial number.

"I don't suppose *you* would have a clue about the origin of this thousand dollar set of designer bracelets."

She continued to inspect them. "Milagroso model 210—pink thulium/praseodymium-plated titanium. These used to be in my equipment box. Why and how would he have them? He never cared much about magic."

"I don't think he was playing Houdini with them. There's a couple of partial prints. You guys are one weird family."

She then spotted the blonde hair, almost imperceptible, on the carpet. But years as a forensic scientist had honed her reflexes.

"A hair . . . here. In the corner."

"Doesn't mean it was the girl's. Could have been left here before, but we'll run the sample."

She ignored the detective, then spied the shiny black object buried in the attractive green shag carpet.

"You missed something else, Marc," she said. "Right here."

"What?" Owens asked. "I don't believe you."

She picked up the AA battery after donning latex gloves. "It is an alkaline battery, likely from the broken remote control over there."

Owens laughed. "A battery? Big stinkin' deal."

"Even a lowly battery can tell many tales." She examined it closely. "Look, it is no longer cylindrical, but now crushed into an ellipsoid. Another important clue that you have overlooked."

"Someone stepped on it—so what?"

"Duh!" She held the crushed battery two inches from Owens' face. "The force needed to crush this alkaline battery on this quaint 70's carpet is enormous—as if a 500-pound weight stepped on it."

"Or a woman wearing stilettos, with all the force centered on the heel, Mendoza," Owens said. "How do you know the force needed to smash a battery, anyway?"

"This cheap generic brand requires nearly 6,200 Newtons to produce this type of deformity. Duracell and Energizer possess a greater resistance to damage."

"I guess I forgot who I was dealing with."

"But what does this message mean?" She looked at the words scribbled hastily on cheap motel stationery with a ballpoint pen:

A GRAVID STERN

"It appears to be Jaime's handwriting."

"So? What the hell's up with that?" Alex asked.

"Gravid stern—a pregnant rear of a ship? It must have a hidden meaning. He likes to write cryptically," she said.

"Does Jay know other languages?" Owens asked.

"Minimal Spanish, that's all. Jaime was not one for academics." She looked at the words and closed her eyes, and finally began writing several words on cheap motel stationery. "There are 1,119 potential English anagrams of those words, most of which are gibberish. I will write the five most likely for our perusal." She finished jotting the words down on the poor-quality pulp:

VERDANT RAG IS
GERARD VAST IS
DEAR VAN GRIST
AND STAG RIVER
DANGER TRAVIS

She paused for another half minute. "The letters form about 375 Spanish anagrams, none of which make any sense. Jaime does not know any other languages, sad to say."

"This is a dumb question, but why wouldn't he just write what he meant?" Owens asked. "Must be some funky Mendoza thing."

"Unless he left it for me. He always claimed to sometimes . . . see things before they happen, but they often come to him mixed up, in anagrams. Those phenomena could never be scientifically proven under rigorous testing conditions. It is possible that he himself was not certain of the meaning."

"Your brother is a clairvoyant?" Owens asked. "No way."

"Not exactly, but some synesthetes are said to have premonitions."

"Sinas-what? You mean the crazy number and word things you can do? He can do that, too? Damn."

"Synesthesia—a blending of the senses. Miguel and Dad do not have it, but Mother, my late grandmother, Jaime, and I do, along with a couple of female cousins. His visions are more surreal than mine, which are science-based. Many are skeptical, but he has interesting abilities as well as I."

Owens circled the last set of words. "Travis? Who's that?"

"I have no idea," she replied. "A green rag? Someone named Gerard or Van Grist? Where is this Stag River?"

"Stag? Might be some men's club or something," Alex said. "You know Jay."

"I'll get the FBI to look up those names," Owens said. "But it sounds pretty bizarre. Right up your alley."

"What about the girl that was here?" Alex asked. "No sign of her, except for that hair."

"We haven't found anything else, but we're still looking. This old carpet's piled pretty deep, and pretty dirty. We'll have to see what turns up on the hair, but it could've been here for days."

Bonnie knew that she had to get to the lab to supervise the evidence they had uncovered. She was the best, and only the best would do when her brother was concerned.

Chapter Thirty–one

San Diego Police Department Headquarters
1401 Broadway St.
San Diego, CA

Alex and Bonnie were walking down the main hall of SDPD with Jackie Levickis when his cell phone rang. He peered at it and instantly recognized the number with the 619 area code.

"It's Wendy's cell phone," he said.

"It is about time. From where does the call originate?"

"How would I know that?" He answered the call and pushed another button to record the audio onto a small digital card. "Wendy?"

"Yeah. What's up?"

"Where the hell are you?"

"Phoenix. Gonna drive up to the Grand Canyon tomorrow."

"We've all been worried sick about you."

"Don't need to worry about me, I'm great, just need some fresh air for a few days."

"I'm coming to get you." He tried to stall for time. "Stay there—I can use my GPS to find you."

"Oh, I won't be here that long. Places to go, people to see."

"Stan wants to know when you'll be home. He and Mom are really concerned about you and the way you've been acting."

"So he has time to get his girlfriend out of there? Yeah, right."

"He doesn't have a girlfriend, you're delusional."

"So are you, you're so dumb. Wake up and smell the roses."

"We'll talk about it, if you'll just stay there."

"Don't give me such a hard time, I'm sorry I called, if you're going to treat me that way."

He tried one more bluff. "Dad's worried about you. He's coming up to visit."

She let out a hearty laugh. "That rotten son of a bitch? I wouldn't see him if he were the last man on Earth. And you're lying."

"Something bad's happened, I'm serious. Jay's been badly hurt and is in the hospital. You need to come back, because he might not make it."

"Jay? Oh, I'm sorry about that, but I can't see him now. Too many things to do. Bye." She terminated the call.

"Well?"

"It sounded like her . . . especially her reaction to the part I made up about Dad coming to town."

"It is not secret knowledge that Wendy despises her father," Bonnie said. "Her surname change is of public record."

"I sincerely hope you recorded that," Jackie said.

"It's on the flash card. What kind of moron do you think I am?"

"We must go analyze it," Bonnie said.

"I have to trace the cell phone, too. I need some expertise here—more than you can provide."

"Humph. The DEA, FBI, SDPD, and other proficient agencies are at our immediate disposal. What more do you require?"

"I need something a lot better than that. Fortunately, such help is readily available in the endomorphic form of Crazy Jim."

"Who the hell is that?" Jackie asked. "Do I want to know?"

"She does not want to know," Bonnie said, crossing her arms.

"My old hacker buddy from college, who helped me dig through Tammy's trash cans, remember? Gone legit now, took over running my old DarTech software company. He'll be here pronto. But the timing of this phone call and the assault on Jay is pretty bizarre."

• • •

Alex, Bonnie, and Jim Krakowski were seated in a conference room with Jackie Levickis and SDPD Lt. Mike Mendoza.

"How is it you want me to help you now, Darkkin?" the portly, balding, thirty–nine-year-old Jim asked. "I am at your service, especially to lovely Agent Levickis here." Jim winked at her. "I'll do whatever she wants me to."

"Hey, watch it, buddy," Jackie said authoritatively.

Jim snickered. "I *am* watching you, trust me."

"Fortunately, you were close by," Alex said. "And conveniently available."

"Lucky for me. Or maybe unlucky, depending on your point of view. Anyway, I don't want to go through any more trash cans, New York or otherwise. Paris might be okay, though."

"I want you to help Bonnie find out if that cell phone call actually originated from Phoenix, and if it really was Wendy."

"I told you I already did, and that seems to be the case."

"Could that have been faked?" Alex asked.

"Anything's possible, but it would take someone pretty talented to spoof a caller ID. What does the Markov models analysis of the conversation reveal, Bonnie?"

"The quality is poor, of course, but it appears to be Wendy's voice in all mathematical aspects."

"So, it was faked, then," Alex said.

She sighed. "Yes, but it could only be accomplished with much difficulty. Only a few people could do that."

"We have to look at all avenues, however improbable," Alex said.

"So, do we really believe big WW is on some mood elevation swing in Phoenix? Can't we get the cops after her, Mike?" Jim asked as he took a bite of a stale glazed doughnut. "She's rather loud and kind of stands out, unless she's become the mistress of disguise again."

The crew-cut Mike frowned. "I can unofficially ask the state troopers to find her, but she's broken no laws, and, as far as I can tell, she's not a danger to herself or others. And Phoenix is a big town, if she's even there, as you say."

Bonnie rose up and punched Mike in the arm, almost knocking him over. "How can you say that, Miguel? She is our family. Jaime has been seriously injured, and perhaps she knows something. The Wendy I know would have turned around after she heard that."

"Hey—I'm speaking as a cop, not as her friend, you know that.

We can't arrest her because she's not showing the expected remorse that Jay's hurt, odd as that seems."

"Like Jim said, do we really think that was her? I don't believe it," Alex said.

"The evidence points to that, Alex," Bonnie replied. "*Pluralitias non est ponenda—*"

"Occam's razor, I know. The simplest explanation is the most likely one." He shook his head. "There has to be something more to this. This thing with Jay right now seems too coincidental."

"I need to go look at some more evidence. The DNA sample of the hair found in Jaime's squalid hotel room is about ready, and I must travel back to the lab."

"That was yesterday. I thought you could do that in an hour."

"Only on television."

• • •

SDPD allowed Bonnie, the former deputy director of the lab, the courtesy of assisting in the investigation. DNA testing results were nearly available the next day, and she was preparing to look at the door hinge.

"Look at this, Brad," she said to the technician to her left. "The metal fatigue marks."

Brad Morgan looked under the microscope. "I don't know what it is you want me to look at."

"The carbon steel—Owens said it was bent or possibly defective, but those marks can only have been produced by stress, by stretching of the steel. Not broken. Electron microscopy will confirm it."

"How can that be, Bonnie?"

"It looks like it was done by the same person who broke into Dr. Bennett's office at Caltech."

"Who?"

"A door that was broken, similar to this one." She looked at her notes from Bennett's office. "What about the hair I found?"

"The strand of hair is female, of course."

"Of course? What is that supposed to mean?"

"I'm sorry, I just meant that there probably was a . . . girl in there with him. Didn't mean anything. You need to stay objective here."

"It could have been another girl who stayed there before."

"Come on, Bonnie. He wasn't there for the free HBO."

"We do not know why he was there."

"I guess not. Anyway, no data with known people we have on file."

"Do you mind if I do some looking? I have other resources at my disposal."

"Be my guest."

She took the DNA data and accessed a "special" database she had accumulated. When she saw the match she fell off her chair.

"Bonnie? You okay?" Brad asked as he helped her up.

"Yes, I . . . just got dizzy for a moment. Vasovagal episode."

He looked at the screen. "What's that? Some other database?"

"Just . . . something else I was looking at." She stared at the DNA profile of the blonde woman whose genetic information she just happened to have on file:

99.3% MATCH
MARY G. WILLIAMS, M.D.
DOB 1/7/72
5547 DAVIDSON BLVD
SAN DIEGO, CA 92126

She couldn't believe it, but the evidence didn't lie. Her best friend and sister-in-law was having an affair with her brother, who was now in a coma, and couldn't tell them what had happened. And who would do something like that to him? The partial print on her missing handcuffs also seemed to belong to her big best friend, not her brother. That didn't prove anything, as Wendy was once her assistant, and had borrowed her magic items before. But she didn't need proof beyond a shadow of a doubt right now.

"Bonnie . . . I've seen her on television and in here with you several times. Isn't she—"

"It is. My wonderful sister-in-law, the Chief of Staff, was in a motel room with my brother."

"I'm . . . sorry you had to be the one to find out."

"Not as sorry as she's going to be when I find her, or as Jaime will be when he awakens. Off her rocker or not, she has some explaining to do. I suppose that casts some doubt on the cell phone call's authenticity."

"But, Bonnie—if Jay was hurt, why did she leave? That doesn't make any sense. I don't think she's strong enough to have done this herself."

"Unless, as we thought, the phone call was a ruse, and she was abducted."

"Abducted? By whom?"

"I do not know. Hush and let me continue our studies."

The other DNA she found on microscopic blood samples and fabric from the carpet was curious. Three males, each with cell karyotype XY. The first had twenty shared paired alleles with her own DNA—clearly her brother's. Another set with only four shared alleles—a random individual, but with several patterns she considered unusual.

She gasped as she looked at the genetic structure and chemical composition of the third individual's—unlike anything she had ever seen before.

"The piece of torn fabric contains a human protein, probably sweat. It appears to contain the amino acids isovaline and psuedoleucine, something not known to be contained in any mammalian protein," she said.

"No way, it has to be a mistake. That's not possible," Brad said. "But you're right—I've never heard of those amino acids occurring in a living organism."

"I have not, either, but those amino acids are real. What in God's name are we dealing with here?"

Brad shook his head. "I have no clue."

She thought long and hard about the connections—two seemingly random assaults on people she knew; one in Pasadena, the other in San Diego, done almost exactly the same way, by someone she reasoned had the strength of ten men. She could buy into the fact that Bennett might have been involved in something classified, but why would someone assault Jaime and take her best friend? What possible value would she be to anyone?

Chapter Thirty–two

Methodist Hospital
San Diego, CA

Alex, Bonnie, and Jackie went to see Stan and Marianne at Methodist Hospital in San Diego. Jay had been taken there after Wendy's disappearance, and was still in a coma. Mike Mendoza and his parents Carlos and Elisa were in the ICU with him. They met them in the waiting room, where they were drinking coffee.

"Stan, Marianne, this is DEA Special Agent Jackie Levickis." The five–seven woman shook their hands.

"Mr. Williams and Ms. Gallinsworth, I'm sorry to hear about this. I assure you, we are pursuing all avenues."

"She had to have been abducted," Alex said. "That cell phone call was fake. It's too bizarre to be merely coincidence."

"There's no proof of that, Darkkin. Until Jay Mendoza wakes up, we won't ever know exactly what happened," Jackie replied.

"Why else would someone engineer that, then?" he asked.

"Don't know. Don't really care, either."

Stan sat down in the waiting room. "I don't know what was wrong with her, Alex. Never seen her like this before."

"What was she doing?"

"Erratic stuff, spending lots of money, not answering pages, was worried about stupid things."

"Like what?"

"One day she blew up because she wanted a bunch of colored

pen refills. Kept bugging me about it until it drove me crazy. Who cares? Then she blew up. I told her we were going to see her doctor, and she flipped out and left, and that's the last I saw of her."

"She always had high energy, you know that. Almost obsessive-compulsive at times," he said.

"Yeah, but you never saw the low times. Sometimes she'd be so lethargic you couldn't get her out of bed at all. Sleep three hours a night for weeks on end, then sleep a day straight. The crying really freaked me out."

"Sounds almost bipolar."

"What?" Bonnie asked. "I did not understand."

"The mood changes. That description sounds like a bipolar person in a manic phase. I guess I could see it sometimes—like a switch suddenly went on."

"*Mania?* That's ridiculous," Stan said. "She never had anything like that before. You're exaggerating. It's not that bad."

"Isn't it? But sometimes there's a trigger. Mid to late thirties is a peak onset time for women. Watching the most powerful man in the world die before your eyes isn't the best memory to have, either."

"You are a radiation oncologist. What do you know of mental illness, Dr. Freud?"

"I know more than you think. I've paid plenty of therapists. You have, too."

"There's something else you better know. We haven't told anyone, not even you, Marianne, but she's pregnant—about six to eight weeks."

"Wendy is up the spout?" Marianne opened her mouth wide. "She certainly didn't tell me."

Alex's face turned white. "Shit, you're kidding me."

Marianne slapped him on the shoulder. "Alex, how crass. Pardon your French, please!"

"Sorry. But I sure didn't know about that, or I would've never gone along with that stunt in the testing center."

"Testing center? What are you talking about?" Stan asked angrily.

Bonnie stepped up. "The mental giant siblings decided it would be useful for Wendy to go into the testing center disguised as a man, to obtain additional information. The whole bit."

"What? Are you insane, Alex?"

"It was her idea, but I thought it would help the case."

"You idiot. Can things possibly get any worse?" Stan asked.

They always could get worse, he knew. "Pregnancy can be a trigger, too. Was she taking any meds?"

Stan took out a blister pack of sample medication—quertraline, brand name Auripex. "I didn't know it, but she had this. Found it in her dresser drawer. Never heard of it."

"Auripex?" he looked at the blue-and-white capsules. "It's a selective serotonin reuptake inhibitor, or SSRI. Why was she taking an antidepressant, and who prescribed it?"

"I called Patty Ashburn, her GYN, who said she didn't. She doesn't see anyone else. I suppose a colleague could have given it to her. I tried to get her to go see Bobbi Elsevier, but she refused."

"Maybe she's seeing another psychiatrist—or, more likely—she got the samples for herself and started taking them."

"Surely not," Bonnie said, opening her mouth wide. "A doctor who treats herself has a fool for a patient."

He sneered. "A lot of doctors don't have the best judgment. That's probably it, then. Some antidepressants can actually cause mania in patients with underlying bipolar II disorder," he said.

"Bipolar II?" Marianne asked curiously. "There are different types of manic depression?"

"It's a milder form of bipolar that often escapes diagnosis. Patients often have episodes of 'hypomania,' or extreme energy and focus, without overtly psychotic behavior. They sometimes are prescribed antidepressants for the 'lows,' and the meds can trigger full-blown manic behavior."

"The samples she took caused it?" Stan asked.

"Possibly. A good practitioner would have considered that, but obviously she prescribed it to herself. She felt better because it got rid of the depression, and elevated her mood, so why would she stop it? Not good."

"But what would she have been doing with Jay in some lousy old motel?" his mother asked. "Wasting money and being obsessed about trivial things sounds like you, Alex."

"Thanks, Mom." He paused for a few seconds. "I hate to talk about my sister this way, but . . . these patients often become hypersexual. Has she been like that, Stan?"

"How do you know about such things?" Bonnie asked. After a few seconds, she then raised her finger into the air. "Never mind, if it is about sex, you will know of it."

"That's kind of private, Alex, but I'd have to say yes to that one."

"There is one other thing I should mention," Marianne said. "Alex, you and Bonnie don't know this, but—"

"It isn't important, Marianne," Stan said loudly, interrupting her. "Why bring it up now? It doesn't help."

"Because it might be important."

"What is it, Marianne?" Bonnie asked, as Stan threw down his hands.

"Well, Wendy and Jay used to date. 1990, or so, before he graduated and went pro."

"Jay and Wendy?" Alex asked. "You must be joking. I knew she worked out with him, but that *has* to be wrong."

"No, it's not. She had a big crush on him. Always full of beans, she was. And you were too absorbed in yourself back then to care, Alex," Marianne said snidely.

"That cannot be true . . . how could I have not known of this?" Bonnie said. "She is my best friend."

"You were what, thirteen, fourteen?" Marianne replied. "You had your own problems, and were just starting to get your own life back together. Why would it have been your business, anyway?"

"Humph," Bonnie said, folding her arms. "I guess not."

Alex shook his head. "But he must've had women falling all over him. How could that have happened?"

"He needed to gain about twenty pounds in his senior year, and saw what she had done with Bonnie in only a year. She went up to USC on the weekends. And that little relationship turned into something else. Wendy can be quite charming, you know. Just like you, Alex."

"Yeah, so what happened with that?" Alex asked.

"They were both so young . . . he went off to pro football, to Wisconsin, and they parted ways. With celebrity came the groupies, the models, the chartered planes . . . he moved on."

"What about Wendy?"

"She was hurt, but eventually met Stan and moved on, too. She wouldn't have wanted that kind of life, and they both knew that. We all have our infatuations, our first loves that never worked out."

"Guess you would know about that," he said, as he couldn't resist sparring with his sharp-tongued mother. "But what does that have to do with anything, Mom? That was twenty years ago."

"Perhaps the infatuation with the past, seeing him again and being around him, triggered something. What other explanation is there?"

But he was much less concerned about *why* they were in the motel together than *who* broke in. He could buy that his sister had lost it, and that Jaime was a playboy—but neither of them was important enough for this kind of assault. Something sinister was underfoot, he just knew it.

• • •

Williams Residence
5547 Davidson Blvd.
San Diego, CA

Alex came by Wendy and Stan's house, and his mother opened the door with hesitation.

"Hey, Mom," he said. "I came by like you wanted. I don't have much time, though. Pretty busy."

"Oh, I'm sure of that. Jake's taking a nap, but this won't take long. I know you are busy with your jet-setting crime solving, which mere mortals like I can't understand." The sarcasm coming from the sharp-tongued woman's voice was cutting.

He frowned. "It's not what you think this time. I'm working with DEA Agent Levickis."

She nodded slowly. "I see—that allows you to justify your work, and makes it less hazardous for those close to you, doesn't it? Just like your father, everything's a childish game."

"So, what's up?" he said as he sat down, trying to change the subject, as she obviously was in one of her bad moods.

"Do you want some coffee?"

"Yeah." She poured him some coffee and added cream. They

then went into the living room and sat down.

Marianne started crying. "Of all the things you've done, I've tried to forgive you. But this time, I don't know that I can, Alex."

"What, you're blaming this all on me?"

"You just never know when to stop meddling, do you? Almost got Bonnie killed a few years ago, as I understand."

"I don't need you to tell me about that. I relive it all the time. And now I'm going to have to live with those consequences for the rest of my life."

"At least you take ownership for it. She lost some memory, but otherwise came out lucky."

"No, she didn't. She's . . . she's having progressive auditory nerve loss from the brain injury three and a half years ago. In a year, she won't be able to perceive anything, even with $250,000 worth of cochlear implants."

She paused for a few seconds. "I'm sorry, Alex. Sorry you didn't learn your lesson. Now Jay might die, and Wendy's probably already dead, because of you, you bastard!" she threw her half-full teacup at him. "Why did it have to be her?"

He got up to dry off his tea-stained shirt and pick up the shattered cup. "Jay's the one who called Bonnie to help. You can't stop her once she's going. Her or Wendy."

She pointed a manicured red fingernail at him. "Oh, I'm so sure you tried to stop it. Don't lie to me."

"I guess I was just trying to help."

"*Help?* You vowed on that altar to be Bonnie's protector, her guiding light, her voice of reason. She's like a brilliant child, yet you and Wendy pull some stupid stunt, like it was some practical joke."

"There's something wrong with her, Mom. It's not my fault."

"Just like your dad, aren't you? Maybe you meant well, but you don't see the danger of your actions before you do them. If Wendy told you to walk off a bridge, would you do it? Can't you be the adult for once in your life? She's mad as a March hare."

"I'm not my sister's keeper. She's the one who started popping pills and went off the deep edge. You've been here most every day for the last several weeks, and you should've seen it, too. Where's your ownership? Nowhere in sight, as always."

"Yes, well, know that she always cared about you. Worried about you all those years you barely spoke to one another. And this doesn't change anything, Conrad Jr. You and your stupid friend Jim. A bad seed, he always was."

"Don't call me that, and don't blame Jim. If Wendy had some personal problem going on, you're the one that should've known. She was closer to you than anyone."

"Again, blame it on someone else."

He shrugged. "Where does that leave us, then? I can't say I'm sorry any more, and can't do anything more to fix it."

"You've done enough, so just stay out of things. I don't know that I ever want to see you again, Alex. Your father caused so much pain for all of us."

"That's my fault too, I guess. You married him. I didn't."

She slapped him with her slender hand, a stinging sensation with which he was quite familiar. He knew she was upset, and was probably transferring the anger onto him; but was she right? Had he been meddling where he shouldn't have been, once again? And how many would pay the price?

"I'll leave now, Mom. But know this . . . I won't rest until I find Wendy, and who beat up Jay."

"Just leave, please. And don't ever come back."

"I'm sorry you feel that way. But you made your own life, Mom, and someday you have to stop blaming me and Dad for it. I've done some stupid shit, but so have you. If you can't come to terms with that, then too bad."

He slammed the door and left and thought about his mother, the good times they once had— but Wendy was always the apple of her eye, and he the inedible seeds. He knew she saw too much of Rad in him when she stared into his blue eyes.

He couldn't repair the damage his father had done. His sister was probably dead, his mother now hated him, just like she did his father—hell, he didn't even want to think about *him* right now. That kind of headache no one needed. He hadn't even heard from him in over three years. One good thing.

Chapter Thirty–three

Darkkin Mendoza Residence
4552 Eagle Point Blvd.
Pasadena, CA

Bonnie and Jim continued working on Bennett's "Magical Horn" CD at her house. She had come to terms with the fact that Wendy was probably off her rocker, and would do anything necessary to try and uncover more information.

"Well? Have you anything yet?" she demanded impatiently.

"Chill out, Square—it isn't that easy. It isn't any operating system I'm familiar with, and I know them all. The most likely candidate is some obscure military operating system. None of my decoders seem to find anything. But what if the title itself is a clue? It sure as hell isn't an audio CD, so why disguise it as that?"

"The title: 'A Magical Horn.' There are, I believe, 5,583 English word anagrams for that, most of which are nonsense. I will write them down."

Jim punched several words into his laptop. "Don't bother. The computer is way faster than you at that." He brought up an anagram program. "No offense."

"Humph," she said as she folded her arms. "Computers are efficient, yet have no personality."

"At least you have that, albeit a prickly one."

"Huh?"

"Never mind." He brought up the list of anagrams and sat back in amazement. "Dang—you're correct, though. 5,583. Most of them are meaningless." He printed the lengthy list and gave it to her.

"Malachi Argon. That is it," she said after looking at the list for a few seconds.

"Huh? A Malachi *what*? Argon gas?"

She leaned back in her chair. "No, Argon is also a man—one of the world's preeminent biochemists and geneticists." She looked at him condescendingly. "Did you not use his textbook in college? 'Argon's Principles of Biochemistry.' A landmark publication."

"Sorry, I don't remember that one. I did mostly computer science and math, when I wasn't hacking into databases, screwing up the Dean's speeches, and playing Robin Hood by disseminating test answers to the masses." He looked at the garbled files again. "Who was this Bennett dude, anyway?"

She rolled her eyes. "Duh! How ignorant you are. He was *only* the world's most preeminent astrobiologist."

"What the hell's that?"

"Astrobiology is the interdisciplinary study of life in space, and combines knowledge of astronomy, physics, chemistry, biology, and geology."

"Life on other planets, like that Mars rock?"

"Yes, but, from my understanding, he did not feel Mars to be the most likely candidate for life."

"What was, then?"

"He was the world's greatest Titan scholar, and felt that it would be the most likely place to support habitable life. One of my favorite scientists, Christiaan Huygens, was quite fond of Latin anagrams, by the way. The most famous is the one, when decrypted, tells of the 'handles' of Saturn: *annulo cingitur, tenui, plano, nusquam cohaerente, ad eclipticam inclinato*."

"Which means? And who the hell cares?"

"'It is surrounded by a thin flat ring, nowhere touching, and inclined to the ecliptic.' The first description of the rings."

"If you say so. But Titan? I guess I do recall that it's the only body to have an atmosphere even remotely like Earth's."

"Correct—despite there being little elemental oxygen, there is much nitrogen, as well as carbon and possibly water ice—the building blocks of life."

"Great, except it's gotta be pretty damn cold out there—what, minus 170° Celsius, at least? I may be just a computer guy, but I know it needs to be warmer than that to form complex organic compounds."

She nodded in agreement. "It is cold, I admit. The peculiar composition of the atmosphere actually *reflects* infrared radiation. Paradoxically, Titan's surface is ten degrees Kelvin colder than it would be if it had no atmosphere at all."

He took a sip of coffee as he stood up to stretch his legs. "An anti-greenhouse effect, if you will. We need something like that here, if you believe that global warming stuff."

"Ah, but you forget the Cronian magnetosphere. While less strong than Jupiter's, the ionospheric plasma along with the solar wind create an effect called mass loading, leading to ionization of the outer atmosphere. This could provide the necessary energy to create complex organic molecules."

"Thus creating life. You really believe life was created that way, like here on Earth?"

She stared at him for a few seconds and shook her head in amazement. "Of course not. Life on Earth was created by God in Heaven," she said confidently.

"God?" Jim laughed for several seconds and slapped his thigh with his right palm. "That's a good one. One of the world's most brilliant young physicists going from ionization of plasma and formation of amino acids to God. What a hoot."

She stood up and grabbed his arm with her powerful right hand. "There is certainly nothing humorous about God, James. No power in this universe is greater than His."

He pulled away with surprise. "Look, I know you almost died as a kid, and can understand having some type of epiphany after what you went through." He shook his head. "But you're a scientist, and can't possibly believe in Genesis and God creating the Earth and all. That's for simple-minded people who can't understand what we can."

"You have made an incorrect assumption—just because I possess a superior intellect does not negate my belief in the spiritual. It is so elemental to me. And we are to God as mere ants are to us."

"I really . . . don't understand."

"Tell me, wise scientist of pure logic—what is the natural pattern of the universe? Towards order or disorder?"

"Is this one of your crazy riddles? I don't know what you mean."

"Does the natural state of matter tend towards less or more entropy, or disorganization?" she asked impatiently.

He thought for a few seconds. "More, I guess. A compressed gas tends to want to expand, for example."

"Exactly—the universe tends towards disorganization. And, as a scientist, to think that random atoms, on Earth or Titan or anywhere else, would just happen to combine to form organized molecules in the form of life, is preposterous. Only the Almighty could accomplish such a magnanimous feat."

"We all made amino acids with simulated lightning, nitrogen, and methane in chemistry class. So what?"

"Hah. A few paltry amino acids do not intelligent life make. I may not take the book of Genesis literally—life was created over a span of billions of years, not days—but some higher power must have caused it to happen."

"What about evolution, then?"

"The Bible was written for the level of knowledge at the time. I do believe in evolution, but that life was somehow originally created by a higher being."

"You have no proof. A scientist should demand that."

She smiled proudly. "That is what faith is all about. You must believe in something you cannot see or prove."

"Okay, then, if he's so benevolent, why did your God make some people defective? Some are born without limbs, some with mental retardation, some blind, others—"

"*Deaf?* More of the defective ones? Let us all be euthanized, so we may be removed from the face of the Earth. That is what *some* would desire." The intense dark eyes pierced into his.

"I . . . didn't mean that, Bonnie. I'm sorry."

"No, you're not really. You are just like my husband, so shortsighted. We don't know God's reasoning, His plan for us, and why He wants things this way. Ours is not to comprehend. Am I less than you because I lack something you have? Do those 'defective' ones have nothing to contribute?"

Jim hesitated. "I guess I see your point."

"That is wise. Perhaps we should now change the subject."

"Works for me." He paused for several seconds and ate half a bag of potato chips. "So, did this Bennett dude really think there's life on Titan?"

"No one knows. I do know they discovered seasonal variations in the atmospheric climate which are similar to Earth's. The methane in the atmosphere and lakes also cannot exist indefinitely—sunlight breaks it down, so there must be some mechanism to replace it."

"But, again, it's too cold for liquid water to exist."

"Perhaps—but there are significant gravitational effects from Saturn and ring remnants going into the atmosphere, enough to keep significant geothermal activity going."

"Assuming God created life, how did it end up on Titan?"

"The most logical way is this: Terran meteorites from millions of years ago."

"What? It's 800 million frickin' miles away. You can't possibly believe that fragments of Earth somehow ended up on Titan."

"Why is it impossible? Martian meteorites have been discovered in Antarctica. And, in 2000, 250-million-year-old bacteria were found dormant in a cave half a mile below the surface in New Mexico. So bacteria might have survived millions of years on Titan."

"New Mexico . . . Titan. Can sure see the similarity there. And Antarctica's just a little bit closer than the ol' murky orange ball."

"Wrong. I have done computer simulations, and I have concluded that a number of fragments from meteor collisions on Earth sixty-five million years ago could have reached Titan."

"The chances of that are pretty remote, don't you think?"

"Perhaps. But billions of tons of debris were thrown into the atmosphere. Bennett had evidence that some fragments from Earth made it into the Jovian and Cronian systems."

"Why not Jupiter's moons, then? They're closer."

"True, but the powerful Jovian magnetosphere emanates enough ionizing radiation to kill anything. And there is no carbon, nitrogen, or water on Europa or Ganymede. Titan is, therefore, the only logical body within our Solar System to harbor life."

"What would it consume? Hydrocarbons? Even I wouldn't eat that. And that's saying a lot." He patted his beer belly.

"The microorganism could have evolved to survive almost anywhere, even to subsist in a hellishly toxic organic environment."

"Huh. Sounds like we need some of those in Los Angeles."

"Before we go, I must know if you took care of those things in my GPS like I asked. They are of the utmost priority."

"Yeah, I remapped the signals, but why? That took a lot of extra work, along with the cell phone."

"And did you swap all my biometric records with those of Tamara Preece?"

"I really had a problem with that, but, yeah. I can reverse it easily enough. Mind telling me what it's all about?"

"I hope I will not have to."

Bonnie made two copies of the CD-ROM, one to take with her, the other to place in a bank safety deposit box, and made a third copy on a miniature flash drive which she hid in her right processor, in a hidden compartment. She didn't trust only having one copy around, whatever was on it.

• • •

The giant moon Titan was one of the oddest places in the Solar System. The largest of Saturn's sixty known satellites was larger than Mercury or Pluto, and far larger and massive than Earth's moon; it contained twenty times the entire mass of Saturn's rings and the rest of its satellites combined. The only Saturnian moon easily visible with a backyard telescope was only fractionally smaller than gigantic Ganymede, the largest of Jupiter's moons.

Titan was first called *"Luna Saturni"* by Dutch astronomer and mathematician Christiaan Huygens in 1655. An expert in optics, he realized that he could improve upon the telescopes of Galileo, and applied himself to the manufacture of better devices. By 1655, he had pointed his new telescope at Saturn to study the rings, and was the first to discover their true shape (Galileo did not realize they were rings). Huygens was one of Bonnie's favorite scientists, mostly because he liked word puzzles written in her favorite language (Latin). In Huygens' day, scientists often used anagrams to distribute news of their discoveries.

Another of his famous anagrams translated into *"Saturno luna sua circunducitur diebus sexdecimhoris quatuor,"* or "Saturn's moon revolves in sixteen days and four hours"—a proclamation that he had discovered a satellite of Saturn. Giovanni Cassini had discovered the next four moons, Tethys, Dione, Rhea, and Iapetus, by 1684. It would be over 100 years before additional moons would be discovered.

But what most intrigued scientists about Titan wasn't its size, but the fact that it had a dense atmosphere, approximately one and a half times as dense as Earth's. The terrestrial planets Venus and Mars had atmospheres, of course, but vastly unlike ours; Venus' was 100 times as dense and contained, as Jasper Bennett had said, toxic sulfuric acid and carbon dioxide. Mars, which lacked a significant magnetosphere, was stripped of most of its atmosphere by the solar wind long ago; its atmosphere was now only 0.7% as dense as Earth's.

Titan's atmosphere was not only of similar density to Earth's, but contained similar gases, such as nitrogen—one of the prerequisites for life. The lack of molecular oxygen was a problem for any future travelers, as was the lack of liquid water. The surface was felt to be an oil company's dream: vast hydrocarbon lakes. Of course, getting there in the first place and getting the fuel back would be more trouble than it would be worth.

Titan was also a much more stable place to live than Jupiter's moons; Io, for example, was torn up with constant volcanic eruptions caused by the massive Jovian tidal forces. The magnetosphere of Jupiter was powerful enough to result in significant radiation to three of the four Galilean moons, eradicating all life there.

But what did the intriguing moon, named after the mythological giants of Greek mythology, have to do with Wendy's abduction (or death, for that matter), Dr. Bennett's murder, and the deaths of President Graham and Senator Orson? And what connection, if any, was there to the juiced-up members of the Las Vegas Conquerors and other pro football teams? These were the many questions racing through the fantastic cerebrum of Bonnie Mendoza.

Chapter Thirty–four

Somewhere over the Caribbean Sea
8:02 AM

"You're so fucking stupid to think you could fool us with that stuff," Tammy Preece said to Wendy, who was seat-belted into a chair in the Gulfstream jet, traveling eastward at Mach 0.8. Her hands were handcuffed together in front, attached to a D-ring in a leather belt.

"I don't believe you actually detected the prosthetics. They were state of the art."

"No, it was pretty good. But you made one mistake. You're left-handed, correct? I noticed that when you signed the consent form."

"Yes, like my father, but so what?"

"In human males, the left testis almost always hangs lower in right-handed persons, with the opposite in southpaws. Your left 'testis' was lower, but, in you, it should have been the right."

"Guess you can't know everything."

"Don't you have any questions for me?"

"Like you're gonna tell me? Who *are* you? I outweigh you by at least sixty pounds, and can beat 95% of guys in a fight. Yet, you threw me around like a rag doll."

"I'm sorry, it was not my intent to harm you. Sometimes I don't know my own strength. And I weigh as much as you."

"How? I assume you have complete androgen resistance, or testicular feminization syndrome, as my brother and I thought. You have negligible facial hair."

"That's right. It was pretty amazing that you figured that out."

"Normally I would be freaking out right now, but I'm not."

"We have given you something to help with that."

She tugged at the steel restraints and looked at the woman who had knocked her around in the hotel. *Mendoza Milagroso* she wasn't, she thought as she considered her limited options.

"You didn't answer me—how were you able to beat me up?"

"Like you, I contain a rare gene that imparts strength and endurance. I have been . . . genetically enhanced, with strength probably twice that of yours. There are others, too."

"Why would you want someone to experiment on you?"

"I didn't want it, I had no choice. I had a progressive neurologic disease that would've killed me. Dr. Argon saved my life."

"Who?"

"You'll see."

She tried to keep her composure and not freak out. That wouldn't help anything right now. "What about that huge dude? The one that killed Jay Mendoza?"

"This whole thing was poorly conceived. We tracked you through a GPS microchip Linda implanted into your brachial vein when you were phlebotomized at the testing center."

"The obvious question next: what's going to happen to me?"

"We will need you for at least a few more months, and will keep you quite safe and comfortable. We need your genetic material, or, more precisely, the material inside you."

"You want my baby? What the hell for?"

"It is our hope that it possesses the genetic material we need."

"My family will find me. You're in way over your head."

"If you are referring to your intrepid sister-in-law, I am afraid she will be dealt with soon. And I do not believe your husband to be a threat to us."

"You're lying."

"I wish I was. She has some interesting characteristics, too, and we have plans for her."

Wendy sat back in the chair and relaxed as much as she could, realizing that she probably wasn't going to get out of this one alive. At least the thoughts weren't racing as much as before. The events of the last few days were merely a fog.

Chapter Thirty–five

Darkkin Mendoza Residence
4552 Eagle Point Blvd.
Pasadena, CA

Bonnie and Jim came back to her Pasadena condo after going to the bank to deposit the CD, and found some unwelcome guests awaiting them—the assistant commissioner of pro football, along with a large, muscular blond man. Their vehicle was nowhere in sight.

"Hey, what's going on?" Jim asked.

"Tamara Preece, this is the last straw. You have broken into my home! What do you think you are doing here? And how did you deactivate my alarm system?"

The five–ten Tammy Preece stared at her. Bonnie thought she weighed maybe 150 pounds, and knew she could take the wiry brunette. She was usually good at sizing people up.

"Don't try it, Mendoza. You don't stand a chance."

Bonnie got into her fighting stance. "I know martial arts, skinny Tamara, and am a skilled boxer. I do not want to hurt you, but I will, if angered—very badly. I killed a man once with my bare hands. I will rip your eyes out first. Then you will die."

"*You* don't want to hurt *me*? How courteous of you. Go on, take your best shot."

Bonnie came at her with both fists, and Tammy blocked them with one hand, then lifted Bonnie with the other and threw her against the wall. Bonnie was used to horsing around with Alex,

Mike, and Wendy, who were all stronger than her, but this was different. Almost inhuman—and Tammy was just as fast.

But she was no wimp—she got up, with the wind knocked out of her. She went towards Tammy again, who picked her up and threw her into the wall again.

It appeared Jim wasn't doing so well, either. She knew that his weight-lifting exercises consisted of lifting twenty–ounce beer cans to his mouth, and his pot-belly showed it. Tammy's male companion sprayed a mist into his face, and he dropped to the ground.

She rose back up and dodged another swing from the taller Tammy, and finally got in one good shot to the solar plexus, which didn't seem to faze her one bit. The big Caucasian man sprayed the mist again into her eyes, kind of like the anesthesia induction she received before her cochlear implant surgery. But she didn't think these two were benefactors, she thought before she drifted off into unconsciousness.

• • •

Bonnie woke up suddenly, and could barely detect the vibration of airplane engines. The hydrocarbon aroma of glycol and jet fuel was piercing, though. She looked at the interior, which appeared to be that of a Gulfstream G550. The hydrocarbon aroma of glycol and jet fuel was piercing, though. She was belted into a chair, with her hands cuffed behind her. Surely they knew who she was, didn't they? *Mendoza Milagroso* used to be, after all, one of the best female escape artists in the world; that was, however, a few years ago, and she was sorely out of practice. Her most recent "fun" uses of those devices usually didn't involve the desire to escape.

Standard size, she realized, as she probed the cold steel with her fingers. She could identify most types by touch alone, as each manufacturer had a distinctive variation in rivet pattern and type of steel. Some were highly polished, while others had a coarser pattern to the steel. Her head was a little cloudy, as she fought to maintain focus as she felt. Ah, so that was it. She felt the plastic retaining locks over the metal bracelets. They had prepared well.

But a good magician was *never* unprepared. If they were going to die, at least they were going to go out with a bang. Of that, she was damn sure, she thought as she gathered her wits and planned her options as she stared at the tough-looking man, holding a gun, sitting across from her. Jim was in a similar predicament, in a seat across the aisle.

The cuffs would be difficult. No ordinary cuffs—she felt and recognized them as ones retrofitted with special Medeco pin-tumbler locks, for high-security prisoners who might have concealed a standard key; she certainly had hidden many of those in her day.

Each lock had seven pins, each which would have to be elevated and rotated at exactly the proper rotational angle to open. And she was very much out of practice; the few stunts she had done recently were with standard devices that were child's play. She knew she probably wouldn't be able to pick them on a table, let alone in them, hands behind her, without a set of special tension lock picks, and those didn't seem to be available right now. After all, she had designed similar devices herself for her own lock company, Milagroso Security.

They had taken her watch and handy wedding ring, the latter which contained a variety of escape devices, none of which were likely to work here. She never sewed the plastic escape key into her clothes any more, but that probably wouldn't work, either. But there was one long-shot option left to try.

"Help me, I think I'm going to vomit," she yelled.

"Oh, tough gal is sick now, huh? Just puke on yourself, bitch."

She actually was able to vomit some greenish gastric contents onto the leather seat. The smell was putrid.

"Shit, Benner, take her to the bathroom. Dr. A won't like her puking on his jet. Hard as hell to clean up."

Benner got her up, unbuckled her seat belt, and took her to the restroom. He unlocked one cuff and locked its mate to a bolt in the small restroom.

"Can you at least close the door? I must pee as well."

"Oh, for Chrissakes. If you pull any shit, I'll shoot your ass."

After the door was closed, she pulled out what she hoped to find. A vomit bag. She needed to shim the cuffs, and remembered something she had always told the recruits at the police academy, whom she used to lecture on escape tactics—using the metal strip to open cuffs. She pulled out a two-inch strip and hid it between her right third and fourth fingers.

To think that the future of the free world might depend on her unconventional use of a barf bag.

Her hands were re-cuffed behind her while Benner dug in his pocket for the double lock activator—a long strip of metal used to keep the ratchets from tightening further. Once double-locked, she could not shim them. But she had a few seconds.

A few seconds was all she would need. With reflexes honed from years of practice, she shimmed the left bracelet off, spun around, and struck him in the face, violently spewing blood and teeth across the cabin. She gasped as she realized she had probably fractured his neck; Alex told her she did something like that three years ago, but she couldn't remember. What she did know was that she was damn good at getting herself in trouble.

The other guards would hear the thuds, but she had prepared for this. She prepared to activate some "additional" circuitry in her aural processors, to activate a self-defense mechanism not even Alex knew about. One which a fellow scientist had designed for her, at her request. Probably illegal, but who the hell cared now? At least it worked better than the laser in the ladies' Rolex she wanted, which weighed about ten pounds, and was impractical to wear. So much for cutting through chain links with that.

"Активировать!" She yelled the Russian word for "activate," which triggered the hidden devices. She had to thank the inventor later—in Russian, of course.

The craft was immediately filled with infrasound from the amazingly compact transducers—extraordinarily painful to all aboard the plane, except, of course, for the one who could not hear. Of course, this switched her processors' modes, so she couldn't process input. The electronic were based on an experimental design of her secret "friend."

It generated a series of low, mid, and high-frequency sound waves of 0.3, 9, and 18.9 Hertz—the three combined produced a frequency of 0.56 Hertz, which created a sense of severe disorientation and nausea. She had tested it before, and it had minimal effect on her; there was a slight effect on her equilibrium center. The others could shield their ears, but it would do no good—the infrasound would penetrate anything that they could use to shield themselves.

The pain was excruciating, to say the least.

"Crap, what have you done?" Jim said, about to vomit.

She took the .44-caliber Magnum from one of the guards and smacked him in the head, and went into the cockpit towards the pilot, who was reeling in pain from the intense sound.

Tammy Preece blocked her way, lunged towards her, and threw a punch, which only knocked her back a few inches; Bonnie then smashed her right fist into Tammy's face, spewing more blood across the cabin. Damn, how did she do that? She finally fired two slugs into Tammy—one in the left chest, the other in the forehead.

"I told you that you would die. You should have listened and stuck to pro football." Forensic scientists were good at knowing how to kill people effectively, and she was damn good with a gun. Rita McPherson appeared to be no threat, and was cowering in the corner, as Bonnie went into the cockpit.

"Do as I say, or die a terrible death, as has Tamara Preece," she screamed at the pilot, who was reeling in pain from the infrasound.

"Turn it off, bitch, or this plane'll crash."

Bonnie made out some of what he had said through lip-reading. "Good. Perhaps that is how it should be, then—to perish in a blaze of flaming glory."

"If you shoot me, there's no one to fly this plane. You'll depressurize the plane, too, if it goes through the cabin, and we'll all die."

She knew he was saying something about the plane being depressurized, but also knew that it was just a myth. Sure, small arms fire might penetrate the cabin, but that wouldn't be enough to completely depressurize the plane, the physicist knew. And she had other plans, anyway. No one would be flying this plane ever again.

"Put it on autopilot." The infrasound batteries would last a couple more minutes, at most, according to the inventor.

"It doesn't work. Whatcha gonna do now?"

She watched in awe as light from the cabin's ceiling lamp split, as it had so many times in her childhood, into the seven Newtonian components of the spectrum; the violet rays swirled and took the form of a shiny, liquid blob, like a lavender ball of mercury. The beautiful chord the light produced was vaguely familiar.

"You are a liar. I know."

"Fuck you. You won't do it. You need me to fly this plane."

"Is that what you say to me?" she said as she fired a round into his left leg, spewing blood across the cockpit. "Apologize to me at once and put it on autopilot, now."

"Oh, shit—you fucking shot me, goddamn it!"

"Do it and I will give you something for the pain."

She approached him again as he put the plane on autopilot. "Okay, I did it. I need something for the pain, shit! You promised."

"Thank you. Mendoza never lies—I have the best thing in the world to relieve it." She then put a bullet through his brain, and he slumped back in his seat. "Permanently."

She went back and released Jim as the battery power in her processors finally decreased to a threshold below which the sonic device would not function. They had about ten minutes' of power left, which she might need later. She had already taken the weapon from the other guard, who was vomiting on the floor.

"I think I'm gonna hurl. Alex said you were fricking crazy. Let me get on the radio, at least I know something about them."

"I caution you—it is quite messy in there."

"Oh, my God," Jim said as he saw blood everywhere. "Did you *have* to blow the dude's brains out?"

"It was necessary. He wanted something for the pain, and I was all out of Tylenol. My remedy, unfortunately, has toxic side effects."

"Shut up. You and your idiotic jokes." Jim fumbled with the controls with blood from the pilot pooling all around them. "It doesn't work, dammit! We're all gonna die."

She scratched her head and stared into his face. "Why does the transceiver not work? Can a computer genius not figure out how to use a simple radio? Hello!"

Jim cleaned the blood off the front and noticed the one-centimeter hole in the front panel and the smoke streaming from the burning electronic circuit boards inside.

"No, I can't, because your bullet went clean through his head and into the radio, dumb ass. Holy shit!"

She put her hand over her mouth. "Oops. I did not anticipate the trajectory properly. My bad."

"Great, just great. So what do we do now? I see you've really planned ahead, Einstein."

"There is no urgency, as the plane is on autopilot. Do you know how to fly?"

"Uh, no, never got around to that. Do you?"

"Are you kidding? I am barely allowed to have a drivers' license, with my positional disabilities. Simply driving to the convenience store can be an all-day adventure. I don't think you want to experience my flying."

"Give me that gun before you shoot something or somebody else." He tried to grab the Magnum from her, but met strong resistance. "Or not." He backed away as she put the safety on and went back out after Rita.

"Where are you going now?" Jim asked. "Forgot. Can't hear."

"To find parachutes," she replied, her back to him. "Parachutes!" she yelled at Rita McPherson as the nauseating sound subsided. "Where are they?"

"What do you mean? There are none here," the red-haired scientist, the one remaining living crew member, said.

She took Rita's red hair and pulled it back. "I know there are three here. I will ask you one more time. I can cause a great deal of pain. I would like to know where the three chutes are."

"I—I don't know, but I'll help you look. Maybe over there."

"Make one false move and it will be your last."

"Chill out, commando. Someone needs to switch to decaf," Jim said. "We don't need any more brains blown out here. I don't think she's too dangerous."

Rita pointed to a closet in the wall; Bonnie opened it and found the three parachutes and took them out. "As I said, there are three."

"How the heck did you know that?" Jim asked.

"I . . . do not know, I looked at Tamara and simply knew it."

"Hell, you can't be serious. I know you've done this daredevil crap, but leave me out of it."

"Put it on. Now—or face a grisly death."

"No way. This isn't some football field you're used to—we're in the mountains. Who knows what's down there?"

"I know what is up *here*. Certain death and destruction."

"Yeah, thanks to your timely intervention."

"A superior fate to the one which awaits us in this aircraft."

He reluctantly put his parachute on as she opened the emergency door at 8,000 feet. "You can't be serious about bringing this gal with us. What the hell for?"

"She is one of their scientists, and can help explain what's in these cases. And I was unprepared before. Once, but never again." She placed the gun in her pocket out and motioned for the shorter Rita to put on the third parachute.

"I'm not doing it—I don't know how to do that," Rita cried.

"Trust me, this aircraft does not have a promising future. I will do everything in my power to make sure you are not harmed."

"I don't know how to do this, God—how will I pull the rip-cord?"

"You should be able to pull it, but I will stay with you until 2,500 feet, and will assist you with that. With some luck, you will drift to safety. If not, well, it hasn't been nice knowing you. Better odds than being up here, though, do you not think?"

"I don't know about that," Rita replied, as she looked out the window.

"It's pretty safe, but we need to avoid the mountains, however." She gathered her processors, the weapons, radios, two cell phones, and a backpack containing a metal briefcase—and proceeded to jump. "You two just stick with me. I've done this a lot."

"Why am I not surprised?" Jim asked.

Bonnie went back to the cockpit and released the autopilot, sending the plane into an eventual meeting with the Smoky Mountains. She pushed a screaming Rita from the doomed plane as Jim followed, and she finally departed, the destination hopefully a plain in western Virginia. She had done it many times before for charity stunts. But this was for real.

And the sensation was, as always, exhilarating. The acrobatic Bonnie Mendoza was flying again, just like in the old days, at terminal velocity of 120 miles per hour—the speed at which gravitational pull equaled atmospheric drag.

She could vaguely remember the last time she jumped for a charity stunt, about six years ago. But this time, there wouldn't be a crowd of onlookers below cheering her on.

Chapter Thirty–six

San Diego Police Department
San Diego, CA

"Jackie," Alex said as he looked at his laptop screen. "Bonnie's GPS just came back on line."

"Her GPS? What?"

"She has a Global Positioning System chip embedded in her right processor. To help her find her way around and so I can find her if she's lost."

"You mean like for people at high risk for kidnapping and such? How, and why now?"

"I assume that she was in a place with shielding and is now out of there. If her power is low, it doesn't penetrate an airplane hull."

"Where is she?"

"Eastern Wisconsin, near Lake Michigan."

"Why would she be there?"

"Must be something to do with Jay and football, that's the only connection." He smirked. "But I seriously doubt if she's there."

"What does that mean?"

"Jim's probably re-mapping the signal. She doesn't want us to know where she's at, and she's trying to lead us somewhere."

She laughed. "That's not possible. You don't understand how it works."

He smirked. "Jackie, I used to run a computer software company, and Jim's several orders of magnitude better than most of your federal buddies with computers. It's the only explanation, and, given who she's with, it's not only possible, but probable."

"Why the hell would she want us to go to Green Bay?"

"Don't know. I guess we'll find out when we get there. But there's only one reason that makes sense. It has something to do with Jaime Mendoza."

"Darkkin, I have one more question."

"Shoot."

"Don't you have a job at a hospital in Pasadena? How can you be gallivanting all over the place and not be accountable? They must be very understanding employers."

"Oh, that. They've been giving me a hard time all week, so I did what comes naturally."

"What?"

"I quit and told them to go straight to hell. Felt great."

• • •

12:00 AM
Somewhere in western Virginia

Bonnie, Rita, and Jim landed in the darkness of the Appalachian Mountains, in a large grassy valley. Bonnie landed about 150 feet away from the heavier Jim, who had landed first. Rita McPherson landed about 100 feet away with a thud. She headed up the hill to find them.

"Are you okay, James?" Bonnie yelled at her husband's friend, realizing then that he was probably too far away for her to "hear" his reply, anyway.

"Yeah, no thanks to you, stupid idiot. You could have gotten us killed. Oh, hell, you can't hear me, anyway."

"Very good." She, interestingly, understood his answer. She found the pair of handcuffs she had brought and cuffed Rita in front after removing her parachute, and proceeded to bury the chutes under some dirt.

"Whatever you are saying, I am certain it is a complaint about how I handled this. Did you have a better idea? Would you rather have stayed with the Argon people, going to do God knows what? I had to make an executive decision."

"*Executive decision?* I wouldn't trust you to mail a letter properly, let alone arrange something like this. I just want to know how you got that sound thing. Like something out of a spy movie."

She could make out most of what he said by reading lips. "I have many weird items. You know that, of course."

He grabbed her arm. "Hey, I'm neither stupid nor naïve, and that wasn't some sappy magic gadget—no one has something like that. I should know about illegal stuff."

She waved her arms. "Trust me, there may be some things you are better off not knowing. This would be one of them."

Jim looked around. "Right now, we need to get somewhere safe. Where the hell are we?" He punched himself in the head. "Ah, why I am I asking the woman who gets lost going around the block?"

She looked up at the sky and located Polaris (the North Star), the pinkish Jupiter just slightly southwest, stars Altair, Vega and Deneb just west of center, Aldebaran and Betelgeuse to the far east.

"Western Virginia, near the Tennessee border. Approximately midnight Eastern time, October second." After she knew the date, her "day aura" was reset, giving everything a kind of indigo tint. Days, like numerals, tended to follow the Newtonian colors of the spectrum: red, orange, yellow, green, blue, indigo, violet.

"How the hell you know that?" No answer. He then grabbed her and repeated his sentence to her face.

"The approximate location of Jupiter relative to the moon at this time can only be there. Crescent moon will not appear until 0100, 0200, across the ecliptic to the east." She took a pair of binoculars she had salvaged from the aircraft and peered at the giant gas planet, seeking the position of the four Galilean moons, which changed by the hour. "Yes, 0500 Greenwich Mean Time. Europa and Ganymede to the left, Callisto and Io to the right. All four visible."

"Right, if you say so. If you can navigate by the stars, how come you get lost driving around the block?"

"My directional problems are complex. I do not have time to explain presently."

"How can you see me so well to read lips in this near-darkness? I can barely see a thing."

"I have had much practice."

"And, for some reason, I can almost understand you now, most of the time. Maybe one gets used to it after a while."

"Shut up. You ask more questions than my husband."

Rita, not seeming to put up a fight, opened her mouth wide. "I never believed them, but the legends about you are true."

"She can't understand you if you're not looking at her," Jim said. "What's true? That she's the world's most brilliant jackass?"

"Her amazing mathematical abilities. There's no way anyone could memorize the positions of the stars or the Jovian moons. She has to be computing it, somehow."

He kicked a clump of dirt into the air. "Yeah, boy, that's a real useful talent. Useful at getting us into trouble," he said as Bonnie walked off confidently, singing some horribly off-key melody. "Who the hell cares?"

"Don't you understand? That's what we wanted to look at, the genetic potential of those abilities."

Jim grabbed the manacled woman. "Listen to me, lady. I'm happy you're so enamored of *Mendoza the Miraculous*' savant-like abilities. They're really useful in a casino, I hear. But wait a while before you pass final judgment on the quality of her decision-making. We're damn lucky to be alive at all; it doesn't mean shit if we're dead."

They walked to an old barn next to a farmhouse, and discovered a 1960s pickup truck inside. "I assume, since you are my husband's friend, that you are skilled in mischief and know how to illicitly start this decrepit old vehicle?"

He rubbed his hands together. "Now you're talking. Where we going?"

"We are going west, to an open plain. The current mountainous area does not meet my requirements."

"West—that's toward Tennessee, if our position's right. What the hell is there, of all places?" Jim laughed as he worked on hot-wiring the Chevy pickup as they placed Rita in the middle. "If you really want to get crazy, we could go visit—"

"Like I stated—you are better off not knowing certain things."

He stared at her. "Oh, hell, how could I have been so dumb—you planned this all along." He grabbed her and stared into her face. "Answer me—you wanted to land here, didn't you?"

She read his lips, as her processors' power was finally exhausted. "I did not plan to be abducted, especially with you, of all people.

But, like any organism, I must attempt to make the best of any situation in order to survive. The current coordinates seemed our most likely chance for the timely recovery of Wendy."

"But, eastern Tennessee—you can't be serious. We're in the middle of frickin' nowhere."

"*De duobus malis, minus est semper eligendum.*" She pointed at him with her right index finger.

"Don't speak Spanish, sorry."

"Latin—'of two evils, the lesser must be chosen.' Do you not agree?"

"Would you stop spouting the stupid quotes? What is it that compels you to do that?" The truck finally turned over.

"If you have a better idea, now is the time to speak up, eh?"

"Uh, don't have one. I'll work on it, though."

"Then silence would be best. But, hopefully, the associates of our abductors believe us to be dead. I have a tentative host in mind, who is good at staying, 'off the grid,' as you say?"

"He's a damn paranoid crazy man, if he's even still alive. How you even gonna find him?"

"A paranoid crazy man with money, a place to hide, and millions of dollars' worth of technology, as I understand. Beggars cannot be choosers, especially in rural Tennessee. And, rest assured, *he* will find *us*."

"I'm going to my happy place to think about something else." Jim gulped for a minute. "Alex made me promise one thing to him on your wedding day."

She put her hands on her hips. "What was that, may I ask?"

"That I was to help take care of you, no matter what happens."

"Humph—I do not need caring for. I can do anything."

He laughed heartily. "I don't think so. You have abilities, but some pretty damn big deficits. If you're in this, I'm in it too, and I'm not going to let you do something suicidal. Stupid, maybe, but not that."

"We probably will be doing both, I regret to inform you."

She removed the two lithium batteries she had cannibalized from their captors' cell phones and sat down in the truck to wire them into her processors; they were well out of the range of cell phone service, so they were useless."This makeshift battery pack must suffice until

I can properly recharge. Fortunately, the voltage is equivalent—8.4 volts."

"You're worried about *hearing* now? You act like you 'hear' me somewhat, anyway. Maybe it's my imagination."

She looked at him angrily. "If I desire to power my devices, it is none of your beeswax. Have an open mind." She pushed the power buttons and now had about an hour of power, she estimated. But she didn't give a hoot about hearing right now; she needed the power for something far more important.

"What's the stuff in that case?" He pointed to the gun-metal Zero Halliburton briefcase Bonnie had strapped to her back.

"I do not know. It is locked."

"That's never stopped you before. Why'd you bring it, anyway? Who cares?"

"I decided it must contain something valuable."

"You have X-ray vision now, too?"

"Quiet." She pointed to the fingerprint pad on the top of the case. "The lock is biometric—I do not have time to deal with it currently. We will have plenty of time at our destination."

"Which is where, exactly? It might be nice to know."

"It might be better if you did not."

"I sure hope it's a surprise."

She started laughing. "We are in for a fun adventure, that is all I can share with you at this time."

Jim laughed back nervously. "I have kind of a dumb question."

"What?"

"Why are we laughing? We don't seem to have a real promising future here. Have you been taking happy pills like WW?"

"Have faith, best friend of my spouse. It is better to laugh than to cry. Felines often purr when contented, but also when in danger, to calm themselves, and, to make a parallel argument, laughter may be soothing as well as—"

"We are in for one long night." He put the crappy vehicle into gear as they drove out of the barn, the occupants of the farmhouse seemingly oblivious to the fact that an odd trio had just stolen their prize plow truck. Luckily, the noise of the old engine was sufficient to drown out the incessant jabbering of the peculiar, slow-spoken physicist.

Chapter Thirty–seven

San Diego Police Department
San Diego, CA

"Alex," Jackie Levickis said. "A Gulfstream was found crashed into a mountain somewhere in western Virginia about twelve hours ago. Air traffic controller said it looked like it was headed east, then diverted south and crashed there. Coast Guard is on the scene. I'm sorry, it looks like your wife might have been inside."

"Oh, shit. What'd they find?"

"Side door torn off. Four dead inside, bodies burned beyond recognition. Three look like they suffered gunshot wounds. Another with his neck broken. It could have been flown on autopilot for a while with the door off."

"Why would they think Bonnie was inside?"

"Dental records of one of the mandibles they recovered match hers, on preliminary reports."

"I don't believe it. Who owns the plane?"

"Weird. It's owned by some government-contracted biotech lab called Argotech Industries."

"Argotech—what the hell's that? It rings a bell somehow."

"Some place that used to do secret biotech research for the government. Got a call from Ken Thornton. You know Ken, don't you? He's director of cyber crime now for the FBI, and an old friend of Bonnie's dad, I heard."

He frowned. "Uh, yeah. Know old Ken pretty well. I don't know why Bonnie or Jim would have anything to do with a place called

Argotech, though."

"He said there was something else you might know something about. They found some weird set of handcuffs with these orange cylindrical locks. I've seen pictures of them before. Why would he mention that?"

He put his hands over his face. "Those are pretty odd ones, I think . . . it can't be possible, but with her, you never know."

"I'm sorry about Bonnie, Alex. If it's true . . ."

"I've learned one thing in the last few years. Don't ever count that lady out. If she's alive, you've got one of the most dangerous human beings in the world out there somewhere, along with my friend who has a great knack for mischief."

"But the dental records—"

"May be totally faked. You don't know that person like I do. They're playing a hunch. But we need to stop them before they get into something way over their heads."

• • •

Two hours later, a fatigued Alex stared at the disgusting green murky suspension of what once might have been considered coffee, as he noticed his cell phone ringing. He spied the Caller ID on his cell phone and woke up with surprise, knowing that the caller rarely used them (or conventional telephones, for that matter) without special accessories.

"Bonnie? What the hell?"

"It is I, husband. I cannot talk long—just wanted to let you know I am alive. Well and alive."

Jackie came up to him. "Trace this call. Stall for time, if you want to help her, Alex."

He nodded. "Where are you?"

"Sheboygan." He knew that she must be using her direct processor interface, since she couldn't "hear" through a normal transceiver. "Very cold up here. I have forgotten how much."

"Call identified, originating from a cell in Sheboygan, Wisconsin. Get a team to the location," Jackie commanded to the agent on the other end of the phone.

"Where's Jim?" he asked.

"James is safe as well. I will see you soon."

"Wait a minute. I need to know for sure that it's you."

"Humph. Of course it is your wife. And tell our noble acquaintance that I will soon deliver his fullers' soap with the brass ring, and tote his seven elements back to him. And tote the seventeenth product to your hand."

He knew she was speaking too fast. That unnerved him. "I don't believe you. Tell me something only you would know."

"Yes, that is only fair. Tell my mother my violet friend Oogly-Googly has come back to visit me after all these years."

"What? Hello?" The call terminated.

Jackie chimed in. "The call came from a cell phone in eastern Wisconsin."

He thought pensively for a moment. "That's where the GPS said she was, but that doesn't mean she's there."

"Mind telling me why she would be in cheese country?"

"I don't want to tell you your business, Jackie," he said, drinking his coffee, "but the likelihood of that call actually coming from there is almost zero. And that can't have been Bonnie, who has difficulty using conventional phones. The speech was too clear and too fast. Must've been faked, just like with Wendy."

Jackie laughed. "They traced it there. That and GPS signals can't be altered."

"If she and Jim Krakowski are involved, they could be anywhere. You don't think they'd be so stupid as to tell you their true location, do you? Jim knows stuff that would make you guys salivate."

She grabbed his arm. "Look, Darkkin, your wife and hacker buddy are in a heap of trouble if they crashed that jet. It belonged to a government contractor, dammit. They're close to being fugitives at this point."

"They were kidnapped, doesn't that count for anything?"

"We have no proof, just like we have none that your sister was abducted. Is your whole family off their rocker?"

"Bonnie's previous career was in law enforcement. Don't you think she knows that? If it's really her, she's playing a hunch."

"We still need to know what they're up to. If you have *any* idea, Darkkin–"

He grabbed her by the arm. "Look, I don't—she may not even be still alive. That's one mind I've never been able to figure out, it's way out of my league." His only hope was that Jim could keep her on the straight and narrow, wherever they were. What was her plan?

"We need to do something. What was the purple thing she was talking about?"

"I have a vague idea, but she often likes to talk cryptically, in riddles. So that we know what's going on, but not too quickly. We need to make a trip."

"Where?"

"Whatever is up there, we need to find out, and the area she mentioned can't simply be a coincidence. How do you like Wisconsin this time of year?"

"Never been there."

"The brats are great, I hear. Right after we make a little side trip to my in-laws' place."

"Your in-laws' home? Why go there?"

"Her phone call was pretty weird—some cryptic things which are likely mathematical in nature. Way over my head, and I'm pretty smart. I only know one person who's even close to her in that department."

"You have some pretty strange family members."

He laughed. "Trust me, we're just scratching the surface. But my main question is this—"

"What?"

"Where on Earth is Bonnie Mendoza?"

Chapter Thirty-eight

Mendoza Flores Residence
5644 Ocean View Rd.
San Diego, CA

Alex and Jackie drove down the suburban side street as he pulled his car up to the driveway of the well-appointed ranch home in San Diego. They exited and went up to the door at 12:30 AM.

Jackie looked around. "*This* is your in-laws' home? Pretty upscale for a couple of academics."

"Yeah. Bonnie's grandmother was a pretty famous musician and composer in Mexico. Always good to have a son and daughter who are millionaires, too."

"Damn, I guess."

The five–seven, early-sixtyish woman answered the door a few minutes later and gave him a hug. "Alex, come in, please. I've been worried to death."

"Thanks. Elisa, meet Drug Enforcement Agency Special Agent Jackie Levickis. Jackie, this is my mother-in-law, Elisabeth Flores." The two women shook hands.

"Alex, you sounded so urgent on the phone. Do we know anything else?"

"Not really. You know about what's happened so far."

"Yes, I know. Carlos has been talking to the police for two days. But you said she called you on a cell."

"It sounded like her, but . . . the speech was too clear and fast. You know how slowly she talks, especially on the phone, if she can use it at all. She's been using my speech-translator computer device recently."

"Of course. Who do you think it was? An impostor?"

"We ran voiceprints on it, Mrs. Flores, using sophisticated methods your daughter herself designed," Jackie said. "The prints are a match. The rate and clarity are a bit better than we'd expect, but her peculiar usage of the English language is rather difficult to emulate. The computer simulated what she should sound like with more 'normal' speech, and it matched." They came into the living room and sat on the couch.

"Her speech is far from normal. It's about half the normal rate, and often difficult to understand. But it is hard to duplicate that voice."

"I know, we're playing a hunch here," he said.

"You said you needed to ask me about something."

"Yeah, it's pretty bizarre, but I asked her to tell me something only she'd know, and she said to ask you about this."

"What?"

"Something about a purple friend coming back to visit, one she hadn't seen in years. Sounds pretty weird, even for Bonnie, if it even was her. Do you know what she's talking about?"

Elisa stared out into space for a few seconds and turned pale. "Purple friend—are you *certain* that's what she said?"

"Yeah. I recorded it and played it back. Why?"

Her mouth opened wide. "You both need to come upstairs. I have to show you something."

They went up the staircase to a storage area, and Elisa pulled out several boxes.

"What's this stuff?" the DEA agent asked.

"Some of Bonnie's old things from long ago. We didn't live here, of course, then, but I kept some of her things after she and Alex got married." They hurriedly perused the many cardboard boxes which were stacked on the floor.

After ten minutes, Elisa finally found the box she was looking for, one which contained many drawings, scribblings, and other things.

"Look at this one." Elisa handed him a poorly-drawn crayon drawing of a young, dark-haired girl standing in a field with a rainbow, with a purple mass on her arm. "Drew it when she was five."

Jackie grimaced. "It's pretty bad, and looks like a two-year-old drew it. She wasn't a very good artist, was she?"

"Horrible is the word for it. But read the poem."

Oogly-Googly is my purple friend
He comes out and visits me now and then
He is without arms, legs, or even a rib
But he jumps up and down when I hear a fib
Oogly-Googly is special to me
No one else can see him, not even my family
I wish you could see *mi amigo* too
He has special powers so true

By Bonita M.
Age 5

"What is it? An imaginary friend?" he asked. "There was that purple blob guy on *Wendy's Science Squad*. Was it the same character?"

"Yes, the purple guy on the TV show paid homage to the real one. Except only Bonnie could actually see the genuine one."

"What . . . is it?" Jackie asked. "I don't understand this."

"Bonnie was always a challenge to us. Having a profoundly gifted child brings its own special challenges, like any 'special needs' child—long before she became deaf. We thought it was an imaginary friend, initially, and humored her. But she kept drawing purple blobs on paper, like any child would draw her surroundings."

"A hallucination?" Jackie asked.

"Not quite. As you know, I am a high-order grapheme-color synesthete, as was my mother. Bonnie and my oldest son are as well, but she has the rarer gustatory and olfactory variety, too. Most synesthestes have differing abilities. Mother was a great musical prodigy. Jaime is an excellent artist but terrible at math. Bonnie and I, to a much lesser extent, have the mathematical and language skills. I was a national Scrabble champion."

"So? I know all that, so why is that important, Elisa?" he asked, growing impatient. He realized where Bonnie inherited the tendency to ramble on about inane bits of peculiar trivia, requiring much filtration and distillation to extract what was important.

"Because of my synesthesia, I had seen several experts in the past, and we had Bonnie see the best. They thought that the blob was a synesthetic manifestation of the most vivid of her childhood senses, the one that imparted exceptional abilities that dwarf what she can do today."

"Which sense?"

"The one she lost, of course—hearing. As you may or may not know, Jaime has some synesthete abilities, particularly *deja vu*, which some people feel to be a form of clairvoyance. Mike, by all accounts, has no abilities, nor does Carlos. The pre-deaf Bonnie had the ability to always know if someone was telling the truth or not. The purple 'friend' would always appear and tell her if someone was lying. It was very creepy."

"You're kidding," Jackie said. "That's impossible, it's just some magic trickery."

"But it's true. Like a lie detector, which detects minor changes in voice, galvanic current, and voice inflection, she could somehow tell. They did experiments with several sets of identical twins. The twins would tell her the wrong names, and there was no way any human being unfamiliar with them could tell them apart with natural senses—but she could in an instant. You have no idea what trouble she got into. The fights at home, the friends she lost. And, to some extent, the ability to predict the near future."

"This thing was real to her?" he asked.

"Yes, but it was never disturbing—she described it as a helpful friend. Oogly-Googly represented the highest level of synesthetic ability achievable by a human being—an actual synesthetic brain construct. It had shape and texture, and, to her, life."

"And I assume that, after she lost her hearing, she couldn't perceive it any longer."

"Correct. She knows of its existence, but it has no real significance, since she can't remember anything. The artificial 'hearing' produced by the cochlear implants apparently can't reproduce it."

"Or can they?"

"That's impossible, Alex. She's had two severe brain injuries. Her mind's largely blank to what happened before age eleven. She had to re-learn everything—speech, how to walk, talk, all of it."

"How many other people would know about this? Wendy?"

"Wendy wouldn't know, as she didn't meet Bonnie until she was thirteen, about 1989. Jaime and Mike would remember. Maybe some old teachers and doctors she saw."

"She's an amazing scientist even without those skills. But with them—"

"She would be a pained and troubled soul, Alex. The visions she saw—she visualized her own illness and pain days before it happened. Didn't know what it was, but she could see the pain, and there was nothing we could do to help her. Losing her hearing was a horrible loss, but you have to take the good with the bad. The loss of that cursed power was a blessing. But the doctors said her hearing would never regenerate."

"I suppose that's one way of looking at it," he said.

"Something else you should know. The doctors never could obtain absolute proof, as it's pretty controversial, but Jaime said he and Bonnie had a special way of communicating."

"Huh? What 'special way?' Secret codes or something?"

"Much more than that. He would, in his dreams, see lifelike visions of her. Talking, interacting, telling him things."

"We all see our loved ones in our dreams, Elisa. You can't possibly believe in out-of-body experiences."

"Not like this, Alex. Carlos and I are both educated people, and don't believe in the paranormal either, but Bonnie could tell us exactly what she told him in a dream, and he could remember it—even if they were separated by hundreds of miles."

"How is that possible?"

"There's no logical explanation, but some scientists believe that very strong synesthetes have psychoportive powers. At least one psychologist thought that Bonnie did."

"*Psychoportive*? You mean like astral projection? That's impossible," he said. "No way."

"Perhaps. But, if Oogly-Googly lives again, and Jay wakes up, it may be a means to communicate with her."

"I certainly hope he does wake up, but I don't believe in phantoms." He stood up and walked around the sofa for a few seconds. "One more thing—she said something about some noble person and 'fullers' soap' before she hung up. Is that a brand of soap she used?"

Elisa thought for a moment. "Fullers' soap? Now *that's* very interesting."

"Why? What is it?"

Elisa pulled out an old black book from one of the boxes. "Bonnie read ravenously as a child and pretty much memorized everything. Knew this classic by heart." She handed Alex the dog-eared book.

"A King James Bible."

"Correct. A fuller is a launderer—in ancient times, one who, for example, washed priests' robes. Fullers' soap is made from alkali, left from the ashes of various plants, which contain potassium hydroxide."

He grumbled. "What is the point?"

Elisa squinted at him. "Why, Malachi, of course!"

"Malachi? What the heck's that? A plant?"

Elisa laughed. "No, a book of the Old Testament. You don't know your scriptures very well, do you?"

"Uh, guess not," he said sheepishly. "Got some catching up to do, it seems."

"There is no time like the present." Elisa thumbed through the old book. "Here it is, Malachi 3:2: '*But who may abide the day of his coming? And who shall stand when he appeareth? For he is like a refiner's fire, and like fullers' soap.*' Curious."

He shook his head. "That's meaningless to me. Refineries and soap? Is she referring to the prophet's name, Malachi, or the numbers? What does 'noble' mean? A king or queen?"

"Don't know, Alex. Puzzles are your thing, I heard."

"She also mentioned something about 'toting seven elements,' I think—whatever that means."

"Toting seven elements. Hmmm," Elisa said as she walked around. "I remember . . . something she really liked as a child."

"What's that, pray tell?" he asked.

"She was really into Euler's totient number function."

"A what?" Jackie said. "I just liked to play with Barbies."

Elisa's eyes opened wide, beaming with excitement. "Leonhard Euler's totient numbers. In number theory, the totient of a positive integer is defined to be the number of positive integers less than or equal to n, that are coprime to n."

"I was really into that stuff, too," Jackie replied sarcastically. "Whatever the heck it is."

Elisa found a tablet of paper and began scribbling numbers. "See, there are many perfect totients, where the sum equals n. The first eight are 3, 9, 15, 27, 39, 81, 111, and 183. 'Toting seven' could mean the seventh totient, or 111."

"111," Alex said. "As I understand, 111 has much significance in numerology."

"Correct. 111 is the smallest repunit composite number and the smallest palindromic number such that the sum of its digits is one of its prime factors, among other things."

"Fantastic. She also said something about the seventeenth, too. What's the seventeenth perfect totient?"

"3,063," Elisa replied instantly. "No logical meaning to me."

"What about elements?" he asked. "She could mean chemical elements, I suppose."

"Atomic number 111?" Elisa asked back. "I'm a mathematician, and don't know anything above 107, bohrium."

His mouth opened wide. "I do. 111 is roentgenium, one of the transuranium, or super-heavy, atoms. Discovered in 1994. Damn."

"So what?" Jackie asked, shaking her head. "What does that have to do with anything?"

He nodded. "It has to do with a lot, because roentgenium was named after Wilhelm Conrad Röntgen."

"*Röntgen?* Oh, no," Elisa said in a desperate tone. "Please don't say that. Let's pray it means something else."

"Unfortunately, I don't believe that to be the case."

"Huh?" Jackie shook her head. "Can't say I've ever heard of the dude. You two have lost me once again."

"Röntgen was a physicist who died in 1923. Discovered the X-ray. But someone else I know always said he was named after him."

"Who?"

"My illustrious, super-heavy father. Crap."

"Your dad was named after some dead physicist? I thought your grandparents made whiskey."

He snickered. "No, it's just a coincidence, but he brags he was really named after the guy. But this *has* to have something to do with him—and that's not a good thing."

"Why is that worse than anything else that's happened?" Jackie asked.

"Just trust me on this one."

"Alex is right," Elisa said. "Where are you going now?"

"Green Bay. Bonnie, or whoever, wants us to go there. Whatever for, I have no idea."

"*Abide by the day of his coming, and who shall stand when he appeareth*? It sounds almost like a threat, Alex. You had best be careful," Elisa said. "She's a juggernaut once she gets going. Can't be stopped."

"Yeah, don't I know."

"You may be way off base, Alex," Jackie said.

"But let's get going. How much trouble can we possibly get into there?"

Chapter Thirty–nine

1:20 AM
Fowler's Bar and Grill
141 Zinctown Drive
Solway, TN

Fowler's Bar, located in the small town of Solway, Tennessee (population 754), was relatively quiet in the wee hours of the humid Saturday morning. The small town, about twenty miles south of Oak Ridge, had few attractions, and this establishment didn't draw too many crowds from surrounding counties.

The few people inside were nursing their beer and whiskey, and a few men were sitting around playing music. The group seemed to center around the six–five, scraggly-bearded man with shoulder-length gray hair, who obviously commanded the respect of his drunken colleagues. A cigarette dangled from his mouth as he busily picked a mandolin, while another shorter, dark-haired man was downing shots of vodka while playing chess with a skinny, sixty–five year-old man at a musty table. The bizarre bluegrass song seemed to have a gospel tone, and its lyrics described man's destruction at the hands of the atomic bomb, one of the lead player's favorites.

Another, obese, six–four man was picking a banjo. Fowler's wasn't one of your better establishments, and was a watering hole where cigarette butts and peanut shells covered the musty old hardwood floor. But the clientele seemed to remain the same most of the time. The rusty old sign greeting visitors at the door dictated the establishment's zero-star service policy, and read as follows:

THIS AIN'T YOUR KIND OF PLACE
IF WE DAMN WELL PLEASE
WE'LL SERVE YOU RATTLESNAKES
YOU DON'T GET IT YOUR WAY
YOU GET IT OUR WAY
IF YOU DON'T LIKE OUR WAY
YOU CAN GET THE @#!%& OUT!

Ralph "~~Lefty~~" "Righty" Fowler, Proprietor

"Hey, Dusty," Rad Darkkin said to his brother. "Get with it, you ain't pickin' very well."

The seventy–year-old, porcine man yelled out. "Well, okay, Rad, you don't have to start no fight over it."

"I'll start whatever I damn well please." Rad knocked over a chair and shoved his shorter brother in the chest.

"Rad, don't start no fight with your bro again," the short, obese, one-armed bartender said. "You guys should get along, and I don't want nothin' broke in my bar."

He gestured with his long arms, making a sweeping motion. "How would one determine if something's broken or not in this shit-hole? And I get your booze for free, Righty, so shut the hell up."

"Yeah, well, I'll call Sheriff Rodney if you don't simmer down. And you guys drink most of the booze and don't pay for it, so where's my benefit? Fat Dusty here just eats my food."

"Aw, shaddup," Dusty retorted.

"This swill ain't food, you shit-assed, one-armed bastard," Rad replied. "And you water down my whiskey by hooking it up to those soda taps. Rodney's probably drunk, anyway."

The vodka-drinking man rejoiced as he captured his unchallenging opponent's queen with his rook. "You will never beat me, even though I am full of this inferior American vodka, my friend," the dark-haired man replied in a Russian accent to his tall, spindly opponent. "Checkmate again."

Rad stood up and ground out his cigarette on the floor. "Hell, that's nothing to brag about. Even Righty's three-legged, one-eyed cat could beat Smiley at chess. The dude barely has enough brain cells left to qualify as a eukaryote."

"Rad, why is the owner called Righty? Such a peculiar name."

"We used to call him Lefty, until the poor SOB lost his left arm in that auger accident." He was nearly oblivious to the electronic device which began beeping on the rusty old metal table.

The sixty–five-year-old, spindly man rose from the chess table, looked at it and pointed to Rad. "Rad, man, this thing's goin' off. What the hell is it? A cell phone?"

"Shut the hell up, Smiley," he said to his cousin. "It's my satellite communicator. Get away from it, you fried-brain dumb ass."

"Satellite? Some high-fallootin' spy thing? Well, you better look at it," Zack "Smiley" Darkkin replied curiously.

"Shit, must be some damn interference again." Rad picked up the palm-sized device and looked at it. "Well, I'll be goddammed. It's about time—I was about to give up."

"What the hell's goin' on, Rad? You get back to pickin', you yelled at me for it." Dusty Darkkin said angrily.

"Quiet, dummy." He put on his reading glasses and looked at the high-tech device, distinctly out of place in such a seedy establishment, and threw Righty Fowler a fifty–dollar bill. "Here's for my Pepsi, you cheap shit. I got more important things to do." He knew his IQ probably exceeded the IQ sum of the other men in the room, excluding his Russian buddy.

"Finally, we do something of value, you stupid old derelict," Viktor Vladimirov said. "We have been waiting weeks for your promised moment of glory. What else does a poor broken-down soldier have to look forward to in this God-forsaken place?"

"Yeah, we gotta fire up the chopper. Good thing I ain't wasted, usually I'd be too drunk to fly."

"What is our destination, my friend?"

"Virginia."

Viktor began singing the Soviet national anthem. "Long live the Soviet motherland, built by the people's mighty hand—"

"Quit singin' that commie song, Vik, and get in the damn truck. It's time to see if your little toy really works."

Viktor put his arm around his larger friend's shoulder. "*Our* toy, Rad, ours. The magnificent brainchild of two old, forgotten warriors, discarded by their governments, working on a secret project they deemed unworthy. We built it together."

"You drunken shit—it had just better work, that's all. Dusty, let's go. You're riding shotgun, after we drop Vik off at the Cave to get the shit powered up and ready."

"I will not let you down. My greatest creation shall be ready, my friend."

• • •

3:00 AM
Somewhere in western Virginia

Jim turned as he heard the military surplus helicopter off in the distance. Bonnie turned suddenly as well, although the aircraft was not yet visible in the dim moonlight.

"What the heck is that?" he said.

"Are you blind? They must know we're here," Bonnie said.

"No, I'm not blind, but you're deaf, and I can't see it yet. How do you know it's even there?" Jim asked curiously.

"It must be Argon's men, Mendoza," Rita said. "They've found us. We're dead."

She laughed. "Rita, the helicopter may be military issue, but I assure you that the person inside is unfit to serve in the armed forces. Like I said earlier, something is better than nothing, I think."

The chopper descended and finally landed in the deserted field, and its occupants turned off the engine and opened the doors.

"Not anything I recognize. Who the hell is it?" Jim asked.

She turned around. "Duh! The GPS in my implant is capable of being tracked."

"By the police? The military?" Rita asked.

Jim grabbed Bonnie by the arm. "So *that's* why you put those cannibalized cell phone batteries in your processors—to power the GPS. But you wanted it remapped to Wisconsin. What good is that?"

"It will be useful to one individual."

"I assume that 'individual' is not your husband, Lt. Mike, or that hot-looking DEA agent. I wonder if she's single."

"No, another person. My GPS unit would not work in Argon's plane, which had shielding. But it's neither the military nor the police. It might help solve the riddle as to where my weapons came from, since you are so curious."

Jim opened his mouth as the ursine figure, in his late sixties, exited the chopper along with his slightly smaller brother. Jim stared at the familiar duo for a few seconds, then pointed at her in disbelief.

"I knew it. *This* is your brilliant plan, the best that stellar IQ of 190 could come up with—the Darkkin brothers? We should've just stayed in that plane and taken our chances there."

The bizarre figure of Rad Darkkin stepped forward, "Heh . . . that was pretty cool. That jet made a pretty fucking good explosion when it hit the mountain, I bet."

"Yes, I am certain it was quite spectacular, Conrad. About two hundred miles from here. Males always like to see objects burn and explode."

"Yeah. 'He dares to be a fool, and that is, heh, one step in the direction of wisdom.' A quotation from James Gibbons. Good to see you again, too. What's it, heh, been, ten years?"

"Fourteen. It has not been long enough."

Rad puckered his lips. "Does your father-in-law get a kiss?"

She jumped five feet through the air, grabbed his shirt, and knocked him to the ground. "Kiss me, Conrad Darkkin, and it shall be your last. I will tolerate pubescent shenanigans from neither you nor your drunken brother." Dusty backed away quickly.

"Heh—just kidding." Bonnie let him up as he turned to Jim and extended his hand. "Jimmy, old pal, what's up?"

"Same 'ol, same 'ol, Rad. Interesting and convenient time to show up. You too, Dusty. Long time no see."

"Yeah," Dusty replied. "I don't know what crazy shit bro's got cooked up, but I ain't seen him this fired up in twenty years."

"As I said . . . the lesser of two evils," she said.

"Who's this lady?" Rad asked, pointing to the handcuffed Rita. "This the only way you could get a girlfriend, Jim? Tie one up?"

"She is a government scientist who works for Malachi Argon. We hope that she will be more help than hindrance in our brave quest."

"Malachi Argon?" Rad's eyes opened wide. "That bastard of shit! You should be careful who you, heh, work for, little lady. It can get you killed," Rad laughed. "Get you killed, get it?"

"What the hell are we going to do now?" Jim asked in a frustrating tone. "Hide out at the distillery? The damn cops are probably looking for us. Please tell me you've thought this through."

"Well, heh, don't blame me for any of this crap. You tell him, sweetie, how I ended up here."

"Yeah, I'm not stupid. You arranged it ahead of time, didn't you, Bonnie?" Jim said to her.

"Humph. Not entirely. Providence happened to put the trajectory of our ill-fated plane over this vicinity of Appalachia. I did know that Conrad was probably monitoring the frequency of my GPS."

"Why would he have been doing that, pray tell?"

"You asked about the sonic weapon device . . . surely you would not believe that I, who is always prepared, to embark on a hazardous mission without adequate defenses."

"Alex know about this?"

"Of course not, as he certainly would not have approved. He might have attempted to deter me in some fashion."

"I might've, too. Thanks for telling me."

"A moot point, as it is now too late."

"It's too late for everybody, I think."

"Heh, get the hell in. Lotsa room," Rad said.

The strange group climbed into the helicopter as Rad flew them back to the "helicopter hangar," an old Quonset hut about ten miles from their true destination. They exited the chopper and entered the old blue 1986 Chevy Caprice station wagon awaiting inside.

"Nice ride, Rad," Jim said as the musty vehicle screeched out of the decrepit building, leaving a cloud of dust behind. "I see you went all out. The Bentley must be in the shop."

"What, you want me to have a, heh, BMW or Hummer out here? Have to be inconspicuous, you know that," Rad said. "This sucker's a revamped, ten-cylinder police interceptor with 420 horsepower. It'll do 185, you underestimate it. Like my helicopter and souped-up van, it absorbs radar, and can't be detected by the smokeys."

"It is primitive, yet suits our purpose," Bonnie said. "I can drive, if Conrad is too inebriated."

"I'll take a drunk Rad over you any day," Jim said.

"Hell, don't worry—I'm sober as a judge, missy. We'll drop Dusty off at the distillery, though. He's got an early board meeting."

• • •

After dropping Dusty off at the D.T. Darkkin & Sons Distillery, the group drove to Rad's "secret warehouse," about two miles west of the factory. They pulled up to the old barn as dawn broke on the Tennessee horizon.

"This is it, Conrad?" Bonnie said, looking at the old barn through the station wagon's passenger window. "The legendary, fabulous Röntgen-Cave? I expected much more."

"Yeah, doesn't look like much, but you of all people should know about illusions, hon. Just you wait."

"I am not your 'hon,' you irritating man," she said in a slightly lower, faster voice than usual. "Watch your tone with me."

Rad pushed a remote control button as the door to the old, yellowing barn door rose. They drove inside as the door closed. "Over here." They walked to the elevator shaft and went inside.

"How long has this fantastic complex been here?" Jim asked. "The Stone Age?"

"Built it in, heh, the late seventies. Needed a private workshop. There are things in here nobody knows about."

Rad opened a secret door after placing his palm on a biometric reading device. They then went down an old elevator and traveled down to the subterranean complex, about twenty feet below the surface.

"Rad, how the hell did you build all this?" Jim asked as he looked around.

"Wasn't cheap, I'll tell you that. Cost me, heh, several million bucks. And there ain't no financing available for this."

"You *are* a lunatic," she said. "Just as I had hoped."

Rad opened the door as they went into the main room. "Well, here it is, folks. Forty–thousand square feet of workspace, on two levels. Living area, kitchen, fully wired for Internet access. Plenty of water, food, booze, and cigarettes."

"Thank goodness," Jim said. "I need a cigarette bad."

"I did not know you smoked, James. An unhealthy habit."

Jim shook his head. "I don't, but I think I'm going to start. That and some hooch may help numb the pain of all this craziness."

"How do you power this?" she asked. "I saw no power wires,

and we seem to be far from the service area of any power utility."

"Heh, the distillery powers most of it, since we're tied into their power grid. Also underground LP gas and geothermics as a backup. I toyed with the concept of nuclear power for a while, but that seemed a little too dangerous and high-maintenance. I did develop a nuclear plane prototype once, but the feds were too worried about people dying if it crashed, the spineless shits."

"What do you do down here?" Jim asked. "Do I even want to know?"

"Work on things I don't want anyone to know about. Me and Vik creating history."

"Who?" Jim asked as the graying, bearded, scar-faced Russian man came into the room.

"Let me introduce my old comrade Viktor Vladimirov." The stocky man shook hands with Jim and Bonnie.

"I am honored to meet such a brilliant fellow scientist," Viktor said as he kissed her hand. "And beautiful, too."

"I have heard much about you as well," she said. "Stellar electronics expert and physical chemist. You were working on adaptive bionics for the Soviet military. You also created the amazing device which disabled out captors on the airplane."

"Yes, young lady. Unfortunately, the great Soviet regime collapsed, with no more money for Viktor and his unique experiments. I am fortunate to have been befriended by one such as Rad."

"We gave him asylum here, but he's still a stinking commie—I don't trust him," Rad said as they both broke out into laughter.

"Where is it?" she asked. "We're wasting time."

"Where is . . . what?" Jim asked. "Everyone's being pretty cryptic here."

"Let's go. Something you, heh, won't believe."

"What about Rita?" Jim asked.

"Hell, let her see it, too. What's she gonna do?"

"She'll probably wish we had left her up in that Gulfstream."

Chapter Forty

The Röntgen-Cave
Solway, TN

"So, this is it, then? It is pretty hideous," Bonnie said, staring at the six–two grey metallic suit held aloft by steel cables in one of Rad's workshop rooms. She had improved "hearing" after restoring her processors' power, and the earlier problems with progressive decline in implant function seemed to have stopped, for some reason. "However, there is no color. It is also smaller and less bulky than I had imagined."

"You're the last person who should be criticizing another's fashion sense," Jim said.

"Hell, this ain't no fashion show, and it's designed to absorb radar and reflect as little visible light as possible. It wasn't designed for looks, dearie. And it's built for speed, not power, to collimate vast amounts of information and process it faster than anyone ever thought possible."

She stared at it intensely. "What weapons does it contain?"

"Shit, it contains the most advanced weapons known to mankind. Some conventional artillery, one gauntlet shoots a limited number of plasma energy blasts; the other, focused EMP."

She stared at the dull, dark grey alloy of the armor's body. "Your claims are impressive. What is its composition? Fullerene-based, I gather, from my initial inspection."

"Yep. The outer shell is laminated C60 fullerite-coated titanium-ruthenium alloy, with an inner core of aggregated diamond nanorods. The hardest damn thing known to man. It'll laugh at a rocket launcher."

She knew that ultrahard fullerite (C60) was even harder than diamond, the former possessing a hardness of 330 GPa (gigapascals); the hardest diamond was only about 230 GPa. The core of aggregated diamond nanorods (ADNR) was the hardest substance known to man, with an isothermal bulk modulus of 491 GPa—over *twice* as hard as diamond. For its mass, it was the strongest substance in the universe. And one of the most *expensive*.

"I don't believe it. You guys are crazy," Jim said.

"Perhaps—but many great inventors were thought to be insane," Viktor said. "I was persecuted for my own theories."

"Hell, check this out." Rad pulled a Colt 45 revolver from his pocket and fired a shot at the suit, as Jim and Bonnie hit the floor.

"You will kill us, you hillbilly dolt! What if the ricochet had struck us?" she exclaimed.

"Heh, not likely. Look where the bullet is." It was on the floor, she saw, right next to it; if it had ricocheted, the force of the point-blank shot would have sent it across the room. "The force is distributed very evenly, resulting in efficient dissipation of small-arms fire."

She examined the slug with the trained eye of a ballistics expert. "It looks as if the force had simply been absorbed at the point of impact. Amazing."

"It's a sophisticated suit of battle armor of Viktor's design, created in the mid-1980s at the end of the Cold War. Never used. I've been working on it as a sort of hobby. It's analogous to the HAL, or 'hybrid assistive limb' suits they've been trying to develop, but have never perfected."

"You have strange hobbies," she said. "I have some of those, too. Great minds think alike, it seems."

"You never know what kind of goddamn toys you might need. Argon's an evil bastard."

"Have you worn it?" Jim asked. "How do you know the damn thing even works?"

"Me?" Rad laughed. "Hell, no, it's for an average-sized Russian guy, I guess. Kept it around for this day. Knew it would come."

"It's always good to be prepared, I guess," Jim said.

"You think about it, if you want revenge. We could go blast the hell out of Argon and his lab, and take care of his ass good."

"So what are you doing with it, then, Rad?" Jim asked. "Admiring your little toy? It looks too small for you or Viktor or me, and we don't have time to be playing with big action figures."

"You think? Of course it's too small for me, dumb ass."

"Why are we wasting our time, then?" Jim looked at it again for several minutes, then back at Rad.

"Don't look at me," Rad said, shaking his head. "She's the one who contacted me—not the other way around."

"Huh?" Jim paused for a few seconds, then opened his mouth wide. "Dammit, Rad, you can't possibly be suggesting that *she*—"

"Of course I am, what's your problem? The Russian computers said that this was the best size to provide optimal speed. Five–nine, 170, 175 pounds. You got a better damn idea?"

Bonnie stared at the gleaming armor. "What can it do?"

"Heh, the armor plate is extremely lightweight, can take any type of small arms fire, armor-piercing and all. Resistant to fire and cold. I've pretty much replaced all the electronics into something you won't believe. It can dissipate energy through an energy-absorbing force field and amplify your strength up to about six times. You can bench press what? One ninety, two hundred?"

"Almost two hundred twenty pounds," she replied.

"Then you'll be able to lift over a thousand, intermittently."

"How's it powered?" Jim asked curiously. "That's kind of key here."

"The complex electronics and such use a sealed plutonium power source. The nanomotors, which power the exoskeleton, use a high-tech lithium-ion polymer. There's a universal charger that can instantly adapt and draw power from almost any source."

"Excuse me," Jim asked, holding up his right hand. "Don't mean to piss on your parade, but if this suit's the bee's knees, why's it in some long-forgotten bunker near the distillery, rather than in military service? Or am I missing something?"

"The exoskeleton is top-notch, but the commies at the time didn't have the technology to control it properly, and we—the U.S. government—still don't. Hard to get sensory input fast enough to operate the thing efficiently. Vik tried to develop liquid-crystal metal armor, but it's not advanced enough yet. It's designed for speed, not power, to be a lethal information-gathering stealth device, to destroy and shut down entire computer banks."

"Alex and I constructed a synesthetic visor a few years ago to help simulate hearing for Bonnie. We had it all mapped out."

"Yeah, I knew about that, and have adapted some of that technology into this suit. Look at it—it's ideal for Bonnie."

She put her hands on her hips and smiled. "It is as demented as I thought it would be, Conrad. I like it."

"You and I are more alike than you know, little girl. That goddamn . . . freak damn near killed your brother, kidnapped you and Alex's best friend. Revenge is something I'm good at. The military has long been interested in synesthesia, the ability to integrate several different senses. It allows much faster response times than normal."

"Then why's it not used more widely, Rad?" Jim asked.

"Technology's too primitive, and true synesthetes are rare. But with Bonnie's native abilities—let's just say that Chi Argon's going to get blown to Kingdom Come."

"Why doesn't the military have it, then?" Jim asked. "You stole it from the government, didn't you?"

Rad shrugged. "Well, yeah . . . nobody wanted the damn Russian thing. Some of the shit I knew about was only known by a small fraction of people. I could've set off World War III if I had wanted to, but I let the damned Russkies and Chinese live. Plus this damn thing's too expensive. About forty million a pop."

"The forty million dollar woman. . . shit," Jim said.

"You should know, *Señora* Mendoza, that the commands are all in Russian," Viktor said. "The readouts, everything."

"Then we need to make certain that I brush up on it, Viktor. Languages are not a problem for me."

"One more thing, a minor one," Viktor replied. "The cerebral electrodes require direct contact with the skin."

"So?" she asked.

"Get me a razor. I will have to shave off your beautiful hair."

• • •

Jim Krakowski watched intently as the wife and father of his best friend, accompanied by robotics and electronics expert Viktor Vladimirov, tested the cornucopia of electronic and mechanical devices in Rad's lab and mapped out Bonnie's brain wave patterns. For a moment, he felt immersed in a strange movie or stage play, but he then realized that, no, this was no nightmare. He knew no Russian, and had no idea what the three were talking about.

He was even more puzzled about how well Bonnie was communicating with them. Sure, the lexical genius could read and write Russian, but Wendy said that it had taken many years of speech therapy for her to talk intelligibly even in English or Spanish; how she had become so proficient in speaking such a complex and different language was beyond him.

He took the downtime to reflect on his past involvements in some crazy hacking stuff, but most of them were pranks—nothing like this. And he was usually the one who needed to be brought down to Earth, the one with the outlandish ideas. He was also the smartest, most of the time. But he thought about the smartest people in the world, and knew without a doubt that at least two of them were in the same room with him right now. Intellect was one thing, though; using it wisely was another. He knew that, above all people. The history books were full of very smart people who made asinine decisions.

There he was—all six–five, 325 pounds of him—thick gray hair down to his shoulders, and a salt-and-pepper beard that hadn't been trimmed in weeks, it seemed. Most people thought Rad to be just a peculiar old hermit, and they'd be partially right; but what lay underneath that facade would probably scare the hell out of most normal people.

There was never a more unlikely candidate for intellectual super-stardom than Tennessee native William Conrad Darkkin. Jim became fascinated with the gravelly-voiced scientist whom he saw many times when he and Alex were undergraduates at Vanderbilt University in nearby Nashville. Rad's father, entrepreneur Dirk Thaddeus "D.T." Darkkin, earned millions of dollars mining zinc and distilling sour mash bourbon in Solway, Tennessee; two of his sons, Derek (now deceased), and Dustin, continued in the tradition. But the other son had different interests, and was no one like any

Darkkin the family had ever seen before.

Rad, an All-State football player in high school, was also a brilliant student; he was the first generation of his family to go to college, and earned his undergraduate degree in atomic physics at Princeton with honors. That enough would have raised eyebrows, but he then matriculated to the Massachusetts Institute of Technology, where he earned his masters' and Ph.D. degrees in nuclear physics by age twenty–four.

Alex always said Rad was a genius, and he spent the early years of his career as a physics professor at the University of Tennessee. After a few years, however, he moved on to become the director at Oak Ridge National Laboratory, but his children didn't know until a few years ago what he actually did there. They had a better idea now, thanks to secret documents given to Alex by a high-ranking FBI administrator (FBI chief of cyber crime Ken Thornton, an old friend of Carlos Mendoza) after a cyber crime suspect had met a sudden, mysterious death by poisoning with heavy water. Rad's involvement could never be proven, but Alex said he knew better.

Alex found out over three years ago that his father did more than do physics experiments in Oak Ridge, and shared that information with he and Wendy. The bizarre Rad was chief of development of some of the nastiest nuclear weapons ever created. In 1975, the U.S. and Soviet Union each had over 25,000 weapons in their arsenals; by 1985, the Soviets had exceeded the U.S. amount, and had over 40,000. Each side had to keep up with the other during the Cold War.

Rad also claimed to have been a quasi-intelligence agent, Alex said after confronting his father; whether or not he had actually accompanied CIA agents on clandestine missions during the 70's and 80's was debatable, as the wild-haired man was fond of embellishment. From what he was seeing, though, it might actually be true.

And Rad, like Alex, was extremely talented at something else—courting beautiful ladies. He finally met scholarly British literature major Marianne Gallinsworth, and married her in 1969. Alex and Wendy came in 1970 and 1972, respectively.

But Rad's occupation provided for many rendezvous with desirable women; his affairs were legendary through his department, much to the disgust of his wife, who, having strong religious beliefs, initially refused to divorce him. Wendy never forgave him for those things, and left Tennessee for San Diego in 1989, never to return. Rad and Marianne finally divorced in 1995, and she moved to Arizona, close to San Diego and Wendy.

All good things would come to an end, though; after retirement from the government in the mid-nineties, he continued working on some contracts through his own corporation, DARC (Darkkin Atomic Research Corporation). It appeared that they might currently be at the space once occupied by DARC, although Alex was never sure exactly where it was..

But the Solway super-genius had reportedly lost a few higher cortical neurons over the years. He was always fond of drink, but it was apparent he was having some mental problems. Alex said he had paranoid delusional disorder; but, at times, "Rad Röntgen" could say some of the most profound things he had ever heard. He apparently wasn't using mind-altering drugs any more, but was still on the booze, it seemed, until recently.

But Jim finally realized something—maybe he wasn't as impaired as Alex thought; could some of the strange behavior have been just an act, to get attention? Surely someone as deranged as Alex had claimed wouldn't have millions of dollars' worth of equipment in some secret lab. Now he was scared even more.

• • •

Jim took a break, then turned his interest to the fascinating spouse of his best friend, a paradox of exceptional intellect and athletic ability combined with amazing deficiencies bordering on impairment—none of them having anything to do with deafness, which was the least of her problems.

The quirky phenomenon named Bonita Mendoza had taken the more traditional route to academic excellence. Born into an affluent, cultured family of high intellectual, artistic, and athletic achievement, much was expected of her. Even then, she was clearly something special. Fluent in five languages by age six. National spelling bee champion at age nine. Celebrated mathematical prodigy. But all those abilities vanished when she almost died after a bout of meningitis at age eleven that left her completely deaf and without any memory. Other than the deafness, she seemed to have suffered no permanent brain damage—but she had to re-learn everything again from scratch. Several years later, she had recovered sufficiently to again rise to academic super-stardom.

She was, among other things, a tenth-order mathematical cipher, a talent exceeded by only a handful of savants, Alex had said. Her cipher abilities were best at algebraic and polynomial manipulations—she was slower at mentally computing, for example, transcendental numbers (e.g., π, trigonometric functions, logarithms, complex exponentiation)—but they were still quite amazing, albeit with dubious use in daily living. The ability to reduce almost anything to a mathematical problem wasn't always useful. But they certainly made her a legendary mentalist.

But the miraculous magician hid her many deficiencies well. The most powerful of the Flores synesthetes was, oddly, bewildered by many simple tasks of daily living, such as telling right from left, balancing her checkbook, picking out clothes (due to her strangely vivid color perception), and finding her way when driving. Because of the latter problem, SDPD had given her a personal on-call driver to shuttle her around to crime scenes, meetings, and the courthouse. Indeed, she often wore a GPS watch which showed direction as well as miles from home—things she always needed to know.

In a way, she was childlike—many experts felt that synesthesia and autism were two ends of the same spectrum. Her childhood doctors thought she might have a high-functioning variant of autism called Asperger's syndrome, as those children were often highly intelligent, had difficulty with socialization, and were prone to extreme verbosity and rambling on about their peculiar interests. But few Asperger's children were stellar athletes; Bonnie's speed at fast motor tasks was in the 99th percentile. She didn't really fit into any established category.

With the aid of many family members and friends, who organized her affairs, managed her money, picked out her clothes, and drove her around, the illusion of perfection best friend Wendy had envisioned was complete. But he had seen enough to know better.

There was always the joke going around that a few members of Mensa International (the exclusive society for super-high-IQ types) were homeless, so brilliant they were unable to deal with the trivialities of daily living; indeed, this lady would probably be one of them, were it not for some luck and the help of caring and affluent family and friends.

He and Alex were pretty good friends in college, and both partook in many drunken fraternity orgies involving lusty, busty coeds. His best buddy had a high libido, that's for sure. And that was most puzzling to him—Bonnie was one of the strangest people he had ever met. He remembered how fondly Alex had talked about her, and the initial picture of her in his mind was quite different from reality.

Honestly, he never really cared too much for the flippant, bossy, obnoxious woman who was prone to speak in prolix sentences of almost robotic precision. He still hadn't quite figured it out; it wasn't her looks, by any means—she was tall, but with an athlete's physique and tiny boobs; her face was kind of pretty, but not like some of the women Alex had dated. It was round and peppered with dark freckles against that brown skin. Her nose had a little bump where it had once been broken, a remnant of a physically adventurous childhood. She looked almost like a teenager, albeit one who could kick his butt.

He smirked as he realized there had to be more than meets the eye with his friend's wife. She was surely a challenging intellectual sparring partner, with whom one could engage in almost any cerebral discussion or contest; but he knew Alex certainly wanted to be physically satisfied. It was sure none of his business, but he knew there had to be something fantastic going on under the bedsheets.

The two unlikely Russian-speaking allies didn't seem to have a nanogram of common sense between them. That meant their, his, and possibly the world's future was in their hands—like two children haphazardly standing in a pool of gasoline, playing with a box of matches. What kind of God-awful foolishness were they cooking up with Rad's vodka-swilling Russian buddy? And how long was he going to survive seeing what they did? Hell, for all he knew, Rad might still have access to thermonuclear weapons.

That's what scared him to death. Rad at least was still around, after a life of living hard, so that was some consolation. The secret spy lab stuff was still a little hard to swallow, though. But there didn't seem to be a lot of other choices right now.

Chapter Forty–one

Lambeau Field
1265 Lombardi Ave.
Green Bay, Wisconsin

Alex Darkkin and Jackie Levickis drove their rented sedan from Austin Straubel International Airport to Lombardi Avenue, on the way to Lambeau Field, on the southwest end of town.

"I assume you've been here several times, Darkkin," Jackie said as he drove down the road.

"Actually, it's my first time here, and I didn't even know Jay was her brother when we started dating. Been to a lot of other pro stadiums, but this one's off the beaten path."

Green Bay was an anomaly in the pro sports landscape, a throwback to the "small-town" teams which dominated in the early part of the 20th century, with towns like Decatur, IL, Canton, OH, and even Muncie, IN having professional franchises at one point. The Packers were a throwback to that era, and were unique in another way: it was the only publicly owned, non-profit pro sports franchise.

No irate owner could pack up and move the team to another city, since the town essentially owned the team, and therefore could, by law, never be moved. The management was elected by a board of directors, employees of the people. The team had survived, despite the smallest market in pro sports, by tradition, smart advertising, and, of course, the sharing of television revenue.

"Dr. Darkkin, it's nice to finally meet you. I've heard so many good things about you," Packers General Manager Edward Ralston said. "I'm so sorry to hear about Jay. I was just starting with the organization when he was here, and wish he could've played a few more years for us."

"Yeah, I bet you wish you could get him back."

"No kidding. He was one of the greatest. Not just as a player, but as a person, too. Did lots of things for charity. I hope they find out who did this to him."

"Thank you. We are still hoping for a speedy recovery."

"What is it I can do to help?"

"We've been everywhere, looking for clues on who could have done this. Jay seems to have left some kind of message, which my wife decoded. And she supposedly made a cell phone call from Sheboygan, although we think that's faked. The only logical conclusion is that it had something to do with the team."

"Your wife, yes. I met her once, a long time ago. A rather peculiar character, far different from her extroverted brother. All-American sprinter for San Diego State in the hundred meters, I recall. Not a bad kicker, either. We let her fool around in practice a bit."

"Yes," he laughed. "Rather unusual. But does the name Travis mean anything?"

Ralston looked through the records, and found something a few minutes later. "Travis. There was a Travis Garno who tried out for the team in 1995, it seems. Defensive end. Not too bad in the speed department, either. Dude never played college ball, either. A frickin' walk-on, but strong as hell."

"What happened?"

"Jay was just becoming a superstar, and seemed to have a lot of influence with the upper brass. He and this Garno didn't get along. Jay convinced them that Travis was a bad seed, that they should get rid of him. Ol' Number 4 felt the same way. He and Jay were pals."

"This Travis ever do anything bad?"

"Bad temper, kind of a loner. No one really liked him, but, no, nothing terrible or anything. Jay seemed to have these feelings about people. And he was usually right."

"A similarity he shares with my wife. His mom says he has the ability to . . . predict the future, in a way."

"Like a fortune-teller?"

"No, things in broad strokes. Couldn't tell you exactly what, but, if he had a bad feeling about something, you'd better listen. But, tell me—what happened to this Garno?"

"Rumor is that he got sick with cancer or something and was never heard from again."

Alex stared at the picture of Travis Garno. Most football players were big dudes, but damned if he didn't look like someone familiar. He couldn't put his finger on it, he thought as they left the hallowed stadium.

• • •

Jackie opened her laptop in the Lambeau Field parking lot and checked all available files of birth records and other files available to her. "This 'Travis Garno' doesn't exist. It must be an assumed name. The Social Security number they gave us isn't even real."

"Why would he do that?" Alex asked. "Fake records?"

"Must be some reason. Maybe this Travis guy didn't want anyone to know what he was doing, trying out for the team."

"Garno. Maybe it's an anagram."

"Anagram? Why?"

"Unusual name." He scribbled some notes on a legal pad. "I'm not my wife, but I'll give it a crack. There should be 120 possible combinations of those letters."

"How do you know that?"

"Magic books for the non-mentalist. There are 5 factorial (5!), or 120, possibilities. Will narrow it to a smaller number of anagrams, since most of them won't make sense."

After a few minutes, he came up with nine potential candidates:

GROAN
ARGON
ORGAN
NAGOR
GARON
GARNO
RAGON
RAGNO
RANGO

"Run one of these names through your federal databases."

"Darkkin, that's stupid. What if it's not an anagram at all, but a fake name?"

"Garno? Come on."

She sighed and ran an extensive search from her laptop, and, after fifteen minutes, came up with some information.

"Combining the name 'Travis' and the others you listed, I come up with a 'Travis Marshall Argon' born in 1971 in Baltimore, Maryland. His age would be compatible with the guy who tried out for Green Bay in 1995. He would've been about twenty-four then."

"Parents?"

"Dr. Malachi and Katrina Argon. What the hell is a Malachi Argon?" Jackie asked. "Something to do with Argotech Industries, the owner of that plane that crashed?"

He thought for a few minutes. "Malachi, the prophet in the Bible verse about the fullers' soap. And the name's damn familiar. Something I remember from a long time ago."

"What?"

"Crazy as it sounds, you just don't forget a name like that. I think it's someone my dad used to know. And that's what the 'noble' meant, I think."

"Noble?"

"Argon is one of the 'noble' gases, meaning that it is inert, and doesn't combine with other gases. The others are helium, neon, krypton, xenon, radon, and eka-radon, or ununoctium."

"If you say so. Chemistry's really not my thing, unless it has to do with drug busts."

He thought for a moment. "Malachi Argon, that's it. The Bible verse, though. Trying to think of a connection there."

"Your dad? Is this guy a fellow scientist?"

"Something like that. I remember reading about him growing up—he was a big shot bio-geneticist. Dad didn't like him at all."

"You said he didn't like most members of the human race."

"Somehow this guy who tried out for Green Bay has something to do with this Malachi Argon."

"I'll try to find out as much as I can about him, Darkkin."

Alex's mouth opened wide. "The '3:2.' The element argon's atomic number is 18. If that's the '3,' then the '2' is 12. Argon's orbital configuration plus 12 equals what?"

"Who knows or cares, Darkkin? You sound like your wife, and we're wasting time."

"[Ar] $3d^{10}$ $4s^{2}$ equals zinc. She also said 'brass ring.' Brass is an alloy made of copper and zinc."

"What the hell does zinc have to do with anything?"

"Tennessee is the world's second largest supplier of zinc—lots of mines there. A place that put me through college is close to one, address 32 Zinctown Drive, in Solway, Tennessee. I don't believe it. And the other riddle—she was talking about roentgenium."

"What fabulous place is at 32 Zinctown Drive?"

"The Darkkin distillery. That's also the 'refinery' in the Malachi verse from the Bible. They refine corn instead of oil."

"Why would she and Krakowski have gone there?"

"It's a place that has lots of Darkkins. In particular, one with a Ph.D. in nuclear physics."

"Why would she lead us on some wild goose chase, with these vague clues?"

"It's how her mind works, and she wanted to leave clues only her family could decipher. And she obviously is involved in something dangerous, and wants us to find her eventually—but not too quickly."

"Where are we going now? The agency wants an update, and they're getting impatient."

"Oak Ridge. The place of my birth."

"Oh, my. This better be good."

"Trust me, it will be an interesting experience."

Chapter Forty–two

The Röntgen-Cave
Solway, TN

Bonnie, Rad, Viktor, and Jim sat down and talked to Rita, who was sitting in a chair, and didn't appear to be too much of a threat, and seemed relatively passive, but it seemed that she didn't want to be an active participant in their little quest to blow Malachi Argon to bits. Rad, in particular, had a problem with that.

"We know Chi was interested in this crazy bio-genetic shit," Rad said angrily. "Always was interested in perverting nature."

"I don't want to answer any questions from you."

Bonnie got in her face. "Then this will be very painful."

Jim tapped her on the shoulder and pushed her aside. "Chill, Square. Look, Rita—it is Rita, right?"

"Yes."

"We're not too bad, or we would've let you die like Tammy Preece or the other lackeys in that Gulfstream, right? Why the heck should we care about you, other than because we're nice guys?"

Rita nodded her head slightly. "I suppose that's one way of looking at it."

"The glass is half full, right? Have a positive attitude here."

"*Positive attitude?* Your setup here is one of the most bizarre things I've ever seen. What craziness is this?"

Bonnie approached her again. "The DNA from your . . . emissary of destruction is peculiar, with some things I have never encountered before. There is a similarity with Dr. Rad here, as well. I am no molecular biologist, but know enough from my forensics training to get by."

"How wonderful for you."

"You listen to me. You miscreants almost killed my brother and kidnapped my best friend. You see those men over there? They don't know a fraction of the ways to hurt you that I can."

"I didn't know about them hurting your brother, I'm sorry."

"Sorry ain't gonna cut it with us," Rad said. "Who the hell is this big dude that I heard about, anyway?"

"Travis Argon, codename Ortho-Man, is Malachi Argon's son. He developed leukemia and went through all the standard therapies, but failed them, including a bone marrow transplant."

"*Argon!*" Rad yelled as he stood up. "I hated that arrogant prick, with his uppity New England upbringing and all. For Chrissakes, I had an affair with his wife. Nice piece of ass."

"Yes, he is a piece of smelly dung," Viktor said. "I knew of him. Despised among scientists, no ethics. Many believed him to be beyond reproach, but his peers knew the true man underneath. The lowest dweller in the carbon cycle—even feces, which serve as fertilizer, have greater worth to the ecosystem than Malachi Argon."

"No offense—but you guys are worried about ethics?" Rita asked. "You seem to take the law into your own hands."

She puffed out her chest. "I will take you into my hands in a moment. But you have not answered about why you desired Dr. Williams. I know she was abducted."

Rita smiled sarcastically. "How can one person be so smart and so dumb at the same time? Haven't you figured it out yet? They need closely matched genetic material to regenerate Travis' bone marrow."

"Huh? Please elaborate." Bonnie shook her head. "I enjoy puzzles, but you are starting to annoy me."

Jim stared at Rita intensely, as Bonnie's light bulb, while amazingly luminous, sometimes took a while to achieve its maximum brightness.

"You *must* be kidding. You expect us to believe ol' Rad Röntgen here is this Ortho-Man dude's father, not Malachi Argon?"

"We . . . found out by accident. Darkkin here's pretty much 'off the grid,' and everyone's forgotten about him. But there's no question. He even admitted just now he had an affair with Katrina."

"Damn straight, and that's the way I want it. Rad is off the grid, deals only with cash, no credit cards, they might find me—"

"Shut up, you egotistical idiot," Bonnie said loudly, having now comprehended the new information. "So *this* is why Travis and Conrad have similar DNA."

"What a genius," Jim said.

She poked her index finger into Rad's chest. "You have caused trouble of apocalyptic proportions by spreading your exalted genetic material across the globe, it seems. Is there any continent upon which your superlative seed has not been deposited?"

"Hell, lemme think." The bulky man thought pensively as he exhaled a cloud of blue smoke from his burning cigar. "Antarctica. No ladies there the one time I went, goddamn it—that was a helluva long two weeks. Shit."

She peered up at him angrily. "This . . . seminal event has paved the way for much destruction at your hands, once again. What price must the human race pay for your selfishness?"

Rad doubled over in laughter. "*Seminal event*? Hey, that's pretty damn funny. And that Katrina was a good lay, that was for sure."

Bonnie slapped him. "You . . . you reptilian Lothario, the pain you have caused your family. No matter, your august coital exploits are not the primary concern here, as we cannot change the past."

Rad looked down at his size fifteen shoes. "I guess I was a pretty shitty husband, gotta call a spade a spade."

"That . . . is putting it mildly."

Rita looked up and took a sip of water. "But we discovered Williams' DNA in that stupid stunt she pulled at the drug testing center. She's pretty messed up. I can see where she gets it from."

Bonnie perked up. "Jaime was right, after all. It all goes back to football and the drug testing center. He always knows."

"Wait a minute. If I had my choice of genetic models," Jim asked, pointing to Rad and shaking his head, "I probably would've shopped around a while longer. He has a couple of good qualities, but tons of bad ones. Perfection *he* sure ain't."

"Hey, look who's talking, you bald, fat—"

"Shut up, Rad," Jim said. "This crap is all your fault."

Rita continued. "Travis was already born, but Malachi found

some unusual genetic patterns, and did some rather outrageous genetic experiments on him back in the late 1990's, when he conceived Project 'Ortho-Man.' An 'orthogenetic man.'"

"*¿El hombre ortodoxo?* Tell me more about him."

"Genes perfectly aligned in the most efficient manner possible—a miracle of modern technology. Strength and endurance more than you can possibly imagine. Trying to create a prototype super-soldier."

"I used to be a forensic scientist, and a microscopic blood sample from the motel carpet revealed amino acids not present in human proteins. I concur that the genetics aren't entirely human. How was this horrific chromosomal adulteration accomplished?"

"Years and years of expensive genetic manipulation."

"What magnitude of expense was incurred? Millions of dollars?" she asked.

Rita laughed. "Not even close. Billions. Many billions."

"Argon could not possibly have funded this himself, and no legitimate source would fund such a perverted project," she said.

"Then he got his own funding," Jim said. "Probably off-shore."

Rad exhaled another cloud of carcinogenic smoke from his Cuban cigar. "Yes, that's it, so clever—a genetic master plan, with me as the nucleus. Heh—me as the nucleus, get it? Genetics?"

"You and Bonnie should go on tour together, after we all get out of jail," Jim said. "But we won't ever make it there, since we'll all be dead. Wendy always warned me about you, but did I listen? No."

"My DNA is, heh, superior, of course, and it's only natural to want to design an army of super-soldiers around me."

"He always was modest," Jim said. "Some things always stay the same."

"We needed undifferentiated fetal tissue of a close enough match to Travis to regenerate his bone marrow," Rita said.

"You are going to experiment on her baby. How sickening!" Bonnie yelled as she grabbed Rita by the neck. "Why hers—because they are related? What has she done to you, louse?"

"I'm sorry, but it's a necessary step to save a life, and create benefits beyond your imagination."

"You better worry about saving yours, and I can imagine quite a bit," she said angrily.

"She has an extremely rare gene found in elite power athletes with large amounts of fast-twitch muscle fibers. We . . . believe the father to possess a similar one."

She laughed. "Are you kidding me? Stan Williams possesses the physique and athletic ability of Gumby. Perhaps you should check your intel and get your money back from Harvard for that Ph.D."

"God, how stupid are you? Why do you think you're so fast? You and the father both carry partial mutations for ACTN7, as well as a different gene, ACTN3, which appears to convey great speed. The combination of ACTN7 and ACTN3, as well as his apparent ability to sense things before they happen . . ."

"I don't get it." She looked around, bewildered. "Are you saying that my brother is—"

Jim fell back. "Now *that* one I don't believe."

"No . . . unfortunately, she is not. I know, somehow, that she is telling the truth."

"How the hell you know that?" Rad asked.

"Is there no dignity in this Darkkin family?" Viktor exclaimed as he took a swig of vodka. "Everyone has sex with everyone else."

Rad let out a guffaw as he doubled over. "You gotta be shittin' me! My saintly little girl, having an affair with the big football jock? I sure as hell need something stronger than this fucking bottle of pop. Even that Darkkin whiskey shit would do."

"Conrad, shut up before I do it for you."

"Haw. Yeah, I bet it's true. Always on her high horse—"

Rad's laughing was interrupted by another sharp slap on the face. "Wendy is surely cognitively impaired and not herself. How dare you think that? Not everyone is as amoral as you."

Jim formed a "T" with his hands. "Time out here to present an alternate universe scenario. Just because big WW said it and believes it, doesn't make it so. She's not dealing with a full deck, I heard."

"Only that she herself said it was his," Rita said. "Why would she lie?"

"I didn't say she did, but she's gone psycho."

"I suppose that's possible," Rita said. "But she improved a lot over the first few days with us."

Bonnie pulled at Rita's shirt. "You best not have hurt her, or I shall show you pain you cannot possibly imagine."

"Her health is in our best interest, you know. She is safe, for now."

Rad continued laughing as Bonnie punched him in the shoulder. "What is so funny? If her statement is true, it is tragic."

"Haw. Just ironic, that's all, little lady."

Rita continued. "It all started after Argon found interest in some moon rocks found in 1970, which contained trace hydrocarbons. There was nothing in them but dead organic material, but it lead him to believe there might be life elsewhere in the solar system."

"Titan, of course," Bonnie said. "It all makes sense now, with Dr. Bennett. He kept it all secret, but knew all along."

"The Cassini mission sent the Huygens probe to Titan, landing in 2005. The probe found hydrocarbon sludge in Ontario Lacus with evidence of primitive forms of life."

"Ontario Lacus—the large methane lake on the south pole?"

"Correct, named because its size and shape resembles Lake Ontario."

"Humph. It would have been useful to perform carbon dating."

"We did. ^{14}C dating showed some fragments to be about 65-70 million years old. About the time the dinosaurs disappeared."

Bonnie curiously found it less necessary to lip-read, despite her processors being nearly dead again. "Your grand tale has many gaping holes. First, sixty–five million years is insufficient time for life to have evolved on Titan, meaning that it originated from someplace else, like Earth. The geologic information from Cassini-Huygens indicated that the surface is actually fairly young."

Rad stood up and walked around. "No, wait. I remember that dumb bastard always had some theory that, when the meteor hit that killed the goddamn dinosaurs millions of years ago, some of the fragments containing life went out into the universe somewhere."

"That's correct," Rita said. "Argon thought that a large meteor might have struck it millions of years ago—possibly fragments of the meteor we think likely killed the dinosaurs on Earth sixty–five million years ago. Most of the fragments probably got sucked into Saturn or Jupiter, but others could have made it to Titan."

"Panspermia," she said. "The transfer of life from one world to another. I have considered this, and Bennett theorized this might be possible, although we have yet to decipher his hidden compact disc."

"Yeah, like she said, Kat spilled that he went all ape-shit in 1970 over some moon rocks that had been discovered to have fossilized remains of organisms. It was classified, she said, and he never found anything else, but he always thought the meteor fragments might've ended up at other places in the Solar System."

She laughed. "But what you describe is impossible. The Huygens probe only transmitted pictures and other simple data, and was incapable of doing those types of experiments. Not carbon dating, and certainly not DNA sequencing. And Huygens did land on the southern hemisphere, but not near Ontario Lacus."

"No." Rita took another sip of bottled water. "There were . . . two Titan probes, but the public was only informed about the one. Argon was so confident that something would be found, he convinced the European Space Agency to build another one, with funding from his 'investors.' The first one suggested the possibility of life high up in the atmosphere, as well. Complex hydrocarbons that were sucked away by Saturn's magnetosphere. Amino acids. The carbon isotope ratio in the methane suggested replenishment from some source, which could have been from biological organisms."

She laughed. "I am skeptical, as amino acids alone do not constitute life. The atmospheric ^{40}Ar (argon) found in the atmosphere could also be found due to geological actions, not biological—from the decay of ^{40}K (potassium)."

"The probe found evidence of amino acids and complex aliphatic hydrocarbons near the equator, most of which are not found in living organisms. A 50-50 mixture of right- and left-handed compounds. But, near Ontario Lacus, they were about 57% L-amino acids, which only occur in carbon-based life forms like us, not random like on the other side." Left-handed, or L-amino acids, were for the most part the only type found in living proteins.

She turned to her wild-eyed father-in-law. "I do not believe this, but is that possible, Conrad? A second Huygens probe with the ability to actually sequence DNA and send the results back to Earth? Does such technology exist? Even I am skeptical."

He laughed. "Shit, I don't know about current space missions, you're the one who was at Caltech and the Jet Propulsion Laboratory for three years, hon. But certainly a lot of things are done that are classified, you know that. It's theoretically possible."

"I was in the theoretical physics division and had limited dealings with JPL. But NASA and JPL were only involved with the Cassini orbiter, the mother ship. The Huygens probe was built by the European Space Agency. But that couldn't have been sent without NASA's approval."

"Of course not, but remember, higher-ups in the military wanted it, though. Research on bio-genetics."

"Who?" she asked.

"Lt. Gen. Brant Gallagher. He has been working with Malachi all this time. The protein, OT-45, derived from the organism we found—*Orthogeneticus titania*—will regenerate nearly any nervous system cells that were damaged. He used it on himself—he had progressive Parkinson's syndrome, and it caused a dramatic reversal."

"You mentioned that Travis had a hematologic malignancy—leukemia, I believe. Argon experimented on him to save him, then?"

Rita gulped. "That's what he said, but I found out something else. He had discovered the ACTN7 gene long before that, and manipulated Travis to make him stronger. The leukemia was the result of his original genetic experiments."

Bonnie stepped back in horror. "This man caused his own son's terminal disease? He should be dismembered."

"Yeah, so, heh, this guy's pretty strong, then?" Rad asked, changing the subject. "Like father, like son?"

Rita stared at the bulky, poorly-groomed man. "No offense, but not really. He can bench press over 1,700 pounds, deadlift 2,800 pounds, smash through concrete—if he has protective armor on, of course. He can survive a fifty–pound drop off a building, the computers estimate."

"Haw. Big deal. What about a, heh, .44 caliber bullet through the brain? Bet the big bastard can't survive that, or a nuke."

"No, he's not invulnerable to firearms. The *O. titania* protein has allowed him some significant regenerative abilities, the ability to combat most human infectious diseases, for example—but not that. But he heals in about the third of the time you do."

"He sounds like quite an investment," Jim said.

"Strength, the ability to ward off blunt injury, limited resistance to toxins and such. His speed is not supernormal, but amazing for a man of his mass. He also has enormous endurance. They want to design an entire set of super-soldiers around him."

"Well, let's just call in the military, the FBI, CIA, Delta Force, or whoever the hell we call to get rid of this dude," Jim yelled.

"You don't get it." Rita shook her head again. "Gallagher's in on it, and it's a secret military operation. You'll never convince anyone otherwise. To them, Argon's a famous, legitimate government scientist. And the really outlandish experiments don't take place at the West Virginia Complex; they take place somewhere else."

"Heh, where—not in the United States, I assume?"

Bonnie looked up, at nothing in particular. "No, it's an island in the Caribbean. I have somehow . . . seen it before."

"How the hell you know that?" Jim asked.

"I . . . don't know, it just popped into my head."

Rita swallowed hard. "She's right. It's not in any U.S. jurisdiction, and they can do what they want. I should've seen it coming."

"Well, my daughter's in there, and we're gonna bust her out."

"It's suicide. They're on an island complex, not the one in West Virginia."

"What I've got designed, you've never seen. You need to tell us how to, heh, get in there."

Rita shook her head. "I'm a biochemist with limited knowledge of the security systems. I know some basics, but you need Willie Chalfant for that."

"Willie Chalfant?" Rad asked. "Who the hell is that?"

"The chief of security. He'd know about the details. He's the one who helped Tammy kidnap you."

"Where the hell is he?" Rad asked.

"I believe he's in Charleston, on vacation for a few days."

"Then we're going to, heh, find him tomorrow night. And it sure is gonna be the worst fucking holiday *he's* ever had. Hope he's got vacation insurance."

"You'll never be able to do it. He'll have a military bodyguard with him, and he's dangerous in his own right.."

Rad laughed hysterically. "Lady, that scares me real bad. There ain't nobody more dangerous than me and my hot tamale here."

She kicked Rad in the shin. "Call me 'hot tamale' again, and you are a dead man," she admonished.

Chapter Forty–three

The Röntgen-Cave
Solway, TN

Bonnie was sprinting eerily down the dimly-lit corridor; why was she running from something? No, wait—she was running *after* someone. Why was she, wearing an evening gown, sprinting after that man in the tuxedo? She was fast, even in heels, and the 170-lb, late-fortyish man was no match for her speed. She caught him and threw him to the ground as he tried to scale a high fence.

He tried vainly to stop her, but she was too fast, as she threw a punch that broke several of his ribs. But she was dangerously over-confident; she slipped on a puddle of oil in the hallway, and fell into the wall. By that time her adversary had found an old screwdriver that he quickly plunged into the right side of her chest.

She fell to the ground, gasping for air. She faintly saw the outline of her brother Mike. God, it was horrible—she was dying, unable to breathe. Then she lost consciousness.

She woke from the dream in a cold sweat. She was sleeping on a cot in a storage room in Rad's underground lab, she remembered. What was this dream, one far more vivid than any she had experienced before? She remembered the police report that was filed after she had attempted to stop Dr. Monte Buechler, a criminal mastermind who had engineered the deaths of dozens of people via the alteration of computer medical records. She was in a coma for over a week, they said, and had retrograde amnesia. Why would she remember this now? On the other hand, she had recently seen strange things long forgotten, like three-dimensional moving violet blobs. Things she shouldn't be able to remember.

She stared at the wall and noticed an odd sensation, not unpleasant, but irritating—something she couldn't remember ever experiencing. It was coming from one direction—right, no, left, she decided, as she looked at the pink anodized bracelet on her right wrist. She looked to her left and saw Jim.

He was speaking her name over and over, she then realized. She put her hands up to the sides of her head. As usual, she had removed her processors, she thought as she saw them lying on the table.

"What's wrong? You having a nightmare?"

"Yes, I remembered something awful, being in tremendous pain. Something that apparently happened several years ago. But that isn't what concerns me the most."

"What do you mean?"

"How long have you been yelling at me? Before I realized you were there?"

"A couple of minutes, I guess."

"Why did you not grab me, then?"

"Uh, something tells me that grabbing you isn't such a good idea."

She walked across the room to the far end. "Say something, softly, and gradually increase the intensity. If I can sense it, I will raise my hand."

"That's nuts." He shrugged. "On the other hand, things can't get much weirder."

"I don't know, but . . . I sensed something familiar, yet alien to me. Something I never remember experiencing."

"Okay." She turned her back to him as Jim began speaking, first in a soft whisper, which he gradually increased in intensity. After he increased the volume of his voice to about a quarter of its maximum volume, she raised her hand.

She turned back around to him. "I detected the same sensation. What were you saying to me?"

"How do you know I was saying anything?"

"You were reciting prime numbers. By the way, you started with one, which is neither prime nor composite. How shameful."

"Sorry."

"Let us go visit our friend Rita, who seems to have some explaining to do."

"I thought you were reading lips pretty well in the darkness. Let's go."

• • •

Jim and Bonnie opened the locked room where they had placed Rita McPherson, and Bonnie woke her up at three AM.

"What's wrong? Don't do anything to me, please. I've tried to do what you say."

Bonnie grabbed her by the arm. "I will do something very bad to you if you do not tell me what you did to me."

"What? I don't know what you mean."

"Liar—I remembered something that has been long gone, and I seem to have a very small amount of native hearing. Last time I will ask—what experiment have you done on me?"

Rita was sweating profusely. "It wasn't my idea, please believe me. I did what I had to do. They wanted to kill you—I convinced Dr. Argon otherwise, that you were of some value."

"What do you mean?"

"We injected you with the *O. titania* growth factor while you were unconscious."

"Injected me, with . . . what is it?"

"OT-45, which causes regeneration of the central and peripheral nervous system."

"Why would you have done such a thing to me?"

"They . . . wanted to do genetic experimentation on you. There were rumors that you possessed precognitive abilities as a child, they said. Before you became deaf."

"Who are 'they,' and how would you know anything about me, a mere physicist?"

"Oh, come on. Dr. Argon and the government has had a file on you for years. You were with the police, surely you know that."

"I should kill you for this!" Bonnie screamed. "Experiment on me, do you?"

"You should be grateful. If not for me, you would probably be dead now."

"Yes, like you will be soon." She let go of Rita and stood up. "What . . . shall happen to me?"

"The growth factor . . . possibly has regenerated damaged neurons, just like with my spinal cord. I anticipated that effect."

She pointed authoritatively at Rita and stared at her angrily. "It has only been a few days. Nothing can do that."

"It's alien technology which can work very quickly. You will likely gain increased hearing over the next week."

"It will restore my hearing to normal? That is ridiculous."

"I don't know how much you'll regain. But think about it, what it can do for you. Make you better. You have a partial mutation for ACTN7 yourself. Your strength alone must be three times—"

"What, I can be a genetic freak, too? I do not need that, thank you, as I was born with enough eccentricities. Understand this, Rita," she said menacingly. "I don't need to be better, stronger, or be anything more than I am. The . . . deafness is a part of me. I need it. It spurs me on to accomplish more . . . do you believe I would be where I am if not for that?"

"Think about it. There's a lot you don't know about *me*."

"What? Why would I care about you, a mere criminal?"

"I was a paraplegic, a woman in a wheelchair until a year ago. Malachi infused the modified protein created from *O. titania* into me, and its regenerative powers restored my ability to walk."

"I don't care and don't need to think about it. I was born again, into a world without sound, when I was eleven. I cannot remember anything else. I am a whole person. Soon my cochlear implants will no longer function, and I will be glad to stop pretending I'm somebody I'm not."

"What about the memories, then, Mendoza? The process can restore brain cells, too."

"Like magic? Hahaha, like magic, how ironic." She snapped her fingers. "Just like that, you have made me whole again? There is always a price to pay for everything."

"Not with this—you can be more than you ever thought possible. Why do you think they wanted you?"

"Hah. Because I was getting in the way."

Rita laughed. "Don't take this the wrong way and pound me, but . . . you flatter yourself with your overblown ego. This thing's so complex you never would have figured it out."

"Untrue—my unmatched intellect would have prevailed, given sufficient time."

"No, they wanted you because of your genetic abilities, to create a hybrid and clone you. Give a replica of Travis your abilities."

She thought about it long and hard. Would it be possible? Her greatest desire was not, as many people thought, to hear as a "normal" person would; it was to recover the memories of childhood lost forever. To remember her first Christmas, her first doll, riding a bike for the first time . . .

But life wasn't magic. It was real. And she didn't want to be some type of genetic freak. Maybe it was too late.

"The changes to me . . . will they be permanent?"

"Probably not. You received one injection, which appears to be regenerating part of your natural hearing. The effects will subside in a few weeks. After about ten to twelve injections, the effects will be permanent, like they are on me." Rita pointed to the case. "That metal case contains two more doses, which can prolong the effects."

"I don't understand," Jim said. "I don't know that much about cochlear implants, but I thought that when they implanted the electrodes, it destroyed any chance for natural hearing."

"I thought that, too," she said.

"How is it possible, then, Square?"

"How is any of this possible? The wonders of genetic manipulation?" She stared at Rita again. "One final question—why did you not tell me this yesterday?"

Rita paused and gulped. "I was terrified of what you might do to me."

"You are right about that—you should be afraid. I should rip your liver and spleen out."

"I can't change what's been done. Killing me won't solve anything."

"Yes, but it will make me feel *so* much better."

"Bonnie, don't," Jim said. "She's right. Whatever's done is done. Enough violence."

"I can . . . help you do this, whatever you're planning to do to Argon."

"Help me? I don't need more of your type of help. How can we trust you now?"

"You have no reason to. But I went into this with the wrong motives and have seen what Argon's capable of. Somehow I see it all more clearly now. I want to help you destroy him."

"Sounds like a plan to me," Jim said. "We need all the help we can get. But how do we know she's telling the truth?"

"She is." She had not noticed the presence of the globular companion that she had seen on the airplane. "I would bet my reputation on it."

"Haw," Jim said. "That's great, because we're betting our lives."

She remembered again the awesome power of Oogly-Googly, the friendly purple protoplasmic blob, whom she had seen on the airplane. She had thought it a fleeting memory of childhood, but now knew the reason for his return.

His presence was linked to natural hearing, which she lost at age eleven. It was a gift of mixed blessing—the ability to tell if someone was telling the truth. Most would give anything to have it. Others would consider it a curse. But Oogly's absence meant she was being truthful.

She didn't like it at all. But there was no going back now. And it was time to take a quick trip to Charleston, West Virginia, to settle a score. She took a second injection of Argon's OT-45 serum with much anticipation about the adventure to come.

Chapter Forty–four

Charleston Town Center Mall
3000 Charleston Town Center
Charleston, WV

After some dinner and shopping the next evening, Argotech Chief of Security Willie Chalfant walked down the West Virginia capital's side street outside the large, multi-level mall on the way to his car. He was, as usual, accompanied by his assistant, a large burly former Army master sergeant in his early forties. Chalfant had a lot of classified information in that head, and never went anywhere without Jackson, a formidable man with a background in Army Special Forces. But he was no slouch himself in the self-defense arena.

He and Jackson walked onto the second level of the parking garage, as he spotted two unfamiliar characters. They tried to avoid the disheveled *Latino* homeless man and the scar-faced, dark-haired man staggering towards them. The latter person was wearing a tattered uniform shirt and swilling a bottle of cheap booze.

"God, get the hell out of my way. You homeless people are disgusting," Chalfant said in disgust. "Go find a box to live in or something."

"*¿Pesos, por favor? ¡Tango hambre!*" the staggering Hispanic man slurred as he held his grungy right hand out. "*¿Me puede ayudar?*"

"Get the hell out of our way, spick, before I smash your butt!" the sergeant exclaimed, drawing his weapon.

"*No entiendo.*" The five–nine male, sporting closely cropped black hair and a poorly trimmed mustache, said with a puzzled look as he shook his head.

"Lookit, Willie," the sergeant said. "This Mexican dude's a few bricks shy of a load. And look at his buddy here," he said, laughing, as he pointed to the overweight man with the scar. "I'll be doing the world a favor, getting rid of them."

"*Я хотел бы бутылку водки,*" the older man said. "I would like a bottle of vodka."

"Vodka?" Jackson exclaimed. "Looks like you've had enough, pal. Go drink some Old Spice or something."

"Aww, be nice and give 'em some money, Jackson," Chalfant said as he flipped a dime to one and fifteen cents to the other. "Quarter to two, get it? Haw."

"*Gracias,*" the homeless Spanish-speaking man said as he proudly held up the shiny dime and nickel.

"Get away," the sergeant said, cocking his firearm. "Last chance, you homeless shits."

The white telephone van pulled up beside them as the door flung open. The seemingly intoxicated Hispanic man then grabbed the sergeant with amazing speed.

"Your last mistake, bum," Sgt. Jackson said. "You try to mess with me, I'll break your goddamn neck." Jackson grabbed the hobo's arm, but showed surprise as he met more resistance than expected.

"You are welcome to try. Go on, take your best shot. You will find it different than you think." The 250-pound man took several swings at the incredibly swift vagabond, who dodged them with ease, as if toying with him. "Not that easy, is it, to fell a homeless man who lives in a refrigerator box?"

"Shaddup, I just need one good strike."

"Ah, but that is one more than you will ever have, you sluggish behemoth." The bum kicked him in the neck and knocked him into the side of the white van. He tried to move, but the hobo picked the large man up, hoisted him over his head, and threw him into the side of the vehicle again, as the van's occupants gaped in awe.

"What the fuck?" Chalfant yelled, pulling his own weapon. He was soon disarmed by the *Latino* hobo's kick to the solar plexus, and was then thrown about twenty feet through the air, into a concrete wall. The hobo then threw the near-unconscious Chalfant into the vehicle, while the raspy-voiced man inside sprayed him with an anesthetic. He quickly lost what remaining consciousness he had.

"Help me hold him down," the hobo said to the big, gray-haired driver of the van, in a higher-pitched voice than he had used a few moments earlier.

"Hell, don't worry. He's out now," Rad Darkkin said. "And, from what I've just seen, you don't need any help. Holy shit."

"Oh, hell, now we're kidnapping people," Jim Krakowski said. "I'm gonna go to prison for life."

"Probably not on your first offense, Jim, and this is better than being dead. But you can always go to South America. I can help you get a, heh, new identity."

"I was just fine until I got involved with you guys. And that big dude's gotta weigh at least 250. How'd M-Square throw him around like that? She lifted him over her frickin' head, and threw that Chalfant dude across the parking lot."

"Don't know. Sometimes the adrenaline flowing gives you greater strength. Shit, I've lifted 700 pounds after smokin' crack."

"No way." Jim shook his head. "I think it's something else, but I don't wanna know what."

Rita McPherson spoke up from the back. "I can explain, Jim, if you want, but the answer should be obvious."

"Not right now, thanks. Going to my happy place again."

The disguised Dr. Bonnie Mendoza and Viktor Vladimirov got inside as Rad Darkkin closed the door, after dragging the unconscious duo to the back. Bonnie removed her wig and mustache as Rad peeled away.

"Hell, Jim, this ain't nothing. Just go with the, heh, flow."

"Jeez, Rad—what if we get stopped by the cops or something?" Jim said nervously, looking around, as Rad tore out of the parking garage at eighty miles per hour. "Slow the hell down! Some security cameras probably saw us."

Rad laughed. "Are you shittin' me? I took care of the security cameras—you think you're working with some goddamn clown? I don't care about the local yokels, anyway. And it's less than a two-hour drive back to Solway, at the velocity we'll be traveling."

"Two hours. A lot of bad stuff can happen, Rad!"

"And you, heh, forget it's night—I have better night vision glasses than you've ever seen. Can drive it in the dark, boy. Infrared and ultraviolet vision. Cops won't catch us, either, because of the vehicle's radar-absorbing devices. In the dark, we're invisible, and this thing can do 180."

"Sorry. I guess I momentarily forgot who I'm driving with."

Conrad Darkkin, sober and off the booze for a month, turned the lights off and donned his ultraviolet goggles. The UV headlights provided vision nearly equivalent to driving in daylight. Jim put on the other pair.

He looked out in amazement. "Ohmigod. It's almost like daytime outside—I've never seen anything like this before. The headlights obviously emit UV to provide additional illumination."

"Yeah, the ambient ultraviolet radiation often needs supplementation. State of the art."

"But why ultraviolet?" Jim asked. "That's pretty esoteric."

"IR works okay, but a lot of CCD and CMOS sensors are sensitive to near-IR and can pick up the lights. The far UV is almost undetectable."

"How much do these goggles cost?" Jim said as he viewed the eerie glow. "They're pretty cool."

"Heh," Rad laughed. "Way more than you can afford. About 950 a pop."

"950 bucks? That's not so bad, I guess."

Rad cackled. "950 *grand*, stupid. And that's at a discount."

The white telephone van roared down State Road 119 at 170 miles per hour on the way back to Tennessee, as the massive driver steered it with amazing dexterity and skill befitting the best NASCAR drivers in the business.

"Dammit, Rad, I just hope we get back from this road trip in one piece."

• • •

The Röntgen-Cave
Solway, TN

Willie Chalfant woke up several hours later to find himself chained to a table in the dimly lit room. His eyes focused as he saw the late-sixtyish bearded man with shoulder-length silver hair come up to him.

"How're we doing? Hope you had a good little nap. The rest of your visit might not be so pleasant." The tall man pulled at the chains. "Trust me, you aren't powerful enough to break those. They are certified by my expert."

"Wh-where the hell am I? Who are you?"

"Heh—I think you probably know who I am, if you know any classified shit," Rad said as he looked into the blond man's blue eyes.

"Some crazy old son of a bitch. I work for a United States government contractor. You're dead meat, whoever you are."

"Haw, I resent that. In any case, I am acquainted with your employer from the, heh, distant past."

He studied the grizzled face as he became more lucid. "You must be Conrad Darkkin. I don't believe it—Argon said you were just a myth. Dead."

"Recognize me now, huh? Let me introduce my friends. You might call them the 'New Darkkin Science Squad.' Vik?"

"Here, Comrade Conrad," Viktor said.

Chalfant stared into the eyes of the scar-faced Russian. "Who the fuck are you supposed to be, Boris?"

"Viktor Vladimirov—former Soviet electronics engineer and bionics expert, at your service. I also enjoy injecting people with drugs and other things. But you can call me Admiral Ampere."

Chalfant laughed. "Is that supposed to scare me? Go on, take your best shot."

"In due time, my friend. Make your own conclusions in a few minutes."

"Where's my assistant, Jackson? Did you bastards kill him?"

"Naw, ol' Jack's just got a bad headache right now," Rad said as he lit his cigar. "Presently, though, you're gonna tell us what we want to know. Meet my friend, Crazy Jim, who loves to hack computers. He would love to hack you up."

"Hello," the portly man said. "I'm sure we'll get acquainted soon. I'm probably the nicest one here. And, by the way, I've done something even my female buddy can't do with her magic tricks."

"What's that, fat ass?"

Jim snapped his fingers. "I made you disappear. You don't exist any more."

"I'm right here, you dumb shit."

Jim shrugged. "Well, you can tell that to the hundreds of computer servers that I purged your very existence from. Social Security number, bank accounts, credit cards, all gone. I gave your 401(k) to the United Negro College Fund and B'nai Brith. They really appreciated the donation."

Chalfant tried to get up, but the restraints held him down. "You know what you can get for kidnapping government contract scientists? It's treason, and you'll get the death penalty."

"*Death penalty*?" Rad approached Chalfant and laughed heartily. "You—you think I really care about that? I was a goddamn spook for the CIA, you worthless piece of shit. I know about more bad crap than you'll ever know, and ate little punks like you for breakfast, loser."

"I've heard about you, but never believed anyone could be so stupid. I guess I was wrong."

"That's what I wanted everyone to think—that I was some crazy drunk dude living in Tennessee—who would've thought me a credible operative? Trust me, I'm a lot of things, but I ain't stupid."

"I'm not telling you anything, Darkkin."

"Oh, I think you will. Last, but certainly not least—meet my brilliant, aristocratic, cultured daughter-in-law, who went to the finest schools and everything."

"I am not particularly proud of being related to him, but what can I do?" Bonnie came up to him, her bald head gleaming like a bowling ball. "We meet for the third time, my tough friend."

Chalfant looked at the cinnamon-skinned woman and opened his mouth wide. "I don't believe it. You're the spick who beat me up in Charleston and threw Jackson around like a rag doll. But you're *dead*."

"I am a ghost, no?" She laughed hysterically. "Humorous—to the end. *Vindicta nemo magis gaudet quam foemina.*"

"Sorry, my Latin's a little rusty, freak."

She broke two of his left hand's fingers as he let out a shrill yell. "Ignoramus. 'No one rejoices more in revenge than woman.'" She pulled out an 18-volt power drill and brought it within a few millimeters of his left eye. "Spick? Freak? You call me that, after what you've concocted?"

"I'll take you on, you south-of-the-border weirdo, if you just let me up."

She laughed as she downed a shot of tequila. "I don't think so. We tried it once, and you did not fare so well. It is not an activity worth repeating, as time is short. Yours has run out."

"Yeah? What the hell are you going to do to me? Talk me to death?"

She stared intently down at him. "We are in for a long discussion. What happens after that depends on what you tell me."

• • •

"I have deduced that you have used Tammy Preece and other women with complete androgen resistance to circumvent the pro football testing system," Bonnie said as she continued questioning Chalfant. "I must assume that the purpose is not to win football games. There must be some biochemical benefit from boosting androgen levels."

"You seem to know it all, don't you, bitch?"

"Shut up. And you have a rudimentary understanding of synesthesia. The mere fact that Jaime carries the gene doesn't mean his offspring will, or that the abilities will be the same. His synesthete powers are vastly different from mine. Not all are beneficial."

"We'll work with the genetics. You'll never figure it out."

"I already have. Their purpose must also be to transmit a DNA-specific poison of some type. Because of the idiosyncrasies of the substance, I suspect that high testosterone levels must be required for it to function, hence your need to augment the levels of Torpin and the other players. But the selection of them makes no sense."

"Yeah, you're a damn genius, but it's too late. The T-fem women can carry it, too, because we injected them with more testosterone than you can believe."

"I still do not understand why you used those football players, though. It is illogical."

"Argon's too clever. You'll never find out."

"Shit," Rad chimed in. "It's so obvious. There's only one reason you'd inject 'roids into losers like Torpin, Edmondson, Yarling, or those other has-beens. And it wasn't to win games."

"What, Conrad?"

"Jesus, figure it out—they killed the fucking President and that Orson dude with that shit. The testosterone must be necessary for the toxin to work."

"What? We thought it was to change the point spread, to gain a betting advantage."

"Haw—a gambler would come to that conclusion. But look at the bigger picture here. No, it must have biological properties other than building muscle. Some sophisticated growth factor, requiring a unique hormonal milieu like that . . . it's the missing piece of the puzzle."

"Okay," Jim asked. "I could buy that, but what does football have to do with it then, if not to alter the course of the games?"

"Man. Don't you, heh, know *anything* about football? The Super Bowl champs met with the President last April, as they do every year. Most of those guys probably shook his hand, including Torpin, and, three days later, he croaks in front of my girl. Why else? You think that pussy Chi Argon gives a shit about something manly like pro football? Those Indy dudes were the delivery method."

She turned towards the restrained man on the table. "Is that it, Chalfant? You killed President Graham using football players?"

He gulped. "No, that's crazy."

The purple companion formed from counterclockwise-spinning swirling mists and began jumping around on her right hand.

"Liar!"

Bonnie rotated the table up ninety degrees, placing the restrained Chalfant perpendicular to the floor. She then pulled out a box containing several rusty knives and walked about thirty feet away from him.

"What . . . are you doing with those?"

"You shall see." Bonnie laughed, then threw the first knife at about sixty mph, which landed in the wooden table about two inches from his right arm.

"Oh, my God. You're nuts."

"Do *not* put me, perfectly coherent, in the same group as my deranged father-in-law. I am a magician, no? Knife-throwing is one of my favorite, yet rarely practiced, pastimes. I hope that you will allow me to hone my skills sufficiently." The second knife flew even faster, landing an inch from his left eye.

"You're going to put my fucking eye out!"

"Relax. You can live with only one eye, trust me. I have lived just fine for many years with no hearing." The third went even faster and grazed the top of his head before becoming imbedded into the board. One more knife left.

"Go to hell. I'd die first."

"I will be happy to oblige you." She took the remaining knife and plunged it into the back of his right hand, which sent blood spewing across the room. Chalfant let out a scream as she grabbed his head by the hair.

"My fucking hand!"

She grabbed his head and knocked it against the table. "Listen here, *diablo*. I will hurt you in ways you cannot imagine if you do not tell me. I was a forensic scientist who has seen death and mutilation beyond your wildest comprehension."

Chalfant was sweating profusely. "That's absurd—they don't care about the President. Argon just wanted to win some money on the football spread. Damn guy spends money like you can't believe. He's addicted to gambling, something you should understand, from what I know."

"Argon gambling, eh?" She looked at him intently. "You are a miserable prevaricator. Do not *ever* gamble with a gambler." She pulled the knife out of his right hand and began to thrust it into the left hand when he interrupted her.

"All right, you damn crazy bitch. Yeah, they killed the President, that damn bastard wanted to put a stop to Argon's research."

"How does the poison work?"

Chalfant shook his head. "It's . . . delayed in its effect, a super-growth factor for accelerating atherosclerosis. It can only be transmitted by direct skin contact. Shut off his coronary arteries in a matter of days. He probably aged thirty years in forty–eight hours."

"So he perished a few days later of a heart attack, like Orson—after Torpin and those others shook his hand."

"Yeah, you're catchin' on. But it all looks like a natural death. Lotta good it does you now, huh, bitch?"

"Is this true, Rita?" she asked the red-headed scientist.

"I don't know for sure. It's possible, but I wasn't involved in any assassination attempt. My understanding was that the football testing was to find a likely match for Travis. But it might be possible to make a poison like that."

She turned and thought pensively for a minute. "The White House barber who died and had the counterfeit money stashed—that must have been where they procured Graham's DNA. And you killed him with the very same poison, linked to his DNA, using a testicular feminization female as a vector, just like with Orson. Tammy Preece must have done that. Amazingly clever."

"Yeah, too bad you didn't figure it out before the Prez croaked. Good riddance to that asshole."

"So why are they still giving steroids to Torpin and the others, if they killed the President in April?" Jim asked.

"They were pretty long-lasting derivatives, take almost a year to get out of the system. And Argon and Gallagher were interested in potential donors for the Ortho-Man project, so the testing lab was also to . . . screen likely candidates."

"I am certain someone suspected foul play. The President must have a battery of regular check-ups," she said.

"But who's gonna prove it, lady? You? You got no proof."

She took another shot of tequila as she looked at Chalfant intently. "And there is more . . . I can see it. But who is stupider—me, or you, who is chained to a table?"

"You think there's something more than killing the President? What more could there be than that?"

She grabbed his head and squeezed. "What do you know, friend Willie?" she said as she began perspiring. "Tell me."

"Get your goddamned hands off me, you bald-headed freak."

"You rotten malefactor," she yelled at him. "You don't like my kind, the blacks, the Asians, or anybody not like you, do you, white man? I can see all your hatred now."

"Right, I hate all your goddamn stinking—" His sentence was cut short as his eyes rolled up in his head and he started seizing.

"Goddamn it," Rad yelled, "What the hell are you, heh, doing to him?"

"She didn't do anything," Jim said. "She just touched him."

"Hell, she did some crazy shit to him!" He went to pull her off Chalfant, but Jim stopped him.

"I wouldn't do that if I were you, pal. The Square's on a roll, it seems. Don't get in her way."

Chalfant stopped seizing, as he stopped breathing. Rad pulled a glazed Bonnie from his body, blood spewing out of her nose. "Get me a towel, dammit!" He took it from Jim and mopped the blood from her face with one hand as he took her pulse from her right carotid artery with his left. "Her heart rate's over 160."

Rad sat her down as she recovered from her little "event."

"Why . . . am I covered in blood? How have I been injured?"

"Don't you know? You had a nosebleed," Rad said, as the blood flow finally started to slow. "What the *hell* did you do to that guy? Some kind of Mexican voodoo shit?"

"I . . . do not remember. I must have hit him with a knife, is that it? It would be unlike me to miss."

"No, the blood's yours. You *did* something to him, gave him some pretty bad heebie-jeebies just by looking at him. Started seizing, and he croaked," Jim said.

"I remember, I saw . . . something horrific in his mind before he died, James," she said as she grabbed his shirt with her blood-stained hands. "An 'ethnic bomb.' Malachi Argon is going to create an ethnic bomb, to wipe out the Asians, Hispanics, and African-Americans of Congress. Like he got rid of Graham."

Rad looked at her, puzzled. "I know a shitload about bombs, but you can't design something like that."

Jim helped Rad clean her up. "Get with the program, Rad—we're dealing with something unknown here. This Titanian organism has given Argon the ability to do things before thought impossible. Like create DNA-specific poisons."

"I hear you, but conventional ethnic weapons are, heh, designed to exploit something else, like the lack of vaccination against an infectious disease or something unique to certain ethnic groups. You're suggesting an actual, deployable device?"

"Yes," she said, with a glazed look in her eyes. "A genetic bioweapon, designed to eradicate certain gene carriers or races. Argon is planning on somehow destroying those who he deems are genetically defective or who would hinder his goals. That is true, is it not,

Rita?"

Rita shook her head. "I swear I've never heard anything about that. There are some theories, that's all."

Bonnie, barely able to stand, looked into her eyes. "I believe you do not know, but it does exist. But we must find those who possess that knowledge."

"Yeah," Rad said. "Argon was rotten to the core, I always knew it, and I'm sure he could be involved in shit like that. But when and where, if you're right?"

She shook her head. "I do not know. His brain did not contain that information."

"Hell, it sure doesn't contain anything now, honeybun," Rad chortled. "Pretty much fried."

She pointed at him wearily. "Do not . . . call me . . . honeybun."

"You seen anything like this before, back in the day, Rad?" Jim asked in disbelief.

Rad thought for a couple of minutes. "Yeah, sort of. It was kind of like the time Smiley dissolved LSD and two different erectile dysfunction drugs together in benzene and smoked it one night."

"Huh. No kidding? How'd that work out for the Smileyman? He get lucky?"

"Heh, not so much—it didn't provide the intended effect, and he was in a trance for about two weeks. He did finally come out of it, though, although he never was the same after that."

"Got it. Message to self: don't ever try that."

Chapter Forty–five

The Röntgen-Cave
Solway, TN

"Don't go through with this, Bonnie, by all that's holy. Whatever crap they injected into you is messing with your mind. We've had our fun, now let's get the hell out of this crazy place," Jim said to Bonnie in their makeshift storage room "lounge."

"'All that's holy?' I was not aware you were a spiritual man, James. You made that clear earlier."

"Today, I am. You have no idea what you're dealing with. It's a life form from another planet."

"Titan is a moon, not a planet, duh! And I really cannot do much about it now, can I—unless I master time travel."

"Yeah, and if crazy Rad said he had a frickin' time machine, you'd get into that, too." Jim put his hand on her shoulder. "*Please* listen to me. You're putting way too much trust into Rad Röntgen and the Russian Vodka-Man over there. Maybe some things are better left alone."

"Well, it is far too late for that now. We are all pioneers on the frontier of a great new discovery."

She then noticed an infernal noise coming from down the hall, which she couldn't make out—something irritating and unintelligible. She veered off into the kitchen area, where Viktor was probably listening to the radio. What was that strange sound? Music? She did have the uncanny synesthete power of "perfect pitch"—the ability to recognize and reproduce exact frequencies. A lot of good it did a deaf woman, though. Today seemed different, though.

She smelled the sound—a C-major, G-minor, then a D-major chord, and finally found Viktor with the old 1970's LP turntable.

He was listening to Rad's family band sulphur-gospel albums. No wonder the horrible sounds didn't make any sense to her. Classical music at its finest.

• • •

The next day, Rad, Jim, and Bonnie were in the laboratory area, where Rad had constructed a crude measurement device.

"Your ability to perceive sound seems to be about twenty decibels lower than Jim, who presumably has normal hearing. About ten decibels better than mine, damaged from years of blasting my fifteen-inch speakers."

"It makes no sense," Bonnie said. "The regenerative properties of the organism are remarkable."

"I guess that's one of the advantages of living in a freezing methane pit—if you can live there, you can live anywhere," Jim said. "Like New York City. But what I can't get is how you're making out our speech."

"Conrad just stated that I am approximately twenty decibels below you. Mild hearing loss. I was a hundred before."

"Yeah, but . . . the cochlear implants are totally different. It took you years to learn to perceive speech with those, right?"

"Yes, but that's because I had virtually no memory before my illness. I did not know what speech was."

"But the patterns in your brain, the mapping, can't be the same. I'm no neuroscientist, but there's no way you should be understanding us so well."

"Music sounds very odd to me. Not like I thought it would be. One of the few remaining memories from my childhood is that of my music boxes I collected as a girl—they were nothing like this."

Jim pulled out one of Rad's scuffed vinyl albums. "This crazy-ass stuff wouldn't make musical sense to anyone, and it's scratched to hell, anyway. Rad should take better care of his things."

"That's great music, I'll have you know. Tragic songs for hard, tragic lives. 'Satan Is Within Ye,' 'Meet Thy Doom with Plutonium,'

'Don't Club with Beelzebub,' 'Americium The Beautiful,' as well as Smiley's other classics."

"But there's only one explanation for this. Somehow, you remember the past."

"Impossible. My past is gone, Jim. I will never remember it."

"That's what they said about your hearing. But your speech seems clearer, faster. You always had that lispy drawl, the kind that most pre-lingually deaf have."

"I am *not* talking differently."

"Oh, yes, you are. Rad?"

"I concur. You used to sound like I did after a few bottles of booze. Much clearer now."

She shook her head. "That cannot be, because I don't perceive things to be any different."

"That's because some of your brain cells have been restored," Jim said. "Languages were transparent to you as a girl, I understand."

"There was nothing wrong with the way I talked!"

"Shit, no offense, but with the big words you use, it can take all day for you to say what's on your mind."

"Rad's right. And I heard you speaking fluent Russian, as well as Vik here can."

"So? I am fluent in many languages. That is no secret."

"Sure, reading and writing it. But speech is different. You're kicking some linguistic ass," Jim said.

"Hell, let's do more tests," Rad said as he continued testing her hearing with his crude audiometer.

"It is odd, like a dull ringing in my ears. It is disturbing."

"What's the pitch?" Jim asked.

"4,573 Hertz." She had the rare synesthetic ability of "perfect pitch"—the ability to instantly recognize the pitch of any sound she could "hear," even though she wasn't particularly musically talented. "Things seem much more vivid than previously."

"Aren't you worried about the permanent side effects?"

"I don't care. If I suffer permanent damage, or even death, that is the price I must pay for my friend, who is not herself."

"Yeah, but—messing around with Rad and his buddies is one thing, but being injected with stuff from Titan is—"

"Reckless, I know. One thing this miraculous organism cannot change. I cannot alter what I did not start, you know."

"We still don't know what you did to that Chalfant dude. Like you fried his brain with the power of your mind."

"It's psionics," Rita said from the back of the room. "Argon had some interest in that."

"Psionics?" Jim asked. "You mean like telepathy, telekinesis, and stuff like that?" He shrugged. "None of that's possible, it's pure fantasy."

"What other explanation is there? Somehow, the restoration of Bonnie's hearing, plus other manipulations caused by OT-45, have resulted in unusually dangerous abilities."

"I don't want them, Rita. Whatever I did, it can never happen again."

"The changes are likely not permanent, unless you continue therapy."

"That is not going to happen. I am concerned about the possible toll on my body if it continues."

"There isn't any. Look at me and Tammy."

"Ha. Char-broiled Tammy is not in the best of shape right now, as she is contributing to the biogeochemical process known as the carbon cycle." She turned towards Rita and stared intensely. "And there is always a price to be paid. You and I have danced with Satan, and there will be consequences, perhaps for all of us."

"*Satan?* That's ridiculous, you don't know that."

She looked up into the air and stroked her smooth head. "There is always a cost; nothing is for free. Rad's old albums will tell you."

• • •

The next day, she stood six–two in the dull grey armor. For what it could supposedly do, it was relatively lightweight—only 130 pounds. The sensor array was fantastic. As Rad had said, the suit provided protection against almost any intrusion. It contained its own thirty–minute air supply, for when the onboard purifiers didn't work. Rad said the Soviets probably spent over forty million dollars developing it—in 1985 dollars. Jim, Viktor, and Rad had spent the last several days manipulating the electronics to adapt to Bonnie's unique processing abilities.

She walked around fluidly in the suit. "It's odd. It seems to move without any lag time whatsoever. Like moving my own body."

Rad's own voice come from the box. A younger version—he thought it more intimidating than the native high-pitched, slow voice of *Mendoza Milagroso,* although her speech was improving.

"It's cortically activated—the latest in cybernetic technology. You could be a quadriplegic, and the thing would still work."

Her senses were quickly adapting to the sensory array. Rad and Jim had altered the hearing sensors to attach to her ears, rather than to the cochlear implant interfaces; but the real kicker was the visual, olfactory, and gustatory arrays. They would serve as surrogates to help compensate for her lack of right-left orientation and direction sense. Right—sweet, left—sour, up—bitter, down—salty.

The sensitive Vladimirov auditory processors could sense up to 110,000 Hz. The best human hearing could go no higher than 20,000 Hz; her own hearing currently seemed to peak at 13,000 Hz, with a twenty-decibel hearing loss, in the "mild" range (as opposed to the 100-dB "profound" loss that she had before). The limit of canine hearing was only about 75,000 Hz. The sensitivity was remarkable, especially given the slow regeneration of something she could never remember—her own native hearing.

"It's—so much," she screamed. "I can't sort it out."

"Just focus. You can control the intensity."

The infrared, ultrasound, and ultraviolet sensors were linked to the olfactory array. Viktor's original technology had been a technological dead end, as there was no practical way for a "normal" soldier to integrate the smells into anything useful, leading to the Soviets abandoning the technology.

But Bonita Mendoza was the physicist who could see and hear odors, hear colors, taste shapes, and, now, see sounds again. She was quickly becoming the most dangerous stealth device on Earth.

"How do we look?" Rad asked through the radio.

"You both look disheveled, as usual. Why?"

"Because the room is, heh, completely dark. You're seeing us through three feet of concrete, in another room."

"This is simulated synesthetic hearing, then?"

"Partially, based on our original assumptions, but part of it is amplification of your own restored hearing. And we'll be able to monitor what you 'see' and 'hear' and give feedback."

"Then phase two is complete. We must now find out additional information regarding the location of their base," she said. "The time for reckoning is near, my friends."

Now it was time to take another trip, the finale in a series of assaults carefully planned by Rad Darkkin to destroy Argotech Industries. She had a little more confidence in her raspy-voiced father-in-law now, although Jim said they were all nuts. Keeping Rad focused was becoming quite a challenge.

Chapter Forty–six

D.T. Darkkin & Sons Distillery
32 Zinctown Drive
Solway, TN

Dr. Alex Darkkin and DEA Special Agent Jacqueline Levickis drove up to the unassuming brick building in the tiny municipality. Darkkin & Sons and the zinc mine were the largest (and pretty much the only) employers in Solway, which wasn't saying much. Business was still pretty good these days, but Alex's uncle Dustin, the president, was always a minimalist, and resisted opportunities for buyouts by larger firms. A large number of family members worked there, and most of them probably still remembered him, even though he hadn't been there in years.

"I don't believe it. Your family owns this place?" Jackie asked.

"Yeah, it's something to be really proud of. Believe me, I've got worse family secrets."

"What would those be?"

"I'm afraid you'll find out soon."

She looked at the brick building. "It's unusual, but certainly a legitimate business. I suppose you get a discount."

He turned towards her. "Get this for irony—I'm an alcoholic. Sure got the genes for it. Kind of hard walking into bars featuring bottles of whiskey with your name on it."

"I'm sorry. I didn't know."

He laughed. "It's okay, I'm not sensitive about it any more. It's not like it's unusual in my family." They walked into the front door of the modest building, and were greeted by a grey-haired woman wearing a pink dress and sitting at an old walnut desk. She hadn't changed much, he thought, since she started working there in the 1960s.

"I don't believe it. Dirk Darkkin, how ya doing?" the elderly receptionist asked him. "Come for a visit, have ya?"

"Pretty good, Flora. This is DEA Agent Levickis."

"*Dirk?*" Jackie asked curiously.

He shrugged. "My middle name. Most of my family goes by theirs. Kind of a family tradition."

"Whatever."

"DEA? We haven't done anything wrong. Oh, this is your wife, isn't it? I heard she was a police big shot. She's sure a cutie."

He laughed. "No, this isn't Bonnie, and that's not why we're here—she's DEA, not ATF. I'm actually looking for my dad. I can't find him at his house in Oak Ridge."

"You kidding? I ain't seen Rad for months. Still alive, I guess, which is hard to believe, the way he lives."

"I need to see Dusty, then. He in?"

"Yeah, but he's in a meeting with some advertising people now—he'll be free in about an hour. You can wait in his office."

"He's available now, Ma'am." Jackie flashed her badge. "You better just go find him, sweetie."

Flora put her hand over her mouth nervously. "All right, come back to his office, I'll get him."

"We'll be waiting," he said. "He better not sneak out the back."

"Is he in trouble, Dirk?" Flora whispered from the doorway.

"Yep, you might say that. Not nearly as much as my dad is."

"Oh, dear." Flora got up and hurried into the rear offices as fast as her arthritic legs could carry her, as Alex and Jackie walked down the corridor to Dustin Darkkin's cluttered office and sat down on the blue 1960s sofa.

• • •

Alex's six–four, 320-pound uncle stormed into his office a few minutes later. "Dirk, what the hell's up? I was in a meeting. You could make an appointment like everyone else, you know."

"Yeah, you're a real important guy, aren't you? Your meeting can wait, trust me. This is DEA Special Agent Levickis."

Dusty backed off from the two, as if he had just touched a hot stove. "Hey, nothin' wrong up here. I'm clean after that DUI years ago, you can check. Ain't none of your business anyway, lady."

Jackie moved towards him, but Alex pushed her gently back as he pointed a finger angrily at his slightly taller uncle. "Shut up. I want to know where my dad is, you son of a bitch."

"What the hell? I ain't seen Rad for, what, a couple of months. You know where he lives now in Oak Ridge. Damn crazy hermit, won't use anything but cash. Don't know where he keeps it all."

"He's not there. I have reason to believe you know something, and you're lying. Ralph Fowler said you, he, Smiley, and some other guy were at his bar a week or two ago, and several other times."

Dusty gulped and began sweating. "You uppity shit, living the high life in California, coming in here to hassle me? Think you're better than us, don't you?"

"If you've got a problem with me, I'm sorry, but I don't have time to deal with your self-image issues now. Where the hell did he go, Dusty?"

"I got no idea what you're talking about."

"Mr. Darkkin, I have the power to arrest you right here and now, for possible obstruction of justice."

"Hey, don't threaten me, brown sugar. I know people."

"*What* did you call me?" Jackie exclaimed. "That's it, idiot."

Alex slammed his larger uncle against the wall. "Dusty, I'll beat the shit out of you, then I'll let Agent Levickis work you over for that last remark. Last time I'll ask—where the hell is he?"

"Listen, Dirk—he told me he'd kill me if I told. I believed him, too. I could see it in his eyes. You know what I mean."

"He can get in line, because I'm going to kill you first." He pulled out two photos of Bonnie and Jim. "Have you seen either of these two people?"

"Okay, okay. Yeah, that's your wife, right? I wouldn't want to tangle with her. As mean as Rad, and that's saying a lot. I remember the other guy, too—your old buddy from Vandy."

"When and where?"

"A little over a week ago. Rad and I flew his chopper and picked them up in western Virginia. They looked like hell, parachuted out of some damn plane that was on fire and crashed into the mountains."

Jackie stared at him. "Conrad Darkkin has a helicopter? You're lying. How? He doesn't even have a credit card or bank account."

Dusty almost fell over in laughter. "Rad's got all kinds of shit, little lady. A jet, too, and probably can get a damn rocket. You ain't got no idea."

"Who else? Fowler said there was some other guy with you."

Dusty nervously took a sip of Darkkin whiskey from a bottle. "Some Russian scientist dude's been hangin' with him. About sixty, named Viktor or somethin', was going on about electronics, robots, and other shit, when he wasn't drinkin' vodka."

"Where'd they go?"

"Don't know where exactly, Dirk, I swear to God. Probably some motel or something, if they ain't at his house. He always bragged he had some lab somewhere, but me or Smiley ain't never seen it."

"They are not, and I doubt they're at a motel. Where is it?"

"I don't know any more. If I did, I'd tell you. Why don't you ask that smart-ass CIA dude who used to be Rad's buddy?"

"Huh? *CIA?* What the hell are you blabbering about?"

"That spook asshole, named Longback or something."

Jackie's eyes lit up. "Alton Lohrbach? The head of the CIA's Directorate of Science & Technology? No way."

Dusty nodded. "Yeah, that's him. Ain't been around in at least ten years, you know."

"Ten years," Alex said in disbelief. "You've met him, huh?"

"Yeah. He was with little bro down here lots of times, a long time ago."

He grabbed Dusty by the shirt again. "Okay, I guess I have to believe you. But if I find out you're lying, you'll see me again."

"O—okay, Dirk. See you."

They stormed out the front door, said goodbye to Flora the distillery receptionist, and got in their rented car and drove off.

"Alex, why are we looking for your father? He's a retired physicist, isn't he? Who cares?"

"That's what I thought, too, but a few years ago I learned the truth, who he *really* was—director of Oak Ridge National Laboratory, where he designed all kinds of high-tech weapons for the military."

"You're kidding."

"Nope. Did some undercover work for the CIA when he was younger. When Wendy, Mom, and I thought he was at some scientific meeting, he was apparently saving the free world from communism. Doing a lot of other things, too, I think. He's smart, he's got tons of cash stashed away, and he's damn dangerous. Who knows what he's up to."

"But why would he be able to find Bonnie when we couldn't?"

"There's only one answer. As bizarre as this may sound, she *wanted* him to find them. And that's not a good thing, trust me."

"Why would she want that?"

"Only one reason someone wants to find Rad Darkkin—to do something very destructive. The two of them, plus Jim, and another scientist we don't even know. I can't imagine what they're going to do, especially if what Elisa said is true."

She pulled out her laptop. "I'm going to find out all I can about this Russian guy your uncle mentioned."

"Feel free to do that, but there's something bad going on around here. I looked up the power data on the distillery from the utility company."

"How'd you do that?" she asked Alex, who stared at her. "Never mind. And why do you care how much power the distillery uses?"

"The Darkkin plant is using about twice the kilowatt-hours the last few months than before, yet their production is actually down a bit, according to the quarterly reports."

"Maybe they went to a different process, or are using some new machine or something."

"Uh-uh," he said, shaking his head. "Someone else is using the excess power. And I'm pretty sure I know who." He looked at the file that Carlos Mendoza's old friend, FBI chief of cyber crime Ken Thornton, gave to him several years ago. "It's time to find a man named Alton Lohrbach."

"I'm going with you."

"You're going to the hotel. I'm flying this one solo."

Chapter Forty–seven

The Röntgen-Cave
Solway, TN

"I am grateful to you for rescuing me from that wreckage of a plane. But I'm not going to help you," Rita McPherson said to Bonnie, Rad, and Jim.

"You will not help? You said you would." Bonnie said. "That is not a wise choice. I do not wish to pulverize you, but you leave me little alternative." She balled her right hand into a fist.

"It's not that I don't want to—I'm scared, and have reconsidered. I did what I did because I believed in helping people."

"What he has done is evil incarnate, and I will—"

Jim stepped in. "We've done this little number before on the plane, so let me be the 'good cop' here. We know you're scared, and ol' M-Square here is a little too theatrical for her own good."

"What? Shut up, you porcine, follicle-challenged—"

He pushed Bonnie back. "Maybe your buddy Argon isn't all that you thought he was, Rita. You think he's such a great guy?"

"He has bypassed some traditional checks and balances, such as Institutional Review Boards, but only for the sake of furthering knowledge. Many of the great scientists—Pasteur, Salk, Banting and Best, to name a few, took some liberties in that area to bring their discoveries to the aid of mankind. Would you deny the world their breakthrough discoveries?"

"Did Pasteur's son murder a professor like Travis Argon killed Jasper Bennett?"

Rita shook her head. "Bennett, the famous astrobiologist? I don't know anything about his death."

"You know of him?" she asked.

"Sure, he's the one who gave Malachi the idea about it, long before the mission. He always thought there was life on Titan, and Malachi paid him a lot of money to be a consultant. But I don't believe Travis would ever kill."

"Hey, he pretty much decapitated the guy, apparently because he had information about Titan that Argon didn't want to get out," Jim said. "Not a pretty sight, M-Square said."

"Bennett worked with us on some preliminary things regarding the discoveries on Titan. But I still don't believe you."

"I hate to break it to you," Jim added, "but ol' Travis is a highly engineered killing machine. Not the future of things to come, as you maintain, unless that future involves extermination."

Rita pondered a minute and drank some bottled water. "You're lying, to manipulate me. I didn't know about the assassination of the President, and that has nothing to do with Travis."

Bonnie stuck her finger into Rita's face. "We are liars? Why, you titian-haired—"

"Cool off." Jim pushed her back again. "I wish it wasn't true, but it is. Bonnie found that Bennett's door was torn off its hinges. He was torn apart, too, like a wild animal might tear apart its prey. I can get proof if you want."

"I . . . can't believe that."

"Believe it, Red. The dude's kinda dangerous."

Rita looked deeply into the dark eyes of Bonnie Mendoza, and thought for a few more minutes. "If what you say is correct . . . which I have no reason to doubt that it is . . . what have I done, and why have I been in denial?"

"You did not do it knowingly. You were duped by Argon, with the promise of walking again."

"I helped kill a man who put Jaime Mendoza in the hospital and kidnapped Dr. Williams. A President and Senator are also dead, along with many others we probably don't know about."

"I guess you thought the means justified the ends. You can help make it right, Rita," Jim said.

Rita began crying. "How can anyone make it right?"

"Then tell us what we need to know to break in there, retreive Wendy safely, and destroy that God-awful place," she said.

Rita laughed. "You must be insane. That thing's as heavily guarded as a military base, with a variety of defensive weaponry. You don't stand a chance."

"Lady," Rad said as he rose up and exhaled a cloud of blue smoke from his cigar. "I've got shit here that no one in the U.S. even knows about. Been saving it for this very day, when someone like me has to make things right again."

"I don't mean to be rude, Dr. Darkkin," Rita said. "But I think you overestimate yourself. In other words, you're insane."

"Look around you," Rad said. "Do any of us, including Mendoza, look like we're playing with a full set of marbles?"

"No. You're all crazy."

"Damn right. But we're not here because we want to be safe. This thing has been planned for a long time, and we're here because we want to kick that SOB's butt straight to hell."

Bonnie held her hand up. "And also to rescue Wendy, stop horrible genetic annihilation, and avoid the end of mankind as we know it. Do not forget about those vital activities."

"Oh, yeah. Gotta focus here, I forgot."

• • •

"The main experimental complex appears to be on this little island in the Caribbean," Rad said while pointing to the computer monitor. "A lot of radiofrequency energy coming from it, my satellite links detect. That *has* to be it."

"How's she going get in there, Rad? Parachute in?" Jim asked. "That thing wasn't exactly designed for swimming."

"No, she can't," Rita said. "There's radar that'll detect it, anything much over the surface. The soldiers will be all over her."

"What is the difference?" Bonnie asked. "What harm can they possibly do to me?"

"Probably none, but you need to get Wendy out of there in one piece. Part of this caper depends on the suit's strengths: stealth ability, speed, and ability to assimilate information and shut down the defenses—not smash everything. And it's *not* completely invulnerable."

"I guess you have a plan, Rad," Jim said. "You always do."

"Hell, yeah. Viktor's buddy is gonna shoot M-Square out of a torpedo tube. It'll go under the radar and get her to the surface without them having a clue."

"The pressure will be too much," she said. "Worse than a space shuttle launch."

"Heh, not hardly, but you'll be safe in Vik's suit. The damn thing was designed for possible space exploration, and it'll protect you against damn near anything, including the eight Gs of a torpedo tube."

"How the hell are you going to do that?" Jim asked. "To shoot a torpedo, you need a . . . submarine, I think."

Rad looked at him blankly. "So, what's your point? Of course we'll be in a sub, you moron. Jesus."

"Are you nuts? Where are we gonna get a nuclear sub?"

Rad shook his head. "Hell, no—not nuclear, that's the wrong boat for this. Vik has a friend in the Russian Navy who'll give us a ride in his Kilo Class SSK 636 attack sub. They're diesel-electric, one of the quietest boats around. They can disappear like a magician." He pointed to her, laughing.

"The U.S. Navy will find us and blow us up, I know it," Jim said. "And I didn't know they had those kinds of subs any more."

"There's still about twelve in service by the Russians, they sold the rest to the Chinese and Middle East, those traitors. And the Kilo is fitted with anechoic tiles which pretty much absorb any sound waves, making it virtually undetectable by active or passive sonar."

"How many more laws can we break, Rad? This suit alone is incriminating, let alone traveling in the sub of another country."

"Trust me," Rad said as he put his arm on the shorter Jim's arm. "I know what I'm doing. And we're pals with the Russkies now, bud, and we'll be in international waters, so what's the problem?"

"What the hell do we do with Rita, and Argotech security dude's assistant? And Chalfant's body?"

"I have a job for Rita. I can get Dusty to take care of our buddy while we're away. Plus, I'll get Smiley to give ol' Willie a proper burial. He used to work at the Solway funeral home, when he wasn't assisting the coroner in autopsies."

Chapter Forty–eight

The Röntgen-Cave
Solway, TN

"We're almost ready," Rad said to the group in the underground lab. "We still need a way to make sure she can shut down all the defenses."

Jim pulled up a chart. "We have the biometrics from Chalfant, which Rita said should get us through most of the perimeter defenses. But we likely will need some passwords that only Argon knows."

"Ol' super math whiz should be able to crack the codes, don't you think?" Rad replied.

She shook her head. "You overestimate my abilities. It is true that I can manipulate numbers easily, but those passwords are likely generated by complex mathematical equations. I can crack them eventually, though, with my cipher abilities."

"Bonnie's right," Jim said. "Those probably use 512-bit encryption, and we need something else to help M-Square. Something from the computers themselves."

"Shit, Chalfant should've known them, right?" Rad asked.

"He does not know them all," she said.

"Uh, I think you meant 'did.' And I don't think we can ask him any more questions, thanks to you," Jim replied.

"Sorry, you know I don't fully remember doing that. But I assure you he was unaware of everything. There are some things Argon must keep to himself."

"There's a lot of firepower likely in there. As good as that suit is, she's going to need a better advantage than that. Any other ways?" Rad asked.

"A password sniffer," Jim said. "That would be the best way."

"What?" she asked.

"A device physically attached to the server, a 'Trojan horse', if you will. It'll filter out the passwords and transmit them to Bonnie before she actually gets in there."

"But I believe such a device must be physically placed in the server. That's impossible," she said.

"Rita can do it," Rad said. "Put the damn thing right in there, then they'll be toast."

"I don't believe you guys," Jim replied. "Anyway, she's been gone for a week. Where would they say she's been? The military's surely combed the area looking for wreckage. There's no way she could've survived."

"They certainly know the parachutes are missing. Any good forensic scientist would have discovered that. They must have been looking for days, and must have given up by now," she said.

"She could've bailed out when we did, but suppose only she survived. Assume that she had a head injury and couldn't communicate with anyone, but was found with amnesia," Jim said.

"Amnesia, how corny. No one would believe it," she said.

"You've had it a couple of times," Jim said.

"That's true. Well, let us develop our plan, Conrad. Get a map so we can plot Rita's timely rescue by the local law enforcement."

"Great," Jim said. "I guess I need to hack into the FBI database to switch around some more records. Another dozen or so federal laws I'm going to break."

• • •

"Rita, will you help us now?" Bonnie asked her.

"I'll do what I can. What do you want me to do?"

"We need for you to somehow get back into Argon's complex. We're going to dump you on the side of the road in West Virginia, and someone will pick you up and take you to the local hospital. You'll have amnesia for a couple of days, but then will 'remember' and tell them to call Argon."

"*Argon?* He'll kill me if he finds out. Right now, I'm alive."

She looked up. "He won't, but we don't really have any other choice. You are a fugitive, and what future do you have?"

"But what good does getting me back into Argotech do? Surely they suspect something's up with Chalfant gone. You don't think you can keep this 'vacation' thing of his up forever, do you?"

"No, but I can re-create his voice synthetically using Markov models and call them. They will never know the difference."

"I guess . . . I could see how that might work."

"But you said that Argon trusts you. Is that true?" she asked.

"Yes, it was Gallagher who was always suspicious. But Argon's no dummy, I assure you. He'll figure it out, eventually."

"Hopefully that'll be too late," Jim said. "We need you to plant this on the server, hook it up through a network port."

Rita shook her head. "It won't work. The computer only allows access through authorized MAC (Media Access Control) addresses. It won't interface."

Jim smiled. "Don't worry, you're working with the best there is. It'll spoof existing MAC addresses and emulate those, to sniff out passwords and transmit them outside to Bonnie's onboard computer. I'll organize the information and send it back before she breaks in. She'll be able to shut down almost all of the computer systems and deactivate the existing passwords so they can't change it back."

"How will it transmit back? That room will absorb most types of radio energy."

"Not this, little lady," Rad said, laughing. "Ultra-high frequency pulsed FM channels, specially encoded. Military doesn't even use them. And the signals don't have to go that far. Once she's on the island, it'll download everything we need to sink that bastard and blow that goddamn island off the map."

She stuck her finger into his chest. "Conrad, I understand your enthusiasm, but *please* do not again forget our primary objective—not the destruction of Dr. Malachi Argon, as gratifying as that shall be—but the rescue of Wendy and the saving of mankind. I hate to keep reminding you."

Rad scratched his scraggly head. "Oh, yeah, Wendy and the future of mankind—I forgot again. Sorry."

Chapter Forty–nine

U.S. Highway 19
Raleigh County, WV

The bare-footed woman wearing tattered and burned clothing made her way to deserted Highway 19, where she climbed up the side of the hill. The debris of wet leaves had left her feet muddy as she staggered down the road. She saw several cars pass in the morning light, which sped up after seeing her. Why didn't they stop for her?

After about an hour, a Raleigh County Sheriff's SUV finally pulled up, and a deputy got out to assist her.

"Ma'am, are you hurt?" the officer asked as he approached her cautiously. "I'm here to help you."

"Oh, my God, thank you," she said as she staggered towards him and fell into his arms.

"Okay, you're all right," he said as he picked her up and took her to the front seat of his vehicle. "Who are you, and what the devil are you doing out here?"

"I need . . . some water and something to eat."

"Okay." He gave her a can of soda he found in the front seat, plus two stale doughnuts, which she ate ravenously as he put a blanket over her shoulders. "Can you tell me your name?"

"McPherson. Rita McPherson."

"Where are you from, Rita, and how'd you get out here? Did you have a wreck?"

"I . . . was in a private plane, a week ago. There was a malfunction and it crashed. Where are we?"

"Raleigh County."

"West Virginia?"

"Yes, Ma'am. South of Charleston. Beckley's the county seat."

She slurped down the rest of the sugary beverage. "I'm from Cairo. I work there."

"Cairo. That's up north, isn't it?"

"Yeah."

He called the dispatcher. "This is Dunsmore. 10-78 out here on U.S. 19, just north of Rawlings Road. Female, early thirties, needs transport to Memorial."

"10-4."

"Miss, we're gonna have to get you to the hospital and get you cleaned up. How long you been out there? That plane crashed a week ago."

"That long, I guess. I . . . parachuted out. I think I'm the only one who survived."

"You've been in the woods that long? Lots of varmints out there—grizzlies, coons, wild dogs . . . you're damn lucky you're in such good shape."

"I couldn't find my way to the road, I kept going around in circles. Thank God I ran into you."

• • •

Beckley Memorial Hospital
Beckley, WV

Malachi and Travis Argon came to Memorial Hospital to see Rita McPherson, and were escorted to her room by the staff, who stared at the bulk of the 450-pound Travis. Rita lay in the bed, with an IV pole infusing Ringers' lactate, and was wearing several bandages over her arms and legs.

"What the hell happened to you?" Argon asked. "We thought everyone was dead. Gallagher's guys have been searching for days."

"I was dazed, roaming around, nothing to eat. Amazingly, the animals didn't get me. I just kept going . . . west, until I finally reached a highway. A sheriff's deputy found me yesterday, wandering the hills."

"My Gulfstream jet . . . what happened?" Argon asked.

"Mendoza got a gun away from one of the guards, shot a couple of people, including the pilot. Tammy got it away from her, but that nutso bitch pulled the emergency exit hatch. We tried to parachute out, I guess Tammy didn't make it."

"They never found her body. They did find Mendoza's—the dental records matched those the FBI had on her, but we couldn't do other testing without drawing suspicion. Damn, she would've been a good experiment."

"Yeah, I heard she was pretty tough," Travis said. "I wish I could've knocked her around, like her asshole brother."

"Shut up, Travis. We don't need that tough-guy attitude. And Mendoza's still alive, I found out. You should've done it right. Cops found evidence in the motel room."

"Yeah, he's just some veg in a coma. Big deal." Travis peered down at his father. "And don't tell me to shut up, Dad. I don't need your shit." Malachi Argon backed away cautiously.

Rita wondered how they had achieved that, with the dental records. The quirky Bonnie Mendoza and pals had several surprises, it seemed. "I don't know about her. They must've died falling out of the plane. A lot of woods here, would take forever to search it, Dr. Argon."

"Yes, I suppose so."

"What about Gallagher? Does he know about this?"

"He was taking a fishing trip for a week or so. We talked to him and let him know. Said he'd be up in a couple of days. It's not as if he can do anything about it."

"Good."Apparently Bonnie's faked voice worked, after all. She looked at the bulky Travis. "You doing okay, my friend?"

"I guess so, Rita. Feel pretty good the last few days. Dad says the counts look normal. Pretty soon I'll be healthy for good, he says."

"Damn right," Argon said. "Right now, you need to go home and get some rest. The doctors say you can come with us."

"I don't want rest. There's a lot of work to do with Travis. I want to help in any way I can."

"You sure you're okay?"

"I'm fine. I just want to get back to the island to help you."

"That's great, Rita," Argon said. "We've lost valuable time. And our new subject is about ready for usage."

Rita gulped as she thought to herself how repulsive this had become. Experimentation on an unborn fetus. But she didn't think anything of it before—why had she changed her mind now? Perhaps contact with the unanticipated powers of Bonnie Mendoza had an effect on her thought processes. But there was no going back now. She had a job to do, even if it meant her life. And she couldn't let them suspect anything.

Chapter Fifty

Methodist Hospital
San Diego, CA

Jaime Mendoza lay in his hospital bed on the early Saturday morning, hooked up to intravenous tubes, although the comatose man was now breathing well on his own. His mind began to spin as if in a wild dream. He was floating in air, looking down at the bright orange landscape, strangely foreboding, yet beautiful. He flew through the thick atmosphere, and landed on what looked like a river bank. He was so light, he noticed, as he walked, with strides about twice as long as normal. The air was cool and misty, although he seemed to be warm, wearing only a T-shirt and jeans.

He noticed that he was younger and thinner—maybe sixteen or seventeen. Where could he possibly be? He looked at the river bank, bent over, and put his right hand into the liquid. Not like any water he'd ever felt—a grayish, frigid, oily liquid that resisted any attempts to hold some in his palm.

He heard the lightning far up in the atmosphere, and gasped in awe at the giant ringed yellow sphere occupying two-thirds of the sky, flattened at its poles and slightly fatter at its equator.

He knew it should be cold here, because the sun was so small, yet he felt warm. He'd had these alien dreams before, but not for a long time, and this seemed so lifelike . . . he didn't think they were possible any more. And they were never so real, like *this*.

He then spied the four-foot, dark-haired girl fishing in the tarry lake. Ah, that explained it. She looked that way the last time he saw her like that in a vision, over twenty-three years ago. He called out to the spindly female.

"I've not seen you like this for a long time. Is that really you?"

The familiar girl turned to him and smiled. "Of *course* it is me. Who else would you expect to see in such a fantastic place?"

"Where . . . where have you brought me?"

She turned around and presented him with the small bluegill she had caught. "I have for you a fine *Lepomis macrochirus*. I remember how much you liked fishing. I recall the times you took me ice fishing in Wisconsin. It was frigid and boring."

He took the cold fish as it wiggled in his hand. "It can't be a fish, not here. This strange pond . . . what is it?"

"It is a special place, named Ontario Lacus."

"Are we . . . dead? Is this heaven?"

"Humph. I don't think either of us is ready for that yet."

"I was worried you were gone forever. I had a feeling."

"Of course we are alive. We are on an alien world which contains many wonders, one of which has allowed me to see you again."

"Where?"

She held her hands out as wide as her forty–eight-inch wingspan allowed. "You see before you the beautiful surface of the largest moon of the sixth planet from the sun."

He looked around and touched her soft skin. "You *are* real, just as I remember. Where have you been?"

"I could no longer visit you in this fashion after . . . I almost died twenty–three years ago. But I am back now, on this special day of science, perhaps for the last time."

"How? They said it was impossible."

"That is unimportant. But rest assured, I am working vigorously on a solution to our mutual problem. You will wake up soon, after our visit, and see Mother and Father."

"You know about what happened?"

"I believe so. The heinous organism known as Travis Argon assaulted you and abducted Wendy. I, with the aid of atypical allies, will soon triumph over the forces of evil."

"You do know. How can this be?"

"As I have said . . . many things have happened. I cannot go back and erase them."

"Wendy—there's something terribly wrong with her. Messed up bad."

"Yes, I hypothesized as much. I hope to encounter her soon. Your last meeting was interesting, as I understand." She smiled.

"I didn't . . . we didn't . . . not there, anyway. I tried to stop her, you have to believe me."

"I know now."

He stared at the sixty–pound girl holding the fishing line and touched her black hair. "You can't be real. You're so small, a mere child. It's impossible for us to actually be here."

"Your perception of me can only be as it last was in your dreams, but I am grown now. Thirty–four."

"What happens now?"

"It is time for me to leave you. Do not despair, as the day of reckoning for many is soon at hand."

"You can't leave me. I'll be alone."

The little girl stroked his face and smiled. "I must, because soon others who care about you will appear. And I have much hazardous business to attend to."

"No, don't leave." She took his hand and started crying as she slowly faded away.

"This may be the last time I will ever talk to you. If it is, always know that I appreciate how much you did for me, Jaime. And you will never be alone, for you will always carry a part of me with you for the rest of your life."

He watched the diminutive, verbose figure fade from existence, like ripples in a pond, as he saw the ominous lightning and methane liquid rain upon the moon. And just then, he woke to see his parents, Carlos and Elisa, in the room, as his blood pressure and heart rate increased dramatically.

"Hey," he said. "Where the . . . hell am I?"

"San Diego Methodist," Carlos replied.

"What . . . day is it?"

"October 23."

"Dang . . . what happened? How long have I been out?"

"Almost three weeks, Jay," Carlos said.

He moved his hands and feet sluggishly. "Am I in . . . one piece?" He slowly looked at his hands, which he balled into fists. "Doesn't look too bad, huh?"

"It would appear so," Carlos said, as the neurosurgery resident on duty rushed into the room. "Your right leg is in a cast. Tib-fib fracture, they had to put screws in. Otherwise, you're pretty lucky."

"I can remember bits and pieces . . . some lousy old motel," he said as he tried to sit up. "Wow. Really woozy."

Carlos pushed him back in the bed. "God, get back down. You need to rest."

"I thought Dani was going to be there, but it was Wendy playing a trick. She was there—my God, where's Wendy?"

His parents looked at each other. "We don't know where she is. That guy who beat you up took her somewhere, we think," Elisa said as she started crying. "She may not even . . . be alive."

"I swear to God, I don't know what was going on, Mom. You'd better find her. She's pretty whacked out."

"We don't know where to start," she said, crying. "We haven't heard anything. Alex and the FBI are looking for her."

"What can you remember?" Carlos asked. "Anything at all might help, son."

"Big dude, Travis, I remember Travis . . . Arlen, Arvin, something like that."

"Argon. Alex found out from some cryptic stuff Bonnie sent him earlier."

"Yeah. He tried out for our team, '95, I think. Big damn dude, strong as hell, but a real ass with an attitude problem. Got sick or something, I think. Some kind of cancer."

"Yes. Travis Argon had leukemia, and his . . . father did some genetic experiments on him, to make him stronger. He's dangerous."

"That's for damn sure. Tammy Preece . . . the assistant pro football commisioner, was there, too."

"Tammy Preece? That's impossible, Jay," Carlos said.

"No, it's not, Dad. She threw Wendy around pretty well."

"But you left an anagram for Bonnie, which led us to Travis," Elisa said.

He thought about his "alien" dream. "Bonnie . . . where is she?"

"We don't know," Elisa said. "She's disappeared too, just like Wendy. Alex said he heard from her, but just once. We . . . we don't know if she's still alive, Jay. A plane crashed in Virginia, and they think one of the bodies was hers."

Jay shook his head. "No, she's here, she just spoke to me. She told me all about it, she—" He paused, looking at his hand. "She's in the Atlantic Ocean, somewhere in the Caribbean."

"You're hallucinating, Jay," Carlos said, shaking his head. "You just woke up from a coma. Bonnie's not here."

"No, don't you remember, little Bonnie . . . told me about Travis Argon, and Wendy, we were on some alien planet, it was all orange and had this oily lake. I could see Saturn in the sky, it was so beautiful, more than you can possibly imagine."

His parents looked at each other. "It's not real," Carlos said. "You couldn't have seen Saturn."

"Yeah, it is, I tell you! How is that possible? I haven't seen a vision of her in over twenty years."

"She might not even be alive," Carlos said. "Alex is out looking for her, but—"

Elisa interrupted after pondering for a few moments. "I just remembered—the date, October 23." She then pointed to the clock, a few minutes after six AM. "Look at the time, Carlos."

"A little after six o'clock. So what?"

"Today is Mole Day. Only Bonnie would know that."

"Mole Day?" Jay said, deep in thought. "She *is* alive, then. But she said something to me, right before I woke up."

"What?" his father asked.

"She said, 'do not despair, for the day of reckoning for many is soon at hand,' then she disappeared, then I woke up. It sounded almost like a threat."

"I have to call Alex," Elisa said, flipping open her cell phone. "Bonnie's still alive, I just know it."

Chapter Fifty–one

Oak Ridge Municipal Airport
Oak Ridge, TN

Alex flew to his and Wendy's birthplace the next morning to meet with the mysterious yet powerful figure his father seemed to know well—Alton Lohrbach, the chief of the Central Intelligence Agency's Directorate of Science & Technology (DS&T). DS&T was the CIA branch responsible for developing and applying technology to advance intelligence gathering of the United States.

He learned from his readings that Lohrbach was born in Philadelphia in 1950 and graduated with a degree in chemistry from Columbia University in 1971. He then joined the United States Navy, where he remained for nine years, leaving with the rank of lieutenant commander. During that time, he served in the Submarine Corps; his biography stated he that he wanted a career in intelligence, and he was recruited into the CIA in 1984 by then-director William J. Casey, and eventually became part of the DS&T, the place where he felt he could make the most difference.

The organization was formed on December 31, 1948, under its original name, the Office of Scientific Intelligence (OSI), by merging the Office of Reports and Estimates with the Nuclear Energy Group of the Office of Special Operations. The OSI remained until 1965, when it was renamed the Directorate of Science & Technology, under the jurisdiction of the CIA.

DS&T provided support to CIA missions via research, development, acquisition, and operation of technical capabilities and systems. DS&T also directed the Foreign Broadcast Information Service and the National Photographic Interpretation Center (NPIC).

The most famous work of the agency was its most notable work, however—its task as a "spy shop," in which some of the most innovative surveillance technology in history—the U-2 and A-12 spy planes, for example.

Alex was surprised how eager Lohrbach was to talk to him when he called; he had expected days of bureaucratic run-around before getting through. But the director said he knew nuclear physicist W. Conrad Darkkin quite well, and was not surprised to receive the call. Lohrbach said it was time to meet the son of Rad Darkkin, one of the most unusual individuals he had met in his life.

• • •

Alex prepared to meet Alton Lohrbach at the small airstrip, a place he had visited with his father, a private pilot, many times. He had expected Lohrbach, for some reason, to be small, not the lanky man he saw walking down the tarmac.

"You must be Alexander Darkkin. I'm happy to meet you," the six–three, sixty–year-old Lohrbach said as he stepped off the plane. He was followed by a pair of black-suited CIA agents.

"Yeah, I wish I could say the same. It must have taken something pretty important to get you out here to meet with me."

Lohrbach shook his hand as they got into Alex's car and waved off his bodyguards. "My pleasure—and, yes, I heard the distress in your voice. Goes with the job."

"You know my dad, I understand."

Lohrbach laughed. "Do I know Rad? Just for the last thirty or so years, that's all. A clever and brilliant mind. You look a lot like him."

"Not really, I look more like my mom than him, but did get some of his height, I guess."

"A unique and fascinating man of diverse talents. Certainly has a colorful family."

"That's one way to put it. He worked with you, then?"

"Yes. Rad headed up our nuclear division, also worked on some nerve gas weapons and other stuff. A man of almost limitless ingenuity and energy. But you wanted to know about what he was doing recently, you said."

"My dumb-ass uncle thinks there may be some secret lab here somewhere. But he runs the distillery, so he could be drinking up the profits. I've considered him neither intelligent nor reliable over the years. On the other hand, the power meters don't lie."

"Power meters?"

"There's far more electricity being used than can possibly be used by the plant. The surges come and go."

The director laughed again. "I don't know what Dusty's told you, Alex—Rad has done some work for us in the past, of course, but nothing recent. He once had his own research facility on the side, called DARC—Darkkin Atomic Research Corporation, but that's not currently operational, as far as I know. The last government contract was over seven years ago, for some reactor coolant specs he was developing."

"I don't understand." They had left the airport area and were now traveling south to Solway in Alex's rental car, as Lohrbach had apparently decided Alex was benign enough to leave his entourage at the airport. "You're being evasive—you're saying he might have some lab out here? If he does, it's stupid to not assume he's up to something sinister."

"Rad was always pretty egotistical. I'm not surprised he's bragging that he's got a secret lab here in Tennessee. And he's more talk than anything else."

"So, this 'DARC' must be near the Darkkin whiskey plant, and he must be tapping off the plant's power grid. Why?"

"I suppose he figured it was a pretty rural area, no one would suspect it. You're a pretty bright guy—you didn't, did you?"

"Guess not. Right under my nose all those years."

"It hasn't been used for anything recently, though, although Rad was tinkering around in it. There were some theories—"

"You mean he's still working on some things for you guys? No way can I buy that bullshit."

"Just stuff on paper, that's all, years ago. One that seemed dead-end, but we let him and this ex-Soviet scientist work on it, to see if there was some technology we could perhaps salvage."

"Who and what?"

"Viktor Vladimirov, a bionics and robotics expert who defected before the demise of the USSR. He and Rad became buddies, I heard through the grapevine. We heard Vlad was dead, though. A lot of people think Rad already is."

"*Viktor Vladimirov? Soviet robotics expert?* That's way too corny for me to believe. What is it they were supposedly working on?"

"This was years ago, but rumor was that Vlad wanted to build some type of high-tech stealth battle armor suit. The idea was good, but it was way too expensive to make—the shell was supposed to be fullerene-based, if you can believe it."

"*Fullerenes*? Buckyballs and stuff like that? That's crazy 'pie in the sky' science fiction." Fullerenes and buckyballs were named after a scientist who developed the geodesic dome, which those carbon molecules resembled—Richard Buckminster "Bucky" Fuller. Fullerenes were discovered in 1985, and were a family of lightweight carbon allotropes with hardness exceeding that of diamond. The buckyball was also the state molecule of Texas, he remembered for no particular reason.

"They also had some problems integrating the sensory input. It never really existed, other than in the development stage."

"You have to be kidding me. He's lost a few marbles."

"I guess so. But some of that was an exaggeration, Alex. The goal was for no one to take him seriously. You didn't. I guess he did cause a lot of problems for your family."

Alex snarled and shook his head. "My mom divorced him and my sister disowned him. You think, Lohrbach?"

"Yeah, I guess I only saw the science side. I'm sorry."

"I bet you're sorry." He turned down a dirt road on the way to their destination. "Do you know of some bio-geneticist named Malachi Argon?"

"Argon?" Lohrbach shook his head. "Never heard of him."

He noticed that Lohrbach had a 'poker face' every bit as good as his gambling-addict wife. "You're lying."

"Why would I do that?"

"Come on. The first rule of gaming is—never con a con man. I know Argon has something to do with this and my wife. I think she may be around here somewhere, if she's even still alive."

"Your wife?" Lohrbach again displayed that inscrutable look. "I don't think I know her."

"Bonita Mendoza—she's a physicist at Caltech. Also a forensics expert, among other things. You must know who she is."

"Right." Lohrbach shrugged and turned towards him. "Look, son, I'm involved with a lot of dangerous stuff. I can't tell you much of it. But I can tell you a little bit."

"What the hell is that supposed to mean? You sound just like my dad, save for the Tennessee accent and lack of cursing."

"We have teams of people who are always trying to gain an edge in technology, and are always looking for people with exceptional abilities."

"You're still being awfully vague, but probably appropriate for a government official. Please continue."

"Oh, come on, Alex, do you think we're stupid? We've had our eye on her for many years, ever since she was a small child. She's not exactly anonymous, and her curious mathematical abilities can be viewed on any children's network channel. DS&T often has interest in child prodigies, most of whom don't pan out, but occasionally you find a gold mine."

"You've been watching Bonnie for years?" Alex shook his head. "That's hard to believe. Impossible, in fact."

"I knew Carlos a bit, as did a few people in the FBI, like Ken Thornton. But, after her illness, the previous people in the agency sort of lost interest. The deafness made her an unsuitable agent, and apparently some of her abilities were diminished."

"Unsuitable agent?" He laughed. "You're a goddamn robot. Are you any better than my dad?"

"At least he knew that life wasn't a cakewalk. Somebody had to do those things."

"Shit, you have a pat answer for everything. Don't expect me to kiss your ass, Lohrbach."

"Trust me, I don't. One more thing . . . would there have been communications between Bonnie and your father?"

Alex shook his head. "I guess I wouldn't be out here if I didn't think that, deep down. All the strange clues suggest that they have teamed up, but it sounds absurd—she couldn't stand him."

"My recent info on her says she's far more dangerous than you may perceive. My guess is that she wanted something from him."

He laughed. "She's about as dangerous as a Chihuahua. All that magic stuff is staged, and the mentalist tricks are mainly valuable for gambling and doing word and number puzzles."

Lohrbach laughed. "Is that right? She's an amazingly gifted individual, on many levels. Knows weaponry, fighting skills, can get out of almost any fix. Thornton once showed me webcam footage of her killing a terrorist with her bare hands. Beat the shit out of him."

"Yeah—I know. But she often thinks like a child. We hardly let her drive, and her clothes are picked out for her every day."

"I really don't care about her fashion sense."

Alex laughed. "Maybe you ought to recruit *her*."

Lohrbach stared at him intently. "Despite my appearances, my reasons for being here are not simply to locate Rad Darkkin, son. At some point, I will likely become Secretary of Defense. I need a person of unmatched intellect, who is beyond reproach, to replace me someday. Someone with the guts to do dirty jobs."

Alex thought for a few minutes and laughed. "Replacement? You'd just better keep on looking. He's sixty–nine, and isn't the most responsible of people. Find someone else with the balls."

Lohrbach laughed heartily and stared back at him. "Is the son of Rad really that naïve, or have I made a mistake in coming here?"

"I have no goddamn idea. Quit talking in riddles."

"And I said 'guts,' not 'balls.' There is a subtle, but important, difference, which you might know, being a physician."

Alex opened his mouth wide and shook his head. "I would . . . never go along with that. This conversation never happened, you son of a bitch. I ought to kick your ass."

"You look like you might, too. I guess you are your father's son, I can see it in your eyes."

"You'd best remember that."

"Whatever you say. But it's not your choice, is it, Alex?"

• • •

Alexander Darkkin and Alton Lohrbach finally reached their destination, twenty miles from Oak Ridge—an old barn on the outskirts of Solway (as if there was actually an inner city of Solway).

"This is it, huh? Secret government lab, you think, Alex?"

"Yeah. My demented dad's play place."

"It's just an old barn."

"Okay, smart guy, you seem to know all about my wife, so it should be no surprise that she likes mathematical puzzles. Here's one for you: she told me about the seventeenth perfect totient number—3,063—which just happens to be the absolute value of the product of a longitude and latitude."

"Where? We're in the middle of nowhere."

He pointed to the old, decaying structure. "Right where that old barn is. And I'll bet anything she's programmed my palm print to let us inside."

"I'm impressed. But that doesn't mean it's anything more than a barn any more, son."

"You kidding me? *Now* who's being naïve?" Alex wrenched the door open, as they went inside and searched for an of access panel of some sort. Alex finally found what looked like a palm-print biometric reader, behind an electrical service panel.

"This is it," he said, as he put his palm on an access panel, which activated a hidden elevator door.

"What the hell? I don't believe it. That sneaky son of a bitch."

"Looks like it still works," he said. "Get in." They went down the elevator shaft to the basement complex and walked in the door. Alex looked around at the vast amount of lab equipment.

"I don't believe it."

He looked at a coffee cup, dipped his finger inside, and tasted it. "Sugar and cream. If it had been down here very long, it would've been putrid."

"Maybe." The director paused for a few minutes. "Look, Alex, I don't know what they're doing. But I do know a thing or two about Malachi Argon. There is the rumor of some type of facility on an island, but we don't have any jurisdiction there. We thought he was just doing some pharmaceutical genetic research. Our intelligence hasn't provided anything which would suggest foul play."

"If that research involves creating a man of superhuman strength, like Bonnie theorized, he's already done it."

"That's science fiction, and I can't believe that. And the agency certainly never authorized any assault on Argon's complex. Your dad isn't that irresponsible."

"Oh, really? I guess you don't know him as well as you say."

"Come now. Despite whatever he's told you, he wasn't a CIA agent, but did go on some secret missions in his weaponry days."

He then saw the trash can filled with unmistakable strands of black hair and picked some up with his fingers. He knew it had been cropped short from her "Jose" disguise as the Las Vegas Conquerors' janitor, but it looked like she had shaved it all off. "Bonnie's hair."

"How do you know that? It could've been someone else's."

"No way. I'd know that thick stuff anywhere. She's been here, Lohrbach, and they've gone somewhere, with your imaginary suit of armor." He then found mounds of technical papers on a table, all in Russian. "Electronics schematics, with notes in Russian. They built their damn robot. You believe me now, smart guy?"

"I don't know what to believe. We need to get up and get some engineers in here to decipher this stuff."

They traveled back up in the elevator to the entrance, and Alex was notified of a voicemail on his satellite cell phone, from Elisa Flores. The phone didn't work in the radio-shielded complex. He quickly dialed his mother-in-law's number.

"Alex. Where are you?"

"In Tennessee, looking for my dad. What's wrong?"

"Nothing—Jay just woke up, and seems pretty good."

"That's great. I knew he'd make it, he's a tough guy."

"He has to tell you something."

"Elisa, I don't mean to put you off, but I'll talk to him later. I'm with an important government official."

"It's about Bonnie—he spoke to her."

"He's hallucinating."

"No, the date today, Alex. It can't be a coincidence. It happened right after six AM."

He looked at his watch and suddenly remembered the "holiday," Mole Day, created in honor of Amedeo Avogadro. It was observed on October 23, from 6:02 AM until 6:02 PM, to commemorate the Avogadro constant, 6.02×10^{23}. The time, 6:02, and date, 10/23, were chosen in honor of the famous quantity, of immense importance in the concept of the mole unit. A chemical "mole" was that number of atoms or molecules of a substance, equal to the number of atoms in exactly 12 grams of ^{12}C. The ultimate geek holiday, for the ultimate geek. She even insisted on abstinence from sex during that hallowed twelve-hour period, he was dismayed to learn.

"Alex? You there?"

"Yeah, I get it now. Let me talk to him." There was a pause for half a minute as Jay got on the phone.

"Alex. Gotta tell you some stuff."

"Man, I'm just happy you're okay. What did your mom mean that you 'spoke to Bonnie?' On the phone?"

"No, in a dream. She took me to the moon Titan and showed it to me, it was so real."

"What do you mean, 'took' you to Titan?"

"As a kid, she could take me to faraway places in my dreams, talk to me, things like that. It was bizarre, there was this orange sky and oily lake, and—"

"You're hallucinating. I'll talk to you later, Jay; I'm glad you're better, but I'm really busy right now."

"No, wait, Alex. She said she was going after Wendy, on some island in the Caribbean."

"That's nuts. We don't know where Wendy is."

"Bonnie does. You need to check it out. Promise me."

"Okay." He ended the cell phone call and pointed at Lohrbach. "Is that possible? Argon on a Caribbean island? Haven't I convinced you that they've been here recently?"

Lohrbach thought for a few minutes. "Yes, there is an island, but I don't know about this. If Rad *is* with Vladimirov, it wouldn't surprise me if he's on a Russian sub somewhere."

He laughed. "Yeah, right. You're making it up as we go along."

Lohrbach's stare was like a laser beam. "I'm dead serious, son."

"You've gotta be kidding. That's out of an old spy movie."

"Welcome to the wonderful world of Rad Röntgen."

"You seem to know a lot, don't you? Got all the answers."

"Knowledge is power, Alex. And I'm pretty powerful."

"Yeah, you're a real dynamo. Well, where to now, Lohrbach?"

"I guess we start looking for island complexes in the Caribbean. I'll call Langley and the Navy."

"Come on. Jay Mendoza's not dealing with a full deck."

Lohrbach tapped on the manila folder in his left hand. "Maybe you don't believe in magic as much as you should."

Chapter Fifty–two

Somewhere in the Caribbean
SSK Vladivostok

The 3,126-ton Russian Kilo Class submarine made its way to the small island in the Caribbean Sea—the site of Malachi Argon's illicit research complex, whose activities were largely unknown to the U.S. government. Inside were the crew, the captain's friend Viktor Vladimirov, Rad Darkkin, Jim Krakowski, and, of course, the reason for their trip—the newly upgraded version of a nerdy kids' superhero—the amazing Bonnie Mendoza. They had gone down to the torpedo room to plot their unique strategy.

"That's it, huh?" Jim asked as he looked at photos taken earlier from the periscope. "How do we know for sure that's it, Rad?"

"Rita gave us the coordinates, and there's a shitload of radio frequency emissions coming from it," Rad replied. "Can't see much from the cliffs through a periscope, but satellite surveillance photos confirm the existence of an industrial area. The peculiar atmospheric emissions suggest a biotechnology complex."

"You will eject my torpedo soon?" the bald-headed woman asked in Russian. "I cannot wait."

"Yes, brave lady. The armor will provide oxygen for at least two hours, and will protect you against the rigors of the G forces. It was designed for space travel, you know," Viktor said.

"After I am expelled, how long until I reach the island?"

"About five minutes. You will scale a cliff, from our surveillance," Rad said in Russian. "After you scale it, you'll find a fence, which is electrified, according to Rita."

"Electrified? Shall I break through it with vast power?"

Rad laughed. "You could, if you wanted to set off the alarms, but there's very little conventional firepower that could hurt that fullerene composite armor. Its design is to simply absorb energy and dissipate it into the ground, where it'll do no harm."

"Thirty feet. I can pole vault over it."

"Probably, but if you miss, it's be a noisy mess. No, after you get to the shore, you'll be able to download data from Rita's Trojan horse, which we'll use from the sub here to control the remote deactivation. We'll see everything you do, and can control the automated functions. Except for your own motor functions, of course."

"Is there an override? In case of malfunction?"

"Yes. You can control it at any time. And don't worry about the signals going back and forth. We'll be able to mask them effectively. Jim and Vik will help you with any directional problems you might have. Be your eyes and ears, so to speak."

"And what will you be doing, Conrad?"

"Heh, supervising everything. And coming in to back you up in case there's a problem."

She laughed. "I don't think that's such a good idea. And I will need no help from you."

"What is this whole thing doesn't work, Rad? Then what?" Jim asked. "Whatever happens to Wendy, if she's even still alive, doesn't matter if Argon succeeds with his plan."

Rad's eyes opened wildly. "If this shit fails, then we send one of my special 'babies' on a one-way ticket to that stinkin' island. There won't be anything left after it gets nuked to smithereens."

"*Nuked?* Oh, crap, you said this wasn't a nuclear sub!"

Rad laughed in a baleful tone. "No, I said the *propulsion* wasn't nuclear—not that it wasn't loaded with nukes. You think I'd get on any sub without thermonuclear weapons? Now who's crazy?"

• • •

Bonnie beamed with excitement as all 320 pounds of her (she now weighed, curiously, 190 pounds, and the armor 130) were loaded into the torpedo tube. At least she didn't have claustrophobia.

She heard the "whoosh" several minutes later as her torpedo was ejected from the Vladivostok; although facing upwards, her sonar sensors provided amazingly detailed forward "vision," and she could see how fast she was going. Eventually, the torpedo technicians guided the device onto shore a number of minutes later.

She got out and pulled the torpedo tube up to a small cave. Sensors online; eighty–four degrees Fahrenheit, wind twelve mph south. She saw the cliff she would have to scale, effortlessly threw up the lightweight but strong Kevlar ladder that she would climb. She moved in the 130-pound armor as effortlessly and quickly as if she were without it.

She scaled the cliff with ease, ascending on the ladder, and rested on a plain, where she saw the electric fence. Vision through the sensors seemed less vivid than her real vision, which was the intent; Rad and Viktor had designed them to provide a more accurate representation of her environment than her "cross-wired" natural vision, feeling that she didn't need any distractions.

The hearing and olfactory sensors were functioning perfectly, and she was "told" to go north by the gustatory sensors, controlled by Viktor. The download icon was flashing, indicating the recovery of data from the device Rita had planted. The readouts were all in Russian, of course, but that was not a problem; it always amazed others how transparent languages were to her. She could adapt to usage of a different language almost immediately.

Her sensors were like an extension of her body, she thought as she approached the pitch-dark fence at nearly forty miles per hour. With the photomultiplier enhancement, she could "see" almost as well as in daylight, however. Detection would be less likely, Rad had said, at night. The fence was "live;" the voltaic sensors detected high voltage, in the "fatal" range (to an un-insulated person). As enjoyable as it would be to break through the electrified fence, it wasn't necessary.

Jim said that he would be able to deactivate the sensors without anyone likely knowing it, at least for a while; someone would eventually spot her, but by that time it would be far too late for anything to do anything about it. The C60 fullerite could shrug off small-arms fire with ease; more sophisticated armaments would likely be repelled as well.

She noticed now that the electrical field had been neutralized. She ran down the field, knowing that the armor would absorb any radar signals; the dull gray color (much to her disliking) also provided effective camouflage in the dark.

It was time to rock and roll, she thought as she entered the now-deactivated lock on the outer door. She could visualize the entire perimeter through the sensors, which were now linked to her helmet electronics.

• • •

Viktor and Jim said he was insane (which was probably true), but there was no way Rad Darkkin was going to let a woman go in there alone—even if it was a woman wearing a forty million dollar armored suit capable of retrieving and assimilating enormous amounts of information. No, even something like that could go wrong, even with Vik and Jim helping her with transmissions. He had been on too many missions to leave everything to chance.

Vik maintained that all the defenses had been deactivated, and he was armed with a variety of assault weapons and Kevlar. He guided the speedboat, which his Russian friends had procured for him, towards the coastline; it was three AM, although he could easily "see" with the aid of radar and night-vision goggles.

He pulled up to the spot where Bonnie must have gone ashore. She did a good job of hiding it, he thought as he found the Kevlar ladder she had used to scale the cliff, using his state-of-the art night vision goggles. Despite outward appearances, he had remained in amazingly good shape; he had been off the booze for two months and had cut down tremendously on cigarettes.

He remembered how it used to be—he seemed forty, no—thirty years old again, as he scaled the thirty–foot cliff, albeit at a slightly slower pace than thirty years ago. He knew he had some help; unknown to the others, he had injected into his deltoid, several days ago, Rita McPherson's last remaining vial of the *O. titania* protein. He already had noticed increased strength and coordination; after all, he did possess the rare gene that helped impart his son, the Ortho-Man, with his unusual strength. He thought it might be his imagination, but his vision seemed a bit sharper, as well. And what else did he have to live for? He was sixty–nine, finally doing what he longed to do for so many years.

His encrypted radio com-link with Jim was active as he went over the cliff and ran towards the complex. All the alarms had been deactivated, he knew as he went through an unlocked door. No blood anywhere—not the way he would've done it; despite her trash-talking, he knew that Bonnie was, in essence, a kindly soul, and didn't want to splatter any brains she didn't have to. The plan was to get the men sequestered into a storage area and lock them inside, which is where most of them seemed to be.

Rad was surprised by a solitary guard who came down the corridor.

"Hold it, pal," Rad said, brandishing his weapon. "Get on the floor and toss down your weapon."

The mercenary soldier hit the floor and put his hands over his head. "I have no weapon, it's gone. That damn thing smashed it."

Rad pulled the man's hands behind him and secured them together with Flexi-Cuffs. "What thing?"

"That damn robot thing, or whatever it was. I'm not paid enough for this shit, man."

"Robot, heh," he said. "I guess you didn't want to mess with it. Good choice."

He went to the room Rita had said to find, as Bonnie was probably preoccupied fighting the abomination known as Ortho-Man and rescuing Wendy. Something might go wrong, and he'd be damned if he was going to be a coward. He was a lot of things—a drunk, an adulterer, and a lousy father—but not *that*.

He found the safe in the room she had mentioned, and affixed a wad of Composition 4 explosive to the door and blew it open. He found the canister, encased in a refrigerant. It was the one thing that could stop Travis, Rita had said, if the new, improved M-Square couldn't.

"Where are they, Jim?" Rad radioed.

"Her sensors indicate they're one floor down, in a large room. Go north to a stairwell, and then down and to the left." He knew that they had mapped out the room from Bonnie's earlier sensor scan.

"Where's Wendy?"

"As far as we can tell from her heat sensors, a person with the approximate mass of ol' WW is in a holding area on the second floor. She sealed off all access to there, so no one can get in or out, Rad."

"What is Bonnie doing now?"

"Sensors indicate a tremendous power drain with battery voltage down eighty–seven percent. Either the consumption is more than we thought, or one of the power packs was damaged. You find what you were looking for?"

"Yeah."

"I still don't believe you made it up there, you damn crazy son of a bitch."

"Heh, you got that right—there ain't nobody crazier than me. But look who's sitting in a Russian sub, Jimmy. You ain't that far behind."

Chapter Fifty–three

Argotech Industries
Caribbean Island Complex

Bonnie stared at the five armed guards who approached her. "Stand down or face the consequences," she said in a synthesized Rad Darkkin voice. "You have no idea what I can do to you."

"Blast him—whatever it is," the team leader said. She laughed as the small arms fire ricocheted off the titanium-ruthenium fullerite armor.

A mercenary soldier fired a taser weapon at her, which attached to the diamagnetic chest plate via a strong adhesive. "Why don't you try 100,000 volts on for size." He activated the device.

The internal electronics of the armor could absorb up to 10,000 amperes of current, and the pitiful little taser didn't even tickle. The current would simply be absorbed by the armor, which was designed to be a poor conductor of electricity. The man's weapon would even provide a small amount of electrical charge.

She then sent back an EMP (electromagnetic pulse) blast, which knocked out all the local electronics—directional, of course. The armor was well insulated against EMP, in any case.

"Stand down. I have no reason to harm you. I realize you are only doing your job, yet I shall not be thwarted in my quest."

"Get out of the way," another soldier screamed from a balcony. He was holding an anti-tank missile launcher.

It was time to see if this hunk of Russian junk really worked. The missile was launched with a loud "whoosh" and was deflected by the Vladimirov armor's force field, which could last only a few seconds. It exploded in a blinding flash, as the energy had been dissipated and a small fraction absorbed. Enough to replace what had been used to generate the energy field.

Additional armed soldiers came after her, and she simply dragged them behind her. "I would advise you to get off me. I will not actively hurt you, but you are likely to get trampled. It is a pregnant woman and an evil one named Argon whom I seek." The powerful electromagnets in her right gauntlet pulled the weapons from their hands, as they gaped in awe.

"What the hell?" a large man asked.

"Get in this room—all of you. I don't want to hurt anyone." She ushered them all into a storage area, which she locked electronically after they went inside. She knew there would be a few random guards still strolling around, but they would be easily dealt with.

She then came to a secured area requiring biometric and typed password access.

"Name, please?" the computer voice asked.

"Malachi Argon." The LCD screen suddenly flashed the message "Name Verified." Jim's Trojan also had transmitted representative voice files from Argon, which Viktor had used to duplicate his speech pattern, so that she could gain access via voice activation.

She then stepped up to a retinal scanner; the computers were able to reconstruct Argon's artificial retinal image, obtained from Argon's own files. The screen flashed the message "Scan Verified."

Finally, she needed to find the password, which Argon apparently only knew himself, as it was not stored on the server. Her visual scanner could determine, from skin oils, which keys had been touched most recently. This would allow her to construct words from the key combinations, by mentally sorting through all anagrams.

She sure didn't need a computer for that. "Orthoman71"—the name and birth year of Travis Argon. Things seemed so clear now—she could think much quicker than before. The dismantling of Malachi Argon's complex would now be child's play.

• • •

Malachi Argon stormed into the examination room angrily. "You better explain this, Rita. A transmitter which has been linked to our computer servers ever since you came here two days ago," he said angrily to Rita McPherson.

"I have no idea what you mean," Rita said as she drew blood from Wendy, who was sitting in a chair. "Can we discuss this in a minute? I have to be careful."

Argon grabbed Rita and threw her against the wall. "You goddamn liar! I trusted you. What is *this*?" He held the domino-sized device in front of her face."

"I said I don't know. I've never seen that thing before, it looks like a network hub or something. Go ask one of the IT guys."

"You want to spend a couple of hours with Travis? That won't be very pleasant."

Rita considered her options and knew she had to bluff for at least a little while. "I already told you I have no idea what you're talking about. I've always been loyal to you."

"We'll see about that. Anybody messes with me, even you, is dead meat."

At that point he received an urgent call on his two-way radio.

"What the hell is it?" Argon bellowed. "No interruptions."

"Dr. Argon, you need to come out here stat. There appears to be an intruder."

"What? Activate the defenses, then. Blast the son of a bitch."

"That's just it—we can't. They've all been shut down. Our computers are inoperative."

"Take him hand-to-hand, then, for God's sake. We must outnumber him fifty to one."

"We tried that, he disarmed them all, and we're locked in a storage area, he reprogrammed the locks or something. We can't take this guy hand-to-hand—it's suicide."

Argon grabbed Rita by her white coat and shook her. "What the hell have you done?"

The bluff was over. "It's what you've done that you'll answer for, you worthless piece of humanity. You can kill me, Argon, but it's all over for you."

"You mean it's all over for *you*. You'll pay the price."

Rita laughed. "I'll 'pay the price'? How corny can you get? The price will be your life."

"What?"

"Your little operation here. Kiss it goodbye, you unethical bastard. I can't stand to sit by and let you experiment on people like Dr. Williams here any longer."

"You forget that this is a government operation. Gallagher's men are out there. What agency's going to believe you, Rita?" Argon laughed. "I'm untouchable."

"It's no agency, and you've lied to me. None of this has been authorized by the government, and this person doesn't care about you, or the law."

"Well, it doesn't matter what you think, because you're going to die soon."

"Not until I've seen you dead. You're about to meet the most dangerous human being alive. And you'll be touched, believe me. Stomped and ripped to little pieces." The guards grabbed her.

Argon laughed. "Travis will destroy whoever it is they sent—you seem to forget about the weapon you helped create."

"That aberration Travis is going to meet his match. And then, may God help you, because *she's* going to tear you both limb from limb. I know—she told me in great anatomic detail how she would do it."

Argon's face turned white as he started sweating. "Get them both out of here," Argon said, turning to Wendy. "And nothing's going to save you, either. Your new friend Rita's going to die, too."

Wendy looked up with extreme clarity, smiled, and stared at Argon as a guard grabbed her. "You'd better be damn scared, dirtbag. Have you ever faced someone with no fear? With nothing to lose?"

"I don't think you're in the best shape to be giving me profound philosophical advice, Williams."

"Perhaps. But you and Adolf Gallagher, wherever he is, should enjoy your last few moments on this Earth. You and my abomination of a half-brother. The days of playing God are over."

Chapter Fifty–four

Argotech Industries
Caribbean Island Complex

The figure wearing the lightweight yet incredibly hard armor met the hulking six–five man in the corridor. Yow, he was *way* bigger than she thought. She'd wrestled with Wendy dozens of times, but he made her look like a shrimp. They stood about thirty feet away from each other and waited, like two Old West gunslingers preparing for the final shootout. This battle likely would cause more destruction than a couple of six-shooters, though, she thought.

She was the aggressor, and made the first statement. "You are adept at assaulting pregnant pediatricians, kindly old professors, and retired football players with bad knees. Perhaps you would like to pick on someone your own size," she said in Rad's deep synthesized voice.

"Back off, whoever you are. Surrender now and I won't hurt you too badly."

"You won't hurt me? How humorous. If anyone dies today, it shall be you, ghastly freak."

"Haw. I'm not a freak—I'm alive because of what my father did. He tried to save my life. Not that it's any of your damn business."

"In case you haven't noticed, I'm making it my business."

"This base is protected by military intelligence. You won't see them, though, because I'll crush that suit like a lobster."

"By the way, Argon is not your father. Your biological father's name is Darkkin."

Travis hesitated a moment. "You lie. Let's settle this, man to man." He ripped the fire extinguisher off the wall, and threw it at her, which she easily deflected.

She laughed. "Right—man to man. That is how it shall be."

Maybe this was a bad decision. Travis was far more massive than she had anticipated, and much faster than she thought. There was no way she would be able to go head-to-head with him with strength alone. But he wasn't nearly as fast as her. Nevertheless, he picked her up as she lunged at him, and tossed her 320 pounds into the wall.

God, he was quick. But she would see it coming next time. The partial restoration of her hearing somehow had given her back, like Jaime, the uncanny ability to sense danger seconds before it happened. She had lost the ability after losing her hearing at age eleven, but was slowly remembering how it used to be.

She rose to her feet and assessed the damage. None she could see. That damn energy field of Viktor's had absorbed most of the impact. But power in the first-generation suit was at a premium, and she would run out at some point. On a negative note, Travis could go on like this for hours, according to Rita.

"Now it's my turn." She tore into him and pummeled him into the wall, striking his body plate with a plasma blast, as he let out a yell. "I have many types of unpleasant energy types for you to experience." Unfortunately, each plasma blast drained a large amount of energy, and she would have power for perhaps two more.

"I can lift two thousand pounds. I'll crush you like an eggshell for that."

"It is impossible to crush an egg, do you not know that?"

"Shut up." He chased her around the large room, while she easily outdistanced him. But he was closing in.

"Perhaps I will crush *you*, and perhaps not. Maybe there is some good in you, and I understand that your behavior may not all be your fault."

"What?"

"Your father is evil personified. He has altered you genetically, for his own benefit—not yours."

"He did it to save my life. It's none of your damn business."

"Perhaps that is a corollary benefit, but he did it to gain favor with General Gallagher."

"Why would he do that?"

"Political reasons. He also has pumped you with enough testosterone to alter your behavior. I see the rage inside."

"Why are you telling me this before I kill you, whoever you are? Trying to psych me out?"

"Because I want you to help me. I need to disable Malachi Argon and the whole place. I need some help for that."

"What makes you think I would help you?"

"Are you so naïve? Who do you think that woman is you brought here? Do you not notice the resemblance? She is your half sister. They want to use her fetus for stem cells. But perhaps there is a way to prolong your miserable, wasted life."

"So? He's a great man, who has helped me, Rita, and the rest."

"He's experimented on them, too. Maybe they wanted it. You don't. But it doesn't matter."

"What I want is for you to die. And I always get what I want."

That might be true, but he had to catch her first. And the fullerite-titanium alloy armor was pretty tough. "You are too slow, and you have to connect with me first."

She had the hang of it now. Travis swung at her furiously, while she could almost see his movements a fraction of a second before he made them. She jumped into him with a strong kick to the neck. He got up, gasping.

"Your time's about up. I just need to hit you once." The testosterone talking. Rita McPherson said the high levels were necessary for his strength augmentation. The worst "roid rage" the world had ever seen.

"And you have no idea what I can do to you." Her mother had taught her something as a child which would serve her well—that knowledge was power of a higher order. And she had the means to destroy the entire complex. But she had to remember her primary mission, which was to find Wendy—not to get revenge on the Argons, sweet as that would be. But this small area was not ideal for speed; it favored the raw power of the Ortho-Man.

They exchanged further blows for several more minutes, and she realized that she was probably going to run out of power before her adversary would tire. Powerful as she was, the armor wasn't built primarily for battle. Her energy was limited by the lithium-ion battery packs that powered the motors; the plutonium cells only powered the electronics. And one of his blows seemed to have damaged one of the main power packs. She had to do something, quickly, as she lacked sufficient energy for another plasma blast.

Her powerful blows, although enough to fell any normal being, were grossly insufficient to down Travis by themselves. He was simply too strong. She had no idea how to activate the bizarre psionic power she apparently possessed, but she seemingly needed physical contact to initiate it, which the armor prevented—if it even would work on him. The plasma blasts might work, if she could somehow recharge her batteries—to deliver a lethal, final blow.

However, her adversary probably wasn't going to let her accomplish that little task. At least she had deactivated and reset all the door lock codes; it was unlikely that even Travis could get to where Wendy was now.

"I'll take your head off, whoever you are," Travis said as he threw her across the room. "Say your prayers."

A prayer seemed like a good thing right now, as the blow had seriously reduced her energy level even more; not a good thing. She would be fortunate just to get away from him, if she had enough power left to get to her feet. She then saw a familiar, if unexpected, large figure storm into the room.

"You say yours, you fucking genetic bastard," the large, gray-haired man said as he burst into the room and threw the canister onto the floor, releasing the cryogenic gas into the air. "I created you, and I'll be the end of you, shithead."

She wondered how the hell Rad had gotten in there, and why—but as long as he was there, perhaps she could take advantage of it. Rita said there was a specific agent to use against him, which she hadn't had time to locate. The father of Travis had bought her a most precious commodity—time.

"You stupid old man," Travis said. "I'm resistant to any toxin or drug, and my Kevlar will shrug off your bullets. Whatever that is, it'll kill you and your little warrior over there before me."

He might be right about that, she thought. Her compressed oxygen was almost extinguished, and she would soon have to start breathing room air. But she knew that Rad, despite his faults, was no dummy, and what he dissipated was probably not toxic to her; if it was what she thought, it might not be too beneficial for him, though. The distraction had also bought her a little time to tap into the 220-volt outlet in the floor; Viktor's universal power converter could draw power from almost any source.

Rad stared long and hard at his genetic son and laughed. "For someone with half of my DNA, you're sure a dumb shit. You really think ol' Chi would've had you around with no way to control you? And good old Uncle Gallagher?"

"*Your DNA*? What are you, old man, crazy? He'd never do anything to me. And I'm going to bust your ancient ass."

"No? Look around you, you fucking idiot. You think he built this multi-billion-dollar complex just for you? Wake up—he used you like he's gonna use Gallagher when he's President. But they won't be playing 'Hail to The Chief' for him now. 'Taps' will be his new theme song."

"I'll break your neck." Travis staggered towards Rad.

"Yeah, ol' Chi was so pathetic, he couldn't stand you weren't his, so he made you over in his own image. Looks like it worked out, heh, real well."

She and Rad watched curiously as Travis started staggering around. "Something's wrong."

Rad laughed. "No shit, Sherlock! Guess you got my brawn, but not my brains, huh?"

"What've you done to me, old man?"

"It's a DNA-specific poison, kind of like what kindly ol' step-dad used to kill the Big Guy. Paralyzes your voluntary nerve centers, I guess. Shit, I really have no damn idea . . . maybe it'll kill you, hopefully. I only pray it hurts like hell."

"Then I'll kill you first," Travis said as he made a final lunge at Rad, punching him in the stomach and launching him across the room. "Die, you old man, whoever you are."

"Agggh," Rad said, spewing blood. "Now *that* fucking hurts."

"No, it is you who will die today," Bonnie said as she made a final heroic burst with fractionally restored power, knocking Travis across the room.

"I—I can't move," Travis said.

She took off her right gauntlet and pressed it against Travis' head. "Soon, you will not be able to think, either, although you may still live," she said to the hulk lying immobile on the floor.

Rad was barely conscious and wheezing in the corner, his chest partially caved in by Travis' blow.

"Don't touch him, are you crazy? I don't know what this shit is I sprayed on him."

She removed her hand from Travis' head as she watched him go into convulsions. She then dropped to the ground.

"Rad—can you speak?" She wearily plugged back into the power outlet to acquire more energy than she had drawn from the half-minute charge before.

"I'm a . . . goner, missy. You did good, though. Kicked that SOB's ass. Fried his, heh, brain."

"You saved my life. He might have killed me were it not for your timely intervention."

"No way, you're one tough-ass bitch. Tougher'n me."

"I will take that a compliment. Stay here, I will procure aid for your injuries momentarily."

After five more minutes of recharging, she then tore off a control panel and inserted a probe into the console. With Jim directing her, she was able to access the main computer and download all of the data, shutting down all weapons systems. She also sealed off the room from entry by anyone else. She knew, however, there was nothing more she could do for Rad, and she left him to find the person she had come for. Her sensor array showed her to be safe.

• • •

She was told by the guidance computer to go down the corridor three hundred and sixteen feet, then through an unlocked door to the left—an instrumentation area where Malachi Argon and an armed guard were standing. The guard turned to fire, but she immediately pulled the gun from his hands with magnetism, then knocked him to the floor.

"Malachi Argon—I have disabled your guards as well as your own genetic monstrosity, whose brain I have reduced to a mere vegetative state. I have shut down your defense systems. I have dealt with them, and now I will deal with *you*."

"I don't fear you, Darkkin," Argon said shakily.

She let out a ballast of loud, bass laughter. Rad had, in typical egotistical fashion, programmed the armor to use his own voice as the default one. "You let my voice box deceive you. I am not Rad Darkkin, but you will wish for that soon, for I am something far worse. Do you prefer this one?" She switched to Argon's own voice. "I will mock you with your own voice."

"Who the hell are you?"

"Someone who has no fear. There is nothing you can do to stop me, and I will not rest until I see you dead."

"Kill me, then."

"Don't worry, I will." She dragged him by his coat down the hall to where Wendy and Rita were being held. She triggered several remote sensors and opened the cell, throwing Argon inside, as Wendy gasped.

"How do you desire to die, Argon?" she said, switching back to Rad's voice. "I will be kind and give you a choice. Electrocution? Beheading? Firing squad?"

Wendy, wearing an old sweatshirt, blue jeans, and sneakers, looked up. "Who or what the hell—"

"Don't panic," Rita said. "Just stay away."

"That voice—but you're too short to be *him*."

"I think you know who I am." She turned towards Argon. "I could have killed your freak of a son, who was defeated by me and the most courageous of men. I will bring you in to answer for the heinous crimes you have committed. You are no better than Hitler, a mere Nazi war criminal." She took a long iron bar and bent it in a circle around Argon, restricting his movement.

"You must like to hear yourself talk. Go to hell."

She threw him down. "The day of reckoning is at hand. You are like the Greek god Hephasteus, who desired his sister Athena, and spilled his seed onto the dirt to create some form of abomination; thusly, you've created yours. You shall therefore pay, and—"

"It *is* you. "Wendy stared in amazement. "There's only one person who talks like that. But it's impossible."

She dragged Argon back down the corridor towards the computer room, while Wendy and Rita waited. "Well? Are you two not coming? I cannot do everything here."

"Sorry. I'm just a *little* off balance," the 242-pound, visibly pregnant woman said as she wobbled down the corridor.

She sneered at the cowering Argon. "I have defeated all your defenses. By the way, I have downloaded all of your data into my memory banks. I know everything."

"That's many terabytes of data. It's impossible. And it's all encrypted."

She laughed. "I don't need your help. My native cipher powers will be sufficient for that."

She mentally raced through all possible combinations of passwords for the encryption and entered them into the computer, and the gray-haired scientist's eyes opened wide as he watched them open one by one.

"That's impossible. No computer can do that," Argon yelled.

She switched to her own shrill soprano voice, laughing as it never had before. "Not a computer. You have just experienced real magic. The kind you can't simulate with a computer. The irony is, you have assisted in my . . . rebirth. And in your death."

"What's wrong with her?" Wendy asked Rita. "What the hell is that armor?"

"It's a creation of your father and a Soviet robotics expert. They risked everything to save you."

"Are the police coming? The military?"

"We're out of any country's jurisdiction, and Argon has the military in his pocket. This was the only way."

"My . . . father helped with this?"

"Yes, he is a brave man who saved us all."

Wendy went towards her. "I need to see your face, to know that you're real."

"Well, do not get too close. I have no idea what my atomic emissions are, as I am partially plutonium-powered; in your state, they could be toxic. And you will see me in a moment, when I take care of this bottom-feeder. Salvation is near."

"The military will have your ass, whoever you are. General Gallagher will—"

"Humph. He will do nothing, except pay for his heinous crimes. Soon, the federal authorities will be on their way to pick him up. They are bound by the laws of law and order. Laws which I am not forced to obey. To think what you did to your son, and might have done to Dr. Williams."

"You can't—"

"Oh, but I *can*. I should kill you, Argon. I want to, so badly," she said, pulling her right fist up. "Who gave *you* the right to experiment, to determine what should be genetically correct? That certain genes are forbidden? That I, a Hispanic with many imperfections, am unsuitable for the Argon Universe? The irony of it all."

Argon gasped. "I never meant to hurt anyone."

Her purple friend was going crazy. "Liar, you goddamn disgusting liar. At least have the guts to admit what you've done before you die."

"We can help each other. Think of what we can do, with our minds combined. You could have everything, Mendoza."

"I already have everything I need. And you think I want you for an ally?" She threw him across the room. "I do not need your puny little primitive mind. One that I am about to reduce to jelly with the power of mine."

Wendy yelled at her friend as she approached Argon angrily. "Don't hurt him with those weapons. This ends now."

Rita held her back. "Don't get in her way."

"She won't hurt me with that armor."

"It isn't the armor I'm worried about. She's deadly."

Bonnie turned towards them. "Why should I not end his miserable life? Your father would want that. And I certainly don't need this suit to kill him."

"Because you aren't that kind of human being, like my father—a person of revenge. He may have engineered your little journey here, but you've got a mind of your own."

"Then perhaps I am no longer the *Mendoza Milagroso* you once knew." She looked around eerily through the eyes of her helmet. "The things I see now, the concepts I understand, are more than you can possibly comprehend. I am different."

"You're still my friend."

"Yes, but there are, within me . . . changes, which were necessary to achieve my goal. There is no going back."

"Hey, I thought I was pretty special, too, and have thought some pretty unique thoughts. Take it from someone who's been there."

"No offense, but you are not a person of good judgment."

"My mind's never been clearer in my life."

"Why did you tell Rita it was Jaime's baby, Wendy?"

"Because it is, and I'm sorry for that. How do you know one way or the other?"

She removed her helmet and looked into her friend's aquamarine eyes. "I know you are mistaken. Whatever delusions you have had, the daughter inside you is Stan's."

Wendy gasped as she saw Bonnie's shaven head and the absence of the aural processors—the quarter-sized magnets on the sides of her head which previously held them in place now stood out more than ever.

"How do you know that, and that it's a girl?" Wendy asked. "I'm so confused."

"Then it is time to rest your weary mind, my friend." She turned towards the cowering Argon. "Not so powerful now, are you, brilliant Malachi? Tell me what I want to know, and you may yet live. Or not. We shall see."

"I don't know what you're talking about."

"Coward! The ethnic bio-weapon—where is it? I know it exists, from the mind of the late Willie Chalfant."

"You're insane. There's no such thing."

Bonnie looked at Argon intensely as she removed her right gauntlet and grabbed his head.

"One last chance. You believed Travis was the most dangerous killing machine alive. But you are wrong—I will put you in a hell beyond your comprehension!" she screamed.

"*You* can go to hell."

She looked at him and started shivering. Wendy tried to pry her away, but wasn't nearly strong enough, as Rita pulled her back.

"*Aieeee!*" Argon yelled, as his eyes rolled back in his head. "My body's on fire. Get it out of my head! It's too much at once!"

"What are you doing to him?" Wendy asked.

"I am doing what is necessary—sending him to Hades. Since it is knowledge he desires, that is what he shall have. Enough to burn his mind to an empty husk."

After about two minutes she turned pale, blood dripping from her nose, as Argon slumped to the floor, lifeless.

"The White House and Congress. They are going to unleash it there," she said as she slumped to the ground. "Radio the military, who are surely on their way already."

"What?" Wendy asked in disarray.

"An ethnic bio-weapon, a genetic device used to target certain races. Argon has created it, and shall soon deploy it at the White House and Capitol."

"You're crazy," Wendy said.

"I . . . know it. They're going to use the ventilation system to distribute it, in about four hours. You have to call someone."

Wendy watched as Argon lay on the ground, seizing. "What is it you've done?"

Bonnie collapsed to the floor, breathing rapidly.

"Bonnie? What's happened to you?" She looked towards Rita. "What has this . . . battle armor done to her?"

"That's not it. It's what I've done that I must answer for," Rita said sadly.

"I don't understand."

"If it's like the other time, she'll be okay. But she didn't accomplish this on her own. We need to go see someone who is dying. It may not be someone you desire to see, as I understand it, but he wants to see *you*."

"Oh, no," Wendy said, trembling. "It can't be. Bonnie? Is that true?"

"It is none other. Go to him, my sister," she gasped as she sat up. "You only have a few minutes left to say your goodbyes."

• • •

Rita took Wendy to the room down the hall, after both donned protective suits. Rad was gasping on the floor, and Travis lay dormant, barely breathing.

"Dad, what the hell are you doing here?"

"It's me, little girl. Haven't . . . seen you in a while. Sorry I've been such a bastard. Tried to . . . make up for it, somehow, the only way I knew how."

She looked at his form lying on the floor. "You're going to make it. You've probably just got some broken ribs, maybe a splenic or renal contusion."

"Heh—don't think so, not this time. Ol' Rad pushed the envelope too far. It had to happen, eventually."

She grabbed for his hand.

"No, goddamn it, don't touch me."

"Why?" she sobbed. "I've got the protective suit on."

"That shit I sprayed on Argon's . . . *my* son . . . was linked to his DNA. It's not just the injury that's done me in, girl, it's this stuff. We're too genetically alike, I can feel it. If this can be transmitted through contact, it could be toxic to you and your baby, even with the suit. Stay away."

"They can't just let you die. I need you."

He shook his head. "There's no goddamn shit they can do for me. And you have the best friend in the world, who risked everything to save your butt. I brought you into this world, about the best goddamned thing I ever did. Wish it made up for all the bad ones."

"Dad?"

"Know this. I'm truly sorry for how I treated your mom. We were from different worlds, she and I—she the cultured Englishwoman, me a goddamned hillbilly with a million dollars of whiskey money in my pocket. How could it have worked?"

"That isn't important now."

"You promise me this. Make sure you find Argon and fry his sorry ass. I just wish I could've done it myself."

"Too late. It wasn't his ass that was fried, Dad."

He looked at his daughter wearily and laughed. "Yeah, I get you. She did it to ol' Orth here before she found you. Where's she at?"

"She's woozy, pretty zonked out in there."

"That . . . happened once before. Appears to takes its toll on her, too." He handed her the radio communicator. "Call . . . Russian sub. Rescue you both. Tell them . . . no nukes."

"Stop it. You're going to be okay."

"No way, I'm, heh, toast. At least I got my last wish, though."

"What?"

"I always wanted to go out . . . on some exotic island, while looking into the deep blue eyes of a beautiful blonde. Looks . . . like I got both of those."

"Don't say that."

"One . . . last thing you gotta have Dirk do for me."

"What?" she cried.

"I want my sorry-ass bones . . . burned up in the Unit 1 fission reactor core in Chattanooga. That's . . . how I always wanted to meet my maker. Disintegrated by gamma rays and alpha particles . . . at the expense of the Tennessee Valley Authority."

"Dad?"

William Conrad Darkkin, age sixty–nine, had breathed his last molecule of diatomic oxygen on Earth. Wendy pressed several buttons on the communicator, and heard Russian in response.

"Hello? This is Wendy Williams. I don't speak Russian. Is there anyone there who speaks English?"

Silence for a few moments. "I don't believe it. It's Jim, Wendy. It looks like things worked."

"Oh, my God. Where are you?"

"Well, I'm in a Russian sub, armed with nuclear missiles, several miles off the coast. You okay?"

"I seem to be the only one who is."

"What do you mean?"

She began crying. "My dad is dead, and Bonnie's in some kind of weird trance."

"I understand," he said. "But the Square will be okay, trust me. I'm so sorry about Rad. But the military's already on their way."

"How is that possible?"

"Jay Mendoza said to look for you guys in the Caribbean, and Alex sent them to find you. Wasn't hard, with all the power and electromagnetic radiation coming from that place."

"Jay's *alive?* I thought he was dead."

"He made it, I guess. Pretty tough. Hey, nice talkin' to you, WW, but we gotta get out of Dodge, 'cause we don't want the United States Navy finding us. Again, I'm sorry about your dad, but I'll see you soon, all right?"

"Uh . . . okay." She felt woozy, finally made it to a chair in the corner, then fell down.

"Wendy?" Rita asked.

"Just a little faint," she replied. "I think I'll be okay. Just get me something to eat . . . and make sure Bonnie's all right. She sometimes needs looking after."

Chapter Fifty–five

U.S.S. Excelsior
Ten miles off Argotech Island

Alex Darkkin, CIA DS&T Director Alton Lohrbach, and DEA Special Agent Jackie Levickis waited on the bridge of the powerful Naval destroyer as the military team radioed from inside Argotech's island laboratory to the ship's captain. The Navy didn't want any civilians aboard, but Lohrbach had used his influence to get them passage to the Argotech complex's island.

"What've they found there, Lohrbach?" Alex asked.

"Not a hell of a lot. There was a lot of electrical activity when they scanned it before, but now it looks almost dead, as if something shut all the power off. Bizarre." He paused as the ship's captain received a call on his radio from a Marine sergeant.

"Skipper—this place has been torn apart by some type of plasma blasts. Bunch of guys knocked out, none dead. This one big dude appears breathing but unconscious, and there's an older scientist who's dead. Blood pouring out of his nose."

"What else?"

"Some pregnant lady identifying herself as Dr. Wendy Williams, a woman scientist named McPherson, and something else you won't believe."

"I'll believe anything when these people are concerned," Captain Bill Ellison said, looking at Lohrbach and Alex.

"A guy inside some Soviet battle armor. Speaks Russian, Latin, Romanian, and a whole bunch of other languages. Likes to talk."

"Who is it?" Ellison asked. "Russian military? Special ops?"

"I have no damn idea who it is. Says he's a United States citizen, but the dude won't let us move him. Says he needs Lohrbach to come inside, and is requesting a laptop and several terabytes of hard drive storage."

"What the hell? Make him get down."

"We, uh, can't, Captain. He used some kind of magnet thing and sucked our firearms right out of our hands. Damndest thing we ever saw. One of Argon's soldiers earlier fired a missile launcher at him, one of the captured guards said. The whole thing exploded, and he absorbed it with some damn force field."

"Can we gas him?"

"We threatened, but he says he has his own air supply, and we don't want to hurt the other two. And no electronics work anywhere around him. He has some kind of EMP device that interferes with them. We're actually using his radio."

"Shit. How many did he kill?"

"Skipper, it doesn't seem that he's killed or seriously injured anyone except for the big dude and the scientist. Men said they all jumped him and he just kept going. He warned them to get off, like gnats on a dog."

"We're going in now," Lohrbach said. "Get me a chopper ride to that island."

The ship's captain put down his radio. "With all due respect, Director Lohrbach, we can't allow you—"

"The hell you can't. Get me Washington, then."

"There's no way you can keep me out of there either, Lohrbach," Alex said. "Whatever she's done, I need to help."

"I can, and I will."

"Me, neither," Jackie said. "We need to see this through all the way. And you have no authority to give us orders, Director Lohrbach."

The captain shrugged as he relented. "Hell, be my guest, then. If you civilians want to get your asses killed, it's your funeral."

• • •

Alex Darkkin, Jackie Levickis, and Alton Lohrbach flew over the small island in the Navy helicopter, and landed on the plain beyond the cliff, where they were met by the Marine sergeant and his team. Lohrbach showed his credentials to the heavily armed men.

"Come on, they're in here. I don't think they're a threat, but be careful. Did you bring what they wanted?" Lohrbach asked.

Alex held the large weatherized laptop and hard drive. "Yeah. I don't think my multi-lingual spouse will disintegrate us."

Rita, Wendy, and the fullerene alloy-encased Bonnie Mendoza walked out of the complex cautiously. Alex gave Wendy a hug, and stared at what he apparently figured must be his wife.

"What the hell is *this?*" Alex asked. "We thought you were dead. What have you done to yourself?"

"It is prototype Soviet stealth battle armor, customized for certain functions. I have been working with the Russian inventor and another scientist well known to my husband here."

"*Vladimirov?* No kidding," Lohrbach said. "We've been trying to find him for months. I guess what we found back in Tennessee was real."

"One more thing," she said, turning to her husband. "One of us did not make it, Alex. His body is inside, and may be contaminated. I did not want to risk further exposure of Wendy to him."

"Oh, my God. Jim?"

"No, James is aboard the *Vladivostok* Kilo Class submarine off our coast. It is armed with nuclear missiles, for Plan B."

"*Vladivostok?*" Lohrbach asked nervously. "Damn, we didn't know she was out here. She has nukes on board?"

"James has assured us that they are departing, their objective attained—shooting my torpedo to the surface."

"I don't believe it. Why?" Alex asked.

"Your father helped me destroy Travis Argon, but paid the ultimate price."

"No. I've got to see this for myself." He ran towards the door, but she stopped him.

"I will *not* let you go in. It may not be safe, and there is nothing further you can do."

Alex fought back tears as he tried to regroup himself. "I just wish I could've seen him one last time."

"We did," Wendy said, patting him on the shoulder. "You would've been proud of him. He kicked some serious ass."

Bonnie moved to the computer. "I regret the loss of Conrad, but there are more pressing matters than his passing. Plug the computer's USB port into my interface here. Do not worry, Rita has tested my emissions since my arrival, and I am safe. I must not power down until I have transferred the data to your computers."

"What program do I use?" Lohrbach said.

"Do not despair, Lohrbach—I am, fortunately, entirely Plug-and-Play compliant." They watched the laptop's LCD display:

> Found New Hardware
> Mendoza Milagroso Mark I Battle Armor
> USB Connection

"What the hell?" Lohrbach said as the armored figure was represented as "Local Disk (E:)" on the disk directory.

"Just drag and drop the files onto that hard drive," she said, as Lohrbach downloaded three terabytes of data onto the laptop.

"What's on there, Mendoza?"

"All the information you need to convict these . . . devils of the worst espionage known to man. Murderers of many. It also contains the means to decrypt a CD-ROM in my bank deposit box. I have sorted the data by relevance."

"And what's on this CD?"

"Information that Dr. Jasper Bennett had stashed away in case he was ever killed, which he was. Data that implicate Dr. Malachi Argon in the cover-up of the greatest scientific discovery of all time."

"Which is—what?" Lohrbach asked.

"The discovery of life on Saturn's moon Titan, the manipulation of which has allowed the creation of the most ghastly perversion of science known to man. And . . . some other things."

"Get to the point. I'm tired of asking questions."

"The names and offshore bank account numbers of Malachi Argon's numerous international 'investors.' You may wish to look them up and pay them a visit."

After the transfer, she powered down the defense mechanisms and removed her helmet. Alex looked at her and gasped. "Why's your head shaven?"

"The electrodes require direct skin contact for optimal communication with the cybernetic circuits."

"Damn, that's messed up," Alex said, grinning and shaking his head. "But kind of sexy."

"I have learned much. But the ultimate goal lies elsewhere."

"Your speech . . . I'd swear it's clearer than before," Alex said.

"Perhaps, one side effect of this mission. There are others, not all of them good."

"No processors. How are you hearing me?"

"My hearing is approximately seventy–five percent normal at this time, but it is only temporary, Dr. Rita tells me, although it may delay the progressive neurological problem which is affecting the functioning of my CIs." She looked up at the sky. "Sounds so loud, colors so bright—is this what normal people see and hear?" She removed the remainder of the armor.

"Chief, what do we do with her? Arrest her?"

"Get that . . . fricking armor, or whatever it is, down to the lab. I'm not sure that there's been a crime committed here. Dr. Mendoza, I hope that you will come willingly."

"I assure you, I am not of danger to you. I have harmed no one except the Ortho-Man and his diabolical step-father. I will come with you, but there is something of far greater importance right now than whether I should be taken into custody."

"What?"

"You must alert the Secret Service at the White House, Director Lohrbach. Argon has engineered the production of an ethnic bioweapon, to destroy Asians, Hispanics, and African-Americans. It will be deployed in the Capitol and White House within the next twenty–four hours. The poison will not act immediately, but will be delayed. An improvement over what he used to kill the President, Senator Orson, and others."

"No way is that possible," Lohrbach said.

"It is true. The commissioner's daughter killed Senator Orson that way, and many others. An Army general's been supplying Argon with information to run his secret biotech program."

"Who?"

"Gallagher. Lt. Gen. Brant Gallagher."

"Are you kidding? He's the one rumored to try and get on the Democratic ticket for 2012. Heavy into scientific research, organ cloning and everything," Alex said.

"Yes. With Graham assassinated, it paves the way for a new President in the next election. Graham's VP, Sam Reardon, isn't considered a real strong candidate."

"You have proof of this?" Lohrbach asked.

"Yes, I have decrypted all the information in Argon's lab. Also, data from a compact disc possessed by Dr. Jasper Bennett of Caltech, who was killed by the Ortho-Man. It is all on the CD in my bank deposit box, and also on a chip imbedded in one of my processors. It contains all the secret information on Titan hidden from the United States government."

"Mendoza, you should know that you're nearly a fugitive," Lohrbach said. "You've acted irresponsibly, albeit patriotically."

"I plead *nolo contendere* to that charge, and you may do what you wish with me. But I believe you will change your tune once you analyze my data. And you need to find the eminently humanitarian General Gallagher, before he unleashes Argon's grand scheme of destruction."

Chapter Fifty–six

The White House
1600 Pennsylvania Ave. NW
Washington, D.C.

The team of Secret Service agents burst into the Oval Office just as President Samuel Reardon was beginning a meeting with the Joint Chiefs of Staff.

"What's the meaning of this interruption, Senniston?" the tall Caucasian man demanded as they were hurriedly ushered out of the Oval Office.

"Let's go, sir. A biological warfare weapon has been discovered in the ventilation shafts of multiple government buildings."

"What the hell?" the forty–fifth President asked. "When was this discovered?"

"Alton Lohrbach just contacted us. He verified that there's a boatload of some type of gas that's going to be injected into the White House and Capitol at noon. A DNA-specific poison, to eliminate certain people."

"DNA-specific poison? Lohrbach's certain of it? Is that even possible?"

"Yes, sir. It's a delayed toxin, apparently linked to the DNA of certain ethnic groups, which could include you. He says a similar weapon was used to kill President Graham and Senator Orson."

"My God," Reardon said as he wiped his brow. "If it's true, it's horrific."

"It is, Mr. President," Lt. Gen. Brant Gallagher said. "I assure you, I'll find out who's behind it."

"Everyone will be escorted out," the senior agent said. "Helicopter's waiting."

The sharply dressed military men rushed out, all except for Gallagher, who was stopped by two agents. "Not you, sir. You're under arrest, General Gallagher."

"What?" he said as he tried to get past the two agents, but was promptly stopped. "I happen to be Vice Chairman of the Joint Chiefs. How dare you?"

"Terabytes of data recovered from Argotech Industries servers implicate you in innumerable acts of terrorism, General."

"I will have your job, whoever you are. Do you know who you're dealing with?"

"Yes, sir. You can call your attorney if you wish. You're sure going to need one." Secret Service Special Agent Senniston read the general his rights as they took him into custody. Several dozen Secret Service and FBI agents had now arrived at the United States Capitol and Congressional office buildings, clearing them out.

• • •

Elmhurst Memorial
Funeral Home and Cemetery
Oak Ridge, TN

A crowd of about two dozen family members had gathered outside on the cold early November morning, as they watched one of their own laid to rest. Conrad Darkkin always had maintained that he never wanted a "stinking funeral," that he simply wanted his body cremated in a nuclear reactor after his death.

Alex knew, however, that the wish was just one of his bizarre rantings, and such a dying request was technically impossible to grant. The best that could possibly be accomplished would be to grind Rad's remains into minute pieces and send him, with the coolant (light or heavy water, or, rarely, a liquid metal such as molten lithium or sodium), through the core and "parboil" his remains; but actual cremation was not achievable. The water going through those dual 830 megawatt commercial BWRs (boiling water reactors) at the

Sequoyah plant was 545 degrees Fahrenheit, after all. Cooked, but not ignited.

So, the family had to settle for a conventional service. He did make certain the body was shielded until he could take it to a linear accelerator and expose it to 100,000 centigray, enough to destroy any remnants of Argon's genetic poison. How fitting, he thought, as he grinned.

Bonnie was wearing a short wig she had purchased in Knoxville, to cover up her still nearly-bald head. Wendy, who was in a wheelchair, was still fairly wobbly from her ordeal at Argotech and her ever-expanding center of gravity. Jim had finally made it back from his new friends at the *Vladivostok,* and had even purchased a new suit.

Even Marianne had come, to his surprise, although the Darkkin family members weren't terribly happy about *that.* Ah, well, he told them all to go straight to hell—just like Dad would've done. After he did that, the family laughed, slapped him on the back, and offered him whiskey, which he politely declined. The teetotaler's refusal of the family brew offended them more than anything.

Alton Lohrbach had even come for the brief ceremony, but quickly left afterwards, not wanting to draw attention.

Afterwards, Alex and the rest of the family left the cemetery and walked down the grassy path to the parking lot.

"My dad always did things his way," he said sadly. "He was a great scientist, and, in his own way, a decent father. He always felt misunderstood, and had a lot of things that seemed to be beyond his control. He was only human."

"Trust me," Jim said. "The Radster went out on top, dude. You all would've been proud of him."

Marianne ignored her son's friend. "Alex, thank you for arranging everything. I am at peace with Rad now."

He scowled at his mother. "Aw, that's great, Mom, I'm *so* happy. Makes my day. I only wish I could've seen him one last time. But I sure wish you were at peace with me."

"What do you mean?" Marianne asked in a bittersweet voice.

He stopped and pointed at the silver-haired woman. "You know what. Today isn't about you, and I really don't want to talk to you right now. Leave me the hell alone." He stepped away from his mother angrily.

"I'm so sorry, the way I felt about him," Wendy said, sobbing, with Stan at her side. "I disowned him, Mom. Even renounced the family name, and I haven't been to this town in over twenty years, except for a couple of holidays. He—he never even got to see Jake."

"I hope you can remember him fondly. I will try to remember the good things and forget the bad," Marianne said.

"But he risked everything, and for what? To save me, that's all," Wendy said.

"He saved a lot of us from some terrible things," Bonnie said. "Without his help, another President and many members of Congress would have perished."

"He wouldn't want us to be sad for him," Wendy said. "I think about how he laughed about death, how each year was going to be his last Christmas. I guess he got his wish—going out with a bang on some Caribbean island, getting irradiated, and buried in Oak Ridge."

They all got into the limousine which would take them back to their hotel in Knoxville. But Alex still couldn't forget the cutting things his mother had said to him at their last meeting, at Wendy's home.

Chapter Fifty–seven

Central Intelligence Agency Headquarters
McLean, Virginia

Bonnie and Alex waited in the anteroom of Alton Lohrbach's office in the large building located in a suburb of Langley, VA. Bonnie could see that her husband was nervous as he fumbled with his visitor's name badge. She had always wanted to come here, but never had the opportunity. Until now.

"Stop fidgeting. It is nothing to be anxious about."

"Yeah, it is. It's worse than being in the FBI office."

"No, hot hardly."

"You really can remember meeting Reagan now?"

"I think so, in bits and pieces. I would have been nine, after I won the national spelling bee. He was a nice man, but merely a human being, like you or I."

"No, he's not. He was the fricking President."

A tall, blond gentleman escorted them inside the intimidating office, where DS&T chief Alton Lohrbach greeted them with a handshake.

"Welcome to Langley, Dr. Mendoza. I understand you have been a guest in D.C. before."

"Yes, many times. I met President Clinton in 1999 as part of a goodwill tour for deaf athletes. I also met President Reagan when I won the national spelling bee. I can remember the latter now."

They took a seat on the plush sofas as an assistant brought them coffee. "I just wanted to thank you for all you've done. You uncovered the assassination of President Graham and Senator Orson, and I have no idea how you figured it all out. I guess you *are* miraculous, as they say."

"I just wish we could have done so before they were killed," she said.

"We can't go back in time—not yet, anyway. But we're working on it."

"I am also amazed that you have allowed me in here after wielding some of the most dangerous weaponry on Earth, against a former government contractor's installation."

"Yes, that was a minor problem which has been dealt with." He handed her a sealed document labeled with the Presidential seal. "President Reardon has pardoned you for all charges that could be brought against you or your 'associates' for unauthorized use of government-owned, experimental deadly weapons against Argon. It was on an island out of our jurisdiction, anyway. In the end, it all worked out. I wouldn't recommend doing it again, though."

"Thank you, sir. Some others helped, too, and one you knew gave his life. What shall happen to Rita McPherson?"

"Dr. McPherson broke a number of laws and engaged in conspiracy against the government. She claims to have no knowledge of the Presidential assassination. However, her testimony and help that she gave you will be given serious consideration. Nevertheless, she needs to pay for her crimes—she knows that."

"I hope that she can salvage something positive from this. We would not be here talking were it not for her unexpected bravery under duress."

"And General Gallagher will likely plea bargain to multiple charges, to avoid the death penalty. He's looking at life without parole in Leavenworth or San Quentin."

"Fun times for him. I guess he won't be running against Reardon for re-election," Alex said snidely.

"No, he won't."

"What shall happen to my . . . Viktor Vladimirov's fullerene suit of information-gathering stealth armor?"

"Oh, yes, that. It's far too expensive to mass-produce, and only a few people with certain . . . gifts could possibly use it. The weaponry is impractical. It'll go back into a storage bin, unless a special *some-*

one wants to work on it." Lohrbach winked at her.

"Humph. It is so ugly, I never desire to see it again."

"Too bad. We'll hold on to it, just in case." Lohrbach turned towards Bonnie. "I'm sorry about your brother. It appears he somehow got mixed up in this by accident. How is he doing?"

"He is getting stronger every day. He will be returning to the sidelines again for tomorrow's game, which hopefully will be a good contest. Rehabilitation, I know much about."

"Right. But, about you . . . your talents are extraordinary, and I would like to explore job options with you. I understand that you are presently an assistant professor of physics at Caltech."

"Yes, to resume official duties soon. I have been quite occupied, as you know, since finishing my doctorate. Special Agent Ken Thornton approached me in the past about the FBI."

"The FBI's a waste of your talents. How about the CIA?"

"It is the same problem as before, sir. My restored hearing is only partial, and temporary—that disability precludes my employment as an agent. In a few weeks my cochlear implants will never again function, due to the degenerative condition of my acoustic nerves. The problem has also been hastened by the injection of the *Orthogeneticus titania* protein into me."

"Not as a typical agent, but as Associate Director of the Directorate of Science & Technology (DS&T). A liaison between the Directorate and the Special Agents. There just happens to be an opening, and I like to plan for the future."

"DS&T? Developing secret gadgets and such? How could this be possible? Others more qualified than me surely must be in line for such a lofty position."

Lohrbach laughed. "There are others in line who'll be pissed, but I'm the chief, so I hire who I want. That person would be you."

She stood up and looked out the window. "That is . . . interesting. But I don't want to become Conrad Darkkin the second. Killing people is not my favorite thing in the world. Historically, it has always been more challenging to build than destroy."

"You'd be saving lives, and would be my second-in-command—using technology to help people. The world isn't all about making nukes and blowing up the world. Despite what Malachi Argon believed, I am all about promoting science. I just want it to be regulated in a better fashion."

"I do not like perverting nature. No disrespect, but if that is what you are asking, Mr. Lohrbach—"

"It isn't. Think of what Argon's advances could do for people with disabilities. You, for example."

She pointed at him angrily. "There is nothing wrong with me, and I certainly do not consider myself disabled. If you are referring to my hearing, in many ways, the loss is a blessing. When Rita infused the Ontario Lacus protein into me, the sensory overload was almost too much for me to take. I do not want to be a genetic freak. Look how Travis Argon and Tammy Preece ended up."

Lohrbach leaned back in his large leather chair and twirled his pen. "Point well taken. Promise me you will think about it?"

"She *has* thought about it, Lohrbach. The answer is no."

"I would prefer she make her own decision."

She thought pensively for two minutes. "Yes, I would prefer that also. I will ponder it . . . the offer is very exciting."

"Do you trust this guy?" Alex asked her. "Tell me."

She looked at the gray-haired Lohrbach for several minutes. "He has an honest soul, beneath his caustic bureaucratic shell."

"Hmm . . . well, is there anything else I can do for you, Bonnie? Or for you, Alex? We and this country owe you a *lot*."

"There is one favor you can do . . . for my sister-in-law. She has been through quite an ordeal and could use some ego boosting."

"Of course. What can I do for the fabulous Dr. Williams?"

"She might enjoy a phone call from President Reardon, if that can be arranged."

"I just *might* have some influence there."

"And your department's support when she is better and runs for Congress."

"She's got it."

Bonnie Mendoza had much to contemplate as the Director left the room. What was her best destiny? To be a research physicist, unlocking the mysteries of a subatomic universe? Being a celebrity, being an ambassador of goodwill? Or being, like her parents, teachers—nurturing the promising young minds of tomorrow?

Those were deep thoughts that would take some time for her to carefully ponder. But now she had to go visit her best friend.

• • •

Two months later
National Institutes of Health
Bethesda, MD

Bonnie and Alex went to visit Wendy at the NIH and walked up to the private room, and were allowed in by the FBI agents who were guarding her room against further unwanted "visitors." The government wanted her monitored closely, to monitor for any unexpected hazards she might have been exposed to at the Argotech complex.

"How are things?" Alex asked. She was now thirty–seven weeks along and visibly showing.

Wendy sat up in her bed and took a sip of juice. "Strange. Like a lot of it never happened. Kind of a fog. A dream."

"How're you doing with . . . you know?" Alex asked.

"Okay. The lithium's not nearly as bad as I thought. It gives me a kind of clarity I haven't had in a long time. I can go to some other meds after she's born, they said. Maybe go off, if they determine it was from the Auripex. It's all my fault, the mess I got you all into." Wendy brushed tears from her eyes with a tissue.

"It is not your fault you have bipolar disorder," Bonnie said. "No more than it is mine I am deaf."

"No, but I precipitated it myself. Took quertraline for depression, when I really was bipolar II, they said. The worst thing a doctor can do—medicate herself. What an idiot I was."

"That is all in the past," Bonnie said. "We cannot go back and change it. If not for that, we never would have found out about Malachi Argon and the Ortho-Man."

"You know for sure the baby's a girl?" Alex asked, changing the subject.

"Yep." She took a drink of water as she showed him the high-resolution ultrasound photo. "Don't see any dangly parts. Pretty conclusive. Bonnie seemed to know it, too."

"How's that?" he asked.

"A lucky guess," she replied. "Do you have a name yet?"

"Dione Cassandra—Cassie for short."

"Why that?" Alex asked.

"Dione is a moon of Saturn, and Cassini the discoverer—appropriate, don't you think? Dione is also the mother of Aphrodite, the goddess of love," Wendy said. "The 'C' is for Dad."

"Yeah." He looked down and frowned.

"How's Jay doing?" Wendy asked.

"They think he'll make a full recovery. Going to need some rehab for a few weeks, but, overall, very lucky," he said.

"I . . . don't know if he'll want to see me, after what they say I did. I almost got him killed. I don't even remember that day."

"None of it was your fault. Everyone knows that," she said. "But what you did accidentally led us to Argon, so some good came out of it. You must view it in that fashion."

"I can't stop thinking about Dad. He . . . he saved us all, in a way. I can't believe he's gone." She started crying. "I tried to love him, I really did. I guess I didn't try hard enough."

"He went out the way he wanted to, sis—in a blaze of glory, saving the world. You know that's what he would've wanted."

"I hadn't seen or talked to him for years. He wasn't even invited to your wedding."

"I know, we hardly spoke any more after I discovered that he and Smiley rubbed out Monte Buechler, the guy who stabbed Bonnie, three and a half years ago. He did some bad things to Mom. He didn't want your forgiveness, only just wanted to do what he had to do, to save you."

"Are the feds looking for his place, to see if he has any more battle armor suits in his little arsenal?"

"He doesn't. Lohrbach and I were there, if you recall, and it was a one-shot deal. Viktor is apparently still on that sub." He took a sip of his coffee. "But are you really going to go through with this thing for Lohrbach? That Ortho-Man dude tried to kill Jay and Bonnie."

"I have to, if possible. I am not one for revenge." Wendy looked out the window. "I hope Stan is okay with this. I'm sure I said some pretty bad stuff to him."

"You're a doctor. You know it's not your fault," he said.

"I never did those things with Jay this time. I don't know why I said that he was Cassie's father. You both believe me, don't you? Bonnie?"

She touched her friend's large hand. "I know it to be true."

Alex perked up. "Hey, I thought your purple buddy was toast."

She smiled. "He is nearly gone. But, even without him, I know it is true because I have faith in Wendy. I have been entirely alone with nothing else to hold onto, but I survived because of faith."

"Bonnie, I have something to tell you," Wendy said sheepishly a few minutes later. "A confession about something I've lied to you about for years. I just can't keep it secret any longer."

"Lied about? What is it? Your previous relationship with Jaime? That was none of my business."

"No, not that," Wendy said.

"Well, no matter, I will forgive you."

"I don't know. It's pretty bad."

Alex put his hand on her shoulder. "She's right. You'd better sit down."

She sat down in the plush armchair of the VIP suite. "Please tell me the bad news."

"Well, do you remember when I told you how successful your *Mendoza Milagroso* merchandise was—the boxed DVD sets, action figures, cereal, vitamins . . ."

"Yes, they were quite successful and earned much money," she said proudly. "Our TV show is legendary. Nominated for a daytime Emmy, you said."

Wendy shook her head. "Uh, no, not so much. Alex?"

"Dear, we have some money because of your investments from gambling earnings and the lock and handcuff design patents, and from my DarTech royalties. And there was no Emmy."

She rose from her chair, then took a step back. "I am *not* as famous as you have claimed? You told me that all 1,000 of the special edition autographed action figure sets were sold."

Wendy looked up. "That's true, but most of them were to me, and 977 of them are gathering dust in a storage warehouse, along with most of the other stuff. Stan is not happy. All of it lost money."

Alex hugged her. "I'm sorry, it's true."

"More of my undiagnosed mania, it seems. The ideas seemed great, but the market just wasn't there."

She shrugged. "Oh, well, it could certainly have been worse."

"But you are still quite a celebrity. You earned quite a lot of money with the magic acts, which went to charity, of course." Wendy looked out the window of the private room. "Stan has been good to me. All those years, the highs and lows, he helped protect me. I guess nobody knows about things until they're really messed up."

"The most important thing is that you have help now. From all of us. You'll need it when you begin your political career."

She laughed and twirled her finger. "*Congress*? Forget it. No one will want a nut case like me now. Damaged goods."

"You might be surprised," Alex said as the phone rang. After several times, Wendy still had not answered it. "Aren't you going to get that?"

"It can wait. It's probably Mom, and I don't want to talk to her now. Right now I want to think of . . . Dad."

"You never know." Alex picked up the phone. "Yes, Ma'am. Who? Dr. Williams certainly *is* here."

"Who is it? Someone from the hospital? I don't want to talk to anyone there right now."

"No, it's a local call, sort of. You'd better take it." He handed her the phone.

"Hello? *Who?* The White House? Is this a joke?" Wendy's face suddenly turned red. "Uh, okay, Ma'am. Of course I'll take it."

"You were saying?" he said as he folded his arms.

"Yes, Mr. President," she said in the highest voice she could muster. "Thank you for calling. I've never been better, thanks."

Chapter Fifty–eight

Darkkin Mendoza Residence
4552 Eagle Point Blvd.
Pasadena, CA

Alex and Bonnie had returned to their Pasadena condominium the next day and were sitting on the sofa, drinking coffee, and reflected on their grand adventures over the last two months.

"How is the hearing?" he asked his wife.

"It seems to decrease a little each day. As Rita had said, the effects are not permanent."

"Maybe you'll be able to use the cochlear implants again."

"Perhaps, Alex; perhaps not. It is not that important. What is most essential is that Wendy and Jaime are okay. I wish we somehow could have saved President Graham. And your father." She started crying. "He was a good man, and saved my life. Thought nothing of his own welfare when he burst in there."

"What about your little buddy?"

"My purple friend only faintly appears. Mother tells me of the stories I used to tell about him, and how much trouble he got me into. A gift of mixed blessings Terrible, in a way."

"Terrible? I think it would be cool."

"You think so? Always to know if someone is telling the truth or not? No one was meant to have such a power. In time, it would have caused me great pain. Mother said it did when I was a child."

"I never figured out how it works."

"It is linked to my own natural hearing. Subtle differences in voice inflections and pitch cause the animated friend to appear. Luckily, he is currently very dim, and will be soon gone. The friendships lost, you cannot imagine. The pitfalls of fooling around with nature cannot be overemphasized."

"You could have taken more injections, you know. Your hearing restoration might've been permanent."

"Is that what you really want? And how do you know the long-term effects of injecting drugs derived from alien life forms? Duh."

"You can't deny that it's improved your speech."

She threw a coaster at him. "Everyone says the same thing. There was nothing wrong with me, the way I was. What I did, I did for Wendy, not for myself, and I did not wish to make myself a playground for Argon's genetic experimentation."

"But it happened, just the same. It's okay to admit something's for you."

"We went through this all before, Alex, in Dr. Traylor's office. I neither need nor want anything more than what I have, as I am blessed with what I have given. I have seen a glimpse of the things I lost, and . . . I am far better off. Who among us should be privileged to know the future, or if someone is telling the truth or not?"

"I guess we've all seen the pitfalls of screwing around with nature. Thank God Argon's gone."

"The problem was not just with Malachi Argon, but lies with the whole world, Alex. The perception they have of people who are not considered 'normal.' I am not normal because I am deaf. Rita is not because she had a spinal cord injury."

"But neither of you were born that way, those things just happened to you because of misfortune."

"It did, nevertheless, and it's the way we are. The whole thing is horrifying. Argon's sickening 'orthogenetics.' Who was he to determine what is and what is not acceptable? We had a guy like that, and look how he ended up."

"Yeah. Adolf Hitler." The Nazi leader had his own ideas on creating a super-race of humans. "But why not eliminate bad genes, if it can help alleviate human suffering? All those kids with cancer and incurable genetic diseases?"

"And who decides which diseases will be cured? You, the all-knowing medical executive? Some ethics committee? Everyone's genetics exposed—who gets insured and who doesn't? A slippery slope . . . once you go down it, you can't ever go back."

"I guess so."

"And, for a brief time, I became someone I didn't want to be—a person of revenge, of violence. What I did to the Ortho-Man, Argon, and Chalfant—was it really right, Alex?"

"You did what you had to do. I don't see any other way to have played it." He paused as he drank his coffee. "The thing we all want to know is . . . did you really visit Jay in his coma? His vision of you at Ontario Lacus? It sounded unbelievably vivid."

"Astral projection? I thought about him a lot when I was in Rad's cave, and wanted him to know what was going on . . . but I cannot honestly say I 'visited' him. Nor can I say I ever did before, as a child. It is possible I was endowed with powers I no longer remember. On the other hand, Jaime is quite metaphorical; you cannot take everything he says literally."

"The things he knew were uncanny."

"He always seemed to have his own precognitive abilities, which doctors have always been puzzled about. I have some great talents, Alex, but still can't believe that telepathy and the ability to project my psyche were among those. I am a scientist and do not believe in the paranormal."

"But it happened." He put down his coffee. "What do you want to do now?"

"I know what *I* desire to do now, Son of Rad Röntgen. I suggest we retreat to the marital chamber."

"Uh, I don't have any insulators handy."

She paused for a minute and looked up. "That is okay, we will not need protective covers."

"Did Oogly-Googly tell you that? He better not be wrong, or he's in big trouble."

Chapter Fifty–nine

Ten weeks later
National Institutes of Health
Bone Marrow Transplant Unit
Bethesda, MD

The robust-looking blonde female infant lay swaddled in a blanket on the cold late March day, dwarfed by the large gurney upon which she lay. Dione Cassandra Williams weighed only twenty pounds, although that was quite large for her age of eight weeks; she was sleeping soundly in the sterile-looking stainless steel bassinet, oblivious to the part she would soon play in human genetic history.

"I admire your humanitarianism, Dr. Wendy Williams, but I don't understand why you're doing this," Bonnie said as she looked up at her friend. "Are you certain you have regained all of your marbles, or do we need to see the therapist again? I have already made an appointment with mine."

Wendy stared at her. "Have you gained weight, or is it just the scrubs? Better watch out. Thirty-five's right around the corner."

"Yes, these horrid surgical gowns make me look ghastly. And my appetite has increased recently, for some reason."

"Yeah. Anyway, bone marrow aspiration is a perfectly safe procedure. I've done dozens myself."

"On an older child, but Cassie is a bit young," Alton Lohrbach said as he looked at Wendy. "I'm glad for the opportunity here, but *why*? Didn't Travis Argon try to kill you and several others, including Dr. Mendoza here? Killed your father?"

"I agree. I would not be as gracious as you," Bonnie said.

"Whatever he is, he's still . . . a human being. And Dad was probably killed by that genetic poison he used to rescue Bonnie."

"He is not human at all, but a ghastly alien perversion of nature, not deserving of life."

She stared down at Bonnie. "Who are you to decide that? He's also a blood relative. And all evidence suggests that the things he did, he was manipulated to do." She dropped her head behind the surgical mask. "I know what it is to be out of control. After what my father did, I couldn't rest if I didn't do this. Whatever's done is done, and we may salvage something positive from this debacle."

"His chance for survival is only about ten percent, Wendy. Even if he lives and wakes up from his vegetative state, he will be subject to federal charges for what he did," Lohrbach said.

"Meaning that you'll experiment on him, right?"

He laughed. "You said that, I didn't—but you know I can't answer that. He's classified, as is everything else having to do with Argon's Titan research. It never existed."

"What you do with him is out of my control, Lohrbach, but I don't believe it was all his fault. We all do things at times we don't have control over. But I have to try my best—that's all I can do."

She watched the hematologist prepare to perform the brief procedure, and knew that it would hurt her baby girl for a few minutes, but also realized that infants' bones were soft and easy to aspirate.

She also couldn't turn back now—what part was she playing in the continued existence of the most fantastic killing machine ever created? Perhaps someone would, somehow, benefit in the end. Her mother always told her that something good had to come out of something bad. And you couldn't get much worse than this.

And she learned there had been a lot of good inside Rad Darkkin. She felt badly that it had taken her so long to realize that, but he made it pretty difficult. Her dad never did anything the easy way.

• • •

The five–seven, platinum-haired woman came up to Alex in the waiting room of the hospital, holding a cup of tea. Bonnie was sitting next to him. She had barely spoken to him since their argument in San Diego three months earlier.

"Alex. May I have a moment?"

"Huh? Why should I stay here and be yelled at again?" He looked at his coffee, refusing to make eye contact with his mother. "I have better things to do."

"Shall I leave?" Bonnie asked. "I do not mind."

"No, please stay," Marianne said. "I have some things I . . . need to say. And I need to ask you some things too, Bonnie."

"What do you have to say, Mom? You pretty much said it all before. Guess things turned out about as well as they could have."

"I'm sorry for that," Alex's acerb mother said quietly. "Understand how upset I was."

He frowned and looked at her as she sat down. "Yeah, you think you were the only one? Wendy's my sister, you know. I don't know why you feel the way about me you do."

"I'm . . . sorry, Alex. I always blamed a lot of things on you, because you reminded me so much of him. I know now that . . . I was part of the dysfunction."

"But I did some bone-headed things. Bonnie too, as did Dad. But they both saved us all."

"And make no excuses for me," Bonnie said. "I am an adult who should know the consequences of my reckless actions."

"I hated Rad, Alex. More than you can know. In many ways, you reminded me so much of him."

"Is that past tense?"

"I guess, and that's unfair. I used to tell Wendy how she should try and forgive him. But I never really did. Never lived by my own advice."

"You can't change it, Mom. Everything's okay now."

"No, it's not." She turned to Bonnie. "You and Wendy were the last people to see Rad alive. I misjudged him so badly."

She put her hand on her mother-in-law's shoulder. "Conrad was a brave man, but had many negative aspects. He was driven as much by his irrational hatred of Malachi Argon as anything. You have nothing to feel regret over."

"I hadn't seen him in over ten years. I know you're good at seeing people's true nature."

"He was a complex individual who was extraordinarily gifted in science and technology. But he had no glory of his own to attain in this caper. I hope that this will redeem his life in your eyes."

"I never wanted him to die. We were unhappy together the latter part of our marriage, but I wanted him to find peace."

She looked at both of them. "He did things his way, as he would have wanted. As irritating as he seemed, he had a sense of goodness in him. I could, for a brief period of time, see the . . . good and evil in people."

"Can you still?" Marianne asked.

"I thank God for many things. One of those is that I am quickly losing that ability. No being was meant to possess such a dangerous power."

She rose up to give Marianne a hug, and pressed down on the wooden arm rest of the chair, snapping it in half.

"What the heck was that?" Alex asked, looking at the wood.

"I guess not everything is gone," she said, sheepishly. "I must remember to be careful."

Epilogue

Six months later
Las Vegas Conquerors Stadium
Las Vegas, NV

The black GMC Yukon pulled up to the gate at brand-new, 78,000-seat Conquerors Stadium on the hot late summer day, for the opening game of the season. The driver opened his tinted window as the gate guard, wearing a name badge identifying him as "Ted," approached suspiciously.

"You can't pull that in here," the twenty–something, reed-thin guard said harshly. "You need to park in the visitors' lot, buddy."

"I don't think so, son," the large, Ray-Ban-wearing man said as he flipped open his identification. "And the name isn't 'buddy.' It's Agent Culbertson to you, Ted, is it?"

The young man gawked at the agent's ID card. "*Central Intelligence Agency?* Aww, that ain't real. You can get in a lot of trouble for that, pal." Ted then went to the back and stared at the license plates which read "U.S. Government," and looked back up, pointing at the vehicle's rear. "For those, too."

"It's real, son. I suggest you call your supervisor, pronto."

"I don't have time for this crap." Ted the gate guard called the head of security on his radio and listened intently on his earpiece. "Mr. Langston, some yahoos are here who say they're from the CIA, and they won't leave. I told them they could get arrested for—what's that?" His thin, angular face turned chalk-white. "Uh, yessir. Sorry to bother you."

"Well?" Culbertson asked.

"Boss says you can, uh, go wherever you want."

"Thanks, sonny." The agent rolled up his window and pulled through the gate, driving to the VIP gate. The two agents in the front got out, checked the area, opened the passenger door, and helped their very important passenger out.

"I do not need help from my entourage," the visibly off-balance Dr. Bonnie Mendoza said to the driver as she plopped out of the vehicle. "*You* are to blame for my inelegant predicament!" she yelled at the man who exited from the other side. "Truly a chip off the old block."

"I believe you had something to do with it, too," Alex Darkkin said, smiling. "And Oogly-Googly really screwed up badly."

"Shut up."

"Do you want a wheelchair, Doctor?" Agent Culbertson asked politely, as her interpreter signed the message.

"I do not! Leave me alone."

"Sure thing, Ma'am."

The gravid Associate Director of the CIA's Directorate of Science & Technology wobbled with her husband and helpers to the special entrance, leading to a private elevator and the VIP suite. They walked up off the elevator to the luxury box at the new Conquerors Stadium for the September season opener. Coach Mendoza was getting ready to start his new campaign, hopefully with a better result than the previous 2-14 season. He proudly made the prediction of being a playoff contender this year, although that seemed unlikely to most.

Bonnie walked confidently into the area, with her hair now shoulder-length; her gait was much wider than it was during her last visit to Las Vegas, as her center of gravity had been significantly if only temporarily altered. She was glad that she no longer had to worry about the aural processors getting in the way of her hair, and having to recharge batteries again. They were met by a clean-shaven, trim Jim Krakowski, who had lost about forty pounds.

"Hey, how's it going? Don't see you guys much any more."

"Yeah. Life in D.C. is pretty busy."

Jim winked at Alex and pointed to Bonnie's midsection. "No lie. Looks like you guys have *really* been busy."

"Humph," she said. "No more jokes, please."

Jackie Levickis, dressed in a navy pantsuit, came up to them. "How's it going, Darkkin?"

Alex looked at her. "Jackie? I didn't know you'd be here." He watched as the DEA agent put her arm around Jim.

"What can I say, bud?" Jim asked as he took a swig of dark imported beer. "When you got it, you got it."

"I don't believe it. You two are an item now?"

"You better believe it, pal." Jim leaned over and whispered in Alex's ear. "She was really turned on after she found out I helped shoot torpedoes out of the *Vladivostok.* These lady agents seem to have the hots for guys like ol' Mr. Danger here."

"Is that right?" He laughed as Wendy and Stan came up, with Jake, now six years old, and Cassie, nine months old, both at the 99th percentile for height and weight.

"Wow, armed men in black outside and everything," Wendy said. "I'm impressed."

"It is unnecessary, but apparently they deem me of sufficient importance to warrant such an escort, especially in my homely condition. They desired to wheel me in here, can you believe it?"

"Cool. You guys want something to eat before I make my grand debut?" Wendy asked.

"Yeah, a hot dog would be great," Alex said.

"Bonnie?"

Alex tapped his wife, who was looking at the field, on the arm.

"What is it?" she snapped.

"*What do you want to eat*?" Wendy signed.

"Four chili dogs with relish, mayonnaise, onions, and mustard, three pickles, and two bags of potato chips. Because of what your brother has done to me, I am ravenous beyond comprehension."

"Ugh. That meal sounds disgusting," Alex said. "Gross."

She read his lips. "No, *I* am disgusting, like one of those egg-shaped children's toys that wobble but never fall down."

"*What to drink*?" Wendy signed.

"A double Darkkin and cola, please. And *dos cerveza.*"

"Yeah, right. Beer and whiskey, huh?"

"Oh, mineral water will be fine, I guess. And a gallon of milk."

"How is it going?"

"My exponentially expanding girth has necessitated that additional funds be allocated for apparel." She plopped on the plush seat. "Oof—I will *never* be the same."

Wendy chuckled as the waiter brought the delectable meal. "No, you sure won't. Get used to the stretch marks. And, take it from me—those chili dogs won't help matters any. The law of mass conservation, I believe you've heard of that."

"I am too hungry to care." She quickly gobbled the four dripping chili dogs, then drank a large glass of milk.

"Hey, that's pretty impressive eating," Jim said sarcastically as he came to her table. "You could give me a run for the money in a hot dog eating contest."

"I am making up for all those days we ate beans and stale peanut butter sandwiches in Conrad's dwelling. Luckily, I can now consume about 6,000 kilocalories daily to maintain my muscle mass."

The cochlear implants had been removed, since they no longer functioned. The protein from the Titanian organism had failed to permanently slow the nerve degeneration. She had the opportunity to secretly inject the protein again, but realized that she was flirting with destiny. She didn't like what she had become, and had another, more important thing to care about right now, and a future to plan.

The genetic experimentation of Malachi Argon had taken its toll. She had learned, in her new position as Associate Director of the CIA's Directorate of Science &Technology, that the Titanian growth factor eventually caused decreased life span and other mutations in those who used it over long periods of time.

Rita McPherson, now back in a wheelchair, was serving her three-year federal prison sentence, in a plea bargain reached between her and the U.S. Attorney General. Malachi Argon was dead, having suffered severe brain injury after his encounter with her. Gallagher was serving life in prison in Leavenworth, Kansas.

A vegetative Travis Argon was still being kept alive in a secret CIA research lab, for what purpose even she didn't know completely. But they assured her that her brief encounter with genetic manipulation hadn't seemed to have caused any permanent damage.

The world simply wasn't ready for widespread gene therapy yet. There were too many ethical dilemmas over who had control over what. And she had seen first-hand the consequences of tampering with life, by a man who thought he was God, using his own adopted son as a human Petri dish.

But other times she realized that she didn't need to be anything she didn't want to be. She had experienced her fondest desire—to remember more of her childhood—and learned that it wasn't the dreamy, wondrous thing she thought it was. It was, like that of most people, rather typical in most aspects.

The purple friend was nearly gone now, and, with it, the abilities it conferred. She was glad—it wasn't something she wanted. Her lispy, "deaf" speech was slowly returning, meaning that her career as a voice-over performer would probably never materialize. But the supplemental strength she had gained hadn't diminished yet.

She watched as her best friend, whose life she had saved, went onto the field to do something she couldn't fully appreciate—sing The Star-Spangled Banner. She could faintly remember music from her childhood now, and knew that Wendy was a talented mezzo-soprano who was ecstatic to sing before the first game, even though the new stadium was only three-quarters full. But hopefully this season would be more productive than the first one; it was unlikely the coach would be placed in a coma again this fall by another Ortho-Man.

Life wasn't about living in the past, because it couldn't be changed. Nor was it about the future, which she couldn't predict. It was about living each day to its fullest. There was so much to be thankful for, with her whole life ahead of her. Things were as they should be—beautifully flawed, for perfection was something no human being should ever be allowed to attain.

And, right now, sending her minions for procurement of additional chili dogs was of the highest governmental priority.

THE END

About The Author

J. Matthew Neal is a native of Indiana and has been a practicing endocrinologist since 1993. He earned undergraduate and medical degrees from Indiana University and a Master of Business Administration degree from the University of Massachusetts. He is currently Director of the Internal Medicine Residency at Ball Memorial Hospital (Muncie, IN) and Clinical Professor of Medicine at the Indiana University School of Medicine. He has over ten years' experience in medical administration and has served in various governance roles in regional medical societies.

Dr. Neal is the author of three medical textbooks: Case Studies in Endocrinology, Diabetes, and Metabolism (Lippincott Williams & Wilkins), Basic Endocrinology (Blackwell Science), and How the Endocrine System Works (Blackwell Science). He has also authored numerous peer-reviewed medical articles relating to endocrinology.

This is his second novel. His first novel, *Specific Gravity,* was released in 2007.